Philip Gwynne Jones was born in South Wales in 1966, and lived and worked throughout Europe before settling in Scotland in the 1990s. He first came to Italy in 1994, when he spent some time working for the European Space Agency in Frascati, a job that proved to be less exciting than he had imagined.

He spent twenty years in the IT industry before realising he was congenitally unsuited to it. Furthermore, an attempt to find a secure, well-paid job with a proper pension had resulted in him finding himself in the IT department of a large Scottish bank during the global financial crisis.

Something, clearly, had to change. And so it was that – following a conversation with a man in a pub – Philip and Caroline left their jobs, sold their flat and moved to Venice in search of a better, simpler future. They were wrong about the 'simpler' bit . . . Philip now works as a teacher, writer and translator; he enjoys cooking, art, classical music and opera; and can occasionally be seen and heard singing bass with Cantori Veneziani and the Ensemble Vocale di Venezia.

PRAISE FOR PHILIP GWYNNE JONES

'. . . as delightful as a Spritz by the Rialto – a must for all Italy lovers'

David Hewson

'A riveting story of deception and corruption'

Daily Mail

'The lively, colourful narrative scuds along as briskly as a water taxi . . . you'll enjoy the ride'

Italia magazine

'An unputdownable thriller'

Gregory Dowling

'Gwynne Jones's talent for evoking place and atmosphere is clear as ever'

Literary Review

'Superb – always gripping, beautifully constructed and vivid'

Stephen Glover

'Clever and great fun'

The Times

'Sinister and shimmering, *The Venetian Game* is as haunting and darkly elegant as Venice itself'

. . . of *Maestra*

Also by Philip Gwynne Jones

The Venetian Candidate

Philip Gwynne Jones

CONSTABLE

CONSTABLE

First published in Great Britain in hardback in 2023 by Constable

This paperback edition published in 2024 by Constable

Copyright © Philip Gwynne Jones, 2023

1 3 5 7 9 10 8 6 4 2

The moral right of the author has been asserted.

A CIP catalogue record for this book is available from the British Library.

ISBN: 978-1-40871-534-5

Typeset in Adobe Garamond by Initial Typesetting Services, Edinburgh
Printed and bound in Great Britain by Clays Ltd, Elcograf S.p.A.

Papers used by Constable are from well-managed forests
and other responsible sources.

Constable
An imprint of
Little, Brown Book Group
Carmelite House
50 Victoria Embankment
London EC4Y 0DZ

An Hachette UK Company
www.hachette.co.uk

www.littlebrown.co.uk

In memory of Auntie Pat, who lent me all those wonderful Agatha Christie books so many summers ago, and of Uncle Colin, who once made my breakfast explode.

Tonight, this frost will fasten on this mud and us,
Shrivelling many hands, puckering foreheads crisp.
The burying-party, picks and shovels in shaking grasp,
Pause over half-known faces. All their eyes are ice,
But nothing happens.

Wilfred Owen, 'Exposure'

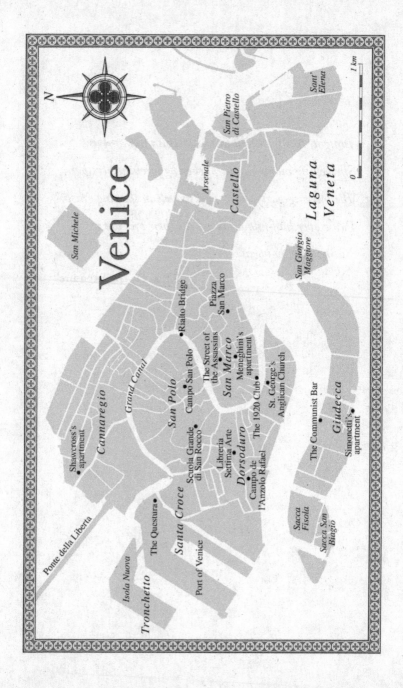

Part One

The Road Trip

Prologue

My breath steams in the air and fogs the windscreen of the Land Rover. I wipe it clear, and my fingers come away damp and stinging with the cold. My body is starting to shake in the freezing air. I could, I know, switch on the engine and turn the heating up, but any noise would seem inappropriate. I don't want to break the silence.

Ahead of me I can see three dark figures, still amidst the white, their silhouettes blurred by the misted windscreen. Again, I wipe it clear, this time with the sleeve of my coat in order to spare my fingers.

I take a deep breath, and pull down the mirror to check my reflection. My image smiles back at me, almost laughing at the absurdity of this act of vanity. Yet this has become a reflex, an act of self-protection. Never appear looking less than perfect. Never have a hair out of place. And, most certainly, never wear the same dress twice.

It's different for men, of course.

I smile back at my reflection. My eyes are a little red, a little tired perhaps, but nothing too noticeable. At least to an audience of three.

Three people. And a dead man.

I should get out of the car. I'd told them I would wait for them here, but it would be ridiculous to come all this way for nothing. At the very least, I owe them that. And, for myself, there would be some sense of an ending.

More importantly, the Land Rover is bone-chillingly cold. I need to get out and move around. I smile back at my reflection, flip up the vanity mirror and open the door.

Immediately the wind wrenches the door out of my hand, and scythes at me through my clothes. Inadvertently I cry out, and one of the figures – I cannot see exactly who it is – turns and looks at me.

I pull myself out of the car, fighting against the wind, my hair whipping against my face and make my way down the track to the cemetery gate. Ahead of me, I can see the great stone cross on which two swords are fastened into a cruciform shape.

The figures are hunched over before the gravestone. Nathan has an arm around Federica, trying to shield her from the wind. Dario checks his watch. I can see from the expression on his face that he thinks we should be going before the weather becomes even worse.

'Nat?' He looks up at the swirling snow. 'We shouldn't leave it too much longer.'

Nathan nods. 'You're right.' He straightens himself up, and shivers. 'We should be getting back. The roads are bad enough, even in that thing.'

Federica holds on to his arm. 'It was a nice idea. Really. Perhaps we'll come back in the spring.' She hears my footsteps approaching, even over the howling wind, as my feet crump in the snow, and smiles at me.

'I'm glad you wanted to come,' she says.

I make my way over to them, unable to stop myself shaking. It is, I tell myself, just the cold.

There are only the four of us there, in the blue half-light of early evening. Four grey shadows cast as we stand, heads bowed, before the grave of a long-dead man. And then, in an instant, there is a flash of red against the white of the snow.

Chapter 1

Nothing says 'Christmas is over' quite like the seventh of January. Even more so when it happens to be a Tuesday. Right up until the mini-Christmas of Epiphany you can kid yourself that the holiday is still rolling on, but in your heart of hearts – if you're an adult, and even more so if you happen to be British – you know that *La Befana* is a poor substitute for *Babbo Natale*.

Federica had left for work, extracting a promise from me that the flat would be back to normal by the time she returned home. In truth, there wasn't all that much to do. We'd given up on tinsel years ago, given that Gramsci saw anything sparkly and low-hanging as a challenge. A tree, however, was something on which Fede was not prepared to compromise. It had to have lights on, it had to be decorated and – above all – it had to be real, even if that meant sweeping up pine needles every day.

I unwound the lights and then rolled them up and packed them away, ready to be stashed in the suitcase under the bed where they would remain until next December. Then I removed the ornaments, one by one, saving the angel for last. Because it terrified me.

The varnish on the face had cracked, its smile was just a little too broad, and the eyes seemed to follow you around the room. Initially, I'd positioned it so that it was facing away from us but Fede had objected. It had belonged to her grandparents, she told me, it was a precious memory of family Christmases and so – in spite of everything – she loved it and the festive season would not be the same without it.

I couldn't really argue with that, and so the angel stayed.

I took it down and tried not to meet its malevolent gaze. I wrapped it in tissue paper and placed it, face down, in a shoe box along with the other ornaments. Then I put the box in the suitcase under the bed, and locked it.

You couldn't be too careful.

That just left the tree. Denuded of its decorations, it cut a sorry figure. A bare Christmas tree, post-Christmas, on a wet Tuesday morning. Yep. The festive season was over, all right.

I wondered how I was going to get it downstairs without shedding needles everywhere. Was a dead Christmas tree the sort of thing that one could just learn to live with? Give it a few weeks, and we'd hardly even notice it was there. But that, I admitted to myself, was going to be a hard sell to Federica.

It needed to be moved. But first, I could treat myself to a coffee, a read of the paper and then, perhaps, I'd have earned myself the right to a morning nap.

I looked at the headline and shook my head in disbelief. Police were still trying to identify a man who'd been found, frozen to death, in an ATM vestibule up in Cannaregio. He'd been there all night. At least one person, it was thought, had made a cash withdrawal without even checking to see if he was all right. The season of goodwill, evidently, was very much over.

I turned to the second page. After a brief Christmas truce, the two candidates for Mayor of Venice had come out swinging in readiness for next month's election.

Anna Fabris versus Giuseppe Meneghini.

Fabris, a university professor of philosophy (typically shorthand for *left wing*) versus Meneghini, a businessman (typically shorthand for *right wing*). Fabris, resident in the *centro storico*; Meneghini on the mainland, but with a desirable pied-à-terre in Venice itself.

Venice would vote in great numbers for Fabris; *terraferma* for Meneghini. So Meneghini would probably win. And nothing, in Venice at least, would change.

I scanned the article quickly. Insults had been exchanged, followed by a despairing plea for civility by Andrea Mazzon, a minor independent candidate with nothing to lose by appearing to be the reasonable one. Or at least as reasonable as a man generally perceived as being an actual fascist could be.

There were others, of course. The *Partito Democratico* on the left, together with at least two variants of the Communist Party. On the right, the *Lega* and the *Fratelli d'Italia*. But Venice seemed to have little appetite for the main parties, this time. This was going to be a battle of independents.

I sighed. Perhaps there'd be something nice on the following page? Perhaps there'd be a photograph of a kitten?

A bar I knew up in Cannaregio, a welcome refuge whenever I found myself in that area of town, had closed its doors for the last time, the great November flood having proved the final straw.

Removing a dead Christmas tree, then, was beginning to look like the least depressing option. I folded the paper up, and tossed it onto the sofa for Gramsci to sit on. At least it would make one of us happy.

I gave the tree an experimental push, and cursed as needles dropped to the floor. Any attempt to move it, it seemed, would end in disaster.

What if I could somehow slide it across the floor? What if I could make the surface just a little bit smoother? I rummaged away in the cupboard under the sink and found a can of furniture polish. Perfect. I sprayed away at the area between the tree and the door. Then I got down on my hands and knees and pushed the tree, ever so slowly, across the near-frictionless surface.

It worked like a dream.

Nathan, my boy, you're a genius.

This still left the problem of getting it downstairs and out into the street, where it would join its equally sorry-looking brothers and sisters in waiting for *Veritas* to come and take them to the graveyard of ex-Christmas trees. But I'd cross that bridge when I came to it. Besides, I thought, pine needles on a dimly-lit staircase might be things that could happily be ignored.

I managed to push it as far as the apartment door and got to my feet. Any sudden movements now could spell disaster. I opened the door, as slowly as I could, hoping there'd be no draught blowing in. Just a couple more gentle pushes and we'd be clear.

My mobile phone, resting on the desk in what passed for my office, began to ring, buzzing and rattling against the hard surface. Gramsci opened one sleepy eye, took in the whole scene, and yowled when he saw his new favourite toy on the verge of being taken away from him. He jumped down off the sofa and raced across the floor, his little paws slipping and sliding on the polished surface, and launched himself at the tree in a last, desperate attempt to prevent me from moving it outside.

Silently, and inevitably, every last needle dropped to the floor.

I sat there gazing at Gramsci in silent disbelief. Then I shook my head, and got to my feet, making my way over to the office to answer the phone.

I stretched my hand out towards it and picked it up.

It stopped ringing.

I looked back at Gramsci, his paws now scrabbling away through the pine needles, as if he had set himself a personal challenge of trying to get them to cover as much surface area of the floor as possible.

He paused, and looked up at me for a moment, before returning to his work.

I sighed, and slumped into the chair behind my desk.

The phone rang once more. I grabbed at it, stabbed at the buttons and shouted 'WHAT?' a little bit more loudly than I had intended.

There was silence on the line for the moment. Then, 'I'm sorry, I think perhaps I've got the wrong number.'

Ah shit.

'Er no, you probably haven't, sorry. It's just my cat is intent on making my life a misery, and now I find myself with a pile of pine needles to sweep up and—'

He cut me off. 'Am I speaking to the British Consulate in Venice?'

'Yes. Yes, you are. Well, sort of. It's the Honorary Consulate.'

'Right. I see.' He paused. 'Is there a proper one I can call?'

'I'm sorry,' I said. 'Just one moment, please.'

I put the phone on mute, and glared across the room at Gramsci. 'This is your fault, you realise?' Then I banged my head gently on the desk, before switching on my brightest smile, and replacing Grumpy Nathan with Sunny Nathan.

'I'm sorry,' I repeated, 'how can I help you?'

The voice at the other end of the line took a deep breath. 'I'm not sure if you can. I've been all round the houses this morning. I've called the police in Venice, but couldn't really make myself understood. Then I called the British Embassy in Rome, and they suggested I call the Consulate in Milan. And then they told me to get in touch with you.' He took another deep breath. 'I'm a bit at the end of my tether to be honest. I think you might be my last hope.'

'Okay. Well I'm sorry to hear that. I'll do all I can, I promise. Just tell me what you need.'

'It's my brother. He's in Venice at the moment, and I'm starting to worry that he's gone missing.'

I nodded to myself, and took out a pen.

'Well, now. I'm sure we can sort it out. People do sometimes just drop out of contact for the simplest of reasons and—'

He cut me off. 'I know all that. I know all that. For Christ's sake, people have been telling me this all morning.' He took another deep breath and then continued, with a slight tremor in his voice. 'I'm sorry. I'm just starting to worry, you understand?'

'Of course.' I clicked at the pen. 'Why don't we start with your brother's name?'

'Shawcross. Anthony Shawcross.'

I scribbled it down. 'And your name is?'

'Stephen. His brother, as I said.'

I put a slash next to Shawcross's name, and wrote 'Stephen' next to it.

'Okay then, Mr Shawcross, how long have you been trying to contact your brother?'

'It's been just over a day now.'

My hand froze, on its way to the paper. 'Ah.'

'"Ah"? What do you mean, "Ah"?'

'Well,' I took a deep breath as I tried to find words that were suitably diplomatic, 'given that the last contact with your brother was relatively recent, I think that does explain why you've been sent around the houses this morning. In all honesty, the police probably won't be interested for at least seventy-two hours. It would be different if there was a child involved but that's not the case here, of course.'

'So you can't help me? Nobody can help me, is that what you're saying?'

'Not quite. These things usually work themselves out, as I said, but there might still be a few things I can do. Can I just ask you if there's any particular reason to feel concerned for your brother's safety?'

Shawcross took a deep breath. 'My brother is a very sick man, Mr,' he paused, 'I'm sorry, I don't even know your name.'

'Sutherland. Nathan Sutherland. Again, I'm sorry to hear that. Tell me more.'

'He's . . .' he paused again, reaching for the words in the

hope that choosing the right ones might somehow make the situation less real, 'very ill, as I said.'

'I see.'

'We told him – that's my wife and I – we told him not to go on this bloody trip. But he wouldn't be dissuaded.'

I nodded to myself. Venice in January could be a cold and lonely place for a single traveller. As if on cue, the wind rattled the windows.

'I understand. Is your brother here on holiday, or is it business?'

'A working holiday, he called it. He was researching our family tree. One of our relatives was killed in Italy during the First World War. Tony had got it into his head that he wanted to stand at our grandfather's grave. I don't quite understand that myself, but this was always more his sort of thing than mine. And so, I told him this trip wasn't the best idea in the world but he said he'd be perfectly fine, and he'd call me every day. Except, well, yesterday he didn't.'

'Okay. Have you tried calling him? It might just be that there's no credit left on his phone and he doesn't know how to top it up. That happens more often than you might think.'

'I've tried that. The phone just rings out.'

'How about social media? Any postings on Facebook, Twitter, that sort of thing?'

'No.'

'Instagram?' I paused. 'TikTok?'

There was a dry laugh at the other end. 'Tony isn't a social media sort of person, Mr Sutherland.'

'What about his employer?'

'Tony's a librarian. At Magdalen College.'

I whistled.

'That's what I call him anyway. He describes himself as an archivist. Apparently there's a difference, but I've never quite worked out what it is. And, no, they haven't heard anything from him either.'

I drummed my fingers on the desk. Missing persons were a rare occurrence and usually had a happy ending. Phones, sometimes, just failed to work or were switched off. It could just be that Anthony Shawcross thought he had better things to do on what might turn out to be his last holiday. And twenty-four hours, really, was no time at all. Nevertheless . . .

'Okay,' I said. 'There isn't all that much I can do given the timescales. But that doesn't mean that there's nothing I can do. I'll start by calling the hospital. As you said, your brother, sadly, is unwell. That'll be the first place to start.'

'Thank you. Is there anything else?'

'Well, do you have an address for him? A hotel, bed and breakfast, something like that?'

'I'm sorry, I don't. Stupid of me. I never imagined it being important.'

'Okay. No matter. Wherever he's staying, they'll have had to register his presence with the local authorities. I can find that out.'

'And the police? You said they won't investigate at short notice.'

'Not officially. But I might be able to call in a few favours. Get things moving, that sort of thing.'

'Thank you. I'm very grateful.'

'It's not a problem. I'll be in touch.'

***

I called the *Ospedale Civile* in Venice, without success. Then I called every hospital within a reasonable distance on the mainland. And then I tried every doctor in Venice that I could think of. Nobody had heard of an Anthony Shawcross. I even rang Father Michael Rayner from the Anglican Church, just in case he'd had an emergency call-out, but without success, and I wasn't about to try every remaining priest in the city on the offchance Mr Shawcross was Catholic.

That only left the *Questura*. I wasn't convinced I really did have any favours to call in, and so I was pretty sure the answer would be little more than a sympathetic sucking of teeth and the suggestion I wait a couple of days.

Still, it was either that or sweep up the remains of the Christmas tree. And it would at least allow me to tell Shawcross that I had indeed done all I could for the time being.

I picked up the phone and dialled.

'*Pronto.*'

'Vanni! My lucky Christmas Angel at the top of the law enforcement tree!'

There was a pause, and then a chuckle, 'I'm sorry, Nathan, is that how the British Honorary Consulate conducts its business over the telephone these days?'

'It's my New Year's Resolution, Vanni.'

'Well, Happy New Year to you, Nathan. And I hope Father Christmas was good to you.'

'He was. Fede bought me a lovely Jethro Tull box set. The remastered *Passion Play* sessions with all the out-takes.'

He chuckled again. 'What a marvellous woman she is.'

'She got me some headphones as well. I think the two might be related. How about you?'

'Socks.'

'Socks? Fantastic. Socks are good.' I paused. 'Anyway, I'm sorry to bother you, Vanni, but I was wondering if I could call in a favour.'

'A favour? Do I owe you any, Nathan?'

'Well, no. But I was wondering if I could have this one on account.'

He sighed. 'That depends. Go on then, tell me what it is.'

'I've got a not-quite missing person.' Vanni, I could tell, was on the verge of sighing again, so I hurriedly continued. 'Seriously ill, apparently, and hasn't been in contact with his brother for over twenty-four hours. Not answering his phone, but no records of him being in hospital. So I was wondering—' I took a deep breath.

'Yes, Nathan?'

'If he's staying anywhere legitimate they'll have registered his passport details. Could you check that out for me?'

'I can do that, Nathan. That shouldn't be too difficult.' He chuckled. 'I thought it was going to be something more complex. What's the gentleman's name?'

'Anthony Shawcross.' I spelled the name out for him.

'Okay, Nathan. Just leave it to me.'

'Thanks, Vanni. You're a pal. Just one other thing.'

'Oh yes?'

'If you find out where he is, would you mind coming with me? Just, you know, in case it's something unpleasant.'

'Ah. I see it's getting more complex already, Nathan.'

'There's lunch in it for you, Vanni.'

He chuckled. 'Just give me thirty minutes.'

Chapter 2

'Thanks for coming out, Vanni.'

'Oh, Nathan, it's the beginning of the year, the city is quiet, and there's a free lunch involved. Of course I was going to come out.' He clapped me on the back. 'This must be a bit unusual for you though, I imagine? Tourists getting themselves in trouble in January?'

'Well, the guy's brother seemed genuinely worried so I figured it was something I should look into. And it saved me from having to dispose of a dead Christmas tree.'

'Why don't you just get an artificial one?'

I shook my head. 'Never going to happen.' I rubbed my hands together. 'Cold out, isn't it?'

Vanni laughed. 'Even after all these years, Nathan, you still need to talk about the weather. What's that line about taking the Englishman out of England?'

'Come on, it's freezing. Can we at least talk inside?'

He nodded. 'I suppose it is a bit chilly.'

I grinned. 'That's it. Now you're getting it.' I took a look around. The icy wind was blowing in off the open lagoon, and along the Cannaregio Canal. Most of the bars and restaurants were still closed and would remain so throughout

January, as their owners headed off in search of the sun during what passed for the low season. 'Where's open?'

Vanni nodded in the direction of Tre Archi. '*Al Parlamento* should be. Come on.'

Cannaregio was a little off the beaten track for me, but *Al Parlamento* was always a pleasure to visit when I found myself in that part of town. It managed to be both modern and cosy at the same time, the polished wooden tables and black ash furniture offset by the ropes that lined the ceiling and walls and gave the bar a vaguely nautical feel.

'Are we properly eating? Or just having *cicchetti*?'

'*Cicchetti* are properly eating, Nathan.'

'Okay. And to drink?'

He shook his head. 'I'm on duty. Just a red wine, please. And a couple of tuna and egg *tramezzini*.'

I made my way over to the bar and looked at the range of food in the cabinet. Meatballs, of course. Small octopuses. Fried crab claws. Sliced meats and cheeses. All of those would be good. But what would be best on a freezing cold day? I smiled, as I saw the rows of crispy orange *arancini*, fried risotto balls. Perfect for getting some heat back into me.

I smiled at the *barista*. 'One of these, please.'

He nodded. 'Which filling?'

'There's more than one?'

'Mozzarella. *Ragù*. Pistacchio and mortadella.'

'Damn, that's difficult. Tell you what, I'll have one of each.' I nodded in the direction of Vanni. 'And two *tramezzini* with tuna and egg for my friend.'

The *barista* raised his eyebrows. 'I think you've done the better, there.'

'Ah, he's a man of simple tastes. Besides, he's at work. He's got to be sensible.'

'Okay. Anything to drink?'

I paused for a moment. A spritz would seem the obvious thing, and yet it was quite obvious that I was having a rather more substantial lunch than Vanni. Perhaps it wouldn't be fair to rub his nose in it by having a proper drink as well. I'd join him in a modest glass of wine.

'Just two *ombre rosse*, please.'

He nodded. 'Okay. You go and join your friend and I'll bring your *arancini* over when I've warmed them up.'

I pulled a chair up next to Vanni. 'So. Did you find anything?'

'I've got an address, that's all. I just hope this isn't going to be something that spoils our lunch.'

I shook my head. 'Nothing is capable of spoiling lunch.'

The *barista* arrived with my plate of *arancini*.

Vanni raised an eyebrow. 'You sure you've got enough there, Nathan?'

'Well, I don't know when I'll next be up here.' I bit into the first, the heat from the molten mozzarella scorching my tongue. I drained half my glass of wine in an effort to stop it burning.

'Good?'

'Very. And you'd have to say it's got some heat back into me.' I looked down at my plate. 'I might give them a couple of minutes though.'

Vanni nibbled at his *tramezzino*. I couldn't help but notice he was looking just a little enviously at my plate.

'Tell you what, Vanni, why don't you take one of these?'

'Oh, I couldn't.'

'You could.'

'No, I really couldn't.' He patted his stomach. 'I enjoyed Christmas a little too much.' He finished the remains of his sandwich, wiped his fingers on a paper napkin, and took a little sip of wine. 'Mm-hmm. That's better. So, let's talk.' He reached into his coat, took out an envelope, and laid it on the table between us. 'Let's have a little look at this, eh?'

He opened the envelope and took out some photocopied sheets. 'Here's his passport. Or, at least, the important bits. Anthony Thomas Shawcross, date of birth June 19th 1958. Next of kin Mr Stephen Shawcross, who seems to be his younger brother.'

Vanni jabbed his thumb in the direction of the Cannaregio Canal, heading out towards the open lagoon. 'Seems he rented an apartment here just a few weeks before Christmas. From a *signor* Righetti who now lives out on the mainland – Mestre, Spinea – somewhere out in that direction anyway.'

'Ah. One of those. An absentee landlord.'

'Exactly. It seems he has a few places around here. Anyway, he's been very helpful.'

'He has?'

'Oh yes. Firstly I told him that I was not from the *Guardia di Finanza*. Then I told him I had a very good friend at the *Guardia di Finanza*. After which he was positively falling over to help me. Now, what else do we have?' He licked his index finger and paged through the photocopies. '*Anthony Shawcross, Librarian. Magdalen College.*' He paused. 'Did I say that right?'

I smiled. 'It's pronounced "maudlin", Vanni.'

'It is?' He shook his head. 'No wonder you English are terrible at other languages. It must take you a lifetime to learn to pronounce your own.' He made little air quotes with his fingers. 'So where's this "maudlin" college, then?'

'Cambridge. No, hang on, what did his brother tell me? Let me check that card again.' He turned his phone back to me. 'My mistake. That's the Oxford spelling.'

'You have two of them? And you spell them different ways?'

I nodded.

'But you pronounce them the same?'

'We do.'

'Should I ask why?'

I shook my head. 'Probably best not to. So, has *signor* Righetti heard from him recently?'

'Ah, well this is where it gets a bit awkward, Nathan. He telephoned *signor* Righetti early yesterday morning.'

'Okay. Anything important?'

'Just wanted to know what the rubbish collection hours were going to be like for Epiphany. So, given that, we can't open a file on him as a missing person for at least another forty-eight hours.'

'Bugger. That's not much to go back to his brother with.'

'Perhaps not, Nathan. But, given Mr Shawcross is supposed to be staying just along the *fondamenta* from here, I figured there'd be no harm in us going along and just paying him a call. And then you can go back to his brother and tell him everything's all right. And I – well I can go back to the *Questura* having had some fresh air and a free lunch.' He swirled the last of his wine, drained the glass and clapped me on the back. 'Come on,' he smiled. 'You're paying, I believe. Now let's get going.'

Chapter 3

Vanni shivered in the cold air that was blowing in off the northern lagoon. 'Bloody cold place to choose to stay at this time of year, if you ask me.'

'Where's our man, then?'

'Just along here. Right at the end of the *fondamenta*.'

'I thought most things along here belonged to the University?'

'Most of that's on the other side of the canal. There are a couple of private houses along here. Both of which belong to *signor* Righetti.'

We passed under the scaffolding of a private residence undergoing restoration. Nobody was at work, it evidently being still too close to the festive season for it to have resumed. A few posters were affixed to the boarding, promoting various local bands or merely being reassuringly rude about the current mayor.

We stopped outside a pair of identical wooden doors, both surmounted by rusted metal lunettes. Similarly, both had a key safe affixed to the wall, next to a white plastic plate with the legend *Locazione turistica*.

Vanni checked his phone once more, nodded to himself,

and moved to the door on the left. 'This one.' He rested his thumb on the buzzer.

There was no answer.

He shrugged. 'Well, I suppose Mr Shawcross might just be taking in the sights. It would be polite to phone him before we go barging in.' He tapped at his phone.

He let it ring for about thirty seconds, then shook his head and hung up.

'What do we do now?'

He looked at his watch. 'Mr Shawcross may be out sight-seeing. Or perhaps he's a heavy sleeper enjoying a long lie-in.'

'Or perhaps—'

'Or perhaps not. Come on.' He tapped at the pad on the key safe, and it clicked open. He smiled at me. 'I told you *signor* Righetti had been most helpful.' He looked inside. 'Emergency key. Excellent.'

He unlocked the door and we stepped inside. 'Now then, what do we have here?'

The entrance hall had evidently been partially redecorated following the previous year's *acqua granda*. The walls had been replastered to a height of perhaps one metre, but had yet to be repainted. To my right, a narrow staircase led upwards; whilst a short corridor led to an open-plan living room and kitchen.

Vanni pointed a finger upwards. 'I'll check upstairs. You take a look in the kitchen.'

'Check for what, exactly?'

'Mr Shawcross, I suppose. Remember, we're just here because we might have grounds to be concerned about his safety.'

'Uh-huh.'

He waved a finger at me. 'And don't touch anything. Just in case.'

I nodded, and made my way through to the living room. There was still a faint smell of fresh paint about the place, and the furniture looked clean and modern. The bookcases I recognised as a popular flat-pack design. The white goods, similarly, were shiny and new. I could only imagine the sort of devastation that last November's floods must have done to *signor* Righetti's property but, fair play to him, he hadn't skimped on trying to put it right.

I took a look at the books on the shelves. There were a few recent Italian bestsellers and a number of guides to Venice, but the majority – presumably thinking about the likely rental market – were dog-eared English-language thrillers. I spotted a faded hardback of *Death in Venice* and du Maurier's *Not After Midnight* – the short story collection that contained 'Don't Look Now'. I smiled to myself. Well, perhaps it was an obligation to read these whilst on holiday in *La Serenissima*.

The kitchen looked clean and well-kept. The dishwasher – I raised my eyebrows, a *dishwasher* no less – had been emptied and the plates stacked in the drying rack. There was even a kettle, a device that most Italians regarded with suspicion, given the likelihood of it tripping a fuse should it be used at the same time as any other electrical device. I rested the back of my hand against it, forgetting what Vanni had said about not touching anything. It was cold.

I'd expected something a little more *Mary Celeste*, but it seemed I was going to be disappointed.

I was about to give up and join Vanni upstairs when I

noticed a cork notice board in the entrance hall. There was the usual selection of business cards pinned up, for local restaurants, bars and pizzerias that delivered. A glossy flyer advertised a regular performance of Vivaldi's *Four Seasons*, a series of concerts that felt as if they might have been running since the time of the Red Priest himself, and would presumably continue until the waves covered the spire of the last church in Venice.

There were two other things that caught my eye. The first was an invitation, printed on thick, high-quality cardboard, that requested the presence of Mr Anthony Shawcross at the inauguration of the new lighting system at the Scuola Grande di San Rocco.

I recognised it at once. After all, a similar invitation was pinned to my kitchen wall, back in the Street of the Assassins.

The other was a map – I looked closer – no, not a map, it wasn't quite detailed enough for that. It was a small pamphlet about Commonwealth War Cemeteries in the Veneto. A basic guide to driving around the sites, with a small photograph and a brief description of each one.

Vanni called from upstairs. 'Nathan, can you come up here for a moment? I think I need your help.'

A large flat-screen TV was fastened to the wall of the upstairs room, while another bookcase held a collection of DVDs. Some old Hollywood classics, cartoons (presumably in the hope of entertaining bored children on a wet day), *cinepanettoni* for the holiday season, and a number of titles unfamiliar to me that looked as if they could have been picked up for a couple of euros or given away free with newspapers.

The furnishings, I noticed, were somewhat more weathered than downstairs, presumably there having been no need to replace them. Vanni was sitting on a beige velour sofa that had seen better days, in front of a wooden coffee table that, evidently, had not come out of a flat pack. Laid out in front of him were a number of yellowed papers, all handwritten.

'What have you found?'

'You tell me, Nathan. My English isn't up to it.'

I sat down next to him, and stretched out my hand. He knocked it away. 'Remember what I said?'

'Sorry.' I took my glasses from my coat pocket, and leaned closer.

I began to read.

Chapter 4

Hello Ma,

Thanks for the cigarettes. Everything arrived safe and, more importantly, dry. There's a joke among the men as to whether they're more frightened of Austrian bullets or Italian cigarettes.

Things are well here. I seem to have made myself useful. Not too many of the brass speak any languages beyond English and shouting. A chap who speaks Italian might go far. A chap who speaks Italian and German might go even further. Well now, your little boy might not have been such a waster after all. It seems I might be in some demand.

Honestly, Ma, it couldn't have come at a better time. They say the Austrians gained a kilometre on us yesterday. Nobody knows how. Everyone says they must be beaten by now. Trouble is they just don't seem to know it yet.

Still, you mustn't worry. It'll be over soon. Everybody can feel it. Except, perhaps, the bloody Austrians and they'll feel it soon enough. That's the thing, Ma. I'd never understood quite how much the Italians hated them before. Some of them were at Caporetto. Dear God, some of them were even gassed at Caporetto. And then there are the Venetians. It almost seems personal to them. No Austrian boots, they tell me, are ever going to tread La Serenissima *again (that's what they call Venice, by the way). So, no, you mustn't worry. I feel it's very much this far and no further. And tomorrow, it seems, I'm being called up to the big house on the hill to talk with the top brass. Who'd have thought it, eh? I hope Father would have been proud of me.*

I'm writing, as ever, to Margaret and the Boy. Could you be so good so as to drop them a line, just in the event of mine not arriving?

Your loving son,

Thomas

'A letter from the front,' I said. 'From the First World War.'

'From an Englishman?' said Vanni.

'I think they were in this area, weren't they?'

Vanni nodded.

'Written to his mother, then. I imagine Margaret is his wife, and the Boy is his son.'

Vanni chuckled. 'The English, eh? Never knowingly over-emotional.'

'Different times, Vanni, different times.'

'Strange, though. I thought letters from the front were censored. Just in case information fell into the wrong hands.'

'I thought so, too. Our mysterious Thomas seems to have been fortunate with this one. Perhaps they thought there was nothing that could be too compromising in there. Or maybe he never got to send it? What do you think he means by "The big house on the hill"?'

Vanni shook his head. 'No idea.'

'What else have you found?'

'Nothing much to speak of. There's a bedroom upstairs. Everything seems normal. Clothes in wardrobes, bed all properly made up. Nothing to indicate that he left in a hurry. Not really anything to indicate he left at all.'

'So he might be back any minute wondering what the hell two strangers are doing sitting in his front room?'

'That'd be good, wouldn't it? But I can't hang around here all afternoon, and I imagine even you've got better things to do.'

'So you're saying we're just going to give up?'

'Nothing else to do. If there's no sign of Mr Shawcross in the next couple of days, well then we'll be able to mark him as a missing person. Until then,' he shrugged, '*boh.*' He looked over at me. 'Anything downstairs?'

'Maybe so. You know there's a big *thing* at the Scuola Grande di San Rocco, tonight?' Vanni scratched his head. 'They've improved the lighting, or replaced it, or something like that. Proper illumination for the Tintorettos after five hundred years. So the great and the good have all been invited to the grand opening. The mayor will be there. The two candidates to replace him. All the great and the good, as I said. And, erm, me.'

'You?'

'Yes. I know it seems a bit odd. But every Consul in the city got an invite and they included me in that as well. The strange thing is, though, our Mr Shawcross has an invite pinned to the wall downstairs.'

'Really?'

'Really.'

'But why?'

'No idea. If he works for Magdalen College he must be quite eminent in his field, I suppose. Whatever that field might be. If he turns up, I'll ask him.'

Vanni grinned. 'Nicely done, Nathan.'

'Only thing is, I don't know what this guy looks like.'

'No problems. We've got that scan of his passport. I can send you a better copy.'

'What do you think I should do, Vanni?'

He shrugged. 'Very much up to you, Nathan. Officially, Mr Shawcross has done nothing wrong and neither can we register him as a missing person for the next forty-eight hours or so. So if he does happen to turn up at this event tonight, that'd be convenient for all concerned.'

'Fingers crossed then. Oh, and there's one other thing. There's a guide to the Commonwealth War Cemeteries of the Veneto pinned up in the kitchen.'

'War graves?' Vanni gestured at the letter on the table. 'And we have this as well.'

'Shawcross's brother said that's why he's over here.'

Vanni got to his feet. 'God, it's getting cold in here. So, what do you know about war graves in the Veneto, Nathan?'

'Nothing at all,' I smiled. 'But I know a man who might do.' I looked at my watch. 'And now, Vanni, I really need to be getting home. Federica will be back in a couple of hours, I need to look my best for tonight and, more importantly, I have a dead Christmas tree to deal with.'

Chapter 5

'Why do you think he invited you?' said Federica.

'I don't know, really. Maybe he just thinks he has to.'

'I mean, you and the mayor have never got on, have you?'

'No.'

'And the last time you met him, you started a fight in the most holy space in Venice.'

I stopped fiddling with my bow tie. 'I did not *start* a fight. I was attempting to *stop* a fight.'

'Do you think he knows the difference?'

'I suspect not.' I went back to work on my tie. Long length on the right side. Bring the left side up and hold in a vaguely bow tie kind of shape. Loop the other side over, make a loose knot. Fold the other side. Poke it through. Adjust to satisfaction.

Oh yes. Don't forget to shout 'Gah!' and start again.

Fede looked over at me and smiled. 'Are you ready, *caro mio*?'

'I'm not ready. I'm not ready at all. I hate wearing evening dress. And I especially hate wearing evening dress to go to an event organised by a man who basically despises me. You know, I wouldn't be surprised if he decided on the dress code just to piss me off. And—'

'Ranting again, *tesoro*.'

'Sorry.'

'Anyway. I've got a present for you. Something guaranteed to make you feel better.'

I smiled.

'And no, it's nothing to do with your horrible music.' She opened the drawer in her bedside table and took out a small box. 'Here you are. Call it an early birthday present.'

I opened it up, and laughed when I saw what lay inside, feeling the relief flooding through me.

'A clip-on. You bought me a clip-on!' I hugged her. 'Best wife ever!'

'Well, not quite. The best wife ever would have given you this thirty minutes ago and prevented all the swearing and getting in a state.'

'Oh.'

'But I thought I'd hold it back for a bit given the shambolic state of the apartment.'

'Ah. The Christmas tree?'

She nodded. 'And before you say "what about an artificial one?", that's not up for negotiation.' Then she smiled again and kissed me on the cheek. 'So why do you think the mayor invited you?'

'He didn't. He invited the Ambassador. But Maxwell's tied up in Rome at the moment and couldn't make it. And while the mayor can afford to be blasé about pissing off little old me, I imagine he wants to remain on good terms with the Ambassador.'

'Why so?'

'Future events. The mayor's got his eyes on the Senate.

That'll mean receptions with the *glitterati*, smiling out from the front pages of *Repubblica*. "Building Bridges with our English friends." Those sorts of headlines.'

'Does William Maxwell really glitter?'

'Only at times of special celebration, as I understand. But he comes with a sufficient amount of stardust to impress the modest social climber. Hence my invite, as a sort of Maxwell-lite.' I offered her my arm. 'Shall we go, *dottoressa* Ravagnan?'

'I think we should, Mr Sutherland. Are you ready to sparkle, then?'

'I'll do my best.'

We sidestepped the carcass of the Christmas tree, and made our way out into the night.

The Confraternity of San Rocco was established in 1478, in honour of the eponymous saint who, it was believed, offered protection from the plague. A saint therefore deserving of a certain amount of veneration in the Middle Ages, and all the more so in a city like Venice. But almost a hundred years had passed before the *scuola* that bore his name was completed and, more importantly, a gentleman called Jacopo Robusti, better known as Tintoretto, was entrusted with the interior decoration. Well, perhaps not so much entrusted. There had, after all, been a competition open to the finest artists in Venice, the winner of which would be given this most prestigious of commissions.

Tintoretto, however, had heard of the concept of 'fair play' but decided he wanted no part of it. And so – with only a modest element of skullduggery, involving installing some of his paintings whilst the canvases of his rivals were still wet – the prize was his.

Crafty fellow, Tintoretto. And yet, who can honestly say that he was wrong? The *Sala Terrena* covered the Annunciation to the Assumption, and more besides. The walls of the *Sala Superiore* detailed the Adoration of the Shepherds through to the Ascension. The ceiling of the same room covered more of the Old Testament than I, at any rate, was able to recall, and made me wonder if it was only lack of space that stopped crafty old Jacopo from illustrating the entire book. And then, in the *Sala dell'Albergo*, Christ looked down from his cross in one of the great Mannerist crucifixion scenes.

Names and *documenti* were being thoroughly checked at the entrance and the presence of policemen with guns made me a little nervous. I didn't think I'd ever get used to that. I remembered how Vanni had reacted when I told him that British policemen normally went about their business armed with little more than a stick.

'Ravagnan, Federica. Sutherland, Nathan.' The security guard smiled and handed our ID cards back. 'Enjoy the evening, *signori*.'

'Thank you.' I craned my head and tried to look at the list of names in his hand, but he frowned and pulled them away. 'Excuse me,' I said. 'I was just wondering if Mr Shawcross is here?'

He licked the tip of his finger and flicked through the pages. 'Shawcross, Anthony.' He shook his head. 'I'm sorry sir, he hasn't arrived yet.'

'He hasn't cancelled or anything has he?'

'Not as far as I know, sir.'

'Ah, well then, hopefully he'll be along later.'

Fede took my arm, and we walked up the great staircase to

the *Sala Superiore*, ready to be greeted. We reached the back
of the line, and I stood on tiptoe to see just who we would be
presented to.

'Oh God.'

Fede looked at me. 'What's the matter?'

'It's him. It's the mayor. I didn't think he'd want to meet
everyone personally.'

'Oh. Perhaps he's forgotten all about your fight in San
Marco. Or perhaps he'll just let bygones be bygones?'

I grimaced. 'Let's hope so.'

I put on my broadest smile and stretched out my hand.
The mayor made to take it and then recognition flared in his
eyes. A smile broke across his face as he changed his gesture
into a wave, and he pretended to be acknowledging someone
on the other side of the room.

Fede gently, but firmly, pulled me away. I turned to stare
back at him, now involved in animated conversation with the
couple behind us. He threw back his head and laughed, then
patted them both on the back as he moved on to the next in
line.

'I don't believe it. Did he do that? Did he genuinely just
do that?'

'Sorry, *tesoro*. Obviously he's not quite over it yet.'

I shook my head. 'The absolute . . . *wanker*.'

I must have spoken a little louder than I intended as
a waiter bearing a tray of prosecco stopped and gave me a
puzzled look.

'Not you,' I said.

He didn't look any the less confused. Federica smiled bril-
liantly at him, and took two glasses.

'Come on, *caro*. Let's go and look at old art. That'll cheer you up.'

She led me to the *Sala dell'Albergo*, where we stared up at the crucifixion. And Christ, fixed to the cross against the background of a thunderous, lowering sky, stared down at us, His body not twisted by the agony of His suffering, but rather radiating strength, and power and light. I smiled to myself. However he might have got the commission, I thought, we could forgive that old rogue Tintoretto for a little *furbismo*.

Federica squeezed my arm. 'How long is it since we've been here?'

I shook my head. 'I can't remember the last time. We shouldn't leave it so long in future. I'd forgotten how wonderful it is.'

'That's the problem of living in Venice. Sooner or later, you risk becoming blasé about everything. This building has been here for over four hundred years, we think. It'll still be here tomorrow. And so we put off visiting again and again. Sometimes, I think, the tourists know better than we do. They only have three days to do everything, and so they *try* and do everything.'

I looked up at the Crucifixion, first with my glasses on and then without. 'I know it's been a while,' I said, 'but I'm not sure I'm noticing a difference. How about you?'

Fede shrugged. 'If you're talking about the art itself, then no. I'm not sure how much better they're capable of making it look; although I imagine there are any number of people willing to have a go. Improving the lighting, rewiring the electrics . . . All that makes a difference, but it's not very sexy. It's more difficult to get socialites in New York help us raise money for that sort of thing. But it's just as important in its way.'

'I guess so. Although I'm just wondering,' I gestured around the room with my prosecco-free hand, '*why*?'

'I don't understand?'

'Well, why not just have a press release? I don't quite see why they're throwing a party for a new lighting system?'

'Because parties are good?'

'They most certainly are.' A waiter passed by with a tray full of drinks. I plucked the glass from Federica's fingers and replaced hers, and mine, with two full ones. He didn't even break his stride. 'But I thought the city didn't have any money, and this must be costing a bit.'

'I imagine it is. But at some point we'll all be asked to put our hands in our pockets and contribute something towards future projects.'

'Oh. I might have known there was no such thing as a free drink. How much are they looking for?'

'About half a million euros, I believe.'

'Do we have that sort of money down the back of the sofa?'

'We don't. But there are people here who might. We're here as representatives of the normal people.'

'And so it's the abnormal ones who'll put up the money, is that right?'

'Exactly.'

I took another look around the room. 'There's a few people here I recognise,' I said.

'I thought there might be.'

I did a quick head count. 'At least six Honorary Consuls, one Consul General, and an actual Ambassador.'

'Is there a collective noun for a gathering of Consuls?'

'There ought to be. Perhaps something alcohol-related. We're a sociable bunch.'

'You seem to be. Now then, tell me about this Mr Shawcross we need to find.'

'Not much to say, really. He's a librarian or archivist or something similar at Magdalen College.' I reached into my jacket and took out the scan of Shawcross's passport that Vanni had mailed to me. 'It's not much of a photo, but it'll have to do. Sixty-something, greying, looks a bit book-ish. Not much more than that.'

'Okay. Shall we split up?'

'Righto. I'll go clockwise and you go anti-clockwise. And then we'll meet back here for drinks.'

'Perfect. Anything else?'

'Yes. If you see someone British, talk to them. They might know something about him.'

'How will I know if they're British?'

'I think we must be very distinctive-looking. At least, that's why I assume people speak to me in English whenever I go into a restaurant.' An elderly couple on the far side of the room raised their glasses and waved and smiled at me. 'Oh no,' I muttered.

'Trouble?'

'The Baldwins. British expats. They live out on Via Garibaldi. Nice enough people, but—'

'But?'

'They keep trying to get me to do things. *Join* things. Foursomes at bridge and doubles at golf. Or is it doubles at bridge and foursomes at golf?'

I smiled back, and I saw them beginning to make their way through the gaggle of people. 'It's too late for me,' I whispered. 'But you can still save yourself.'

Fede gave me a quick peck on the cheek. 'Be brave,' she said, and disappeared into the crowd.

The waiter, seeing the tiredness in my eyes, swapped my empty glass for a full one.

'You look like you need that,' he said.

'I do.' I paused. 'Are you supposed to say things like that?'

He shrugged. 'I'm not sure. It's just nice to know my work's appreciated.'

'It is. Very much. Thank you.'

'Take another. It'll save me coming back.'

'I always knew there was something I liked about this place.'

The Baldwins had, eventually, decided it was time to move on to other people.

As I'd explained, an incident of a few years previously where a shard of glass had gone through my shoulder made it impossible to play golf, and bridge nights, unfortunately, turned out to clash with my weekly – and non-existent – phone call to the Ambassador. It was getting hard to keep track of excuses, though.

Federica was deep in conversation with an elegantly dressed red-haired woman on the other side of the room. There was something familiar about her, but I couldn't quite put my finger on it. She wasn't one of my diplomatic buddies, and neither was she part of the expat community. One of Federica's work colleagues, perhaps? At any rate, I was sure I recognised her.

I felt a hand on my shoulder and turned to see a very large man by my side, with a shock of dark curly hair. Instinctively, I wanted him to think well of me. I hoped I hadn't been staring. But then his eyes crinkled as he smiled, just like Dario's did.

'My wife,' he said.

'Oh right. Mine too.' I shook my head. 'Sorry, wrong thing to say. I mean the other one is my wife.'

His smile grew even wider. 'I knew what you meant. Do they know each other?'

'I honestly have no idea. They seem to be getting on well though.'

He stretched out his hand. 'Gianluca Casagrande.'

'Nathan Sutherland.'

'Your Italian is good, Mr Sutherland.'

I smiled. 'Well, it ought to be perfect after all this time.'

'So what brings you here tonight? Apart from your wife, of course.'

'Well, I normally come to these sorts of things as her plus one. She's been involved with various restoration projects over the years. But tonight, for a change, she's my guest.'

'I see.' He smiled. 'Are you in the arts yourself, Mr Sutherland?'

'Me? No, I wish. I'm the Honorary Consul for the UK. Oh, and call me Nathan, please.'

'Of course. Naaathan.' He stretched out the first vowel as if trying it on for size. 'Is my pronunciation correct?'

'Perfect. My apologies, I know it's not an intuitive name for Italians.'

'The Honorary Consul.' He looked around. 'It seems we have quite a diplomatic corps here tonight.'

'Well, I think it's stretching it a bit to describe me as a diplomat, but thanks for the compliment anyway. So, what brings you here? Apart from your wife?'

'Well, we pledged a little money – not as much as we would perhaps have liked – towards the restoration. But mainly,' he grinned, conspiratorially, 'we're here for my wife to meet and greet.'

I looked across the room to where the red-haired woman was shaking hands and smiling in the midst of a group of minor diplomats all of a certain age and all of whom seemed pleased in the way that only men of a certain age can be when an attractive woman seems to be paying them an unusual amount of attention.

And then my mind flashed back to that morning's headlines in *La Nuova*.

'Oh,' I said. 'So that's—'

His chest might have puffed out. Just a little. 'Anna Fabris. Yes.'

'Wow. That's your wife.'

'Who might just end up being the next Mayor of Venice,' he grinned.

'My goodness.'

He smiled. 'I don't know what that would make me. Venice's First Gentleman, perhaps? Venice's *first* First Gentleman for that matter. Have you met her?'

I shook my head.

'Well, let's rectify that.' He waved across the room to his wife. 'Anna, *cara mia*. Come and meet my new friend.'

Anna smiled and nodded at her group of new diplomatic confidantes, then made her excuses and walked over to join the two of us.

'*Cara*, this is Nathan Sutherland. Our esteemed English Consul in Venice.'

She smiled, and offered me a hand to shake. '*Piacere*. So you must be the husband of *dottoressa* Ravagnan?'

'That's right.'

'Well you have a very charming wife, Mr Sutherland. She's been telling me all about you.'

'She has? Oh.'

'Don't worry. It was all good. Well, most of it.' She saw the expression on my face. 'I'm sorry. I'm just teasing.'

'And I keep telling you that's a bad habit, *cara mia*.'

'It is. One day I'll say something to the press, they'll take it seriously and then *pffft* – all this will be over. It's such a shame, though. Having to be so terribly boring and normal all the time.'

Federica joined us. 'Did you have a nice chat with your friends, *tesoro*?'

'Nice enough. Which means I've managed to escape both the golf circuit and the bridge circuit again. For the time being at least.'

'The hard life of the diplomatic service?' said Anna.

'Very much so. The endless round of parties becomes wearying after a while.'

Gianluca brushed something from Anna's shoulder, and nodded in the direction of a couple of press photographers. She rolled her eyes. 'Okay. It seems I have to go and sparkle for a moment. Lovely to have met you both. See you later.'

We exchanged kisses and they made their way over to the waiting press pack.

'They seem nice,' I said. 'Both of them.'

'Mmm-hmm,' said Fede.

'Ah. What does *mmm-hmm* mean?'

'Nothing bad. Just means I'm thinking, that's all. And they do seem nice. I'm also thinking that she seems very clever, and capable and charming and – well – all those qualities we don't normally associate with being Mayor of Venice.'

'Do you think she could do it?' I said. 'Become mayor, I mean.'

Fede took a deep breath. 'Perhaps. God knows, I think the city could do with her. Not another businessman. Not another party apparatchik from the left or the right, or a lunatic nationalist. I think she'd be very good for us. The only trouble is—' She broke off, and sighed.

'Is?'

'She's an intelligent, honest woman. None of those things are in her favour.'

Chapter 6

My nemesis the mayor walked past us, beaming and laughing and repeatedly patting the back of the man at his side.

Fede gave me a discreet little elbow in the ribs. 'That's him,' she said, 'Giuseppe Meneghini. The mayor's Chosen One, just following one half-step behind him.'

'I don't know much about him.'

'I'm not sure anyone does. Not really.'

'So who does he line up with? Politically, I mean?'

'He says he's completely independent. "I'm not a politician, I'm a businessman." That sort of thing.'

'Oh, I see. Like the mayor?'

'Exactly like the mayor.'

'Why do people keep falling for this bullshit?'

'Because we're Italians. We like businessmen because we like to dream that we can be like them and be fabulously successful and not have to pay very much tax. But mainly it's because we really hate politicians.'

'Why do you think he went to the trouble of organising all this? The mayor, I mean?'

Fede shrugged. 'Can you think of a better place for a party?'

'Well, no.'

'And it'll look fabulous in *La Nuova* and *Il Gazzettino*.'

'Sure. But what's in it for him? I mean, he's not standing again. He's either going to be called upstairs as President of the Region or the Senate if he's lucky. Is it just an ego thing? One final chance to beam out at us all from the front pages over our coffee and brioche.'

'Well, I think you're right. It is an ego thing. But I think it's more than that as well.' Fede gestured around her. 'Look who's here. Businessmen. Religious leaders. Scholars. All the great men of the city, and,' she frowned, 'even a couple of women as well. Oh, and you of course.'

'Don't spoil it.'

'Sorry. But it's just his chance to say "Look what I've done. You thought I didn't care about Venice, but I've managed to replace the lighting in one of the city's most beloved spaces without the taxpayer having to put his hand in his pocket. Look how wrong you've been about me all these years." And more than that.' She looked discreetly to her left and then to her right. 'Anna Fabris is here. And so is Giuseppe Meneghini. The mayor is going to want a photograph with his anointed one, isn't he?'

'But Meneghini's just another businessman. Do they even have any shared values?'

'They share enough in that they're not Anna Fabris, an unreconstructed leftie who, worst of all, happens to be a woman. No, *signor* Meneghini is Mr Mayor's Anointed, and he's the one who'll be on the covers of tomorrow's newspapers.' She frowned. 'That's putting me off the idea of breakfast just thinking about it. Could be worse, though. Andrea Mazzon might be here.'

I grasped for the name, and failed. 'Remind me,' I said.

'The Demon King, *caro*. I think perhaps even Mr Mayor might have decided that he really didn't want to be sharing newspaper headlines with someone like him. That's something to be thankful for, at any rate.'

'Oh *him*.' A little lightbulb flashed on in my brain. 'The pantomime fascist. But only the hardcore nutters are going to vote for him, surely?'

'The hardcore nutters might just be enough to get him into a coalition. Depending on whether he wants to get into bed with Anna or with Meneghini.' She made a face. 'Eww. And that's an image I don't need in my head.'

There was a screech of microphone feedback, making not a few of us jump and not a little prosecco leap from glasses. Giuseppe Meneghini looked embarrassed, but only for a second before the beam reestablished itself on his face.

'*Signor* Mayor, *egregie signore, egregi signori,*' he paused to nod at our new friends and, if anything, his smile grew ever wider, 'dear Anna, dear Gianluca. It's so wonderful to be here tonight. So wonderful, in fact, that I hope you will forgive me for having arranged a little surprise for the occasion. As some of you know, I've always loved the incredible, rich musical heritage of this city. And so, when I heard about tonight's event, I contacted my old friend *maestro* Franzoi of the Ensemble Giovanni Gabrieli in the hope that we might attempt to make this evening even more special. I'm delighted that he accepted, and even more delighted that he has allowed me to take part as well. And so now, can we give a warm Venetian welcome to the Ensemble, who've been most patient in waiting for us.'

He started to clap, and a grey-haired man in a loose black shirt made his way up the stairs and into the hall, with the expression of someone attempting to look embarrassed whilst secretly being quite pleased. He bowed, deeply, and then joined in with the applause as his singers – perhaps thirty of them, male and female in equal number – made their way into the hall and dispersed themselves around the room.

Meneghini beamed, and took his place in the circle.

The *maestro* bowed and smiled once more, and took out a tuning fork which he tapped against the back of his hand and then held next to his ear. He frowned, momentarily, and then hummed a couple of notes, looking at each section of the choir in turn. A few of them nodded back at him, as if to indicate that they'd got it. He closed his eyes for a few seconds, and then raised his right hand.

Giovanni Gabrieli. *O Magnum Mysterium*. Alessandro Striggio's *Ecce Beatam Lucem* might have been more appropriate; but Striggio, as far as I knew, had never come any closer to Venice than Ferrara and so was not to be considered a right and proper representative of *La Serenissima* for an occasion such as this.

It was good, all right. No, more than that. To stand in a room illustrated by one of the great Venetian masters, suffused in the gentle light that reflected off the golden panels on the ceiling, listening to Gabrieli's timeless music was more than good. It was special.

I thought for a moment that *O Magnum Mysterium* would have been more appropriate before Christmas, but then shook my head, annoyed at the silly, uncharitable thought. Besides, prolific as he had been, it was entirely possible that Gabrieli had never got around to writing something for a wet Tuesday in January.

The last notes died away and, as an added touch, the lights dimmed leaving us in near darkness and complete silence. But there's always somebody who has to be the first to applaud and, more importantly, to be seen to be the first to applaud. The mayor shouted *bravi*, started to clap, and the moment was broken.

The lights came up, *maestro* Franzoi smiled, bowed, and indicated each section of the choir in turn.

'So what did you think?,' said Anna.

I shrugged. 'It's good. He's good. I've got to give him that.'

Fede glared at me.

'I'm just being honest, okay? I think he's probably shored up his vote amongst lovers of Renaissance polyphony.'

'And elsewhere?'

'And elsewhere,' I took a deep breath, 'well, I can't speak for everyone but it's entirely possible they'll all think he's a showboating prick.'

Anna looked shocked for a moment, and Gianluca looked around, afraid that somebody might have heard. And then Anna laughed.

'We can only hope so, Mr Sutherland. I'm afraid I can't do anything to compete with that. I've got no voice at all.'

I felt a tap on my shoulder. One of the black-clad male singers, tall, burly and ferociously bearded bent down towards me.

'I heard what you said.' Even though he was whispering, he had a bass voice like the very wrath of God.

'Sorry. Just ignore me, I don't know what I'm saying.' I

managed to restrain myself from adding 'and please don't hit me.'

'You're absolutely right, you know? The prick didn't even turn up for any rehearsals. The *maestro* says he made a donation and so,' he shrugged, 'we put up with it.'

'Oh, right. I've got to say though – and I'm no expert – he sounded pretty good to me.'

'He is. That's what makes it worse.'

Meneghini walked over to us, grinning from ear to ear. 'Anna! Gianluca!' He kissed them both.

Anna smiled at him, likewise Gianluca, although perhaps with more studied politeness. 'I didn't know you could sing, Giuseppe.'

Meneghini grinned again, and pretended to mop his brow, Pavarotti-style. 'I really didn't think I could do it, but the *maestro* carried me through.'

'So is this the start of a whole new career for you?'

'No, I think this is the first and last time. Besides,' he lowered his voice, 'I don't think I'll have time once I'm mayor.' Gianluca stopped smiling, and Meneghini threw his hands in the air. 'Joking. I'm joking!'

Anna pretended to punch him. 'Now Giuseppe, we said we weren't going to talk about this.'

'I know. I know. I'm sorry. My God, but I could do with a prosecco.' He reached out and grabbed a glass from a nearby waiter. '*Grazie, capo*. And cheers everyone.'

I raised what little remained of my drink, and Meneghini frowned. 'No no, that won't do at all.' He snatched the glass from my hand, scurried after the waiter, and returned with a full glass. 'Here you are. You can make a proper toast with this one.'

I raised my glass and smiled. 'Well, cheers then.'

His ears pricked up at my accent. 'An Englishman?'

'Giuseppe, this is Mr Nathan Sutherland. He's the English Honorary Consul in the city. This is his wife, *dottoressa* Federica Ravagnan.'

Meneghini nodded. 'Delighted to meet you both.' He took a hearty drink of prosecco. 'My goodness me, that's better. There was quite a thirst on me. And that's after only four minutes of Gabrieli.'

'I'm a Ring Cycle man, myself,' I said.

He looked confused for a second and then clapped me on the back. 'English humour. I love it. Mr Sutherland, I've always wondered about this, but what does an Honorary Consul actually do?'

'Well, sometimes I wonder that myself.'

'No, don't be modest. I really would love to know.'

'Well, the Embassy is in Rome, of course, and the Consulate General is in Milan. I kind of deal with more local stuff. If someone's lost their passport, or been robbed, then I sort them out as best I can. Similarly, if they're in trouble with the police I can advise them on lawyers and interpreters, and liaise with their families back in the UK.'

'Does that happen very often?'

'Not very much. We're a law-abiding bunch in the main. And despite what you might have heard about the Bad Lord Byron, I'm not sure Brits really come to Venice to behave badly.'

'I'm very glad to hear that. You make it sound quite exciting, though.'

'It can be. It can be frustrating as well. Sometimes you're

dealing with people who are angry or upset, and you realise that you just can't help them. And other times, of course, you might have to tell people bad news. If someone has died, for instance. Or if someone's gone missing.'

'Oh. Does that happen often?'

'Rarely. But it's upsetting when it does.' I figured it was worth asking about my misplaced Englishman. 'Incidentally, one of my compatriots was on the guest list for tonight. A Mr Anthony Shawcross. I was very much hoping he'd be here, but I haven't seen him. I don't suppose any of you know him?'

Meneghini rubbed his lower lip. 'Shawcross,' he said, slowly, trying the word on for size. 'No, I think I'd remember a name like that. Anna, Gianluca?'

They both shook their heads.

'Is he one of those people who's been unfortunate enough to need your services?' Then he grinned. 'That's sounds terrible. I don't mean it like that.'

'I genuinely don't know. He might be one of those rare missing persons. I hope not. I think he's in Venice for some sort of historical research. And so I very much hope he's cloistered away in a remote library somewhere and not picking up his messages.'

'Well, I very much hope so too.' Anna and Gianluca both nodded.

'Giuseppe. My dear fellow. What a delightful surprise.' The mayor walked over to us and hugged Meneghini to him, kissing him on both cheeks. Then he turned to Anna and kissed her hand. He nodded at Federica, ignored Gianluca, and flashed me a smile that could have curdled milk. 'Giuseppe, you must come with me. The press are over in the – oh, what do they call it? The room with the big crucifixion.'

'That's the *Sala dell'Albergo*,' said Federica.

He ignored her. 'As I said, the press are waiting. They'd like a photograph of us both.'

'Of course.' Meneghini smiled. 'Anna, Gianluca, lovely to see you again. *Dottoressa*, Mr Sutherland. I do hope we meet again soon. Oh, and I do hope you find your Mr Shawcross as soon as possible.'

The mayor was halfway across the room before he realised Meneghini was not directly behind him. He turned, and might have tutted, before jerking his head in the direction of the *Sala*; as if to indicate that he was, after all, still mayor, and Meneghini merely an aspiring one.

Fede sighed. 'I think I've seen enough. There's not enough prosecco in the world to make this bearable.'

Anna put a hand on her arm, rolled her eyes and smiled. 'I understand. Hopefully we'll meet again soon.'

Fede took my arm, and we made our way downstairs. Behind us we heard the flash of cameras as the Mayor of Venice and his Anointed One shook hands and smiled and beamed, as Christ looked down on them from his cross.

Chapter 7

'Is that Mr Shawcross? Mr Stephen Shawcross?'

'Speaking.'

'Ah, good morning, sir. It's Nathan Sutherland here again. The Honorary Consul in Venice.'

There was a momentary silence on the end of the line, followed by 'Oh Christ.' He took a deep breath. 'Okay, tell me the worst.'

'Well, there is no worst. Not as we understand it. The good news is that your brother is not in hospital and doesn't seem to have been taken unwell. The last news we have of him is from two days ago, when he telephoned the landlord of his apartment.'

There was another long pause. 'And so what does this mean?'

'Well, for the moment,' I cleared my throat, 'it means there's very little that we can do. Given his recent contact, the police won't consider opening a missing persons report just yet.'

'Christ.' His voice rose. 'So my brother could be lying incapacitated in his apartment and no one would know?'

'No, we know for sure that's not the case.'

'You do? How?'

'I called around there yesterday afternoon. He's not at home. I suspect he's left the city for a couple of days, probably searching out your grandfather's place of rest, as you said.'

'Do you mean you actually physically looked around his apartment?'

'Yes.'

'How did you manage that?'

'As I said yesterday, I called in a favour.'

'From the police? So they are involved now?'

'Not officially. As I said, we have to wait—'

He cut me off. 'Christ. The stories we hear about Italy. They really are all true, aren't they?'

'Mr Shawcross, I assure you everybody is doing all they can.'

'No. No, I'm not sure they are. And if they are, well it's not enough. I'm sorry Mr Sutherland, but I'll have to take this higher.'

I attempted to stammer out some sort of apology, but he spared me the embarrassment by hanging up. I assumed taking it higher meant only one thing, and stared at my phone as if challenging it to ring.

It took perhaps five minutes until the familiar number flashed up on the screen.

I put the phone down, pushed my chair back from the desk and sighed. Fede put her arms around my neck, and kissed the top of my head.

'Better?' she said.

'Much,' I sighed.

'Would a coffee help?'

'Immensely. Maybe a *caffe corretto con grappa*? Or a spritz would be even better.'

'It's half past nine. Isn't that a bit early, even by our standards?'

'I've seen plenty of people drinking spritzes at nine thirty.'

'Yes. And are they people you'd aspire to be?' I said nothing. 'I'll get you a coffee. It sounds like you're going to have a busy day, so tell me all about it.'

I rubbed my forehead. 'Well, that was Maxwell on the phone.'

'Happy Maxwell or Angry Maxwell?'

'Manageable Maxwell. I must have thrown in the right number of "Excellencys". But he wanted to know how I was getting on, of course. And the only information I had to tell him was that Anthony Shawcross might actually be missing, but the police won't do anything as yet.'

'Well, there we go then. Job done?'

I sighed. 'Not really. Wouldn't you know it, but William Maxwell only happens to be an Honorary Fellow of Magdalen College? More than that, he says he actually remembers Anthony Shawcross from his time there.'

'Oh. And what does that mean?'

'It means I really need that coffee.'

Fede made her way to the kitchen, immediately followed by Gramsci. In the meantime I looked through the pile of scribbled notes on my desk. Shawcross had been invited to a prestigious event and failed to turn up. Nothing particularly suspicious about that. Had it not been for the free prosecco I might have sat it out myself.

Nobody by the name of Shawcross – indeed, no British citizen of any description – had been admitted to the local hospitals. He'd left no social media footprint at all, but that didn't seem out of character. And, less than two days ago, he'd been in touch with his landlord. If one could put his illness to one side, there really was, as far as I could see, no particular need to worry about him. But, then again, I wasn't family.

Fede returned from the kitchen with a mug of tea for herself and a steaming thimbleful of black coffee for me. I sat back, closed my eyes, and breathed it in. 'Ahh, that's better.'

'Better than a spritz?' Fede noticed the newspaper on my desk and turned it to face her.

'You might be right. I can feel the synapses starting to fire already.' I opened my eyes and clapped my hands together. 'Because there's one thing I might be able to do.'

'Uh-huh?'

'Yes. It's to do with that map I found. With the Commonwealth War Cemeteries.'

'Mm-hmm.'

Fede, I noticed, had more than half an eye on the newspaper headlines, and the *mm-hmm* sound was a reliable indicator that my words were, perhaps, falling on stony ground.

'Fede, I have something very important to tell you.'

'Mm-hmm.'

'It's about me. Well, about us actually. About what might happen in the event of my death. I've decided to leave all my worldly possessions to Gramsci.'

'Mm-hmm.'

'I mean, it's nothing personal. We've had a splendid time

together and I'm really very grateful but – well, you know – Gramsci was there first, after all.'

'Okay.'

'And I'm sure your mother would let you move back in, so it's not as if you wouldn't be provided for.'

She nodded. 'That's nice.' Then she looked up, and frowned. 'Did you just mention my mother?'

'Ah-hah! You weren't listening, were you? I knew that would get your attention.'

She opened her mouth to protest, but then grinned. 'Oh, I'm sorry, *caro*. I was just looking at this. It might be important.'

'It is?'

'More about the election. There's been another opinion poll. Anna's got quite a lead over Meneghini. I'm starting to think it might actually happen.'

'That'd be good, right?'

'It'd be fantastic. *She'd* be fantastic.' She looked down at the newspaper again, and shook her head. 'But we've been here so many times before. We always end up being disappointed. Anyway, I'm sorry. Tell me what you've found.'

'There's the letter we found at his apartment. Dating from the First World War. And then the map showing the Commonwealth War Graves in the Veneto. Now it might just be that Mr Shawcross is doing a tour of them and that's taken him out of contact for a few days. Some of these places are pretty remote. He might not be able to get a signal.'

'Hmm. Maybe not. How many of these places are there?'

'A lot. Now that might have been a problem. However,' I smiled, 'I know a man who might just be able to help me.'

Chapter 8

Ad nominum honorem

I traced my fingers over the inscriptions etched into one of the side panels that flanked the great bronze doors of St George's Anglican Church in Campo San Vio.

Granezza.

Barenthal.

Cavalletto.

'Lovely aren't they?'

I jumped. Father Michael Rayner, the Tall Priest, had appeared without me noticing.

'Forged in the *Arsenale*, from British artillery from the Crimean War. Swords into ploughshares, you might say. They were restored back in 2015. Those names were barely legible before. And now – well, they'll outlast us all. Certainly me. And that's as it should be.' He clapped me across the back. 'You wanted to see me, Nathan?'

'I did, yes. There's something I'd like to talk to you about.' I rested my fingers on the bronze panel again. 'About this. About war graves in the Veneto.'

He nodded. 'I'd be glad to help. If I can. A relative of yours?'

'No. Nothing like that. It involves a person who might have gone missing.'

He frowned. 'A job for the police, surely?'

'You'd think so.' I sighed. 'Vanni's a good chap, but this has only been a couple of days and so the *Questura* won't register him as officially missing. The guy's apartment bill was paid up to the end of the month and they've got no idea where he might have gone to. All I've got to go on is a name and the fact he was researching Commonwealth war cemeteries in the area. I thought he might have come to you.' I gestured towards the bronze panels. 'Given these.'

Rayner shook his head. 'No. Nobody's been in touch. But it's entirely possible he just didn't know about us. We're not as visible as we should be. Perhaps we need more of an online presence, as I understand we have to call these things.'

'Perhaps so.' I stamped my feet and shivered. 'Cold out here. Any chance we could talk about this in Church Pub?'

'Maybe later, Nathan. I think we might have something in the church itself of interest to you.'

'Oh good.' I stamped my feet again. 'Is it warmer inside?'

'Marginally. Come on.'

We walked down the *calle* that led, invitingly, in the direction of Church Pub. For a moment I hoped that Rayner had changed his mind, and this could all be discussed over a spritz and a porchetta focaccia, but he stopped at the side door of the church and reached for the keys in his pocket. He must have caught the disappointed expression in my eyes and chuckled. 'Come on,' he repeated. 'It won't take long. And if you're good I'll let you buy me lunch.'

'Terrific.'

He led me into the vestry and flicked on a few lights. 'There's something here that might interest you,' he murmured. 'Come on. Let's go upstairs.'

The spiral stairs to the organ gallery were, as I remembered, perilous, unlit and dimensionally unsuited to someone of the height and build of Michael Rayner, and I wondered quite how his ministry in Venice had managed to survive so long. We were halfway up the stairs when I heard a dull thump, a cry of 'Ow' and a whispered curse of 'Buggeration.' Followed, shortly, by a 'Sorry', as if his employer might have heard and disapproved.

We emerged into the organ gallery. Rayner rubbed his head, and combed dust from his hair with his fingers.

'Do you do that every time?'

'Pretty much.'

'I thought you'd have got used to it by now.'

'No. I just try and avoid coming up here. I have churchwardens – nice, short churchwardens – for that.'

'And the organist?'

'We have a policy of not employing excessively tall ones. It's served us well so far. Come on, let's have a look in the archive.'

'The archive? Is that what we're calling it now?'

'It's what I'm calling it. If the Frari has one, well, so can we.'

He unlocked the door at the far end of the gallery, and waved me through. As I remembered, the archive at St George's was not one to rival the great state archives of Venice. There was little more than a bookcase with old registers of services, and a single volume that recorded baptisms, marriages and deaths amongst the small Anglican community. But nevertheless, in its own quiet way, this too was a tiny part of Venetian history and so – despite fitting comfortably into a small IKEA bookcase – it deserved to be dignified with the title of 'archive'.

Rayner noticed me scanning the shelves with my head tilted to the side, the better to read the titles on the spines of the volumes.

'Not there,' he said. He pulled up two chairs to the writing desk underneath the far window, and sat down. 'Come on.'

The desk was old, and and had evidently suffered the attentions of woodworm. The leather top was scratched and scuffed with age, whilst the wood itself was clumsily inlaid with an Art Deco pattern. He caught the expression in my eyes. 'This was a gift. From the Sisters of San Giuseppe up in Cannaregio.'

'I thought they'd all moved out to Padua or somewhere?'

'They did. We inherited a few things from them. Altar linen, for example. All terribly elaborate and ornate and not really our thing at all. Nevertheless, it was a gift.' He tapped the surface of the desk. 'And so was this. So I don't really feel we can just get rid of it.' He patted my chest. 'Now, shift your chair back a little, eh? Just so I can open this up.'

He pulled the top drawer open, not without some effort. Then he reached inside and pulled out a large book, bound in light brown leather, with dull oval gemstones set in silver affixed to the cover.

He placed it on the desk, and ran his sleeve over it to brush away a fine layer of dust.

'So, what do we have here?'

Rayner ran his hand across the cover once more, but this time with a look of genuine reverence in his eyes. 'It's our Book of Remembrance, Nathan.'

'Wow,' I said. 'But isn't this valuable?'

Rayner shrugged. 'Better to say invaluable. As a historical document, that is.'

'Shouldn't it be under lock and key? Instead of just in a drawer?'

'Well, nothing short of a piece of field artillery is going to get through the bronze doors downstairs. The side doors are stout enough. And the door up here is always locked, even if one could fight one's way up the spiral staircase.'

'Nevertheless, if it's of historical value?'

'Nathan, you'd have to be some sort of monster to want to steal something like this. And besides—' He looked embarrassed for a moment and stared down at his shoes.

'Besides?'

'It's too big to fit in the safe. Now, come on, let's take a look.'

He opened the cover, and turned to the frontispiece. '*To the Glorious Dead*,' he said, shaking his head. 'I always struggle a bit with that, if I'm being honest.'

He leafed, ever so carefully, through a few pages inscribed in beautiful gothic script.

Name upon name upon name.

Rayner slipped his spectacles on to his nose, and picked one out at random. 'Andrews, Henry. Private, 4th Fusiliers. Died, 17th April 1917. Age 23.' He shook his head. 'There are about twenty names on every page, Nathan. And about four hundred pages in this book. Every Remembrance

Sunday, we pick out and read perhaps ten names at random. Which means it'll take us almost one thousand years to read out every one. And this is just one book, in one small chaplaincy, in one tiny corner of the Diocese of Europe. *Kyrie Eleison.*'

I couldn't think what to say.

'So,' Rayner continued, 'what's this gentleman's name?'

'Shawcross. Anthony Shawcross.'

'Unusual surname. That's good.'

'It is?'

'Of course. Smith or Jones would be rather more difficult to track down. But I imagine there can't be many Shawcrosses. Now, some of the entries here record the final resting places of the dead. And if we can find that then we'll have narrowed down the location as to where your chap might be.'

'Oh, I see. That's very clever.'

'Thank you.' He leafed through the pages, as carefully as he could. 'It's terribly fragile. We have to be so careful with it. Now then, here we are. *Shawcross, Robert. King's Fusiliers. Died November 1916, aged 17. Buried Granezza. Shawcross, Thomas. British-Italian regiment. Died June 7th, 1918, aged 30. Buried Monte Cavalletto.* Mm-hmm.' He removed his glasses. 'But which one is your man?'

'Thomas. We have a letter from him. Where's Monte Cavaletto?'

'It's up in the Northern Veneto. On the Asiago Plain.'

'You've been there?'

'A couple of times. For Remembrance services, that sort of thing. The nearest town is a place called Calvene.'

'Any hotels there?'

'It's a small place, but there are a couple. Last time I stayed at the *Antico Borgo*.'

'Would you recommend it?'

'I would, yes.' His eyes narrowed. 'What are you planning, Nathan?'

'A road trip.'

'Nathan, Monte Cavalletto's cut off at this time of year by the snow. I don't fancy your chances of getting out there.'

'No, but there might well be some trace of Anthony Shawcross. And that's enough to be going on with. At least that's something I can tell his brother. Not to mention the Ambassador.' Rayner gave me a quizzical look. 'He's taken kind of a personal interest in this. Old school tie. That sort of thing.'

'I see. And how are you going to go about this? There's no public transport out to Cavalletto.'

'I'll have a word with Dario. He's got a car. Or, at least he's in a car share with a mate. Do you fancy coming along with us?'

Rayner shook his head. 'If you don't mind, I'd rather not. And I'm sure I'd only get in the way. When are you planning on doing this?'

'Dunno. Depends when – or if – Dario's free.'

'Oh good. So we have a bit of time then.' He closed the book, and shut it away within the drawer. 'Time, at least, for you to buy me lunch.'

Chapter 9

'You're sure you're okay with me doing this?', I said to Fede. 'I mean, you could come along if you want to?'

She smiled at me. 'Like *padre* Michael, I think I'd only be getting in the way. No, it'll be nice for you and Dario to have a boys' weekend together.'

I pretended to huff. 'This is official consular business, you know? We're not going on a hunting and fishing trip.'

There was a buzz from the door phone.

'*Chi è?*'

'*Ciao, vecio*, it's me. All ready to go?'

'Almost. Come on up for a minute.'

Dario was flushed pink, whether from the cold or from a more-than-usually excessive bout of puppyish enthusiasm. He hugged first me and then Federica who gave a little shriek.

'My God, Dario, you're freezing.'

'Am I? Yeah, I suppose it is kind of cold out there.'

'Do you want a cup of coffee? Something to warm you up?'

'That'd be good.' He frowned. 'Do we have time?'

'Nathan hasn't finished packing yet.'

I gave a little cough. 'I think you'll find I haven't started packing yet. But it won't take long. It's only a couple of days after all.'

Dario frowned. 'You're going to need a proper padded jacket at least, and some decent boots if we're going to be doing any walking.'

'I assumed we wouldn't be. Everyone tells me Cavalletto is cut off at this time of year.'

'You never know. Winters are getting milder.'

'Anyway, we probably won't need to go out there. I imagine we'll find Mr Shawcross holed up in the library amongst the old books, or in front of a toasty fire at his hotel.'

Fede looked at me. 'You know, Dario's right. You should take some proper clothing with you. Just in case.'

'I haven't *got* any proper clothing. The whole point of this trip is just to get a little more information which I can pass on to the relevant authorities and Mr Shawcross's brother. I'm not anticipating hanging around a remote graveyard in the depths of winter.'

Both Fede and Dario were staring at me now.

I threw my hands up. 'Okay, okay. I'll take a scarf. And some wellies. And some thick socks. I think that's the best I can do.'

Fede looked at Dario. 'You will look after him, won't you?'

Dario nodded. 'Don't worry. I'll keep an eye on him. Make sure he doesn't get into any trouble.'

I waved my hands. 'Excuse me? Nathan's still here. And perfectly capable of looking after himself if it gets a little cold.'

Fede rolled her eyes. 'I'll make coffee. You go and pack, *caro*.' She turned to Dario. 'Make sure he's got everything, will you?'

Dario grinned. 'Come on then. Let's check out the socks drawer, eh?'

'So, you know how to get there?'

Dario drained his coffee and nodded. 'Sure. It's not all that far. Not much more than a hundred kilometres.' He looked over at Fede. 'We could probably be there and back by tonight, really.'

She smiled. 'It's okay. He'll only fret if he feels rushed or if he doesn't have enough time.'

Dario grinned, and then reached into his pocket. He took out a Touring Club Italiano map of the Asiago area, and spread it out. 'I've marked a few places,' he said. 'There's a *birrificio* just five kilometres out of Calvene which is supposed to be worth a visit. Now, that's no good if we're driving of course, but there does seem to a be a bus once an hour from the centre of town. Over here,' he jabbed at the map, 'there's an *agriturismo* that Vally tells me is one of the best in the area. So I thought maybe dinner there tonight. And then if it's good I'll go back with the girls – anniversary, birthday, something like that. Hey, maybe we could all go back? Oh, and if we've got time I'd like to stop in Vicenza.'

'Vicenza?', I said, fearing I was losing track of the conversation.

'Sure. Great vinyl record shop in Vicenza. *Vinyl Vicenza*, it's called.' He frowned. 'Or is it *Vicenza Vinyl*? Anyway, they always have a January sale so I figured we should try and drop by there.'

Fede smiled and patted him on the back, before turning

to me. 'I see you've got a busy few days of official consular business ahead of you then, *caro*.'

'Erm, well . . .'

'It's all right. Really. Have a good time. Tell me about that *agriturismo* when you get back, maybe that's somewhere we'll need to go one day.'

Dario folded the map away. 'Okay, *vecio*, I think we're good to go.'

'Grand. There's just one thing I need to do.'

Fede smiled. 'You mean, kiss your wife goodbye?'

I frowned. 'Ah. In that case there's two things I need to do.' I kissed her, and then went to the sofa, where Gramsci was perched. I laid my hand – gently and carefully — on his back, feeling the rise and fall of his breathing. A low sound came from his throat, which might almost have been a purr.

'Listen Grams, it's like this. I need to go away for a couple of days, okay? And I know that's going to be a bit weird, because I haven't done that before. But Federica's going to be here to look after you. So she's primary care giver now, all right? And I won't be long. And maybe I'll try and bring you something back from Calvene. So are we good?'

There was no sound except the occasional rumbly purr, as his chest rose and fell.

'He's asleep, Nathan,' said Fede.

Tronchetto is neither here nor there, and very few places – with the possible exception of Piazzale Roma – say 'you have reached the end of Venice' quite as uncompromisingly. An artificial island, created in the 1960s, much of it served as a car park for tourists and commuters. A number of businesses were also housed there in buildings whose architecture could best be described as 'functional'. To the best of my knowledge, the island hosted precisely one bar and caffè, which made me think that making decisions as important as where to go for lunch or post-work drinks must be a little dispiriting.

Nevertheless, the Christmas lights were still twinkling away, doing their bit to add a little post-festive cheer. They would remain in place until the end of *Carnevale*, still almost two months away, the council having decided it was more economical to leave them in place instead of taking them down and putting them up again a month later. Besides, I thought, in the midst of a cold and dark January, couldn't we all do with just a little bit more twinkliness?

Dario led me to a bay on the ground floor of the car park, occupied by a silver Mercedes.

I whistled. 'Nice,' I said.

He nodded. 'It is. Unfortunately it's not ours.'

'It's not?'

'No.' He sucked his teeth. 'I always leave it here, though. Or hereabouts. And so does Paolo, whenever he uses it.'

'You sure you told him you needed the car?'

'Sure I'm sure. I guess he's just parked it somewhere else.' He tapped away at his phone, and held it to his ear. It rang, and rang, and I could see his expression darkening.

'*Ciao*, Paolo. It's Dario here. Listen, we're at Tronchetto and I can't see the car anywhere. Can you give me a call back and let me know where it is? It's kind of important, okay?' He hung up, and dropped the phone back into his pocket.

'Not there?'

'No. Guess he could be in a meeting or something.'

'So what do we do? I know you said it wasn't a long journey, but I'd hoped to make it further than Tronchetto before nightfall.'

He patted my shoulder. 'No problems, *vecio*, no problems. It'll be here somewhere. We'll find it eventually.'

'Okay. So what are we looking for?'

'It's a silver Fiat Panda.'

'Mm-hmm.' I nodded. 'The Fiat Panda, correct me if I'm wrong, is the most popular model of car in Italy, isn't it?'

'I think so. But don't worry.' He took the key fob out of his pocket, held it above his head, and pressed it. 'Eventually we'll hear the car unlocking, right? Come on, let's start on the top floor and work our way down.'

I shook my head, and followed him up the ramp.

'See, that wasn't so bad, was it?' said Dario.

I looked at my watch, and bit my lip. Still, as Dario had said, Calvene was only one hundred kilometres away.

He tossed the keys to me, and I caught them almost without thinking.

'What are you doing?'

'I thought you might like to drive. It'll be a bit of a novelty for you.'

'Dario, I haven't driven a car in over ten years.'

'All the more reason for you to practise then.'

'Seriously Dario, I don't know if I can even remember how.'

'It's like riding a bike. Once you know how to do it, you never really forget.'

'Yes, but the consequences of doing so are kind of serious when doing a hundred kilometres an hour on the *autostrada*.'

He smiled. 'Give it a go. You'll be fine.'

I made it as far as the exit from the car park before Dario made me pull over. We wearily changed places, and Dario pushed the seat back as far as it would go, his large frame incongruous in the space.

'Sorry,' I said. 'About the wing, I mean.'

'Don't worry. It'll polish out, I guess.' Then he smiled. 'Anyway, one hundred kilometres to go, and I've got a late Christmas present for you.'

'You have? Shit, I didn't know we were doing that. I haven't got you anything.'

He shook his head. 'Doesn't matter.' He slid a CD into the player, and a familiar whooshing sound came from the speakers followed by a thundering eight-bar riff.

I grinned. 'Hawkwind! You shouldn't have!'

He gave my shoulder a gentle punch. 'Of course I should. After all, we're in a Silver Machine, aren't we?'

I didn't think Dave Brock and Robert Calvert had had a Fiat Panda in mind when they wrote it, but I supposed we were.

Dario dropped a few coins into the self-service till at the toll gate on the exit from the *autostrada*, the barriers raised, and we continued our journey across the Venetian plain.

He checked his watch. 'About halfway there,' he said.

I nodded. 'It's strange, you know, being surrounded by so much space.'

Dario looked confused. 'I don't get it?'

'Think about it. In Venice, how often do we see wide

open spaces? You know, proper, open fields and green spaces. Stretching ahead into the distance.'

'Grey motorways. Factories. Uh-huh. You miss that?'

'I don't miss it. It's just, well, a novelty you know?'

Dario had been unusually quiet on the journey, and a singalong to 'Master of the Universe' had been half-hearted at best.

'You all right?'

'Sure.'

'It's that front wing isn't it? Look, I'll pay for it, I promise. Well, if you can just polish it out that'd be nice of course, but if you can't—'

He shook his head, and drummed his fingers on the wheel. 'It's not the car, Nat. I told you, don't worry about it. I'll just tell Paolo it was like that when we found it.'

'What is it then?'

'You been reading the newspapers? About that thing over in China?'

'Oh that. Sounds kind of like SARS or bird flu. That sort of thing.'

'You're not worried about it, Nat?'

'China's a long way away.'

'We're not in Marco Polo's day now, *vecio*. The world's a smaller place.'

'So you are worried about it?'

'A bit. I'm probably over-reacting. It's just with the flooding last year, and then everything we hear about the environment every day and now this . . . I'm worried about my little girl, I guess is what I'm trying to say. What sort of world are we leaving the kids, eh?'

I sighed. 'It doesn't look good, does it? But kids are adaptable, Dario. They're tougher than we think. They'll put things right. Everything that we managed to bugger up.'

He frowned, ever so slightly. 'And you know that, how?'

I grinned. 'I don't. But I thought it was something you needed to hear.'

He looked cross for a moment, and then laughed. 'Ah, listen to me, eh?' He looked down at the CD player. 'Look, have we maybe had enough Hawkwind by now?'

I tried to keep the disappointment out of my voice. 'Sure. What do you have in mind?'

'Genesis?' I looked at him with suspicion in my eyes. 'Gabriel era, okay?' he added.

'Then Genesis it shall be,' I said.

The mournful opening refrain of 'Selling England by the Pound' sounded out as the road started to climb, leaving the featureless plain behind us. Dario started to sing, softly at first, and then with growing enthusiasm as we made our way through the forested roads that led to Calvene.

I smiled. He was, evidently, feeling better.

Chapter 10

'Is this the place?'

'Guess it must be. Looks like the only hotel in town.'

Dario got out of the car, slipped, and grabbed at the door to steady himself. 'Frosty out here. Mind your feet.'

I stepped out, sliding my feet experimentally over the surface of the road. Snow had been cleared recently, leaving behind patches of icy residue.

I took a look around. The street was lined on either side by anonymous modern buildings, and dominated by the *campanile* of the church that towered over its surroundings. Snow was starting to fall again, and the sight of the hotel in the grey half-light made me feel as if we were in a low-budget remake of *The Shining*.

I couldn't help feeling a little disappointed. 'You know, I was expecting something more.'

'More?'

'A bit more, I don't know, mountain-like. Traditional. Cosier, if you like.'

'There was a big flood here back in the nineteenth century. Most of the town centre was swept away. So what we see here has all been rebuilt.' He nodded at the bell tower. 'Even that.'

'How do you know all this?'

'I looked it up.' He grinned, the corners of his eyes crinkling as they always did. 'Look, you might think I spent all my time checking out places to eat and drink. And, yes, I did spend quite a lot of time doing that. But I also thought if we were coming here for an important reason then I ought to learn something about it.'

'Wow. I'm impressed.'

'You did the same though, right?'

'Right. Yes, of course I did. Of course. Anyway,' I said, changing the subject, 'let's get checked in and see what we can find out.'

The receptionist, a moustachioed little man with an optimistic comb-over, smiled at the two of us. Then Dario swept the snow from his coat and on to the polished wooden floor and the smile vanished.

'*Signori?*' He made a great play of running a finger down the ledger in front of him. 'A room for the night? We have two doubles, one twin remaining.'

'Ah, maybe we will. Later.' I said. 'In the meantime, though, we'd just like to ask after one of the guests.'

He removed his glasses, and stared at us without saying a word.

'It's another Englishman. Anthony Shawcross.'

He shook his head. '*Signor Shawcross, sì.*' He looked at me with suspicion in his eyes.

'Is something wrong?'

'Nothing wrong.' He licked his finger, and turned over a page of the ledger. 'But we haven't seen him since Tuesday morning.'

'But his bill has been paid?'

'We require our guests to pay in advance sir. *Per colpo di qualcuno, non facciamo credito a nessuno,*' he smiled.

'But you've checked his room? He's not there?'

He shrugged. 'The room is made up every morning, sir. There's no sign of him having slept in his bed.' He frowned. 'Are you a friend of his?'

'I'm afraid I don't even know him. But I do know Mr Shawcross has been out of contact for a few days. Could we perhaps take a look around his room?'

The little man drew himself up to his not particularly considerable height. 'I'm afraid we couldn't allow that, sir'.

'I know, but I really am concerned about him. We'd only be a few minutes.'

'*We?*' He left the question hanging in the air, as he turned to stare at Dario.

I jerked my thumb in his direction. 'He's my designated driver.'

Dario rolled his eyes at me. 'As my friend says, we'd just be a couple of minutes.'

'I'm sorry, but I don't know who either of you are. As far as I know you've just walked in off the street thinking you might be able to steal from my hotel and,' he stared at Dario as another sheet of snow slid from his shoulders, 'melt all over my clean floor.'

I sighed, and was in the act of reaching for my business card when Dario placed a hand on my arm and shook his head. He took out his wallet, and slowly, deliberately, placed five twenty-euro notes on the counter.

The little receptionist met his gaze and then turned to the

pigeon hole cabinet behind him. He took down a key and placed it on top of the pile of notes.

'Five minutes,' he said.

'Well, I can see why *padre* Michael stays here, *vecio*. Do you think they're all as friendly as him?'

I stared at him. 'Dario, what did you just do there?'

He shrugged. 'Didn't seem like he was going to let us in.'

'Dario, that's the moment at which I take out my consular identity card, say something about "diplomatic business" and allow my natural warmth and charm to do the rest.'

'Oh. And does that work?'

'It does.' I paused. 'Some of the time.'

'Hey, my way worked as well though, didn't it?'

'Except that now you're one hundred euros down.'

'Yeah, but I assumed you'd be paying me back?'

'You what?'

'You know, expenses and all that. Like in the movies.'

'Oh terrific. Terrific. Come on, give me the key before our time's up and he wants another hundred.'

He passed the fob over to me. I weighed it in my hands. Wooden, bell shaped, with a rubber strip around the middle. 'Blimey, not much chance of forgetting to leave this behind is there?'

I opened the door and we stepped through. Shawcross's room, as we had been told, had been made up.

I shivered. 'They've turned the heating down.'

'I guess the guy's not using it, so they think they'll save a bit of money. Okay, so where do we start? Before we get into trouble for the whole "breaking and entering" thing?'

'Technically speaking we're just "entering". And the guy gave us the key, didn't he?'

'Uh-huh. I'm just thinking what Mr Shawcross might say if he suddenly comes back to find us turning his bedroom upside down.'

'We're not going to turn it upside down. We're going to search it carefully. And if he does suddenly come back, we'll apologise profusely. Then I'll call his brother and tell him the good news. And then we can go for a splendid dinner together, happy in the knowledge that justice has been done.'

'Okay. That's a plan I can get behind.' He clapped his hands together. 'So, what are we looking for?'

I shrugged. 'Anything that might tell us where he is.' A suitcase stood on a luggage rack in the corner. 'I'll start with that. You take a look in the bedside cabinet. Then maybe the wardrobe.'

There was, I told myself, every possibility that Anthony Shawcross had checked himself into another hotel for a couple of nights and was just holding on to this room as a base. Presumably he'd have taken some sort of overnight bag with him though? Nevertheless, I felt I should take a quick look at his suitcase without actually tearing it apart.

There was little of interest to be found there and I repacked it as carefully as I could. Dario, I noticed, seemed to have given up and left the room. I heard him moving around in the bathroom.

'Dario?'

'Nat?'

'Do you really think you'll find anything in there?'

'Maybe. Just a hunch.'

I shook my head and turned my attentions to the bed-side cabinet and the stack of paperbacks on top of it. *The White War. Life and Death on the Italian Front. Caporetto and the Isonzo campaign. Hell in the Trenches.* Hemingway's *A Farewell to Arms* was also present, presumably as a source of light relief.

There was something else. A small pamphlet for the Villa Godi Malinverni. I'd never heard of it before and flicked through it. It was just a few kilometres away and – according to the blurb, at least – was generally reckoned to be the first large-scale work by Andrea Palladio.

I turned it over. There was a contact phone number which had been circled in pen, and a 'how to find us' map which, amongst other points of reference, indicated the Commonwealth cemetery at Cavalletto. This, too, had been ringed in pen.

'Nat,' called Dario. 'Come and take a look at this.'

I slipped the pamphlet into my pocket. 'What is it?'

'I took a look in the bathroom cabinet.'

'Erm, why?'

'Running out of places to check, basically.' He waved his hand at the contents of the cabinet. 'Painkillers. Steroids. And this.' He held up a packet for me to look at.

'Lumakras? What's that?'

'I've just googled it. It's an anti-cancer drug. For lung cancer, specifically.' He shook his head. 'The guy at reception told us that Shawcross's room was last made up, what, two days ago? So he's headed off without painkillers, without his medication?'

'He might have taken a supply with him.'

'Mm-hmm. Okay, he might have. But look,' he swept his hand in an arc to indicate the rest of the bathroom, 'shampoo. Toothbrush. Shaver. Unless the guy had two of everything there's nothing to indicate he wasn't planning on coming back the same day, is there?'

I shook my head. 'Hell, Dario, this doesn't look good does it?'

'It doesn't, *vecio*. What have you found?'

'A map of the area. He's marked off the road to Cavalletto.'

'Shit. Do you think he tried to get there?'

'I think maybe he did.'

'So what are we going to do? Call the police? Tell them there's a vulnerable guy gone missing?'

'We could do. But technically he's not gone missing. And even if they're interested, we could waste hours there giving statements.' I went over to the window and stared out. 'It'll be dark in a few hours. I don't think we've got time to waste.'

'Nat, if he's been out there for two days in these temperatures he'll be dead already.'

'Maybe so. But I think we need to try.' I nodded at the map. 'Do you think you can get us out there?'

He took a deep breath. 'For a journey like this, I wouldn't usually choose a Fiat Panda. But we can try.'

I nodded. 'Okay then. Let's get going.'

Chapter 11

We gave the key back to the receptionist, who looked at us as if hoping we'd have something exciting to tell him. When we said nothing, the look changed to one of disappointment.

'Okay,' I said, 'I think we'd like two rooms for the night.'

He shook his head. 'No singles available *signori*. As I said, two doubles, or one twin?'

I looked across at Dario. 'Do you snore?' He shook his head. 'Okay, we'll take the twin.'

'One twin room. *Va bene, signori. Documenti?*'

We took out our ID cards and passed them over. The receptionist flicked through them, his eyes passing from the photographs to our faces. He nodded and tapped at an open book on the desk. 'Names and addresses in the book, please.'

'You still use a guest book?'

He shrugged. 'The manager doesn't want to spend money on computers. Waste of time, he says.' He turned to the pigeon hole cabinet behind him. 'No VingCards either. Again, waste of money he says.'

I scribbled my name down, and passed the pen to Dario. 'We'd like a table for dinner as well. Should we book?'

He shook his head. 'But the kitchen closes at ten o'clock.'

'Okay, we'll be back around nine. If not before.'

'Before would be better.'

'Then before it is. Come on Dario.'

The receptionist shook his head as if not quite believing that we were going to be back at all. Then he picked up Shawcross's key, and hurriedly replaced it in its pigeon hole, as if embarrassed to have been complicit in our little undertaking.

'Pretty, isn't it?' I said. 'I mean, the town may not be all that much to look at, but you can't fault the view.'

The Asiago Plain stretched out to our right as Dario steered the Panda ever upwards, along a narrow road lined with bare, snow-covered trees.

'Pretty. Uh-huh,' he muttered.

'How're you finding it?'

'Okay so far. But this is a Panda, not a Land Rover. How much further?'

I looked at the map. 'Just another few kilometres.'

He nodded. 'Okay, we should be all right as long as it doesn't get any worse. It should all be downhill from here.' The snow was falling more heavily now, and he switched the wipers to double-speed. He shook his head. 'Nat, a sick man drove out here in weather like this? It doesn't make sense. *Jesus*. Hold on.'

I felt the rear of the car sliding away from us as Dario fought with the steering wheel.

'Shit. Hold tight.'

The upcoming hairpin bend turned back on itself almost one hundred and eighty degrees. On the left, the road dropped away precipitously. The barrier on the edge was bent back on itself. Ominously, a faded bunch of flowers was tied to it.

'Shit,' Dario repeated. Then, almost as if forcing himself to do so, he slackened his grip on the wheel. The rear end continued to slide away from us, as the car slid ever further towards the edge of the road. Too terrified even to close my eyes, I dug my hands into the seat as my right leg pumped away at an imaginary brake.

Then Dario dropped his hand and pulled on the handbrake. The rear end slid away further and, for a moment, I thought we'd gone too far. Then he released the brake, gave the wheel the lightest of touches, and we were safely out of the bend.

Dario repeatedly tapped on the brake, ever so gently, and brought the car to a halt. He cut the engine and we sat there, breathing deeply.

Dario broke the silence. 'Bloody hell.'

'Bloody hell, indeed.'

'That was close.'

'No kidding.' I patted his shoulder.

'Friend in the army once showed me how to do that.'

'That was smart. How many times have you done it?'

'Including this time?'

I nodded.

'Once.'

The road ahead, for the time being at least, looked relatively straight. 'So what do we do now?,' I said.

'Well, we could carry on. Slowly. Or—'

'Or?'

'I could try doing a three-point turn and we'll go back the way we came.'

I shivered. 'No. Let's not do that.' I took another look at the map. 'It can't be far now. Just a few kilometres.'

'A few kilometres in a vertical direction?'

'Don't even joke about it.' I took a deep breath. 'Come on. We can still get there before it gets dark.'

'Okay. Let's do it.' He turned the engine on and we made our way –slowly – along the snowy trail.

Dario drew the car to a halt at the entrance to a single-lane track leading down through the trees.

'Are you sure this is the place?'

I looked at the map again. 'I think it must be. Come on, let's get out and have a look.'

We stepped out into the freezing air, our breath misting immediately. A small, wooden arrow pointed in the direction of the track. I wiped the snow from it with my sleeve. *Cavalletto. Cimitero Inglese.*

I shielded my eyes against the bright winter sun, and looked along the track. And there it was. Perhaps half a kilometre away, its whiteness making it difficult to distinguish from the background of undisturbed snow, lay the Commonwealth cemetery of Cavalletto. Rows of white gravestones encircled by a stone wall, and dominated by a giant stone cross.

'I guess that's the place, then,' said Dario. 'Do you want to go down there?'

'I think we need to.'

'We'll have to walk. I don't think we can risk getting the car down there.'

'Do you think it's safe?'

'Probably not. But we're going to anyway, aren't we?'

I nodded. 'Come on then. Let's just take it easy.'

There were, I noticed, no car tracks. Shawcross, perhaps, had come to the same conclusion we had, decided it was too dangerous, and simply turned around. Yet why had he not returned to the hotel? Was it possible he'd simply spun the car off the road at some point between here and Calvene, and was even now lying injured – or worse – at some lonely spot unfrequented by passers-by?

It wasn't a pleasant thought.

The snow was deep, almost to our knees. Dario, at least, had proper boots and waterproof gear, whilst I shivered in my Wellington boots. It would not, I knew, be wise to spend any more time out here than necessary.

Dario grabbed me by the elbow. 'There,' he said, pointing towards the near wall of the cemetery.

A flash of red amidst the white. At first I struggled to make out its shape and then, as I squinted and shielded my eyes, I recognised what it was. A car, half covered with snow.

We half-walked, half-slid towards it. It was a Land Rover. If this was how Shawcross had arrived, he'd evidently not been taking any chances. Dario cleared the snow from the windscreen and peered inside.

'There's nobody there, Nat.'

I looked back up the trail to where we'd begun our descent. The only prints in the snow were ours. Similarly, the white covering of the graveyard looked pristine.

'No tracks except ours, Dario. It must have snowed since he arrived. Question is, just how long ago was that?' He shook his head.

I turned through a full circle. No sound at all, save for the crump of my boots on the snow. I cupped my hand to my mouth. 'Mr Shawcross,' I called out. The words echoed back at me from the snowy hills. 'Anthony Shawcross,' I shouted again.

Silence.

I looked at Dario. 'I suppose the Land Rover could belong to whoever keeps the cemetery in order?'

He shook his head. 'They'd be too smart to come out here if it looked like the weather was going to change.'

I nodded. 'You're right. Well, given we've come this far shall we have a quick look around?'

Dario shrugged. 'Couldn't hurt, I suppose.'

We made our way along the track to the iron gates in the wall. They were, as I had expected, padlocked, but the wall was only a metre high and – even in the snow – would not be difficult to scale.

A small noticeboard was fixed to the gate. The cemetery, it explained, was generally open from April to November. Outside of those months it would be impossible to guarantee access due to the unpredictable weather. Private visits could be arranged by telephoning a certain *signor* Rossi in Calvene.

I tested the gate, expecting it to be fastened shut but, to my surprise, it swung open. I bent down to look at the padlock, and found it open, the chain swinging free.

I looked up at Dario. 'Whoever's been here hasn't locked up behind them. Which means they either forgot or,' I shielded my eyes from the sun once more, the better to scan the graveyard, 'they're still here.'

The cemetery was small, and it seemed impossible that anything could be hidden from us. There were, perhaps, fewer than one hundred graves.

I walked midway along the central row, looking down at the headstones at random. Private James Walker, aged twenty-three. Corporal Robert Nash, aged twenty-seven. Private Michael Stone, aged twenty. All so young.

A cold and lonely place to lie, I thought. Perhaps it would look different in the summer, with the sun shining down on the green of the surrounding hills and the sound of bird-song in the trees but here, now, in the middle of winter all that struck me was the silence and the sense of loneliness and loss.

I looked up at the great stone cross and the bronze long-swords fixed to its front that accentuated the cruciform shape. I shook my head. There was something about the imagery of a weapon being used as a symbol of remembrance that didn't sit well with me. Then I looked back around the graveyard and upon the rows and rows of simple white headstones, and thought, perhaps, that this was not about me.

A cold and lonely place to lie.

'Nat,' Dario called out. 'Over here.' He was crouched at the foot of the Cross of Sacrifice.

'What have you found?'

He motioned for me to crouch down next to him. Then, with his right hand, he gently swept away the snow from the dark object half buried in front of him.

We'd guessed what it was before he'd even half-cleared it.

He swept the snow from a black woollen hat, covering grey hairs. Gently, respectfully, he continued to brush away.

Tonight, this frost will fasten on this mud and us.

Pale, grey, lifeless eyes stared back at us.

Dario breathed deeply. 'He's dead, Nat.'

'Are you sure?' The question sounded ridiculous as soon as I'd uttered it.

He nodded, sadly. 'I don't know how long he's been here. But he's dead. He couldn't have lasted long. Not like this.'

I reached for my phone. 'Okay, let's call the police.' I looked at the signal bar. Nothing. 'Can you try yours?'

Dario took out his mobile and shook his head. He held it above him, squinting at the screen. 'No signal. Let's go back to the car and try there.'

I turned to stare back at the body that lay in front of the Cross of Sacrifice, eyes open and staring into nothing but the endless white.

'What about him?'

'There's nothing to be done, *vecio*. Come on, let's get out of here before it gets dark.'

All their eyes are ice, But nothing happens.

I bent over Shawcross's body, scooped up a handful of snow, and let it trickle through my hand as slowly as I could manage, in order to cover his eyes. Then I shuddered, and turned to follow Dario back up the track to the blessed warmth and safety of the car.

Chapter 12

'Dario Costa?' the *ispettore* asked.

Dario nodded.

'And Mr Nathan Sutherland?'

'That's me. *Naaathan*,' I corrected him and then wished I hadn't. 'Sorry, it's a difficult name for Italians, I know.'

Dario shot me the briefest of glances that quite clearly meant 'please stop talking'.

'*Documenti*.'

We took out our ID cards. The *ispettore* seemed to take an excessively long time in checking mine, and eventually gave it back with a look of disappointment on his face.

It had been a long evening, and I feared the prospect of dinner was receding into the distance. We'd finally managed to call the *polizia* in Calvene from the car, at which point they'd told us to wait. And then, after they'd arrived, they told us to report to the station back in town. Just to complete a few formalities.

My stomach rumbled, and the *ispettore* shot me a glance.

'Hungry?'

'Just a bit.'

He yawned. 'Me too. Tired as well. So let's get this over with, eh, and we can all go home for a nice dinner and a good sleep. So, once again, just tell me what happened. You know the dead man, I understand?'

I shook my head. 'I don't know him. I know who he is. He rented an apartment in Venice over a week ago and hasn't been heard from for a couple of days.'

He frowned. 'I don't understand why this is your business. Are you a friend of the family or something?'

I took out my business card. 'I'm the British Honorary Consul in Venice.'

He took the card from me, and turned it over in his hands. 'Venice. That's a long way from here.'

'It's the nearest Consulate. And, as I said, Mr Shawcross had been in the city prior to making his way to Calvene.'

'I see. Well it's very good of you to come out all this way, Excellency.'

I assumed he wasn't being serious. 'You don't have to call me that. And as to why I came out all this way, well that might be because the police didn't seem to be taking it seriously.'

Dario winced.

The *ispettore* raised an eyebrow. 'We didn't?'

'I'm told the police aren't able to investigate until a certain period of time has passed.'

'Okay. Okay. I'm sorry if we're not quite as efficient as your famous British bobbies.' He put his head to one side. 'Is that the right word?'

'It is.' I smiled.

'Oh good.' He tapped his pen on his pad. 'Now, might I just ask what led you to the British cemetery?'

'We knew Mr Shawcross was searching for the grave of his grandfather. It didn't take long to work out where that was.

When we found he wasn't in his hotel, well, we decided to take a look.'

'You didn't decide to call us first?'

'We didn't think we had time. Mr Shawcross, as I understand, was not a well man and appeared to have gone out without his medication.'

'Oh, I see.' His eyes narrowed, ever so slightly. 'How could you know that?'

Dario, I could see, was barely restraining himself from putting his head in his hands.

'The concierge very kindly let us look around Mr Shawcross's hotel room.'

'He did? What an agreeable concierge.'

'Indeed.'

The *ispettore* scribbled away some more. 'Okay. I think that's all we need to know.' He paused. 'For now.'

'Of course.' I smiled at him. 'You'll be in touch with me as soon as you know anything, of course?'

He looked genuinely taken aback. 'You want *me* to keep in touch with *you*?'

'Well yes, of course. If we're correct, the body in the graveyard is that of a British citizen. It'll be my job to inform his relatives and to arrange the repatriation of the body. With your cooperation, of course.'

'*Our* cooperation?'

'Of course. The consular service in Italy is proud to have an excellent relationship with the law enforcement agencies.' I smiled again. 'And so we're always eager to cooperate as much as we possibly can.' I paused. 'After all, phoning distraught relatives is a difficult job at the best of times. All the more so in a foreign language, I imagine. And, even by Italian standards, there are a distressing number of forms to be completed when it comes to repatriating a body. We're always keen to spare the police forces work like that.'

He nodded, and might have smiled. Just a little. 'I think I understand.'

The smile never left my face. 'Excellent.'

He slid our documents back across the desk to us. 'We'll be in touch.'

'What was all that about?' said Dario.

'What was all what about?'

'All this, "you'll be sure to keep in touch with me, won't you?" business.' He shook his head. 'Nat, he's an unfriendly cop. If you meet an unfriendly cop, you make sure you're nice to him, all right?'

I waved a finger at him. 'Ah, but what did he think of us?'

'That we were a couple of jerks?'

'A couple of jerks who'd interfered with a crime scene. Exactly. But now what are we?'

'I'm guessing we're still a couple of jerks. No, worse than that. We're a couple of rude jerks.'

'No. We're a couple of jerks who are going to do their best to save him from having to do any more work than necessary.' Bureaucracy, I was slowly coming to learn, was something that could be leveraged to work in one's favour. 'And so, because of that, we're now people that he feels the need to be nice to. Or, if not actually nice, at least not actively unpleasant.'

Dario smiled. 'That's very good. That's very clever. Hey, maybe you're finally becoming Italian?'

'Maybe I am. So tell me Dario, after a day like this what would be the most Italian thing to do.'

'Dinner?'

'Dinner!'

'I'm sorry, *caro*. It sounds like you've had a tough day.'

I sighed. 'It's not been great. I mean, it's kind of what I'd been expecting but it was still a shock. The poor guy. Dying all alone in the middle of nowhere. Just snow and ice and the howling wind.'

'Well don't think about it too much. You'll give yourself nightmares. How's Dario?'

I looked across the bedroom to where Dario, with a big smile on his face, was singing 'Shine On You Crazy Diamond' down his telephone.

'He's singing to Emily.'

'Oh, that's lovely.'

'Isn't it? Come on then. Tell me about your day.'

'It's not been too bad, surprisingly. I think Gramsci and I might actually be becoming friends.'

'Really?'

'Well, it's more that I'm bribing him with food. Which means it'll be your responsibility to get him back on a normal diet when you return.'

'Oh hell.'

'Well, it's an incentive to come home soon, isn't it?'

'Tomorrow afternoon, I hope. There's just one more thing I'd like to do here. Shawcross was interested in a place called the Villa Godi Malinverni. Do you know anything about that?'

'Oh, there. How interesting. I think it's Andrea Palladio's earliest work. He mentions it specifically in *The Four Books of Architecture*. I've never been there but I probably should. Do you think it's important?'

'It might not be. There's probably nothing that needs investigating. The likelihood is that poor Mr Shawcross was overcome by the cold, found himself all on his own unable to get a phone signal and— Well, just fell asleep. That's probably all there is to it. But this villa seems to have been important to him and so I'd just like to check it out, that's all. If nothing else, they might remember him. It'll be something else to tell his brother about how he spent his last day.'

Fede sighed. 'Ah, nothing's ever simple in Nathan World is it? Do you think all Honorary Consuls go to this much trouble for their citizens?'

'I'm going the extra mile, that's all it is.'

'And I'm sure they appreciate it. So what did you and Dario get up to tonight?'

Dario had driven us out to the *agriturismo* that he'd found, and dinner had been a splendid plate of sliced *sopressa vicentina*, followed by *bigoli* with a *ragù* of duck; after which we'd made a heroic assault on what appeared to be the Italian Cheese Mountain.

I decided that perhaps Fede did not need to know about this. 'Nothing much. Just pizza and a beer, that's all. How about you?'

'Oh, I decided to cook for once.'

'Really?'

'Yes. I made myself a very nice risotto with honey and Castelmagno cheese.'

'Seriously?'

'Of course.' She paused, and then burst out laughing. 'Pizza and beer, of course.'

'Oh right.' I immediately felt guilty.

'So just the same as you then.'

'Oh yes. Exactly the same.'

She laughed. 'You really are a terrible liar, Mr Sutherland.'

'Sorry. It's just that Dario and I— Well, it'd been a bit of a difficult day and we'd skipped lunch. And it might be that we pushed the boat out a bit more than we should have and—'

'It's all right, *tesoro*. You don't have to justify it. I'm happy that you had a nice time.'

'Oh good.'

'I mean, I'd have been even happier if I'd been there to share it with you, but I don't mind. Really.'

'Well, that's very kind of you.'

'Not at all.' She paused. 'After all. It'll be you settling the credit card at the end of the month. Won't it?'

I laughed. 'Of course I will. And we'll do something nice when I get back. Promise.'

'I'll hold you to that. Good night then, *tesoro*. Love you.'

'Love you too.'

I hung up. This was turning out to be an expensive trip.

I found it hard to sleep that night. Every time I closed my eyes, I saw the frozen expression of Anthony Shawcross staring back at me.

Eventually I gave up, and switched the bedside light back on, sitting myself up. Stupidly, I hadn't brought anything to read. Even more stupidly, I hadn't brought anything to drink, and the hotel room came supplied with one of those disappointing minibars that only contains small bottles of water and expensive tubs of mixed nuts.

I picked up the brochure for the Villa Godi Malinverni and flicked through it. There was more to it than Palladio. The villa had served as the headquarters of British Command during the war. That explained Shawcross's interest. Perhaps his grandfather had been stationed there.

I flicked further through the pamphlet. Plenty of details about its construction and about Palladio, most of which slid off my eyeballs as I realised, gratefully, that I was falling asleep.

I woke up with a start, woken by the sound of the brochure sliding to the floor. Sleepily, I reached over the side of the bed to pick it up.

Something had dropped out from between the pages.

A bookmark.

I picked it up, and then groped for my glasses in order to be able to examine the logo. Slightly jokey in design, it showed the Lion of St Mark with a book held between its paws. *Libreria Settima Arte.* A bookshop in Campo Santa Margherita.

I yawned and checked my watch on the bedside table. Nearly two o'clock. Which meant I'd entered the zone where, even if I were to fall asleep immediately, it wouldn't be enough. Oh well. There'd be coffee in the morning and hopefully Dario would let me sleep in the car during the drive home. I looked across at the other bed, where he snored gently but non-distressingly, and smiled.

I placed the brochure at the side of the bed, with the

bookmark on top of it. And then something caught my eye. A note had been scribbled along the side. It was difficult to read, and I pushed my glasses as far down my nose as possible, whilst holding the bookmark near to the light.

The Visconti Box???

Chapter 13

Something was insistently prodding at my shoulder and I half-opened an eye. Still dark.

'Not time to get up yet,' I muttered, sleepily.

The prodding continued.

'Grams, I'll get your breakfast in a couple of hours. It's still dark outside.' I assumed the regular defensive position and pulled the covers over my head.

Gramsci started to vigorously shake my shoulder which was a new trick for him. I sighed and properly opened my eyes.

Dario put a finger to his lips. 'Shhhh.'

'Dario? What's going on?'

'Just listen, *vecio*.'

'I don't get it. Listen to what?'

He put a finger to his lips again and jabbed a finger towards the wall.

Somebody was in the adjacent room and, by the sound of it, moving furniture around. Shawcross's room.

Dario padded over to the door. I got out of bed and joined him.

The door creaked as he pulled it open, and he winced, but

the sounds from the next room continued unabated. Dario nodded at me, and we crept out into the corridor.

There was nobody else around. An occasional blade of light shone under the door. Whoever the occupant was, then, was using a torch instead of the overhead light.

Dario laid his hand upon the doorknob, and the floor-board under him creaked.

Immediately the light shut off.

Dario mouthed the word 'Shit' and looked back at me, inclining his head towards the room.

I nodded back at him.

He twisted the knob to the left, pushed the door open and took a half step inside. The rear window was open, and pale moonlight shone through. I blinked, as my eyes struggled to react to the darkness. Then the door slammed into Dario's face, and he fell to the ground.

I dropped to my knees. 'Christ, are you all right?' The door juddered backwards from the impact of the blow, and I looked up at a figure silhouetted in the moonlight.

He made to kick me in the face but I managed to roll aside, catching the blow in my shoulder. Immediately, he jumped over me and ran down the corridor towards the stairs. I scrambled to my feet and ran after him, throwing my arms around him in an effort to throw him to the floor.

It was one of the stupider things I'd done in my life.

He drove one elbow back into my stomach, whilst raking his heel down my shin. As I bent over, trying to catch my breath, he spun me round, twisting my t-shirt around my neck until I began to choke.

Then he smiled at me, and flexed his fingers. Despite the

pain, I noticed something on the back of his hand. A tattoo of a little man wearing a bowler hat.

Then the little man came to greet my face at high speed, and I dropped to the ground.

I heard footsteps thundering downstairs and the sound of the front door slamming. I shook my head to try and clear it, and got to my feet.

'Dario? You okay, man?'

'Yeah, I'm okay'. He rubbed at his forehead, and his fingers came away stained red with blood. He winced. 'How about you?'

'Okay, I think.' Then I noticed blood dripping from my nose onto my shirt. 'Well. Okay-ish, I suppose.'

We heard the sound of a car receding into the distance.

'Do you want to follow him?'

'We'd never catch him up in time. Besides, I'm in pyjamas. It wouldn't be dignified.'

'*Che cazzo*?' The receptionist, tying the cord of his dressing gown around his waist, made his way down the corridor. He looked us up and down, then through into Shawcross's room. 'What the hell have you been doing?'

I flicked the light on. The room had been not so much torn apart as pulled apart. Slowly, methodically, so as to make as little noise as possible.

'*Signori*, this is very bad. Very bad.' He shook his head as if trying to stress quite how bad this was.

'This wasn't us, you realise?' I said.

He scowled at me. 'Very bad,' he repeated.

'Seriously, it wasn't us. What, do you think we just decided to have a fight in the middle of the night in the room next door? I don't care how badly he snores, nothing gets me out of bed at three in the morning.'

'I do not snore, Nat,' said Dario.

'Yes you do. It's okay, it's not something I'd punch you for.'

'Oh, thanks for that.' He looked at the receptionist. 'You don't have a night manager, here?'

'*Nossignore*. Not at this time of year.'

Dario rubbed his forehead, and winced again. 'And you keep the door open? So anyone can just walk in?'

'For our guests, *sissignore.*And Calvene is a peaceful place. No trouble here.'

I shook my head. 'So what do you think he was after?'

'Don't know, Nat. I mean, we gave this place a good look over earlier didn't we?'

'Uh-huh.' I yawned. 'Okay, I'm tired. I don't think there's anything more for us to do, is there?'

The receptionist scowled at us both again, and motioned us out of the room before locking the door. He dropped the key into the pocket of his dressing gown and made his way back to his room, where he turned and shook his head at both of us.

I looked at Dario. 'I think we're going to have to leave a big tip.'

He nodded. 'The guy in the room. Did you see his face?'

'No. He was wearing a balaclava or something. Although he had a weird tattoo on the back of his hand – looked like a little man wearing a bowler hat. Does that mean anything to you?'

Dario shook his head. Then he stretched and yawned. 'You got the time?'

'I think it must be the back of three.'

'Time to turn in again, I guess.' He looked more closely at my face. 'You're going to have a nice bruise or two coming up in the morning.'

'And you've got a cut straight across your forehead.'

'You know what this means?'

'Yes. It means we're going to have a hell of a job explaining to Fede and Vally how we managed to acquire these in *Vicenza Vinyl*.'

He grinned, and then the two of us laughed and made our way back to our room.

Chapter 14

'Nat, man, you looked tired.'

I yawned. 'I feel tired. Couldn't get back to sleep and when I finally did it turned out it was time to get up anyway.' I rubbed my face. 'And I've had a rubbish shave as well.'

Dario grinned. 'Federica's going to think we were out clubbing or something.'

'She's going to think we were out fighting or something.'

'Well, we were.'

I shook my head, and tore open a sachet of sugar which I dumped into my coffee. 'Clubbing. God, the very thought of that makes me feel tired. How did we manage it when we were young?' I looked at the sugar caddy in front of me, took out another sachet, and repeated the operation. I stirred and stirred, breathing in the aroma and feeling its gentle warmth upon my face. 'Oh, that's better.' I took a sip. 'Ah, inject that into my veins, why don't you?'

'It's just a coffee, Nat.'

'Oh Dario, don't ever say it's just a coffee.'

'So do we have a plan for today?'

'Well, I think you have a visit to *Vicenza Vinyl* lined up.'

'Or *Vinyl Vicenza*.'

'Whatever it may be. So there's that. And then tonight I ought to try and make a nice dinner for myself and Federica.'

He shook his head. 'Why don't you just go out for pizza?'

'Nah, she did that last night. And I know she'll say that it's fine and that pizza two nights running is fine but,' I shrugged, 'I'll just feel like I'm burning valuable Hubby Points for no reason if I do that.'

'So that's it?'

'Not quite.' I pushed the brochure across the table to him. 'There's this place. I'd like to have a look at it.'

'Villa Godi Malinverni,' Dario read. 'Any reason?'

'The place was used by British Command during the First World War. Which, I guess, would have made it of interest to Anthony Shawcross. I'd just like to ask a few questions.'

'Do you think they'll remember him?'

'They can't get many visitors at this time of year. Least of all foreigners. I reckon it's worth a go.'

'Okay then. Well, I'm all ready to go. You got your stuff?'

I prodded the bag at my side with the toe of my shoe. 'Yep. I'm ready.' I got to my feet and glanced towards reception. There was nobody there. I took our key out and laid it on the desk. 'We should probably leave him something, you know. He let us bribe him. And he didn't give us too much of a hard time about last night.'

He shrugged. 'If you like.'

I took a twenty from my wallet, and laid it under the key fob. 'Come on then. Let's go.'

Dottor Riccardo Pasin was well-dressed, elegantly spoken and gave every impression of being a man who was far too polite to take obvious offence at having been called early in the morning in order to arrange a hasty private tour. He opened the great front doors of the Villa Godi Malinverni with a disappointingly normal Yale key, and motioned for us to wait outside.

I heard the beeping of the security alarm being deactivated and then he waved us inside, arms spread wide and a smile appearing on his face with the same facility as the lights he'd just switched on.

'Welcome to the Villa Godi Malinverni of Andrea Palladio,' he beamed, and ushered us inside. 'It might be a little cold, I should warn you. Normally I'd have slightly more notice before opening up and I'd make sure the heating was on,' he gave us the gentlest of rebukes, 'but I'm sure we'll warm up soon enough. And the interior is so splendid, I'm quite sure you'll completely forget about the temperature.'

Even to untrained eyes such as mine, the villa was something of a marvel. If truth be told, the outside was perhaps not all *that* striking, but it was evidently the work of the young genius who had begun work upon it whilst still in his mid-twenties. Looking out upon carefully maintained parkland, and down upon the Asiago Plain, British command could not have chosen a lovelier – or more strategically useful – position in which to hole up. Indeed, the gardens – in a classical nineteenth-century English style of paths and rivers and ponds – would, I imagined, have made them feel very much at home.

Very few people, I was sure, knew quite as much about Andrea Palladio as did *dottor* Riccardo Pasin. I was pretty sure that no one, for that matter, knew as much about Pietro and Marcantonio Godi, for whom the villa was constructed. Or about Gualtiero Padovano, Battista Zelotti and Battista del Moro, the three painters responsible for the frescoes in nine of the rooms. Or about Antonio Caregaro Negrin who designed the gardens, centuries after Palladio's death. Quite simply, Riccardo Pasin knew the history of every last arch, stave and pillar in the Villa Godi. And, by God, he was going to let us know about them.

Once you've done a few guided tours of Italian houses you kind of get the picture of them. They may not start on time. They may very well not end on time. They will last precisely as long as your guide thinks they need to in order to best convey the maximum amount of useful information to you with a maximum of clarity.

This, of course, is a fine and creditable thing to do.

It also means that you should make no firm plans for lunch.

I was about to follow Pasin into yet another beautifully frescoed room, when Dario put a hand on my shoulder to hold me back.

'How many more of these?', he whispered.

'I'm not sure. I've lost count.'

'Which one's this?'

'I'm pretty sure this is the Room of Sacrifice.'

'I thought that was two rooms ago?'

'That was the Room of Triumph. At least I think so. It definitely looked more triumphal than sacrificial.'

There was a gentle *harrumph* from the door. 'I'm sorry gentlemen, is there something in this room you'd like me to explain in greater detail?'

'No, no.'

'No, thank you. Everything's quite clear.'

'Any questions, gentlemen?'

Dario's shoulders had been slumping slightly, but he suddenly snapped to attention, for all the world like a student at the back of the class who's been caught using WhatsApp.

'I, er, I don't think so. I think it's all very clear. And yes, we've both definitely learned a lot.' He turned to look at me. 'Haven't we, *vecio*?'

'Oh yes. Absolutely.'

We stood there in silence for a few moments. Pasin looked a little disappointed.

'Well,' he said at last, 'I hope it's been an informative tour.'

Dario and I nodded as one.

'It's a pleasure to be able to open up at this time of year. This is normally such a quiet period. And very few foreign – I mean, very few non-Italians.'

I smiled. 'I believe you had one just a few days ago. A gentleman called Anthony Shawcross.'

'Oh, was that the name? I forget if we exchanged names. A lovely gentleman, he seemed to be. In that particularly English way.' Then he looked confused for a moment, and looked at me with just a hint of suspicion in his eyes.

'I'm the British Honorary Consul,' I said. 'We've had some bad news.'

'Bad news?'

'I'm afraid he's dead.'

'I'm so sorry to hear that.' He paused. 'Now I think of it, he really didn't look terribly well. Poor man.'

'He was okay when he left you, though?'

'Yes. Or, at least, well enough. He said he was hoping to see his grandfather's grave down at the war cemetery. I did try to put him off. It can be dangerous trying to reach there at this time of year, you understand?'

'Is that why he was here? To find out about his ancestor?'

'Yes. Now the war isn't really my field of expertise. I was a little disappointed to discover that he wasn't here to discover more about Palladio, but there we go.' He looked at us with a touch of sadness as if we, too, had been disappointing visitors.

'Can I ask exactly what he wanted to know?'

He gave a thin smile. 'Can I ask why?'

I shot Dario a warning look, just in case he felt like taking another one hundred euros from his pocket. 'It's just that I'll need to inform Mr Shawcross's family. It would be nice for them to know how he spent his last day.'

'Oh. Oh, I see. Well, the villa, you may know, was used by British Command during the last months of the war.'

'So I understand.'

'The Prince of Wales himself was a guest for some time, I believe. Anyway, Mr Shawcross wished to know if there were any records of his grandfather having been billeted here.'

'And are there?'

Pasin coughed. 'This is a little embarrassing for us, I'm afraid. I'm told there were records left behind which were collected by a local historian.'

'Oh right. Could we meet him perhaps?'

'That would be difficult. He's been dead since 1953.'

'Ah. And the records?'

'Disappeared around the same time. There are stories that,'

again, he coughed, 'things were sold which perhaps ought not to have been sold.'

I shrugged. 'Different times, I suppose. Any idea how we might go about tracking down records of those who might have been stationed here?'

'I'm afraid I have no idea. I'm really not the best person to ask, as I said to Mr Shawcross. I know about the Prince of Wales and the Earl of Cavan but I have no idea about regular soldiers. Indeed, I don't even know how one would go about investigating such a thing.'

'I see. That's a pity.'

He smiled. 'I don't wish to sound harsh. But the villa is almost five hundred years old. Imagine that. And so a few months during the war – even with an illustrious guest such as His Royal Highness – really isn't of such importance to us.'

I nodded. 'Of course. Well, thanks for your time. We do appreciate it. Don't we, Dario?'

'Oh, we do.'

I smiled at him. Then we shook hands and Dario and I made our way outside, leaving him to lock up behind us.

'So what do you think?' I said.

'I think that's the longest guided tour I've ever been on. How about you?'

'Likewise. Mind you, I'm pretty sure I could answer almost any question on the life of Andrea Palladio now.'

'Do you want me to test you?'

'No.'

We drove on in silence, as Dario manoeuvred the Panda

along the icy roads. Then we were back on the *autostrada*, and I could see his shoulders relax as the roads became easier.

'There's a copy of *Master of Reality* in the glove box,' he said.

I fished it out and slid it into the CD player. We both smiled and nodded along in rhythm to the opening track.

'So, are you happy now?' he said.

I took a deep breath, and then shook my head, slowly. 'No. Not really.'

He sighed. 'Go on then, *vecio*. Tell old Dario about it.'

'Part of me wants to believe that he was just a guy who was badly ill who wanted to stand at his grandfather's grave and pay his respects whilst he still could. And then, just as he did so, he became overcome by the cold and just sat down and fell asleep. That's what I'm going to tell his brother, unless I hear anything different from the police.'

Dario nodded. 'I'm waiting on the *but* here.'

'Someone broke into Shawcross's room last night, remember?'

He shrugged. 'Could be a coincidence. Guy finds out the hotel isn't properly locked up at night and decides to try his luck.'

'Too much of a coincidence, surely? Anyway, there's something else. I found a bookmark from a shop in Campo Santa Margherita. There's a note scribbled on it about something called the Visconti Box. What do you reckon that is?'

'I don't know. Something to do with the film director?'

'You know much about Visconti?'

He laughed. 'Nat, I've got a five-year-old little girl. Never mind Visconti, I'm lucky if I get to watch anything that isn't

Peppa Pig.' Then he frowned. 'Shit, that reminds me. I'll have to get her a present.' He turned his head towards me. 'So what are you going to do, Nat?'

'I don't know. Maybe I'll go along to that bookshop. And maybe do a little bit more research on the Villa Godi. But now – right now, Dario – I think it's time for *Vicenza Vinyl*. Or *Vinyl Vicenza*.'

Dario grinned, and turned up the volume on the stereo as we made our way towards Vicenza.

Part Two

The Visconti Box

Chapter 15

'I'm so sorry.'

I have heard these words so often in the past week that they have ceased to have any meaning. But people, I know, are trying to be kind.

I hug the woman in return. She lays her head on my shoulder and I feel her cheek, moist with tears and sweat, against my own. Her hand against my arm feels clammy and soft. For a moment I almost recoil before I remind myself that she, too, is only trying to be kind. She has come out on a filthy, baking hot Venetian summer's day to say goodbye to my father.

She releases her grip and steps back, dabbing at her eyes. I vaguely recognise her but cannot for the life of me think of her name. Someone from father's workplace, I think. I imagine, then, that I cannot have seen her since his retirement. No wonder her name has slipped my mind.

I look over towards Grandfather. The young priest is crouching by his wheelchair, holding his hands and talking earnestly and just a little bit too loudly about the joy of the Resurrection in baby-talk Bible language. I feel the anger rising within me — Grandfather is neither deaf nor an idiot — but I choke it back.

I walk over to the pair of them, and gently move the priest to *one side. I crouch down by Grandfather, put my arms around him, hug him. I feel his body shaking with grief for a moment, and then he pulls away. He holds my face in his hands, his eyes red. Were I not there he would, I know, cry until there were no more tears left in him. But Grandfather will not allow himself to do that. Not in front of his little girl. He is now just a few months from his one hundredth birthday, and, once again, he has become the head of our family.*

I blink back my tears. I should, I know, try to be brave like him but, try as I might, I cannot force a smile onto my face. The words stumble, brokenly, out of me. 'Oh nonno *Alvise, this isn't right.'*

The old man looks back at me. He shakes his head. The smile does not leave his lips, yet I can see the pain etched on his face. 'No,' he says, 'no, it isn't. But it is has happened. Our memories will not always be sad ones, Anna.'

I lay my head on his shoulder and cry, softly, for a moment as he strokes my hair. Then, gently, he raises my head and nods towards the young priest, now earnestly in conversation with Gianluca. 'Listen to me,' he says, and nods in his direction, 'I should be doing his job for him.'

I look over at Gianluca, and catch the touch of desperation in his eyes. Then I look back at nonno *Alvise and we both laugh, wiping away the tears as we do so. The young priest looks over at us and frowns. Our minds, evidently, should be on higher things, yet he remembers that it is not his place to tell us exactly how we should be mourning and so he turns and makes his way through the crowd, in search of someone who might be more receptive to his platitudes. And then I remind myself, yet again, that he, too, is only trying to help.*

Gianluca walks over to us, tugging at his collar. 'We're nearly ready.'

I look over to the side of the canal. Father's coffin is ready to be lowered onto the boat that will take us on our last journey together, out to the cemetery island of San Michele. There will be no grand family mausoleum for him to rest in. He will merely be filed away, respectfully and neatly and then, perhaps ten years from now, his remains will be exhumed and moved elsewhere. I should find this more upsetting than I do. Perhaps I will, but this is a problem for a future Anna to face.

Neither of us have moved. 'Anna, nonno Alvise, we're nearly ready,' Gianluca repeats. Nonno has always been merely Alvise to Gianluca until now. But from today, perhaps in deference to his new status in the family, he will be Grandfather.

I get to my feet, whilst Gianluca looks down at him. 'Nonno, are you sure you want to come with us?'

His tone is not unkind but I feel a flash of annoyance. We have talked about this, over and over. Gianluca tells me it will be too much for the old man. Perhaps it will be, I reply, but that is his decision to make.

Gianluca crouches down next to him and, once more, tugs at his collar. He looks uncomfortable in the heat, and I feel sorry for him. He is not used to wearing a suit and tie. This morning he joked that his one good shirt must have shrunk in the wash.

'Nonno Alvise.' Grandfather smiles at Gianluca, and he reaches out to pat his hand. 'Are you sure you want to come? It will be hot and difficult at the cem—' He corrects himself, hurriedly. 'On the island.'

What he means is that it will be difficult to move Grandfather around in his wheelchair on the gravel paths of San Michele. And Gianluca doesn't want things to be difficult. Not today.

Grandfather shakes his head. 'I don't want to, boy,' he says, his voice dropping to a low, bass grumble. 'But I'm going to. When they put my son away, I'm going to be there with him. Right up until the final moments.'

'Of course.' Gianluca gets to his feet, but his smile is a little too tight, a little too forced. Grandfather has made things a bit more difficult than they needed to be.

We make our way over to the side of the fondamenta. *The hoist on the rear of the water hearse lowers father's coffin into the boat. It sways for a moment until two members of the undertaker's party reach out – slowly, reverently – to still the motion until it settles with the gentlest of thumps.*

Gianluca offers me his arm, to steady me as I prepare to step aboard.

And then I see it. On the nearby bridge, two tourists, a man and a woman, are staring – no, gawking – at us. The man raises his mobile phone in front of him.

He's photographing us. My father's body is being taken away for the last time, and this man, this stranger, is photographing us. I shake off Gianluca's arm, and stare right back at them.

The man continues to click away on his phone. The woman has noticed my gaze, and is tugging at his arm, a look of concern on her face.

Grandfather, thank God, is turned away and cannot see what's happening. For a moment, I want to scream. Today I bury my father, his body eaten away by the cancer contracted in a filthy factory in Marghera. And for these two strangers, this final moment, this act of farewell, is something to be photographed as a memory of their vacation.

In perhaps a week's time – perhaps also for years to come – these images will be shown in – where? New York, Paris, Moscow – to bored friends and relatives, politely suffering through an endless evening of holiday reminiscences. My father, reduced to the same status as a gelato on the Zattere.

No. I do not want to scream. I want to fly at them, claw at their stupid faces, bright red from too much sun, tear the phone from his hands and throw it into the canal.

I breath deeply, screw my eyes shut, and bend over, resting my hands on my knees as I try to block it all out. Giuanluca rests his hands on my shoulders.

'It's all right, Anna. I'll fix it.'

Before I can stop him, he's striding across the campo and over the bridge. The woman is tugging more urgently at her partner's arm now, but he shakes his head, his phone still trained on the water hearse, fascinated by the scene unfolding before them.

And then Gianluca is with them. I see his left hand close firmly around the phone and turn it away. His fingers are closing around the man's. I am afraid, for a moment, that he is going to hurt him, but then he turns to the woman and puts on his sunniest smile, waving with his other hand as if merely directing them to the nearest café or gelateria.

He releases his grip on the phone and, still smiling, leans in just a little towards the man. The tourist is, if possible, an even brighter shade of red now. He jabs at the keypad and then holds the phone out towards Gianluca, for him to verify that the offending photographs have been deleted.

Gianluca continues to smile, and gives a little bow of

acknowledgement. He pats the man on the back, nods politely to the woman, and then makes his way back to us.

My legs feel a little unsteady, both from the heat and from the scene, but Gianluca is there to calm me.

'All done,' he says.

I cannot quite find the words, and so just nod in acknowledgement. I try to smile. 'Thank you.'

'It's all right my love. I'm always there to fix things. That's what I do.'

The priest and funeral party are looking at us. I look back over to the water hearse crew and nod at them. Then I take a deep breath, crouch down next to Grandfather, and take his hands in mine.

'I think it's time for us to go, nonno,*' I say. And the old man smiles.*

Chapter 16

'Flowers!' said Fede, her eyes brightening. She kissed me on the cheek. 'Thank you, *caro*. How nice.'

'Well, Dario and I stopped in Vicenza for a bit of shopping. It was either this or an old Jethro Tull B-sides compilation that I found. Did I choose right?'

'You did. That almost makes up for you being in a fight.'

'Oh.' I rubbed my forehead. 'You noticed.'

'I did. I thought it best just to assume there was a good reason for it. Am I right?'

'Well, to be honest it wasn't really a fight at all, more—'

She shook her head. 'Later, I think. Now, let me find a vase for these.' She paused and looked at me. 'Do we own a vase?'

'We've been together nearly six years. I must have bought you flowers before now.'

'I'm sure you have. I think I wrote it down. Anyway, we must have one somewhere. So, did you have a good time?'

'I'm not sure that's quite the word. I think I told you most of it on the phone, but I probably skimmed over quite a lot.'

'Oh. Okay. Let me find a vase and then I'll make us a spritz and you can tell me all about it.' She paused. 'No. You make us a spritz and then you can tell me all about it.'

'How's Gramsci been?'

She nodded towards the sofa. 'Quiet. Mercifully so.'

I walked over and carefully – ever so carefully – scratched his tummy.

'Hello Grams. It's me.'

Silence.

'Have you missed me?'

Silence.

'I'll bet you have. Still, I'm back now.'

His eyes flicked lazily open, and his teeth latched on to my finger. He wrestled it, slowly, from one side to another before releasing it, and closing his eyes again.

'I'll make us that spritz,' I said.

'Oh, that poor man,' said Fede, after I'd brought her up to date.

'I know. It must have been a lonely place to die. But – it's strange, I know – there's also a great feeling of peace there.'

'So what now?'

'I think the police will be happy to treat it as an accidental death. I'll ring Stephen Shawcross – oh, and Maxwell I suppose – and tell them what's happened. Then I guess I'll do whatever paperwork I can, and wait until they inform me if the body can be repatriated or not.'

Fede picked up on the tone in my voice, and frowned. 'What do you mean "happy to treat it as an accidental death"?'

'Well, look at it from their point of view. A man in very poor health decides to drive out to a lonely spot in a blizzard and doesn't make it back. He wasn't particularly dressed for the cold. Who knows, maybe when the storm was at its height he just couldn't find his way back to the car?'

'It's possible. Come on, it's more than likely.'

'I know it is. But there are things about it that don't sit quite right. The break-in at the hotel. Why Shawcross's room in particular? And what's the Visconti Box, for another thing?'

'The Visconti Box?' said Fede.

'He'd scribbled it on a bookmark. I'm wondering if it's a reference to Luchino Visconti.'

'Oh yes?'

'The director, I mean.'

Fede frowned. 'Oh, top mansplaining there, *caro mio.*'

'I'm sorry. I didn't think you were that interested in cinema.'

'Just because I don't care for films with vampires, zombies, or giant gorillas does not mean I'm not interested in cinema.' She took out her phone. 'Hang on a moment. The Villa Godi Malinverni? That's where you were, right?'

'Uh-huh.'

'Okay. That rings a bell, I think. Should be easy enough to check.' She tapped away. 'Villa Godi. Visconti. Ah, there we go. Easy.' She held the phone out towards me.

I craned forward to see it. '*Luchino Visconti. Senso. 1954. Farley Granger. Alida Valli.*' I paused. 'Oh, I know Alida Valli. She was in *Eyes without a Face*. And *Suspiria.*'

Fede rolled her eyes. 'If you say so. Anyway, she also was in Visconti's *Senso.*'

'Which I have not seen.'

'Because it doesn't have black-gloved killers with open razors? Or giant gorillas.'

'You make my taste in cinema sound so vulgar. So, go on then, tell me more.'

'The ballroom scene was shot in the villa.'

'Oh right. So what's it about then?'

'What?'

'This film.'

Fede paused. 'I don't actually know. I've not seen it.'

I laughed, and wagged a finger. 'Ah-hah!'

'Oh, I'm sorry, if I'd known it was the sort of thing we were ever likely to have in common I'd have made more of an effort. Hang on a moment.' She flipped up the lid of her laptop and tapped away. 'Here we go. It's on RAI Play.'

I paused, with my spritz halfway to my lips. 'It is?'

'Yes.' She patted the sofa next to her. 'Come on then. It seems it's important. Let's watch it.'

'How long is it?'

She squinted at the screen. 'Only two hours.'

'Oh right. Two hours of Italian art cinema. Er, do we have to do it right now?'

'Well, you said it was important. And anyway, it's got that actress you like from *Suspiria*. That'll help, surely?'

I got to my feet, seemingly having painted myself into a corner. 'Can I at least fix us another drink first?'

'Of course you can, *caro mio*.' She patted the sofa again. 'But don't be too long. It's not a short film and it does seem to be getting rather late.'

Poor Alida Valli, by now quite insane, wandered the streets of Verona crying her ex-lover's name out into the darkness. Moments later, Farley Granger, his face turned to the wall, was riddled with bullets by what looked like most of the Austrian army, and crumpled lifeless to the ground.

Fine flashed up on screen, the credits rolled, and then we sat in silence for a few moments before Federica turned on the lights.

'So. What do you think?'

'It's good. No. More than that. It's great. Glad I've seen it.'

'I thought you'd like it. Now. Would it honestly have been improved by the addition of a maniac in black gloves?'

'I think Visconti could have pulled it off.'

'I suppose if anyone could, he could. So, did this help?'

'Well it's opened my eyes to Italian art cinema.'

'Uh-huh. Anything else?'

I shook my head. 'I don't know. I mean, I can see the links with Venice – the opening scene at *La Fenice* – and I suppose we have the Italians versus the Austrians. But that seems a hell of a stretch to the First World War. And it also seems a stretch to me as to why this would have been so interesting to Anthony Shawcross.'

'Maybe there isn't any connection?'

'But there's that bookmark from *Settima Arte*. The Visconti Box, remember?'

'A different Visconti?'

I shook my head. 'Too much of a coincidence, if you bear in mind that *Senso* was partly filmed at the Villa Godi.' I yawned. 'Anyway, this is all something to worry about tomorrow. There'll be awkward conversations to be had with Shawcross's next of kin. And maybe the police up in Calvene. But after all that, perhaps I'll go along to *Settima Arte* and see if they remember talking to an Englishman about Luchino

Visconti.' I bent down to kiss the top of her head. 'You know, Benito Mussolini once described Alida Valli as the most beautiful woman in the world?'

'Did he now?'

'He did. You'd have to say, at least the old monster was right about one thing.' I kissed her again. 'Well. Almost right. The second most beautiful woman in the world perhaps.'

Fede smiled at me. 'Trying too hard, *caro*. But thank you anyway.'

Chapter 17

Vanni and I sat in the warmth of the bar *Motondoso* and I wondered just what had happened to my old friend over the past four days. I looked at what he was drinking.

'Hot chocolate?' I said.

He frowned. 'A man can drink what he likes for breakfast, Nathan.'

He tore open his brioche and a dark chocolatey goop oozed out.

'Nutella?'

He nodded. 'I've got a bit of a sweet tooth at the moment. It's just,' he took a deep breath, 'well if you must know, I've given up the cigars.' He waved a finger at me. 'And don't go thinking this is permanent. This is just as a favour to Barbara.'

'Early birthday present?'

'Not so much.' He sipped at his hot chocolate, leaving a tiny drop at the corner of his moustache.

I wasn't quite sure if I was allowed to dab it away. 'You, er . . .' I made a little motion with my finger.

He scowled and dragged the back of his hand across his mouth. 'Oh, I'm sorry, Nathan. Old Vanni isn't quite cutting such a *bella figura* after Christmas, maybe? While Nathan is in perfect shape, of course.' He reached over and jabbed me in the stomach.

'Ow!'

Vanni harrumphed, tore into his brioche once more, and dipped an end into his hot chocolate. He popped it into his mouth, and dabbed – excessively I thought – at his moustache. 'Everything okay, Nathan? Wouldn't like to think I was offending your delicate British sensibilities in any way.'

'Everything's fine, Vanni.'

An awkward silence fell between us.

'So,' I said. 'It's all going well then? No mood swings or anything?'

Vanni rubbed at his forehead. 'Oh God, Nathan, I'm finding this hard work.'

'I know, man. I've been there.'

'But I said I would, and so I'm going to do it. Even if it kills me.'

'And everyone who works for you?'

'Especially them.'

'And your friends?'

'Them as well.'

'Sorry. It's a bit shit, isn't it? If it's any consolation it gets better after a while.' I paused. 'I've got to say though, I'll miss those passive smoking sessions in your office.'

Vanni sipped at his hot chocolate, and then took a deep breath. 'Look, I told her it wouldn't be forever. It's just – well, there's this thing she's worried about. You know she works at the *Ospedale Civile*?'

I nodded.

'There's this thing that's going around. In China.'

'Oh yes. I was talking about that with Dario. Might be like SARS. Something like that?'

He shook his head. 'Nobody really knows, Nathan. All I know is that Barbara is concerned. It's not just the flu, she says. It could be serious. She's worried. Seriously worried, I mean. Says I need to look after myself a bit better. Just in case. Which means cutting out the cigars.'

'Blimey. Well done you. Got to say, I hadn't really been giving much thought to this.'

'Me neither. But,' he sighed, 'if it keeps my wife happy, then I'll do it.' He poked around, miserably, with his tea-spoon at the base of his cup.

'You know what, Vanni,' I said. 'I'd like a hot chocolate as well. And, to hell with it, I'm going to have a Nutella brioche on the side. Will you join me in another?'

'Are you sure?'

'Absolutely.'

'Well in the absence of a good smoke I guess the sugar will keep me going. Thank you, Nathan.'

I waved at the *barista*, and then tried to mime 'two hot chocolates and two Nutella brioches please' at him. He looked confused, wandered over, and I repeated the order out loud.

'So,' said Vanni, 'you didn't want to meet just so we could eat breakfast together?'

'No. I've heard nothing from Calvene. How about you?'

'About Mr Shawcross? Nothing directly. As I've said before, we're not very good at talking to each other. But I imagine the results of the post-mortem will take a couple of days to come through. And this is in a small town, just after Christmas. We can't expect it to be like the movies.'

'I suppose not.' I shrugged, and tore off a piece of my brioche, sucking the Nutella off my fingers. I always found *signor* Ferrero's magic concoction a little too sweet for my liking, but, I had to say, this was absolutely hitting the spot.

Vanni saw the expression on my face and grinned. 'You know, perhaps I could get used to these after all. Now then, Nathan, why don't you go over what you found at Cavalletto again?'

'So that's it?'

I nodded. 'Pretty much. We found Shawcross frozen in the cemetery. And a scribbled reference to something called the Visconti Box. What do you think that is?'

Vanni shook his head. 'First things first. From what you were saying the unfortunate Mr Shawcross was a very sick man?'

'So his brother told me. And we found a whole load of stuff in his hotel room – you know, heavy duty medicines and the like.'

'Okay.' Vanni nodded. 'So, putting ourselves in the shoes of a *poliziotto* from a small town like Calvene: is it not entirely possible that having driven out to Cavalletto – a difficult journey that he'd been advised against making – Mr Shawcross, a seriously ill man, was simply overcome by the cold and froze to death?'

'Sure it is. But then there's the fact that someone broke into his room that night.'

'If I understand correctly, Nathan, that's something you did as well.'

'We didn't break in. We just came to an arrangement.'

Vanni grinned but shook his head. 'Look, Nathan, if Calvene come back to us and say that Shawcross's death was accidental – and I suspect they will – well, that's pretty much an end to it, I think.'

'You think I'm overthinking this?'

'Oh, when do you ever do that, Nathan?'

'Never. Well, hardly ever. So you wouldn't mind if I were to check out some of the things Mr Shawcross seemed to be interested in?'

'No. Why should I mind?' But his eyes narrowed. 'What sort of things?'

'The golden age of Italian cinema.' I smiled.

Chapter 18

People often ask me what it is I actually *do*. Sometimes I tell them that the job of an Honorary Consul is to be a Professional Deliverer of Bad News. Oh sure, it's nice when you can help people – actually help them. Reunite them with missing possessions. Get them hospital treatment. Get them home in the case of an emergency. But sometimes you can't do that. And in the very worst of times, you have to be the person who picks up the phone, telephones someone in the UK, and delivers Bad News.

It's never as difficult as the first time. But neither does it get very much easier. There's denial of course ('who put you up to this?') and, understandably, anger ('why can't you tell us more?'). You do get used to those. And if somebody wants to shout at me, well that's okay if it makes them feel better for a few moments. If it gives them back some sort of feeling of control.

What you never get used to is the sound of crying. When you can't think of any words to say. When you realise that, at the end of the day, you're just a bloke who translates lawn-mower manuals, with a business card that makes his other job sound more important than it actually is.

No, you never really get used to it. And perhaps that's a good thing.

Stephen Shawcross was one of the easier calls I'd had to make. He was upset, naturally, but possibly not all that surprised. His brother had been seriously ill, and – although this journey had been of great importance to him – he had always thought it seemed ill-advised. I said, as I always do, that I would be in touch as soon as I had further information from the police.

My phone conversation with the police in Calvene was similarly brief and efficient. There was, it had been discovered, a slight wound to the front of Anthony Shawcross's head consistent with having slipped on the icy surface in front of the Cross of Sacrifice. Given Mr Shawcross's state of health, and the adverse weather, it seemed reasonable to assume that he had quickly fallen unconscious and succumbed to the cold. There were no suspicious circumstances – indeed, why should there be? – but, nevertheless, they were waiting on further results from the post-mortem. They would, of course, be in touch regarding the results and the procedure for returning Mr Shawcross's remains to the United Kingdom.

So there we were. Accidental Death of an Archivist.

There was no reason then to waste a morning at *Settima Arte*. No reason at all. No point in heading out into the cold.

Oh hell.

I grabbed my coat and made my way downstairs. I was just a few steps past the Magical Brazilians when I smelled the aroma of fresh coffee and pastries.

Well, it would be silly to head off on an empty stomach, wouldn't it?

'*Ciao*, Ed!'

'*Ciao*, Nathan! The usual?'

'Too early for a breakfast spritz, Ed. Even for me. *Macchiatone* and a brioche, please.'

'Everything all right, Nat?'

I got myself a brioche with *frutti di bosco* from the cabinet, as part of my five-a-day. 'Well, everything's just a little bit better now.'

I heard the welcome hiss of the Gaggia, and then Ed passed my coffee to me. I tore open a sachet of sugar and emptied it into my cup. Ed looked at me quizzically as I stirred my drink.

'It's just the usual stuff, Ed. Sad news about a British tourist.'

'Oh. Is this something you have to sort out?'

'It is, yes. But thankfully this one seems straightforward.'

'Sorry, man. Doesn't sound like fun.'

'It isn't.' I sighed. 'But you know what? With the number of visitors to this city the amazing thing is that it doesn't happen more often. That's something to be grateful for, at least.' I finished my coffee. 'You know what, Ed, I think I'll have another.'

'You sure, Nathan?'

'Absolutely. I can't be expected to be my usual ball of dynamism and energy on a single coffee. Tell you what, let me get you one as well.'

'Cheers, man. That's nice of you.'

I slipped him a couple of euros, and he dropped one into his pocket. 'I'll save that for later,' he winked.

I noticed a copy of *La Nuova* on the bar, its headline facing towards Eduardo. Even upside-down I thought I recognised the face on the front page.

'You mind if I take a look at that?'

He shrugged. 'Go ahead.'

Anna Fabris smiled back at me from the cover. As well she might. The most recent opinion polls showed her at around fifty-two per cent. Enough, crucially, to win in the first round of votes without recourse to a second round, or *ballottaggio*.

In theory, nobody really liked the idea of the *ballottaggio*. It took up even more time, cost money and ensured that the only news item on the front pages over the following weeks would be yet more of the two leading candidates kicking lumps out of each other. It also meant that there was always the possibility that the candidate with the most votes from the first round – perhaps falling only a few hundred short of outright victory – could still conspire to lose as the dark, shadowy forces of the minor parties promised to deliver their votes as they jockeyed for position in a possible future administration. This, everyone agreed, was unfair on the candidate who might be considered the moral victor in such a situation. Unless, of course, their candidate went on to win. In which case it was perfectly fair.

'D'you think she could do it?' said Ed.

I shrugged. 'I don't know. Maybe.'

'I hope she does. She seems all right. Just – honest – you know. That'd make a difference.' He tapped the photo of Meneghini. 'This guy, however – he's just another business-man and we know what that means and what we'll get if he gets in. Just more of the same. All he's got going for him is that he's pals with the current mayor.'

'You sound like you've made your mind up?'

'I'm pretty sure. She sounds good. She's saying all the right things. Trying to make this city liveable for residents again. Protecting the lagoon. Affordable housing. It all sounds good.'

I nodded. 'I think you're right.' Then I looked at the front page again, and shook my head. 'But those numbers aren't there yet. She's got to win outright first time. If not, the nutters and headbangers who vote for Andrea Mazzon will be lining up behind Meneghini.'

'So, are you going to vote for her, Nat?'

I shook my head. 'I would. But I don't get a vote any more.'

He put his head to one side, and frowned. 'You did last time. I remember you bitching away the next day when the wrong guy got in.'

'That was then, and this is now.' I paused. 'We had this Brexit thing, remember. I don't get to vote any more.'

'Oh right.' He shook his head. 'Sorry.'

I shrugged. 'It's what happened. I should get on with applying for Italian citizenship, I suppose. It's just—'

'Ah. You don't like the idea? Hard to let go of being British?'

'No. It's just I'm very lazy.' I drained my coffee and gave him a smile. 'But I suppose there's something resembling work that I should be getting on with. I'll see you later, Ed.'

'*A dopo*, Nat.'

At least we always had January.

The tourist season expanded year-on-year. There had been a time when the profession of gondolier had been an honourable, well-paid but effectively seasonal job. Nowadays, if you so wished, you could effectively ply your trade all year round, gliding your passengers around the canals and singing them possibly non-Venetian songs in the merciless heat of an August day or in the chilly February fog.

The first visitors would arrive *en masse* for *Carnevale*. Then, perhaps, there would be the gentlest of respites until the Easter holiday. By late spring the streets would be ever-busier, until the chaos of summer when those Venetians who were able would flee the city to the blessed cool of the mountains or, perhaps, the beaches of Croatia, seeking respite from the heat, the humidity and the hordes. Autumn, whilst generally more manageable, was prime-time for those without school-age children. And after that, of course, was the run-up to Christmas. The off-season became a little less off every year.

But at least we still had January. We didn't know for how much longer, but it was there for now. Life in the city seemed just that little bit more manageable. Seats became available on the *vaporetti* and walking the narrow *calli* became less akin to a contact sport. Everything became, blessedly, that little bit quieter. A little bit less like hard work. Indeed, on those mornings when Gramsci insisted on waking me at an unholy hour in order to be fed, I would occasionally walk the shady streets in the early morning fog, the only sound being those of my own footsteps and thinking to myself that – despite the random irritations of an unfriendly cat – I was a lucky man.

January was also the quietest time of year for consular business, as the number of British visitors plummeted. It was an unwelcome surprise, therefore, to find myself having to deal with a case just two weeks after Christmas.

Many of the bars and restaurants in Campo Santo Stefano

were closed, and would remain so until February, as those owners who had been fortunate enough to make some proper money during the lucrative tourist season took themselves off to warmer climes.

I stopped at the apex of the Accademia Bridge, and rested my elbows on the rails, looking out upon the Grand Canal. *Vaporetti* and delivery boats made their ways back and forth, and even a few gondoliers were ferrying their visitors around. From my vantage point, I could see a young couple snuggled up together against the chill and almost envied them. Further out, towards the *bacino*, the church of the *Salute* was semi-visible in the mist. I looked up at the skies. They were clearing, slowly, and by midday the fog would have burned off and Baldassare Longhena's great church would again dominate the skyline at this end of the canal.

I made my way down the other side of the bridge, leaving San Marco behind me and moving into the *sestiere* of Dorsoduro. I crossed over the Rio San Trovaso, heading towards Campo San Barnaba where Indiana Jones had once unexpectedly (and implausibly) emerged from a non-existent manhole. The smell of fresh coffee came from the bar *Ai Pugni*, near the bridge of the same name. I fought off the temptation to stop for a second breakfast and crossed into Campo Santa Margherita.

I hadn't been in this part of the city for some time. There were any number of half-decent or more-than-decent bars to be found but I was starting to find the crush of the night-life hard work these days. There was, perhaps, just a slightly desperate edge to the need to be seen having a good time there. I increasingly found myself preferring the more family-oriented atmosphere of Campo San Giacomo dell'Orio where

Dario, Vally and Emily lived. Campo Santa Margherita, I had to admit, was no longer aimed at people of a certain age. People like me, that is.

The *campo*, whilst not exactly busy, still showed more signs of life than one might have expected. The bar outside the Italian language school was doing a brisk trade in coffees, whilst those traumatised by the morning's experience were seeking solace in something a little stronger. Kids from the nearby art school, presumably on a break, were chatting, flirting and smoking. Three people manned a fish stall, as locals of both a human and avian nature jostled for the best of what remained.

There had been three fish stalls in Campo Santa Margherita when I arrived in the city. Now one, only, obstinately remained. The thought made me sad. I usually went to the Rialto market to buy fish from Marco and Luciano and wondered if I should have given more custom to those who had plied their trade here. But there is, after all, a limit to how much fish one can eat.

Libreria Settima Arte was next to the butcher's shop, similarly closed for post-Christmas holidays perhaps in the expectation – possibly unwarranted – that people might be thinking of reining it in a bit following two weeks of festivities.

I'd never been in the bookshop before, but I liked the look of it. It was tiny, with warrens of book stacks crammed together, but things had evidently been curated with care. There was also, I couldn't help but notice, a cloud of cigarette smoke hanging in the air, and the presence of a half-empty pack of MS by the till suggested that the proprietor had a relaxed attitude to the smoking ban.

Cinema, evidently, was their thing. No genre, actor or director, it seemed, was too obscure for them. I did wonder how much of a market there might be for an expensive hardback on the silent films of Francesca Bertini, or how many casual visitors would decide to take home a volume on Pier Paolo Pasolini as a souvenir of Venice, but perhaps there was still enough reverence for 'The Seventh Art' amongst locals to keep the shop ticking over.

Within five minutes, I was convinced this was the greatest bookshop in the world. Within ten minutes I was prepared to ask if I could work there. For free, if necessary. I picked up volumes on Hitchcock, Mario Bava and Dario Argento and took them to the cash desk before I remembered the actual reason for my visit.

The man behind the counter was almost completely concealed under multiple layers of clothing, wrapped up almost as perfectly as Claude Rains in *The Invisible Man*. A woolly hat was jammed onto his head, whilst a scarf covered the lower part of his face. His hands, in fingerless gloves, appeared blue with the cold.

'Chilly, isn't it?' I said.

He might have shrugged. Then he looked through my purchases and, I thought, nodded approvingly although it was hard to be absolutely sure.

'I've not been in here before,' I said.

He grunted, noncommittally.

Conversation, it appeared, was going to be a little difficult. I looked around, and smiled. 'It's a lovely shop,' I said. 'I must come here more often. It's just it's a bit out of my way. I live in San Marco.' Shopping out of one's own *sestiere*, I had come to learn, was frequently seen as venturing into that area of the map marked 'Here be Dragons.'

'Well, they've got bookshops over there. So I hear.'

It was impossible to see if he was smiling but communication, of a sort, had been established.

'Have you got anything on Visconti?' I asked.

He looked at me, blankly.

'*Luchino Visconti.*' I stressed the words, perhaps a little too much. 'Have you got anything about him?'

'I know his name, you know.'

'Sorry.'

'Anyway, we do.' He waved his hand. 'Over there. Under V.'

I wandered back to the shelves and cast my eye over them. 'Any books about *Senso*?' I called back.

He peered over his glasses at me. 'Why do you want to know about that?'

'Well, it's a very good film.'

'Uh-huh.' He shuffled out from behind the counter in order to join me. 'We did have one.' He ran a finger along the shelves, murmuring the titles under his breath. 'We did have one,' he repeated.

'Perhaps you sold the last one, recently. To another Englishman?'

He started, and stepped back from me, scowling all the while. 'Hey now, what's this all about?'

'Nothing. If a man wants to buy a book on Visconti, why shouldn't he?'

'You know how many people come in here in January?'

I shook my head.

'You're the first one today. Just before Christmas another

Englishman came in wanting a book on Visconti. You remember these things.'

'Did he say why?'

'Mister, I don't ask why people buy books. That's not how bookselling works. You think if someone comes in and wants a biography of Napoleon, I ask if he's thinking of invading Venice?'

'I suppose not.'

'No. And if somebody comes in wanting a biography of Luchino Visconti, I just think, hey, maybe this guy just really likes Visconti, you know?'

'Okay. Okay. So there is a book on *Senso*. We've established that. Could you tell me the title?'

'Sure. You want to buy it?'

'I think I do.'

He tapped away at the computer terminal on his desk. 'Here we go. *Beyond Neorealism. Luchino Visconti and Senso*. Professoressa Susanna Barichello. Edizioni CaFoscari.'

I frowned. 'I don't think I know her.'

'She's a professor. At Ca'Foscari university. Edizioni CaFoscari is the university press.'

'Okay. Can I buy a copy?'

He tapped away. 'The other Englishman had our last one. I can order one in but it'll take a couple of weeks.'

'A couple of weeks?'

'Sure. Specialist book. Small print run. The guy was lucky I had one in stock.'

'Ah-hah!' I waved a finger in the air. 'But there must be an e-book, surely?'

He looked at me, more in disappointment than in anger,

shaking his head. 'Never, ever, say that to a bookseller, *signore.*'

'Oh. Okay, I'm sorry. I'll have a physical copy then.'

'Hardback?'

'Why not?'

'That'll be eighty-five euros.'

'You what?'

'Eighty-five euros. It's a specialist book intended for libraries. But it's really well produced. This is a book for a lifetime.'

'I'm not surprised. Eighty-five euros is taking years off my life. Isn't there a paperback?'

He shook his head. 'I told you. It's an academic book. It's mainly aimed at libraries.'

'But you sold one to the Englishman who came in before Christmas?'

'What can I say? He looked like an academic. Look,' he sighed, as if taking pity on me, 'you could always just go and see the author. If there's something particular you want to know.'

'I can?'

'Sure. I know her. Susanna Barichello is still at Ca'Foscari. She teaches the Cinema in Italian course.'

'Oh right. Thanks. That's very useful. Do you think she'd speak to me?'

He shrugged. 'Why wouldn't she? Although maybe don't tell her you only want to speak to her to save spending money on her book.'

'Hmm. Fair point.' I smiled at him. 'Okay. Thanks for your time.'

I turned to leave, and he coughed, gently.

'Your books?'

'Oh yes. Thanks.'

I scooped them up and was about to turn away again, when he coughed once more. He pointed at the till.

'Ah. Sorry.' I put the books down and fished out a credit card. We stood there in that awkward silence that exists whilst waiting for the Point of Sale terminal to connect to the bank, both of us hoping that no awkwardness would ensue that would necessitate me having to go to the bank and return with cash.

Eventually, mercifully, the terminal bleeped its approval and he tore off the receipt and passed it to me. And so, having spent rather more money than I'd intended, I felt able to ask the question that had been the real reason for my visit.

'Do you know anything about something called the Visconti Box?'

His eyes narrowed, and he paused before replying. 'Is that the name of a book?'

'I don't know. Can you tell me?'

He sighed and tapped away at the terminal, before shaking his head. 'Nothing of that title, no.'

'Anything in a different language that might mean something similar. Could you just check?' I craned my head across the counter in order to get a better look.

'Mister, there's nothing in French, Italian, Spanish or English. You understand?' He yanked at the monitor, turning it away from me, and sending a small pile of books toppling. He grabbed them just in time, and pulled them back, swearing under his breath.

'I'm sorry,' I said. 'I'll get out of your way now. But you really have been most helpful, thank you.'

He scowled at me again as I made my way to the door, my purchases tucked underneath my arm. 'Why are you so interested, anyway?'

I looked back at him and grinned. 'Maybe I'm just a guy who really likes Visconti?'

Chapter 19

Gramsci was curled up on top of my pile of new purchases, his chest slowly rising and falling and an occasional gentle snore escaping.

'He looks very comfy there,' said Fede, turning her head on one side in order to examine the titles. 'Oh, I didn't realise there was a book about Dario Argento that you didn't have.'

'Neither did I. This was a bit of a find. This is him in conversation with John Carpenter.'

'My goodness.' She paused. 'That's good, then?'

'Extremely so!'

'Oh, I'm glad.' She gave me a quick squeeze. 'Do you think you should be letting him sleep on top of it?'

'It seemed the path of least resistance.'

'So, tell me then. What have you discovered?'

I took a deep breath. 'Not very much, to be honest. It might just be that Shawcross was interested in the Villa Godi Malinverni simply because it was the British HQ during the war.'

'And Visconti?'

'I was starting to think that maybe that's not so strange. Mr Shawcross seemed like an educated fellow. Exactly the sort of person who might be interested in Luchino Visconti and *Senso*.'

'An educated man, indeed.' She smiled at me. 'You hadn't seen it before, had you?'

'Oi!'

'Only joking, *caro mio*.'

'Anyway, I've been doing some research. On the Visconti Box.'

'Oh yes. And have you found anything?'

'Erm, well, sort of.'

'Sort of?'

'I found a DVD box set on Amazon.' I coughed. 'I have to say it looked rather good. So I bought it. And, well, there was a second volume as well and so—'

'Okay. I get the picture. Anything else?'

'Not really. Although it turns out that a company called Visconti also make fountain pens. Which come in a special box. The Visconti Box, see?'

'And, let me guess, you bought one of those as well?'

'No, I managed to fight off that temptation.' I tapped my chest. 'Iron will, you see.'

'So what now?'

I yawned. 'Well now, I think it's time for dinner. No, scratch that. Now, I think it's time for a spritz. And then it'll be time for dinner.'

'Lovely. What are we having?'

'Pumpkin and ricotta lasagne. Can you imagine anything more perfect for a cold winter's night?'

'I'm trying and failing. But beyond dinner, what are you going to do?'

I shrugged. 'Well, I guess I'm going to see this Professor Barichello and see what she knows.'

'Maybe there's nothing to know about?'

'Part of me thinks that. And a large part of me wants to believe that. That the poor guy just slipped and fell. Thirty minutes later he'd have been dead. Maybe not the worst way to go. And he'd kind of accomplished what he'd come to achieve, being with his grandfather.' I paused. 'And yet there's also that part of me that isn't sure. I can't help thinking it would have been a hell of a cold and lonely place to die.' I got to my feet, yawned, and stretched. 'God, listen to me. I'm even making myself feel cold. Spritzes will definitely help.'

'They absolutely will. Anyway, sleep on it tonight. Maybe you'll feel differently in the morning.'

Professor Susanna Barichello leaned across her desk to shake my hand.

'I hope I'm not interrupting too much?'

She smiled. 'Not at all. It's nice to break up the day.' She tapped her computer screen. 'I've got a dissertation to review.'

'Oh. Anything interesting?'

'*The role of gender in Italian cinema 1920–1950*. So, yes. Most interesting. Now what can I do for you, Mr Sutherland?'

'I wonder if I could talk to you about Luchino Visconti. About *Senso* in particular.'

She smiled. 'Well, I'm always happy to do that. Indeed, I published a book on *Senso* just a few years ago. Is this research for an article?'

'Nothing like that, I'm afraid. I have to admit it's a film I saw for the first time just two days ago.'

I thought she'd look disapproving, or at the very least disappointed, but she closed her eyes and smiled in pure pleasure. 'Ah, but I envy you that. I can't think how many times I must have seen it. How wonderful to be able to experience it for the first time. Did you know they used the *La Fenice* scenes for reference in reconstructing the theatre after the fire?' She opened her eyes and looked at me, evidently expecting me to wax lyrical.

'I didn't know that. Anyway, I enjoyed it very much,' I said.

She nodded, but the corners of her mouth turned down, as if she'd been expecting something a little more effusive.

'Anyway,' I continued, 'this is all about a British citizen, a Mr Shawcross. He was found dead at the war cemetery in Cavalletto a couple of days ago. He'd been visiting his grandfather's grave and got trapped when the weather changed. Among his possessions was a bookmark with the words *The Visconti Box* scribbled on it. I just wondered what that could be?'

Barichello smiled again. 'I thought you told me you were the Honorary Consul, not a private investigator?'

'Well, sometimes the two roles overlap. But seriously, it's just for any information that I might be able to pass on to his family, regarding his final days.'

'The Visconti Box. Well, I suppose that does make things sound terribly mysterious. But it's really not quite so much of a mystery as all that. Visconti directed the ballroom scene at the Villa Godi Malinverni near Calvene. While he was there, he came into possession of a box of papers from a local historian.'

'Papers?'

'All sorts of things. Mainly letters and documents from the war period.'

'Why would Visconti have been interested in that?'

'He worked with the resistance during the Second World War. He sheltered partisans. He helped British prisoners of war to escape across the border. I think, perhaps, if the opportunity had been there, he might simply have been interested in reading about the experiences of a normal, working-class soldier from an earlier time. Especially if it was linked with the very ballroom in which he'd been working. Or perhaps he thought it might give him ideas for a future project. I don't think that's so likely though. That type of film wasn't the sort of thing likely to interest him. Not at that stage in his career.'

'I see. So Shawcross, perhaps, thought some of those documents might relate to the fate of his ancestor?'

'I imagine that's possible.'

'Fascinating. Is it possible to have a look at the contents?'

'Much of Visconti's legacy has been digitised. But, unfortunately, that's not the case in this situation. It passed into the hands of Franco Zeffirelli. The two of them were partners you understand? At least for a time. When Zeffirelli passed away last year some of his possessions were due to be sold at auction. Including something the newspapers called the Visconti Box. Imagine that. A gift from Visconti to Zeffirelli.'

'Priceless, I imagine?'

Barichello waved a hand in the air. 'Beyond price. To a collector.'

'You don't know who bought it?'

She grinned. 'I put in a bid myself but, sadly, the university don't pay me quite enough for me to have a realistic hope of acquiring something like that. As it happens, it was withdrawn from sale at the last moment. If you're interested, you might try Fabio Simonetti.'

'Who?'

'He has the *Libreria Settima Arte* in Campo Santa Margherita. He's something of an expert on Visconti.'

'He is? I was there only yesterday and he denied having even heard of something called the Visconti Box. He got rather cross when I mentioned it.'

Barichello laughed. 'Ah, Fabio can be like that. You must have caught him on a bad day.' Her expression changed, and she looked sad. 'But I'm sorry to hear about Mr Shawcross. I hope it was some comfort to him, to stand at his grandfather's grave.'

I stood up to shake her hand. 'I hope so too,' I said.

There was a knock at the door, and the briefest of pauses before it opened and Gianluca Casagrande walked in.

'Okay Susanna, I'm done for the morning. Marco, Alessandra and I are going for lunch at *Ae Oche*. Fancy joining us?' Then his face burst into a broad smile. 'Mr Consul!'

'*Dottor* Casagrande.'

'Call me Gianluca, please.'

'Of course. And call me Nathan.' I grinned. 'Mr Consul sounds terribly serious.'

'Nathan it is then.' He looked over at Professor Barichello. 'Susanna, any objections to Nathan joining us for lunch?'

She smiled. 'Of course not.'

'Are you sure? I don't want to drag the conversation down too much.'

Barichello smiled again. 'Oh, don't worry. I promise I don't talk about Ugo Falena and Luigi Maggi outside of the lecture hall. Mind you, try not to sit next to Alessandra. She does tend to go on about deconstructionism and Derrida as soon as she sees an opening.'

'Oh right. Well, I'll try not to get in the way.'

'Excellent.' Gianluca grinned and clapped me on the shoulder. 'Pizza and beer it is then.'

Gianluca didn't even look at the menu, but smiled up at the waitress. 'Pizza Margherita, as always.' He looked over at me. 'Now, Marco and Alessandra here are just about to tell me how boring this is.'

The two professors nodded as one.

'But,' Gianluca continued, 'they'd be wrong. Because the Pizza Margherita is like Hemingway's prose. Simple, clear, direct – no messing about. Perfect as it is.'

'I have to say, I hadn't thought of it like that before.'

'What are you having then, Nathan?'

All eyes, I suddenly noticed, were on me, as if I were under pressure to choose a literary pizza.

'Pizza *Inferno* for me.' Suitably Dante-esque. It seemed like a safe choice.

Gianluca grinned and sipped at his beer. 'So what brings you out to Ca'Foscari on a cold January afternoon, Nathan?'

I sighed. 'Well, it's a bit sad really. You remember when we met the other night? I said I was looking for a British citizen that had gone missing? A Mr Anthony Shawcross?'

Gianluca frowned. 'I remember the name.' Then he snapped his fingers. 'Wasn't he found recently? Up north in the Veneto.'

'He was, yes. In the Commonwealth cemetery at Cavalletto. He'd been caught by a storm, it seems. The poor man was frozen to death.'

Gianluca stiffened. 'You were there?'

'I'm afraid I found him.'

'God, that must have been horrible. The poor man, indeed.' Then he frowned. 'I'm not sure I see the connection with Professor Barichello?'

'Oh there isn't one. Not really. It's just that I found he'd scribbled a reference to something called the Visconti Box. I wondered what it might mean.'

He shrugged. 'Is it important?'

'Almost certainly not. But it might be some extra information I can pass on to his family. About his last days, you know?'

Barichello drained the last of her beer. 'I'll see what I can do to find out who put it up for sale. It's probably not possible, but I know various collectors who might have an idea. I can ask around, discreetly. Gianluca, you know Fabio from *Settima Arte*?'

Gianluca nodded.

'He was very rude to Mr Sutherland, but he'll be nice to you. Why don't you ask him?'

'Well, I can try, I suppose, but you know what Fabio's like.'

Barichello smiled. 'Fabio's never been quite the same since the smoking ban. So there we go. Our own little treasure hunt. Who'd have thought that in 2020 so many of us would still have such an interest in Luchino Visconti?'

'So many?'

She frowned, as if she'd revealed a confidence. 'Well, you. Mr Shawcross, of course. And Andrea Mazzon sent me an email on the same subject recently.' She shuddered. 'Awful man.'

Professor Marco raised his eyebrows. 'Mazzon? Never had him down as a film buff.'

Barichello shrugged. 'I don't imagine he is. Obviously, he's from the opposite side of the political spectrum to Visconti. I wonder if he wanted to find out if any public money had been spent on trying to acquire the archive. People like him always get angry about things like that. I think they enjoy it.'

Gianluca nodded, and checked his watch. 'Well, it's been a lot of fun. But now I suppose we really ought to be getting back.'

I reached into my jacket, but Barichello stopped me. 'No need, Mr Sutherland. We come here almost every day. They give us a generous discount.'

'That's kind of you. I have to say, if I I'd known academia was like this I might have paid more attention at university.'

We all laughed and got to our feet. Gianluca clapped me on the back once again. 'I'll be in touch, Nathan, okay?'

Chapter 20

'You look tired,' I said to Fede.

She yawned and stretched. Gramsci, on the sofa beside her, repeated her gesture. She looked down at him. 'We've had a tough afternoon, haven't we Unfriendly Cat? Well, I mean, it's probably been tougher for me. Your contribution, to be frank, has been disappointing.'

'So what have you been up to?'

She tapped her laptop. 'I've been doing some work for you.'

'The Visconti box?'

'Exactly. I thought that just searching for "Visconti box" was far too vague and of course it's just going to bring back DVD sets and expensive fountain pens. Pages and pages and pages of them. So then I tried to refine it down. I tried searching on *archive* and *Senso* and eventually I got it down to this. Come on, come and take a look.'

I perched myself on her knee as she brought up a webpage from the *Guardian*.

Visconti Box withdrawn from sale.

A box containing an archive of papers belonging to the great

*Italian filmmaker Luchino Visconti, expected to fetch a signifi-
cant amount of money at auction in Rome, has been withdrawn
from sale at the last moment.*

*The box is believed to contain a collection of material from the
Villa Godi Malinverni, in the Veneto area of Northern Italy, in
which Visconti filmed the ballroom scene for his 1954 masterpiece,*
Senso. *Rumours have persisted for years as to its possible contents.*

*'It was very exciting to think that the contents might finally
come to light,' said Professor Susanna Barichello of Venice's
Ca'Foscari university, and an expert on Visconti's life and works.
'They have been the subject of much discussion in academic circles
for almost half a century. What light do they shed on the filming of*
Senso? *Do they add any more information to the background of*
Le Notti Bianche? *But more than that, there have been rumours
of all sorts of things that might be discovered. We must bear in
mind that – at this point in history – the Villa Godi Malinverni,
from where the contents originate, was undergoing a great deal of
restoration. What Visconti seems to have acquired is a veritable
jackdaw-like collection of papers. It's believed that there might
be letters and diaries by soldiers stationed there during the First
World War. There might even possibly be some original papers by
the villa's architect, Andrea Palladio. Whatever there may be,
I have to say I'm desperately disappointed today. I just hope the
current owner will have a rethink or at least make them public.'*

*The so-called Visconti Box was to be auctioned by Christie's
in Rome.*

'Letters from soldiers,' said Fede.

I nodded. 'Barichello said as much to me. I guess that
explains why Shawcross was so interested in this.'

'Maybe. But any number of soldiers might have passed through there. The odds against any letters – even if there were any – belonging to his grandfather would seem to be pretty high.'

'True. Did you find anything else?'

Fede smiled. 'I did. Take a look at this.'

She tapped away at the keyboard, but was interrupted by the door phone buzzing.

'I suppose I'd better get that,' I said.

'I suppose so.' She patted my stomach. 'Anyway, it'll give my knees a rest. I'm sure you're a bit heavier than you were.'

'Sorry. I know, I should get on to my post-Christmas workout.'

'You have a post-Christmas workout?'

'Well, it's something I think about every year. I think that counts.' The entryphone buzzed again. 'All right, I'm coming.' I made my way over to the door. '*Chi è?*'

'Ciao, Nathan. It's Gianluca.'

'Gianluca? Come on up.'

I buzzed him in, and heard him making his way up the stairs. Federica looked over at me and slowly, but deliberately, closed the lid of her laptop.

Chapter 21

'Nathan. It's good to see you again.' Gianluca Casagrande checked his watch. 'It must be, oh, hours since the last time.' He grinned.

He stood in the doorway, immaculately dressed but wet from the rain outside. He swept it from his hair, sending a spray through the air. Gramsci yowled as a few drops of icy water landed on him, and he scurried under the sofa.

'Oh, I'm sorry.'

'It's okay. He'll sulk for a bit, that's all. He'll be out when it's time for dinner.' I looked at my watch. 'Which probably means about thirty minutes from now. Although any time is dinnertime to Gramsci.'

He smiled. 'Gramsci? Interesting name for a cat.' He started to unbutton his coat. 'Can I hang this up? Hopefully away from anything else. It's a bit wet out there and I don't like umbrellas. They're horrible in narrow little streets and they always end up getting lost or stolen.'

'Sure. Go ahead. Coffee? Or is it a bit late in the day for that?' He tried to put on a brave face and failed. 'Or something stronger?'

'Oh, that'd be good. Better not tell Anna, though. I'm

always telling her about not being seen drinking in public, so she'll think I'm a disgusting hypocrite.' He grinned. 'Which is true, of course.'

'Well, you have an audience of two people and a cat. So I'm not sure that counts as "public". But we'll be very discreet. Is a spritz good?'

'They're always good, thank you.'

I went through to the kitchen and fixed us three Spritz Nathans.

'How is Anna?' I heard Fede say.

'She's fine, thanks. Tired though. I'm not sure either of us realised quite how much work this would be. And it's emotionally draining, you know? How every little thing gets pored over and scrutinised.'

'I can imagine.'

I returned with the drinks. 'So, what can I do for you, Gianluca?'

'Well, firstly my apologies for coming round at this hour and drinking your booze. It's just that when I finished work at the University I thought perhaps it might be nice to have a little chat somewhere a bit more discreet than a pizzeria.'

'Er, sure. Of course.'

'Would you like me to go?' said Fede.

'Oh, dear *dottoressa*, of course not. This isn't anything that I can't say in front of both of you.' He ran a hand through his damp hair again. 'Nathan, you told me at lunchtime that you were involved with the discovery of the body of the British gentleman?'

I nodded.

'I was just wondering,' he continued, 'if you ever managed to speak to him?'

I shook my head. 'I'm afraid not. I wish I'd been able to. I'd have warned him about going up to the cemetery at this time of year.'

'I see. I see.' He tapped his fingers on the table. 'I'll be honest, the main reason I'm here is that we were talking at lunch about that reference to the Visconti Box, and Andrea Mazzon.'

'Oh yes,' said Fede. 'Anna's rival.'

Gianluca smiled. 'I'm not sure if rival is quite the word. He's not polling in substantial numbers.'

'No, but he doesn't have to. He's polling about three per cent. That might be enough to make him kingmaker. Or queenmaker, if that's a word.'

Gianluca shook his head. 'It won't come to that. At least, I hope to God it doesn't come to that. Imagine having to work with him? I was just wondering, Nathan, were you thinking about speaking to him?'

'I don't know. I hadn't really thought. The only reason to is that the box might contain some memorabilia relating to Shawcross's grandfather. That would be of interest to his family. So I might have a chat with Mazzon, I suppose. Just on the off chance he knows where it is.'

Gianluca rubbed his forehead. 'I was afraid you might say that. But, seriously Nathan, I wouldn't do it.'

'No?'

He shook his head. 'Seriously, I wouldn't. Mazzon's not a nice person.'

'Well, if the polls are correct, approximately three per cent of Venetians seem to think he is.'

'I know. And that's part of the problem with this bloody city. Again, I wouldn't go near him. Mazzon knows some very unpleasant people.'

'I only want to ask him about some letters from a long-dead British serviceman. Nothing contentious there, I'd have thought.'

He shook his head. 'I would just be very, very careful about how you approach him. That's all.'

I opened my mouth to speak, but then Fede put her arm around me and rubbed my back in a way that clearly meant 'please stop talking'. She smiled at Gianluca, and then ruffled my hair. 'I'm afraid he's always like this. Never wants to let things go. Always has to go the extra mile.'

'Well, there are grieving relatives to think about.'

'I know, *caro*, and that's very noble of you, but really you've done all you can. And there's that huge translation project you were telling me about.'

I looked over at her and caught the expression in her eyes. 'Oh, that thesis translation? Well, yes, I suppose time is pressing on that, now.'

'And so, given January is your quietest month, you really should be finishing that off now instead of paying house calls on fascists.'

'I suppose that's true.'

'Rent has to be paid, after all.'

'It does,' I nodded.

Gianluca smiled at me. 'There we go, Nathan. Your wife has spoken. They always know best at the end of the day, don't they?'

'Oh, they do.'

'What's this thesis about, if I can ask?'

'Conrad,' I said.

'Hemingway,' said Fede.

There was an awkward pause.

'Conrad's influence on Hemingway,' I said.

'Oh. Right.' He smiled. 'I've written a few papers on Hemingway in my time. I'd very much like to have a look at it. Once you've finished, of course.'

I smiled back, as best I could. 'Of course.'

I got to my feet. 'Can I offer you another spritz?'

He checked his watch. 'It's a pleasant thought, but I'll have to decline I'm afraid. But it's been lovely to see you. We must get together some time. All of us, properly.'

He kissed Federica on both cheeks, and then myself. 'Have a good evening both.' He bent to look under the sofa, from where Gramsci was peering. 'And you too, kitty.'

I held his coat for him. 'See you again, Gianluca. Best to Anna.'

I closed the door behind him and turned to Federica. 'So,' I said, 'it seems I now have to invent a thesis.'

'Sorry, *caro*, but I thought it best to interrupt you. You see there was something else I found. Take a look at this.'

She went back to her laptop and flipped up the lid. 'Here we go,' she said, 'good old RAI.'

'What is it?'

'It's the auction for the Visconti Box. It's a clip from the news, from not long after the death of Zeffirelli. It would have been quite a big story.'

I clicked on the website and waited as the video loaded. As frequently happened with RAI, the news piece had been clumsily edited, meaning that the same video footage was repeated multiple times until such point as the narration finished. Numerous friends of Zeffirelli, we were informed, had been present, although none were believed to have actually bid. The camera panned around the room, as the reporter told us that the lot had been withdrawn at the last minute. The footage was repeating itself for the third time when Fede grabbed my hand.

'Now wait,' she said.

'What is it?'

'Just pause it for a second.'

'Uh-huh.'

'No, it's gone too far now. Rewind it ten seconds. Now let it run on. And stop it here!'

I paused the video.

'Look,' said Fede.

'I'm looking. But what am I supposed to be looking at?'

'Just look. What do you see?'

I shrugged. 'I don't know. Just a big crowd of people?'

'Don't be useless. Keep looking. Who do you see?'

I moved the video on a few seconds, and then replayed it once more. Still nothing leapt out at me. I tried again, and then started as I spotted a familiar face.

'Wait a minute. That's Anthony Shawcross.'

Fede turned to look at me. 'Seriously?'

'Yes. I thought that was who I was meant to be looking at?'

'No. Which one is he?'

I moved the cursor, and circled it around Shawcross's face. 'That's him.'

'You're sure?'

'Absolutely I'm sure.'

'Okay. Now this is weird. Because that's not who I meant. Take a look at who's standing next to him.'

I peered more closely. 'Bloody hell. That's Gianluca, isn't it?'

Fede nodded. 'It is.'

'And this?' I tapped the screen, at the frozen image of a gaunt, ascetic-looking grey-haired man. 'I keep thinking I should recognise him.'

'You should. That's the Demon King himself. Andrea Mazzon.'

I whistled. 'Anthony Shawcross. Gianluca Casagrande. Andrea Mazzon. All at the same auction. This seems a bit strange.'

'Isn't it just?'

'Rewind it once more. Can you zoom in on Gianluca this time?'

'I can try.' She tapped away at the keyboard. 'What's he doing?'

'Freeze it. Just for a moment.' The image was hard to make out and yet, once my eyes had cleared, obvious. 'He's patting Mazzon on the back.'

'What for?'

'Who knows. Can you get any closer?'

She shook her head. 'This is as good as it gets.'

It was enough. Gianluca, with his hand across Mazzon's shoulders, was smiling broadly.

'What's he got to smile about?' said Fede.

'I wonder.' I shook my head. 'Oh hell. I don't want Gianluca to be a bad guy.'

'Perhaps he isn't, *caro*. I hope not, anyway.'

I looked again at the image. Gianluca Casagrande, with a broad smile on his face, clapping the shoulders of a man who, only five minutes ago, he had suggested I avoided speaking to for my own safety.

'There's something that needs checking out here. Isn't there?'

Fede nodded. 'There is, *caro*. Oh, I think there is.'

Chapter 22

Hello Ma,

Well, look who's been called up to the big house on the hill! Only your little boy, Thomas!

Ma, you'll never guess who was there. Only the Prince of Wales himself! They say he's been there for some time now. They're trying to keep it secret of course. Which makes me worry that this letter won't reach you. Oh well, we must hope for the best as I was bursting to tell you. I wish Father could have seen me though. His lad lining up to shake hands with the future King of England, imagine that.

The crazy thing is, that wasn't the reason I was there. I don't think a humble captain usually gets called to meet a member of the Royal Family. It seems the brass have got a bit windy about the way the campaign's been going in the last couple of days. The Austrians have got further than anyone thought possible.

Now, you mustn't worry about me! Everybody is convinced they'll be pushed back eventually, and probably sooner rather than later. But here's a thing! They're sending me to Venice for a couple of days. Just two of us, myself and one of the Eyeties. Can't tell you more, but I'm tremendously excited of course.

I'll be back by the time you read this with lots of stories, I'm sure.

Your loving son,

Thomas

PS

I'm re-reading this letter now. I'm sorry Ma, I can't imagine they're going to let this one through. I'll send if off though, just in case. And, in any case, I'll be able to tell you all about it soon enough. Everyone has a feeling now that it can't be much longer.

I've written to Margaret and the Boy. Give them a hug from me when you next see them.

Chapter 23

I put the phone down. An *agente di polizia* from Calvene had just informed me that the results of the autopsy were in and, as far as could be determined, Anthony Shawcross, lost, weakened and confused in the snowstorm that had hit Cavalletto on the afternoon of January 7th, had died of hypothermia.

So that was it. No mystery. Just a very sick man who'd ignored all the advice he'd been given, and paid the price.

I closed my eyes, and tried to imagine it. The confusion, the hopelessness when everything around you has turned to white. And then, perhaps, you sit down and just close your eyes. Nothing but the howl of the wind and the icy flakes cruelly snatching at your face. In a lonely, lonely place.

I snapped my eyes open as Gramsci hopped up on to the the desk.

'Ah, you see puss, you're a very lucky cat aren't you?' I leaned back in my chair, stretching my arm over my shoulder in order to tap the window. It was cold to the touch. 'You have a nice warm apartment. Comfy sofas to destroy. Whereas out there,' I rapped on the glass again, 'there are, sadly, a lot of very cold kitties. And people.'

Ah well. Everything had been carried out according to the

book. I telephoned Maxwell, who seemed grateful for what I'd done. I wasn't sure I'd actually done all that much but, on the other hand, had Dario and I not been there it was possible that Shawcross might have lain under the snow for weeks.

That just left his brother to deal with. Stephen Shawcross had been upset, of course, when I'd broken the news of Anthony's death to him, but unsurprised. He'd given me the impression of a man who'd been expecting bad news for some time.

'Mr Shawcross?'

'Speaking.'

'It's Nathan Sutherland here. The Honorary Consul in Venice. We spoke just a few days ago.'

'Of course. It wasn't a conversation one would easily forget. Is there anything new to tell me?'

'Well, this is just to say that the *polizia* in Calvene have just been in touch with me regarding the result of the autopsy on your,' I bit my tongue, 'regarding the investigation into your brother's death. And, well, it confirms their original hypothesis.' Hypothesis? Had I really just used the word hypothesis? Did I automatically become a little more pompous when I had to deliver bad news?

'Meaning?'

'The official reason for your brother's death is given as cardiac arrest as a result of severe hypothermia. Even though his car was less than a hundred metres away, he'd have been absolutely blind given the intensity of the storm. And, given his state of health, they assure me that he would swiftly have fallen unconscious and . . . and . . .'

My voice trailed off. Never got any easier.

Stephen Shawcross took pity on me. 'I understand.' He took a deep breath. 'Well, thank you for all you're doing, Mr Sutherland. I'm sure it can't be easy for you either. So, what happens now?'

'I'm afraid there are going to be quite a number of forms to complete.'

'Ah. Well, you're in Italy of course.'

'It's not just that. There are quite a number of hoops to jump through in the event of repatriating a body.' I paused. 'If that's what you want to do?'

'I think so. He always wanted to be buried with our parents.'

'I understand. Now, I can do most of the work for you on completing these forms – these, sadly, are things I've had to do a number of times. Then I scan them and send to you for signature. Then you return them to me, I pass them on to the relevant authorities and then, well, then we can get things moving. I do have to warn you that it might well take some time.'

'I understand.'

'I also have to warn you that it will be expensive. Unless your brother had the requisite insurance, of course.'

'I'm afraid not. Insurance was impossible to come by, given his health.'

'I understand. I'm sorry.'

'But actually I'm glad you mentioned that. There's something you might be able to help me with.'

'If I can.'

'It's just that – look, Tony and I spoke on a number of occasions last year about what I was to do when he died.

Now, most of it will be dealt with by the solicitors but there were a number of other things.

'Some of these were just a bit silly. Like the emergency credit card in the biscuit barrel at the back of the cupboard. But some of it was more important stuff like access to bank accounts. Passwords. Access to his email. Things like that.'

'I understand.'

'I remember the first birthday after Mum died. We both got a reminder from Facebook. It seems silly, but it shook us both up a bit. And that happened every year thereafter, of course. No way to stop it. Now Tony didn't want that to happen again. And he'd also read all sorts of accounts of relatives not being able to access the deceased's email and the like. So he made sure I had access to everything. For emergencies only, of course.'

'A wise man, your brother.'

'He was. Anyway, I logged on to his bank account. Just to be absolutely sure as to where I stood with regard to funds for – well, getting the old chap back home for one thing. And there was a transaction there that I found a bit confusing. Something I don't quite understand.'

'Okay. Was this something your bank could advise you on?'

'That might be difficult. The transaction involves a bank in San Marco – that's part of Venice, right?'

'It's one of the six *sestieri*, yes.'

'So, it's a payment made to the Rialto branch of Unicredit, and the customer's name is Mazzon. Andrea Mazzon.'

'What?'

'Andrea Mazzon. You sound surprised?'

'No,' I lied. 'It's quite a common name, that's all.'

'I wouldn't have thought anything of it, but the amount is significant.'

'Can I ask just how significant?'

He paused for a moment. 'Twenty thousand euros.'

I whistled. Pretty significant. 'Mr Shawcross, do you have any idea what this was for?'

'None at all.'

'Do you have the date of the transaction to hand?'

'I can find out. I think it was mid-December, or thereabouts.' He sighed. 'Look, I suppose I could go through his emails. I don't feel happy about doing that, but I'd like to know what this transaction was for. And it's not just about the money, it's more that this is kind of a big unsolved question hanging over my brother's passing, and I'd like to know what it's all about.'

'Of course.'

'And, again, I know this is none of your responsibility and I feel a bit cheeky asking you this, but is there anything you can do at your end?'

Oh, I think so.

'I'll do what I can,' I said.

'Thank you. I'll be in touch.'

'Likewise.'

I spun round in my chair. Twenty thousand euros, transferred to the bank account of a candidate for the mayoralty. I scratched Gramsci behind the ears. 'Well now, Fat Cat. I think we might just have a little bit of a problem here, eh?'

Accidental Death of an Archivist. I wasn't quite so sure any more.

Chapter 24

There were a lot of Mazzons in the *Pagine Bianche*, but only one Andrea. At least in the *centro storico* of Venice. If I was to look much further afield, things would start getting complicated. I'd just have to hope he was the right one.

There was no number listed. It was happening more and more these days. People no longer saw an advantage in having a fixed line and were moving towards simply depending on their mobile phones. More than that, ever-proliferating automated spam calls were leading more and more people to simply not list their number. But Mazzon, at least, had left his address listed.

Andrea Mazzon, Demon King and darling of the extreme right, and unlikely candidate to be Mayor of Venice. Academic and writer, with a particular interest in the First World War.

He was born in the early sixties, but dressed as if he hailed from two decades earlier. Rock and roll, it seemed, had very much passed him by. His father, surprisingly, had been a member of the Communist Party; a partisan and poet, it seemed, of some distinction.

The more I read about Mazzon, the more I understood why he did not make his telephone number public. He had, it seemed, strongly revisionist opinions about Italy's twentieth-century history. In a country where many people, secretly or otherwise, still harboured a nostalgia for the days of Mussolini, this was perhaps not so exceptional. He had gone further, however, by describing the actions of the Italian partisans in the Second World War as 'akin to a terrorist organisation, organised solely for extreme political means, that served no purpose other than to prolong the war in Italy.'

Andrea Mazzon, the son of a partisan. Family reunions, I imagined, must have been very tense affairs indeed.

There are things you do, and things you do not do if you are in any sort of public life in Italy. And one of the things you do not do is to criticise the partisan movement. The fact that Mazzon had chosen the previous April 25th – Liberation Day – to make his statement had only made it worse. Following a storm of protest, he had been dropped by his publisher; although columns by him still occasionally surfaced in certain areas of the press who knew articles by him would serve as clickbait for advertising revenue.

He was also, of course, standing as a candidate in the mayoral election. There was no chance of him being elected directly, but there didn't need to be. All he had to manage was third place, and thus allow himself the luxury of being kingmaker in the event of a *ballottaggio*.

The only image I had been able to put together of Anthony Shawcross was of a slightly fusty, unworldly academic. The two of them seemed unlikely collaborators. But Mazzon – unpleasant as his opinions seemed to be – nevertheless appeared to carry proper academic weight as a historian.

I checked the address once more. Campo de l'Anzolo

Raffael, in the *sestiere* of Dorsoduro. A nice part of town, not too far from the Zattere, and close enough to the pubs and bars of Campo Santa Margherita, in the event of Andrea Mazzon proving to be an unexpected night owl.

It would be worth talking to him. The trouble was, from the little I'd read, I was pretty sure we weren't going to get on. Perhaps I needed some more information first?

My two elderly communist buddies, Sergio and Lorenzo, would surely know more about him than I could find in the newspapers. Perhaps they'd even have known his father? They would also, I imagine, have 'strong opinions' to express but I was pretty sure I'd be able to filter out the essentials.

There was just one thing. I'd have to play *scopa* with them. I checked my wallet and counted its contents. I sighed. I'd need to get some money out first.

'Hey, look Sergio, the bank's open,' smiled Lorenzo.

Sergio grunted, tried to look serious and failed, and came over to give me a hug.

'Long time no see, *compagno*. Not since the *acqua granda*.'

I looked around the Giudecca Communist Bar. Nothing very much seemed to have changed since I was last there, although Pino, the elderly *barista* whom we affectionately referred to as 'Lorenzo's dad', had been replaced by a young woman.

'What happened to Pino?'

Lorenzo shook his head, sadly. 'Not with us any more. He's moved on to a better place.'

'Oh.'

'The Milan Bar, I mean.'

'Turncoat,' grumbled Sergio.

'He said he enjoyed working here but he wanted to go somewhere with a little more life to it.'

Pino, as I remembered, seemed to have spent most of his time dozing behind the bar. The thought of him having to fend off dozens of raucous *rossoneri* fans screaming at the football on television seemed hard to imagine.

'Anyway, this is Bianca. She's a student at Ca'Foscari. She's much better.'

'Pleased to meet you, Bianca. I'm Nathan Sutherland.'

She smiled. 'Oh, Sergio and Lorenzo have told me lots about you. You're the English Honorary Consul, is that right?'

'British. Just to be absolutely precise.'

'Oh I'm sorry. I keep getting that wrong.'

'No worries.'

'What can I get you?'

'Spritz Campa—'

Sergio cut me off. 'Why don't you get us a half litre of red, eh, Bianca?' He sat down, shuffled a pack of cards, and grinned at me. 'No, make that a litre. Nathan might be here for a bit.'

I peeled the penultimate note from my wallet, and passed the pile to Sergio and Lorenzo who smiled and divvied it up between them.

It left me with ten euros. Oh hell, I might as well buy another round then. I nodded to Bianca.

'Same again?'

'I think so.'

I turned back to Sergio. 'This place doesn't look any

different. I can't believe it. Not after what happened last November.'

'It wasn't easy,' said Lorenzo. 'There was filth from the lagoon everywhere, as you can imagine. It took weeks to dry out properly. Then there was replastering to be done, of course. Rewiring. Replacing all the electrical goods.'

Sergio grunted. 'Yeah, it took a bit of work. But, you know, there were two of us.'

He didn't appear to be joking.

'Anyway, *compagno*,' he continued, 'you didn't just come over here to drink wine and give us money, did you?'

'Er, no. There's something you might be able to help me with.' They both nodded. 'What do you know about Andrea Mazzon?'

Sergio, as expected, started to turn the shade of purple that he reserved for the discussion of people on whom he held 'strong opinions'.

Lorenzo merely smiled. 'Well, let's just say he's not a regular visitor to this club.'

I wasn't sure anyone, apart from myself, was a regular visitor but I let it pass.

'Did you know his father?' I asked.

Sergio sighed. 'A little. We both did. He was a quiet man. Kept himself to himself. His wife died when she was still quite young, leaving him at home with the boy. He came in here a few times when he was older. I liked him well enough. Never really understood his poetry, but Lorenzo tells me it's very good.'

Lorenzo smiled. 'Oh, it really is, Nathan. You can see the influence of Cesare Pavese, even though I don't believe they ever met. You're familiar with Pavese?' I shook my head. 'Oh, now, you really must read him. Let me know next time you're going to be over here, I've got a few volumes I could lend you.'

Sergio rubbed his forehead. 'Lorenzo?'

'Sorry. Carry on, Sergio.'

'Did he ever talk about his son?' I asked.

Both of them shook their heads. 'I think he knew it wasn't quite the sort of conversation for the club,' said Lorenzo.

'Bit of an elephant in the room, I imagine?'

Sergio took a draught of his wine. 'I'm just glad he died before his boy said what he did about the partisans.'

Lorenzo shook his head. 'Well, they do say people become more right wing with age, Sergio.' Then he smiled. 'Fortunately we have you to help balance things out.'

'Cheeky bastard.' Sergio grinned and playfully punched his old friend in the shoulder. 'Anyway, *investigatore*, what's your interest in Andrea Mazzon?'

'It's like this. I found a British academic frozen to death at the foot of the cross in the war cemetery at Cavalletto. And it's almost certainly a tragic accident.' I paused.

Lorenzo smiled again. 'Except you think it might not be, is that right, Nathan? Come on then, tell us all about it.'

'His name was Anthony Shawcross, and he'd been researching his family. There's a Thomas Shawcross buried at Cavalletto. Anthony had a couple of letters from him. He'd written something about "being called up to the big house on the hill". Now, I think that must mean the Villa Godi Malinverni. It was the centre of British Command for a period during the war.'

Lorenzo nodded. 'Ah yes. A lovely place. I haven't been

for many years though.' He sighed, and looked thoughtful. 'I wonder if I ever will again?'

'Lorenzo, if you can help me I'll drive you there myself. Actually, no, that'd be a bad idea. But I've got a mate who'll drive you. Anyway, Shawcross, it seemed, had been in touch with Andrea Mazzon about something called the Visconti Box and something that happened to his grandfather during the war. And I'm just trying to work out what that could be.'

Sergio grimaced. 'If I wanted to know about a dead relative from the war, the last person I'd ask would be Andrea Mazzon. He'd only say bad things about them.'

'I gather he has, shall we say, *revisionist* opinions on that period.'

'He has opinions, *compagno*, that would see his sorry fascist arse kicked all the way to Caporetto and back if he ever wandered in here.'

'Not a fan then?' Sergio considered going purple again, then caught the expression in my eyes and realised I was joking. 'Look. When I was researching the Visconti Box I saw a photo of Mazzon and Shawcross together with Anna Fabris's husband. What sort of link could there be between them?'

Sergio refilled our glasses. 'Who knows?'

'I mean, Shawcross wasn't a politician. Gianluca Casagrande isn't a historian. I wonder what links them?'

Lorenzo coughed. 'Well now, Mr Shawcross, you said, was interested in military history. *Dottor* Casagrande is a Professor of English Literature I believe?'

'He is. He ordered a pizza the other day because it reminded him of Ernest Hemingway.'

'There we go then. A shared interest in the First World War. Indeed, I have to say that – unpleasant as he might be – *signor* Mazzon is something of an expert in the field.'

'I've been reading up on him. I'm finding it hard to understand why a guy like him might actually end up having an influence on who becomes the next Mayor of Venice.'

Sergio shook his head. 'You'd think it impossibile, right? But it's been coming for a while, now. The trouble is,' he sighed, 'the trouble is nobody takes an interest in politics any more. Not really. Nobody buys proper newspapers and the TV news is a joke. That's what lets people like Andrea Mazzon get a foot in the door.

'You see, about five years ago, he was just a guy who turned up on late-night talk shows to be pompous about music or art or stuff like that. But then he started appearing on football shows. Seriously. Being a pundit. That sort of thing. You ever watch *Dribbling*?'

I shook my head. 'Not much of a sports fan, really.'

'Quite right, Nathan,' said Lorenzo. 'There are far better ways of filling the day.'

'Well yes, there's Jethro Tull, the Marx Brothers and being manservant to my cat. Go on, Sergio.'

'At first, people think he's a bit of a joke. Here's this academic, with an accent that's even posher than Luca di Montezemolo, and he's on RAI every week talking about football. Lazio. Well, *of course*, he'd be a Lazio fan. And people start to think, hey, this guy sounds a bit strange but maybe he's really one of us. Maybe,' he almost spat the words, 'he's a *character*? You know what I mean?'

I nodded.

'And so then he decides he wants to go into politics as an independent candidate and he's definitely not a fascist, oh no. He's not *CasaPound*, he's not *Forza Nuova*. He's not even the *Lega* or the *Fratelli d'Italia*. No, he's just a centre-right politician.' He drained his glass and shook his head. 'Except he's not.'

'No?'

'Trust me, *compagno*, I've seen photos of the people who hang around with him. And there are some weapons-grade bastards there.'

'And so, what, you think he's going to be in some position of power after the next election?'

Sergio shook his head. 'I don't know. He doesn't need to win much in the way of votes. Just enough to drag Meneghini over the line, and then he's got him by the balls.'

'Meaning?'

Sergio gestured with his thumb in the direction of the lagoon. From the outside, I could hear the rain pattering against the glass.

'Meaning he gets to tell Meneghini what he wants. You think it's bad, now? With the cruise ships? Any sort of environmental protection will go out of the window. Houses for the kids? Jobs that don't involve tourism? They'll be gone. Because that's what these people are like. They don't care. They just see Venice as this magic well of money that you can go to, day after day after day. Except one day, you go and you find the bottom's dropped out of the bucket.'

'And you think Meneghini would go along with it?'

He shrugged. 'Why wouldn't he? It doesn't matter how people vote in Venice.' He grabbed my hand and jabbed it in the vague direction of the mainland. 'It's people over *there* that matter to him.'

We sat in silence for a while, listening to the rain patter.

Lorenzo cleared his throat. 'I think what Sergio is trying to say is that being an academic and historian does not stop one from being an absolutely unholy prick.'

Sergio and I, glasses halfway to our mouths, stared at Lorenzo. He shrugged. 'Sorry. Sometimes these things just have to be said.'

'More drinks, *ragazzi*?' asked Bianca.

'Lorenzo's just sworn for the first time since 1973. I think maybe we've had enough.'

'Okay then.' She checked her watch. 'Look, I've got an essay to write by the end of the week, can I just head off?'

Lorenzo smiled. 'Of course you can. And thank you so much for looking after us.'

'Look, if you want to stay on, just be sure to switch the lights off and slam the door behind you. If you change your mind and have more drinks, just leave the money on the bar.' She glared at Sergio. 'Not like last time, okay?'

'I told you, that was a mistake. I went to the cashpoint, the door slammed behind me and I couldn't get back in to pay. All right?'

She walked up behind him and shook him by the shoulders. 'Joking.' Then she turned to me. 'And Lorenzo's right about Mazzon, you know. He really is an unholy prick.'

'You know him?'

'I study Twentieth-Century History. I went to a lecture by him once.'

'Not good?'

'Oh the lecture was all right, I suppose. I mean, I didn't really agree with it, but you couldn't honestly say it was rubbish or anything like that. He does know what he's talking about. It was just about the way he talked to people. There was some problem with the audiovisual stuff he wanted to use. Now, this always happens. If you have a one-hour lecture, you can pretty much guarantee there'll be ten minutes of messing around trying to get the sound adjusted properly, or the smart board to work. So the *tecnico* comes in, and he's trying to get everything up and running, and nothing's happening and Mazzon smiles at us all and says "I think there's a lesson here, ladies and gentlemen, about paying attention in class. Or you might end up like this poor fellow."

'And a few people laughed, but mainly there was this really awkward silence. Because we all know this guy, you know? And I just thought about that thing they say that you can judge people by how they treat others.'

'There's another one,' I said, 'that I prefer. "Be nice to people on the way up. Because you'll be meeting them again on the way down."'

'I hope that's true,' she said. 'All right, comrades, see you tomorrow.'

'When will we see you again, Nathan?' asked Lorenzo.

I opened my wallet and stared inside. 'The next time I get paid, I suspect.'

Chapter 25

I knew little about Andrea Mazzon beyond what I'd read and what the comrades had been able to add, but Campo de l'Anzolo Raffael seemed like exactly the sort of place he'd live. A *palazzo* on the Grand Canal, I thought, would be just his thing but almost certainly out of reach financially. The remoter areas of Castello and Cannaregio were perhaps just a little bit too blue-collar, and the Lido – well, the Lido had cars, and Andrea Mazzon generally gave the impression of someone who thought it had all been downhill since the invention of the internal combustion engine.

No, Campo de l'Anzolo Raffael seemed far more his type of place. Residential, relatively quiet and the sort of place where a man could go about his business whilst his neighbours pretended not to know who he was.

I checked the address I'd been given. A modest three-storey building in pale terracotta that faced the eponymous church. There was also, I knew, a splendid restaurant in the *campo* and wondered if Mazzon spent much of his time there.

I rang the bell and waited. And waited some more. I swore under my breath. I should have made an appointment but, given the lack of a phone number, coming out here seemed to be the only way to actually meet him.

Rain was falling more steadily now, and I pulled my coat around me. I'd try once more and, if not, I'd have to give it up as a bad job and try and think of another way.

The door opened, just as I was about to ring the bell one final time, and I jumped back. An elderly man, with two dogs and a shopping trolley, looked me up and down.

'He's not here,' he said.

'Erm, who isn't? Sorry?'

'Andrea Mazzon. That's who you've come to see, isn't it?'

'It is. How on earth did you know that?'

'Mister, I've lived in this house for over seventy years. I know everybody that comes and goes. And if there's someone I don't know – especially in the last few weeks – I assume it's going to be for him.'

'Right. Do you know when he'll be back?'

He checked his watch. 'Should be about ten minutes now, by my reckoning.'

'Uh-huh. Do you actually know where he is?'

He made to gesture in the direction of the church but realised that the presence of his dogs and his shopping trolley made that difficult. He settled for a nod of the head instead. 'He'll be in there. Says his prayers, he does, every morning. You can set your watch by it.'

'Wow. He must be very devout.'

'Oh I'm sure he must be. Leastways, he never gets bored of telling people he is.'

'Right.' I paused, wondering if this would be a question too far. 'What's he like as a neighbour, then?'

He frowned. 'Mister, you're not from the papers are you?'

'No, I'm not.'

'Only I don't want any nasty stories being attributed to me. I've got to live in the same house as him, after all.'

'No, really. I'm the British Honorary Consul. I just think he might be able to help me.'

He shrugged. 'Didn't know we had one. That sounds very grand.' Then he smiled. 'Anyway, *dottor* Mazzon is just fine as a neighbour. Most of the time, anyway. The worst thing he does is play his classical music just a bit too loud. Just so's we can all hear it. Showing off, I call it. But that's not the worst thing in the world, I guess.' He looked up at the skies, and shook his head. His dogs were starting to get fractious and whined as they looked up at him. 'Anyway, nice meeting you, sir. Now, the weather's not going to get any better so if I don't take these two out now, I never will.'

He closed the door behind him, and made his way across the square. I joined him, until we reached the entrance to the church.

'I think perhaps I'll wait for him inside. At least that'll get me out of the rain.'

He grinned. 'Probably very sensible, sir. And if you do get the chance to say a quick prayer, say one for me, eh?'

'Oh, depend on it.'

He gave me a wink, and carried on across the square, the two little dogs yapping away happily.

A tall, ascetic figure in black was seated at the front, moving the rosary through his fingers.

I sat at the back so as not to impose on what, I assumed,

was meant to be a private moment. A private moment that he made sure his neighbours all knew about. I shook my head. That seemed uncharitable. Nobody goes to church every day unless they really want to be there.

Or, perhaps, unless they really want to be seen there.

There was another figure beside him, a shorter, stockier man in a heavy black jacket and woolly hat. Sensible fellow, I thought, as I shivered with the cold and hoped that *signor* Mazzon's prayers would not be long ones.

Woolly-hatted man got to his feet and patted Mazzon on his shoulder before striding, slowly, towards the back of the church, resting his big hands on the back of each pew as he passed by them, as if testing their strength.

He paused, blowing on his hands and then rubbing them together to keep them warm. Then, smiling to himself, he cracked his knuckles.

The sound, in the silence of the church, made me start. Then I noticed the tattoo on the back of his hand, and forced myself not to jump again. It was the same image of an angry bowler-hatted man that I had last seen approaching my face at great speed in Calvene.

I looked away from him and bowed my head as if in prayer, listening as the sound of his steps receded. Even violent men with aggressive-looking tattoos were allowed to go to church, I reasoned. Nevertheless, the coincidences were piling up.

I could no longer hear the sound of footsteps, and so I opened my eyes and gazed up at the ceiling. Angels in armour, cheered on by a cloud of *putti*, despatched bat-winged figures to hell as clouds scudded across a pale blue heavenly sky. St Michael, again? Perhaps. Those old Venetians really did love their military angels and wars in heaven. But why Michael in a church dedicated to Raphael?

'If you don't mind me saying so, you're looking in the wrong direction.'

I gave a little jump.

'I'm sorry. I didn't mean to startle you.' The tall, thin figure of Andrea Mazzon looked down at me. 'You seemed quite absorbed in that.'

'I was, yes. There's something familiar about it.'

'Francesco Fontebasso.' He rolled the *r* and stretched out the vowels for maximum sonorous effect. '*The War in Heaven*. Often mistaken for Tiepolo but, really, it's far too crude for that.'

I clicked my fingers. 'Fontebasso. Of course.'

Mazzon looked surprised. 'You know him?'

'I wouldn't say we were close. But I know of him. My wife knows him better. She worked on a restoration of a work by him in the Accademia.' Mazzon looked at me, quizzically. '*Dottoressa* Federica Ravagnan.'

He nodded, and raised his eyebrows. 'Oh yes. I've heard of her. She's quite brilliant, I understand.'

'Well, I think she is. I hope I tell her that enough, anyway.'

He nodded, yet looked confused as if unsure as to whether I was joking. 'As I was saying, that really isn't the right direction to be looking. In Angelo Raffaele, one shouldn't look directly upwards, but rather over there.'

He took my hand and raised it, to point at the organ loft. He crouched down next to me, bringing his face close to mine, and whispered. 'Guardi. *The Story of Tobias*. I come in here every day, you know? And I don't think there has been a single occasion when these little works have not moved me to the brink of tears.'

I nodded. 'They are lovely, aren't they?' I offered him my hand. 'My name's Nathan Sutherland. I'm the British Honorary Consul.'

He shook it. 'Andrea Mazzon. And so what, may I ask, brings the Honorary Consul to this part of Venice on a cold and wet January morning?'

'Well, I was rather hoping to meet you.'

'Oh, really?'

'Yes. I was wondering if we might be able to have a chat about Anthony Shawcross?'

'Shawcross? My goodness me, that poor man. I met him once or twice, as you may know. And then, of course, I read about him being found up at Cavalletto.'

'Yes. I was the one who found him.'

He shook his head. 'Terrible. The weather can be unpredictable at this time of year. I've only been there during the spring. What on earth was he doing there?'

'He wanted to visit his grandfather's grave.'

'But why now?'

'He was a very sick man. Quite simply, he didn't have time to wait.'

Mazzon shook his head. 'He never looked particularly well, but he never told me anything and I thought it would have been indelicate to ask.'

'Anthony Shawcross was researching the history of his grandfather during the Great War. And, as I understand, few people know the history of the conflict in this part of Italy as well as you do.'

He gave a little shrug. 'Well, that's as maybe. My enemies wouldn't say so.'

'Did he ever ask you about something called the Visconti Box?'

Mazzon smiled, ever so faintly, and took a deep breath. 'Ah, I think I'm beginning to understand now.' He looked at his watch. 'Look, I'm not sure if this is a conversation for church. Neither do I think it's appropriate for a café. Why don't you come up to my apartment? That's possibly a better place for unpleasant conversations.'

Chapter 26

Mazzon led me back across the square, and opened the door of the *palazzo*. I was about to close it behind me, when I heard a 'Just a moment' from outside.

It was the elderly gentleman with the two dogs and a *carrello* now bulging with shopping. I held the door open for him.

'Thanks.' He nodded at Mazzon. 'Good morning, *dottor* Andrea.'

'Good morning Bruno. Can I give you a hand with that?'

'Oh, that's kind, thanks.' He nodded at the dogs. 'I've got my hands full with these two little devils.'

Mazzon dragged Bruno's trolley up the stairs, and positioned it outside his apartment door. 'Okay there?'

'Just fine thank you, *dottor* Andrea.' The two little dogs jumped up at me, again and again, excited by having a new stranger to play with. 'Renzo! Lucia! Stop that!'

'It's okay,' I smiled.

'They like strangers. I'm getting a bit long in the tooth now to play with them as much as I ought. They probably think you're going to throw balls for them.'

'Aww. Some other time, I'm afraid.'

Bruno looked over at Mazzon. 'One of your musical friends, *dottor* Andrea?'

'Oh my goodness me, no.' Mazzon raised his eyebrows. 'Although, are you musical?'

'I can manage a little bit of Jethro Tull in the shower, but I'm no expert.' They both looked confused. 'Never mind.'

Mazzon smiled. 'Never mind, indeed. Lovely to see you, Bruno. Enjoy the rest of your day.' He nodded at me. 'Mine is the apartment directly above.' He led me upstairs. 'I'm afraid my cleaner doesn't come until tomorrow, so you'll have to excuse the mess. Come in, please.'

Mazzon closed the door behind me and then, rather to my alarm, turned the key in the lock. He must have seen the expression on my face. 'Oh, don't be alarmed. I'm in the habit of locking the door. There are people in this city who don't wish me well, you understand?'

I nodded.

'Well then,' he continued. 'I suppose we ought to have this difficult conversation. I have to say I'm a little surprised that the British diplomatic service directly involves itself in debt collection.'

'Debt collection?'

He ignored me. 'Now, there are some items here of value which you may find of interest. Just take what you need. Everything, that is, apart from my books. I'm sorry, but you really will have to take those from my cold, dead hands.'

'*Dottor* Mazzon, you're mistaken. I'm not here for that.'

'You're not?'

'No. Do I look like a debt collector?'

He smiled. 'I have to say I'd been expecting someone

rather more fearsome. But you are here regarding the matter of the twenty thousand euros, I imagine?'

'Only because I've been speaking to Mr Shawcross's brother and he happened to comment on this rather large transaction.'

'Well I can clear that up for you. I'm glad we've avoided an awkward conversation. Now, would coffee be good?'

'Coffee is always good. Thank you.'

Mazzon disappeared into the kitchen, and I was left alone. I wasn't sure if I should sit down or not. Instead, I wandered over to the bookcases.

He was well-read, I had to give him that, although there was surprisingly little fiction, and nothing as far as I could see by authors who were still breathing. As well as Italian, he appeared to read English, German and Russian. Most of the titles were unfamiliar to me, the vast majority seeming to be volumes on the First and Second World Wars.

I wasn't sure if I was allowed to touch them or not, but drew one out at random. I flicked through a few pages, and then replaced it hurriedly, as if my fingers had been burned.

There was a cough from behind me. 'I'm sorry, I didn't ask you if you'd like sugar?'

'Sorry?' I said, my mind being elsewhere.

'Sugar?' he repeated.

'Oh yes, thank you. One spoonful.'

He dropped a sugar cube into an espresso cup, and placed it on a table in between two leather armchairs. 'Sit down, please.' He gestured at the bookshelves. 'It's a modest collection, perhaps, but I'm quite pleased with it. Sadly, the number of books one can own are constrained by the size of one's apartment. I hate to think of how many I've had to give away over the years. There's something dreadful about that, don't you think? Like giving away pieces of one's own past.'

I nodded. 'I understand.'

He smiled. 'Did you find anything of interest?'

I hesitated for a moment. I scanned the shelves again for the volume that I had taken down, but was unable to locate it. 'There was something, over there. I can't remember the title but—'

His smile grew even wider. 'Yes?'

'It was,' I took a deep breath, 'well, I recognised the name of the author. He's a Holocaust Denier.'

He nodded. 'Oh, quite possibly. You don't remember which one?'

'You have more than one book on – that?'

'Of course. I'm an historian. Specifically of the first part of the twentieth century. It's impossible to examine that period – properly examine it – without exposing oneself to such material. Whatever one might think, it is something that needs to be confronted. History isn't just about reinforcing one's own prejudices, Mr Sutherland.'

I shook my head. 'God.' He winced, ever so slightly. 'I'm sorry. No offence.' I noticed a plain metal crucifix affixed to the wall, the sort of thing you might see in any public building in Italy. His faith, then, was more than just an affectation for the voters.

I thought I should move the conversation on to safer ground, but hated myself for doing it. 'This must be a lovely area in which to live.'

He nodded, as if to indicate that he was perfectly aware

of what I was doing. 'It is.' He got to his feet, moved to the window and pulled aside the curtain. We looked out onto the rear facade of Angelo Raffaele. 'It's not the most spectacular church in Venice, but it suits me. And there's no denying, it's very convenient.' He noticed the expression on my face, and smiled. 'When I was a little boy, Mother used to make me go to church every morning to say my prayers for the day. Before school. Even in the middle of winter. I've never quite got out of the habit.' He shook his head. 'Father hated that, of course. He hoped I'd put all that God-bothering nonsense, as he put it, behind me after she died. But I never did. Perhaps that's why I never had any time for my father's politics.'

He sighed, and shook his head. 'This is a fine place to live in general. Everybody here in the *palazzo* keeps an eye out for each other. It's a decent area. People with what we might call refreshingly old-fashioned values. There are a couple of *sagre* and *feste* in the summer months, but nothing too wild. No, it suits me very well. And where do you live, Mr Sutherland?'

'San Marco. The Calle dei Assassini to be precise.'

'Oh yes, I think I know where that is. Not too close to the *piazza*, thank goodness. I think I'd find that unbearable. It's a tragedy that the most beautiful place in the city is now a no-go area for its residents.'

I looked down at the restaurant on the corner, the Trattoria Anzolo Raffaele. 'I'm very jealous of you living so close to that,' I said.

'I'm afraid I don't go there unless I'm entertaining. Oh, don't get me wrong, I'm told it's excellent. It's just that I've never been much of a foodie, if that's the right word.' He chuckled. 'Mother used to say that if it weren't for bookshops I'd never leave the house at all.'

I smiled. 'So, you were going to tell me about Anthony Shawcross?'

'Anthony Shawcross and the case of the missing twenty thousand euros. My goodness, that sounds like the title of some trashy thriller, doesn't it? But it's really not as mysterious as all that. So before I begin, can I ask what you know about the Visconti Box?'

'Not a great deal. I've spoken with various people about it. Professoressa Barichello at the University. Oh, and the gentleman at *Settima Arte*.'

He nodded, and then smiled. 'It sounds terribly dramatic, doesn't it? But I'm afraid it really isn't as exciting as all that. Visconti filmed the ballroom scene in *Senso* at the Villa Godi Malinverni. The story has it that he read up on its history, and discovered that the Prince of Wales, no less, had stayed there during the last days of the Great War. Perhaps that sparked the germ of an idea for a project. I think that image, that concept, of dancing in the ruins might have appealed to him.

'The British left the villa in some haste at the end of the war. I doubt we'll ever know exactly what might have been left behind. But there was an archivist in residence at the time, long dead by the time our great director appeared on the scene. Visconti acquired a box of papers – drawings, letters, diaries and photographs – shortly after he completed filming. From one of the late archivist's relatives, I believe, who didn't really understand the value of what he was letting go. But, for whatever reason, the project never evolved into anything concrete.' He smiled. 'Perhaps Visconti simply found the decline of the Italian aristocracy more interesting than that of the English. No offence.'

'None taken. And so what happened to it?'

'It passed into the hands of Franco Zeffirelli. He and Visconti were *close* for a while.' He gave a little shudder, deliberately I thought, in the hope of provoking a reaction from me. 'It was auctioned in Rome towards the end of last year. Or at least it was supposed to be.'

'So I understand. I seem to have missed that.'

'It was in mid-December. Not long after the *acqua granda*. Like everybody else in Venice, I imagine you had other things on your mind. Anyway, Mr Shawcross and I had exchanged emails regarding the British presence in this part of Italy during the war.' He paused, and smiled. 'Emails, yes. And people say I don't live in the twenty-first century. Well, I was able to give him some information, and then I heard about the auction of the Visconti Box. Now, the expected asking price was beyond both of us but we thought we could combine our finances on this. Hence the money in my account.'

'And then the box was withdrawn from auction at the last minute?'

'Yes. Infuriating, of course.' He saw the expression on my face and held up a hand. 'This was not long before Christmas. Now, I might have mastered email but the intricacies of internet banking are beyond me, I'm afraid. That'll need an appointment with my bank and that, as you probably know, isn't so easy in the days just after the festive period.'

'I wasn't going to say anything.'

'Yes, you were. And rightly so. I'll make sure Mr Shawcross's brother receives the full amount within a couple of days.'

'Well, that's good of you. Thank you.'

'Not at all. Might I say you've been the most polite debt collector I've ever had.'

'You've had more than one?'

He smiled. 'Teasing.'

I got to my feet. 'Well, thank you for your time, *dottor* Mazzon. And for the coffee, of course.'

'My pleasure, Mr Sutherland.'

'There's just one thing, though.'

'Oh yes?' Again, he raised his thin eyebrows by perhaps a millimetre.

'Why are you doing this?'

'I don't understand?'

'Standing for mayor. I mean, I don't really know you of course, but it seems to me you'd far rather be here or in a library, researching and writing away.'

He chuckled. 'Good point. Very good point. Would it sound so ridiculous if I said it was a sense of duty?'

'Erm, well . . .'

He waved a hand. 'No, no. You don't have to lie. Sometimes I wonder why anyone in this wretched country would want to be a politician. Everybody hates you and your career is almost certainly going to end in failure. But it's as banal as that, I'm afraid. This city has been good to me, and so I want to put something back. Moreover, it's a city with a history of being badly run. I think I can do something about that.'

'You can?'

'Yes.' He chuckled. 'I mean, let's look back over the years. We're not exactly talking about the finest minds in Italy, are we? Either we're talking party men or businessmen, and both of those have failed. I don't have any of that baggage. When I say I'm independent, I mean it.'

I took a deep breath. '*Dottor* Mazzon, some might say that you do carry quite a lot of baggage.'

'They do?' Those eyebrows, again. 'What do they say, Mr Sutherland?'

There was no point in dancing around it. 'They say you're a fascist.'

'Dear Mr Sutherland, anybody in Italy who's even vaguely to the right of Che Guevara gets accused of being a fascist at some point. For an independent thinker it's practically a badge of honour.' Then he turned off his smile. 'But what do *you* think?'

I took a deep breath. 'As I said, I don't really know you. But I do think you're a man with a regrettable collection of books.'

'And I assure you I'm really not as terrifying as all that. You may call me a fascist. I prefer to say I believe that there are certain values – certain important values – that we've lost. And as a result we've become a harder, cruder, less gentle people. Trying to recover those values seems to me to be important.'

'Such as?'

'Simple things. The importance of faith. The importance of family. Not much to object to there, surely?'

'I think that depends on whether you mean just one faith and one type of family?'

He chuckled. 'Well then, perhaps we should leave it there for now.'

'Do you seriously think you can get one of the other candidates to work with you?'

'I don't think they'll have any choice. There's virtually no chance of either Fabris or Meneghini winning in the first round. They'll have to come to me. Now, I'd rather it was Anna, but Meneghini will have to do.'

'Anna? You'd rather work with Anna?'

'Of course. She's far more intelligent than Giuseppe.' He put a hand to his mouth and pretended to yawn. 'He's just another businessman. No imagination. No real intelligence to speak of. There's nothing to him beyond empty sloganeering. "A mayor for all the city". That's all he's got. His only advantage over Anna is that he has better taste in music. That's the one thing I suppose you could say we bond over. Nevertheless, he's going to win.'

'You seem very sure of that.'

'I am. Anna, I imagine, will just shade the first round of votes. But she won't work with me – neither will her supporters – for the reasons you described. But Giuseppe – he'll come round. I'm very sure of that.'

'We'll see. Again, thank you for your time *dottor* Mazzon.' As I reached the door, I turned to look at him once more. 'You really are very confident, you know? Considering that an awful lot of people don't seem to like you very much.'

He smiled back at me. 'They don't. But I think enough people do.'

Chapter 27

I mooched around the flat, trying to avoid annoying Gramsci, and wondered what to do. Because, on the face of it, there was little left *to* do. I'd call Stephen Shawcross within a couple of days, just to be sure that Mazzon had indeed reimbursed the money, and that, really, would be that. An accidental death with nothing further to be done beyond the bureaucracy. And yet, a man with a tattoo who'd sat next to Andrea Mazzon as he said his prayers was, almost certainly, the same man who'd punched me in the face in Calvene. I shook my head. Too many coincidences. Or I really just was that unlucky.

I heard the rattle of keys, shortly followed by the door slamming. Gramsci yawned and stretched, and pricked up his ears. He wandered over to see what was going on, and looked disappointed when he saw that it was only Federica. Still, given that he'd gone to the effort of getting up, it was probably time for post-lunch lunch. Or was it pre-dinner dinner? He went and sat down next to his bowl, and looked up at Fede with the saddest little expression he could muster, and gave a piteous little *m'yeep*.

'Hello Unfriendly Cat. *Ciao, tesoro.*' She kissed me on the cheek. 'Your cat needs you.'

I shook a modest number of kitty biscuits into his bowl. Gramsci made his 'is that all?' face.

'That's all. You can have a little more later if, and only if, you're good. Understood?'

Gramsci rubbed himself against my legs and then flopped over, waving his paws in the air.

I sighed. 'Okay. Just a little more. But make it last.'

He munched away, happily.

'As I was saying. Make it last, okay?'

Fede looked at me, and shook her head. 'I can't believe you're still falling for that old one.'

'Sorry. Is it a bit pathetic?'

She nodded.

'Anyway, how has your day been?'

She brightened. 'It's been good, you know?' Federica was currently working on a short-term contract at the Palazzo Querini Stampalia, trying to put right some of the devastating effects of November's flood. 'I think we're getting somewhere. I'm not saying it's back to normal, nowhere near, but there's progress. I can't imagine they'll be keeping me on beyond the end of the month. But it seems there might be the chance of a bit of work at San Polo.'

'Oh yes?'

'There might be some restoration needing to be done on the ceiling. You know, the ship's keel roof?' I nodded. 'Hasn't been touched for two hundred years. They'd like a few of us to do some investigatory work up there.'

'Scaffolding, hard hats, the usual?'

'The usual.' She flopped down onto the sofa. 'And so, how has your day been?'

'Well, I had coffee with a fascist. So I guess you'd say it's been *interesting*.'

She rubbed her forehead. 'Okay. It sounds like this is going to need a spritz.'

'So, then. What did you think of him?'

'Well, I have to say he wasn't quite what I was expecting.'

'No jackboots? No black shirt?'

'No. He seemed, well, his reading material aside, kind of normal.'

'Normal. Uh-huh.'

'Normal-ish, anyway. Okay, the guy wears his religion on his sleeve. But otherwise normal-ish. Difficult to reconcile with the fascist Demon King that I was expecting. He was polite. Made me coffee. Didn't try and convert me to Christianity. Or fascism for that matter.'

Fede set her glass down. 'But that's the problem, isn't it? Fascism doesn't arrive with guys wearing Iron Crosses. It arrives with harmless-looking, slightly sad middle-aged men like Andrea Mazzon.'

'That's another thing I don't get. Who's going to vote for this guy? I mean, seriously?'

Fede sighed. 'You'd be surprised. He makes a great deal of his faith, as you know. That plays well with one section of his audience. He talks about family – *mamma* in particular – quite a lot. That plays well with another section.'

'So he's the fascist it's okay to like?'

'The cuddly fascist. That's his image. The harmless middle-aged man who loves his country, his mother and his church. In no particular order. He turns up on television chat shows, uses lots of long words and – instead of thinking he's some kind of appalling elitist snob – everyone thinks he's a "character".'

'I still don't know what's in it for him. I mean,' I shrugged, 'just, why?'

'I imagine being Mayor of Venice might pay better than being an historian, *caro*.'

'Is it that important? I mean, I know we make a big deal about it, but is it really that important?'

'It could be. To us, I mean. A good mayor might genuinely make things better. Better for the environment. Better for the kids who live here. Jobs that don't involve tourism. The chance that one day you might actually be able to afford an apartment here.' She sighed. 'But I've given up on all of that now. Sometime shortly after I gave up on Santa Claus.'

'Even Anna Fabris?'

Fede put her head to one side. 'Okay. She might be good. She might actually be really good. But I'm not putting money on her winning. If she doesn't win the first round outright then the nutters and fascists will transfer their votes to Meneghini as the least-worst option.

'You know what I think? I think perhaps Anna genuinely does think she could make the city a better place.' She shook her head. 'An intelligent female candidate, with ideals. In Italy. Oh God, how brilliant would that be? As for Meneghini, I've seen no evidence other than that he's an entitled idiot who just likes the idea of swanning around in a sash for a few years, in the hope that it might get him noticed enough to have a chance to become President of the Region or, God help us, even a Senator.'

'And Mazzon?'

'He worries me. I think, like Anna, he thinks he can change things.'

'I guess so. But he's not going to be Mayor of Venice, is he? Nobody seriously believes that for a minute.'

She shook her head. 'No. But that's not important. All he has to do is get into bed with Meneghini.'

'But what could he realistically do? In terms of actual power? It's not like he could actually pass any laws or anything.'

Fede sighed, again. 'He wouldn't need to. He could just make things more difficult. Withholding funding, that sort of thing. Providing refugee services? He cuts that. Any sort of provision for the LGBTQ community? He cuts that. Historic buildings sold to oligarchs, or turned into hotels? He does that. Ever bigger ships in the Giudecca Canal? Bring it on. And, let's be honest, he could get away with it.' She paused. 'Did you ever hear of a guy called *lo sceriffo*?'

I shook my head. 'Before my time, perhaps?'

'Perhaps. Only by a little, though. He was Mayor of Treviso. Liked to go by the nickname of the Sheriff.' She shook her head. 'It's always nicknames like that, isn't it? Inadequate little men, choosing these macho aliases. The Sheriff, the Punisher. It's always stuff like that. Pathetic.'

'Go on then. Tell me about him.'

'He was mayor for eight years. Eight years where Treviso was represented by a man who told his voters that the city was turning into a casbah. That he wanted a campaign of ethnic cleansing against gypsies. Oh, and who gave a fascist salute during a council meeting for good measure.'

'Bloody hell.'

'But, as I said, he was mayor for eight years. Meaning he was re-elected. If there wasn't a limit on the number of terms, he might still be there. Because once these bastards are in, once they've got their feet under the table, it's bloody hard to shift them.'

'So what does this mean?'

'It means, *tesoro*, that Andrea Mazzon is not the sort of person I want to see having any sort of influence in Venice at all.'

'I know.' I shrugged. 'But what can we do about it?'

Fede smiled and patted my arm. 'Oh we'll think of something, *tesoro*. We'll think of something.'

Chapter 28

'*Pronto?*'

'Mr Sutherland? Mr Nathan Sutherland?'

'That's me. How can I help?'

'My name's Giuseppe Meneghini. You might recall we met just a few days ago. At the Scuola Grande di San Rocco.' He chuckled. 'I hope you haven't forgotten my singing voice?'

Gramsci hopped up onto the desk, and I scratched him behind the ears. 'Well, that's not something one forgets in a hurry, *signor* Meneghini.'

'I was wondering if perhaps it might be good to meet up. To have a chat, that sort of thing.'

Gramsci looked up at me, his eyes narrowing. I nodded at him, and put my fingers to my lips.

'Erm, well I don't see why not? Could I just ask why, though?'

'Well, it just seems like something we should do.'

'This isn't anything political, is it? If it is, then I probably shouldn't. I mean, it'd probably be okay but I'm not sure the Ambassador would be that keen on it.'

'Oh?' There was a note of surprise in his voice. 'But I understood you met with Andrea Mazzon recently.'

I wondered how on earth he could have known that, but I managed to keep the surprise out of my voice. 'Ah well. That was a little bit different. I suppose we'd call it consular business.'

'Well, that sounds most mysterious. But this is just dinner so I'm sure the Ambassador won't mind.' His voice was light, jocular even.

'Oh right. In that case, then yes, we'd be delighted.'

'Ah. Perhaps just the two of us though. This time, at least.'

'Hmm. Well, okay. Where and when?'

'Are you free tonight?'

'I can be.'

'Excellent. Tell you what, why don't we meet at my club?'

'I'm sorry?'

'My club. The 1920 club, not very far from you.'

'I didn't even know there were any private members' clubs in Venice.'

'We're very discreet.' He chuckled. 'We don't tend to do the sorts of things that would get us into the papers.'

'Well now I'm intrigued. Tonight it is, then.'

'At eight o'clock or thereabouts. I have a couple of meetings this afternoon but I should be free in good time. If I'm not, don't worry, I'll leave instructions for you to be let in.' He chuckled again. 'You won't be left out waiting in the cold.'

'So, whereabouts is this place?'

'Ah good point. We're not in the *pagine gialle,* either. Okay, can you find the Fondamenta del Traghetto San Maurizio?'

'I, erm, think I probably can,' I said.

He picked up on the uncertainty in my voice. 'Look, you'll be coming from the direction of Santo Stefano, I imagine?'

'Uh-huh.'

'Okay, so you head to Campo San Maurizio. You turn right just before you come to that museum of musical instruments. Go straight down the *calle*, right to the end, turn right and you'll be there.'

'Ah right. Okay, I can place it now.'

'It's a small *fondamenta*. Just the one building. The doorbell you want is the one with Rilke on it.'

'Rilke? Seriously.'

He laughed. 'Seriously. *A stasera*, Mr Sutherland.'

He hung up. I raised my eyebrows at Gramsci. 'Well now, Fat Cat. What have I done here, I wonder?'

'So you're going for dinner with another fascist then?' said Federica.

'I think that's a bit unfair. Look, I've been reading up on the guy and, sure, he's a bit more right wing than I might like but there's no indication he's an actual fascist.'

'Maybe not, with the emphasis on the *maybe*.'

'He's just a businessman. That's all he is.' Fede rolled her eyes. 'Look, I'm just going for dinner with the guy. I'm not going to let him use my image on election material.'

'And is Andrea Mazzon going to be there? Did you think about that?'

'He didn't mention anyone else.'

'You've had coffee with an actual fascist, and now you're going to spend the evening with the man who's prepared to enable him.'

'This is just dinner.'

'It'd better be. I don't want to see photos of you in tomorrow's papers.'

'Look. If there's anyone else there, anyone at all, I promise I'll leave. Promise.'

'Really?'

'Absolutely. Look, I've got no more time for these bastards than you have. But the guy was polite, he sounded nice enough and, well, I think it might seem a bit rude if I pulled out now.'

She shook her head. '"It might seem a bit rude",' she repeated. But then she smiled. 'Oh dear, all these years in Italy and you're still far too English, *tesoro*.'

I kissed the top of her head. 'Are we okay then?'

She nodded. 'You go and do what you have to do. Just be careful, okay, and try not accept any more invitations.'

'I promise. And now, I think, I need to go and iron my black shirt.'

I ducked, and the cushion that Fede had launched at me whistled past my head.

It was a chilly evening and the streets were dark as I made my way to Campo San Maurizio. The eponymous church that gave the square its name had long since been deconsecrated and now housed a museum of musical instruments. I paused, and scratched my head as I looked at the neoclassical facade. Had I ever been in? I genuinely couldn't remember but thought I probably hadn't. A shame, and a bit of a waste given that entrance to the museum was free, in a city not prone to giving things away.

I took the first *calle* on the right, made my way to the end, and then stopped. Meneghini had been right. There really wasn't much of a *fondamenta* at all. But, even by Venetian standards, there was one hell of a view. Opposite me, across the Grand Canal, lay the Palazzo Salviati, its mosaiced exterior seeming to glitter in the moonlight. To my left was the long low profile of the Guggenheim, its white Istrian stone shining. And further along, dominating the skyline, was the church of the Salute. Yes. It was a very, very fine location for a private members' club. How had I not heard of this place?

As Meneghini had explained, there was only one doorbell. *Rilke.* Engraved beautifully, in a flowing script, onto the polished brass bell plate.

Why Rilke? I buzzed, waited, and the door clicked open. A floating staircase in white stone, almost Carlo Scarpa like, led up to the first floor where a lift awaited me. I nodded to myself. That made sense. I imagined the ground floor would easily flood in the event of *acqua alta*. It would, therefore, make little sense to have anything depending on electricity at ground level.

The lift smelled of nostalgia; of cigar boxes and hotels in old films. There were just two buttons, 'Clubroom' and 'Restaurant'. My finger hovered over 'Clubroom' but then, at the last moment, I changed it to 'Restaurant.' Meneghini had specifically mentioned dinner.

I stepped out of the lift, and into the 2020s. You wouldn't describe it as flashy or glitzy *per se*. Simply that it was evidently the work of people who had no truck with the belief that there was such a thing as too much white marble and chrome. The immaculately polished floor gave the impression that you would slip if you so much as dared to step on it.

A white-jacketed waiter moved towards me. At Florian, or at Quadri, he would have sported a neat Marcel Proust moustache. Such things were *passé* at the 1920 Club, where hipster beards were tolerated. I took a look around the room and the staff. No, not tolerated but positively encouraged.

I took a tentative step out upon the marble and swivelled my foot as if stubbing out a cigarette, just to test what the surface was like. If the waiter's smile wavered, it was only for a moment.

'Sir?'

'Ah, good evening. My name's Nathan Sutherland. I'm here to—'

'Of course, sir. *Signor* Meneghini has just arrived. Your coat?'

'Thanks.'

I let him take my coat, but first transferred my wallet to my jacket. Over cautious, perhaps, in an environment like this, but why take chances? Again, the ghost of a frown passed his brow, displeased perhaps at my gesture having demonstrated a lack of respect, but it passed in an instant.

'This way, please, sir.'

I followed him to a table in the corner where Giuseppe Meneghini got to his feet and smiled at me.

'Mr Sutherland?'

'*Signor* Meneghini?'

'That's me.' He stretched his hand out and we shook. Neither a wet flapping fish, nor a bone crusher designed to show who was the alpha male. Just a regular shake.

'What can I get you?'

'Oh, I don't know.' I looked down at his glass. 'What have you got there?'

'A Manhattan.'

'Okay. I'll have a Negroni. Thanks.'

He smiled, and motioned the waiter over. 'My friend here would like a Negroni.'

The waiter nodded, and switched his smile on. 'Of course, sir. Any particular Negroni?'

'Erm, a Negroni Negroni. Is there a choice?'

The frown returned, momentarily. 'We have the classic Negroni sir, or, if you prefer, Negroni *sbagliato*, Negroni with Aperol, alcohol-free, Scotch Negroni, Vodka Negroni, Kiwi Negroni . . ..'

I held my hand up. 'Remind me again, what's a Negroni *sbagliato*?'

'Spumante instead of gin, sir.'

'Okay, thanks. A classic Negroni please.'

'Flaming?'

I shook my head. 'I don't think we need to go that far.'

Meneghini motioned for me to sit down. 'Simple pleasures, I see, Mr Sutherland.'

'It's just I don't see any point in messing about with something that's already effectively perfect. One third gin. One third vermouth. One third Campari. There's nothing to go wrong with it. You could make it whilst drunk. In fact I've frequently made one whilst drunk. And then people think they have to mess about with it and make one with whisky or Aperol or, God help us, the Negroni *sbagliato* – the *mistaken* Negroni – well, never has a cocktail been more mistaken in its life.'

I suddenly wished that Federica had been by my side, to dig me in the ribs and tell me that I was, perhaps, ranting on a little too much about what was, after all, only a pre-dinner drink. But Meneghini just smiled.

'Sit down, please. I made sure we had a window.' He tapped the glass and grinned at me. 'Take a look at that. Not bad. Not bad at all, eh?'

I could only agree. 'That's one hell of a view.'

The waiter arrived with my drink and we chinked glasses.

'Your health, Mr Sutherland.'

'And yours.'

He tapped the menu. 'Now, let's think about ordering. The steaks are good. That's what I'm having.'

'Beef in Venice?'

'Trust me, these are as good as anything you'll find in Florence. The chef got some special grill in. Very excited he was.'

'Okay. Then I'll join you. How do you recommend them?'

'Medium rare.' He grinned. 'He's a good chef, but a bit of a purist. Ask for one rare and he'll just show it the flame.'

'Medium rare it is then. Are we doing antipasti?'

'The *pesce crudo* of the day is always very good. You're okay with raw fish?'

'I'm very okay with it.'

'Excellent.' He motioned the waiter over. 'We'll share a plate of the fish to start, and then two steaks medium rare. With perhaps some mixed vegetables on the side.'

The waiter smiled. 'Of course, *signor* Meneghini.'

Meneghini tapped the side of his glass. 'But maybe give us ten to fifteen minutes first, eh? I don't want to rush this. And my friend, I'm sure, wouldn't want to rush his Negroni.'

'Of course, sir. And to drink?'

'A half of the house white with the fish, and a half of the

house red with the steaks.' He looked at me. 'I hope that's okay?'

'Of course.'

'I mean, it's tempting to split a bottle between us with each course but I've got a busy day tomorrow and I imagine you do as well. Oh, and the house wine is perfectly good.' He paused. 'I'm afraid I don't know much about wine. Do you?'

'I think wine knows more about me.'

He smiled. 'So, raw fish followed by steaks. I think that's what they call the caveman diet? "Surf and Turf", in English, is that right?'

I smiled back. 'It is.'

'Good. My English is a little,' he waved his hand this way and that, 'a little shaky. I am trying to improve it.'

I looked out of the window once more, and then around at the interior. 'You know, I had no idea this place was here.'

'Well, I'm not that surprised. We're low key here and have been ever since we started, as I understand.'

'In 1920?'

'Indeed. I imagine there'll be some sort of centenary event this year. A suitably discreet and low profile one, of course. '

'What's with the whole Rilke thing though?'

'I believe he stayed here on his last visit to Venice. He had a circle of friends here and they kept meeting after he left. Then it kind of became a businessman's club.'

I looked around, approvingly. 'I like it. I don't suppose you'd be interested in translators as well?'

'As a matter of fact we might well be. I understand the English section of our website needs some attention and—'

He caught the expression on my face. 'I'm so sorry, that isn't what you meant, was it?'

'It wasn't, no. It's fine. Easy misunderstanding to make.'

He rubbed his forehead. '*Oddio*, now I'm embarrassed.'

'Don't be. It was only a silly joke.'

'Well anyway, I'm afraid it's rather difficult to get in. I'm only here because I inherited my membership from my father. Everyone here descends in one way or another from that original group of friends who sat and listened to Rainer Maria Rilke declaiming his poetry.' He smiled. 'Listen to me. That makes us sound all a bit apostolic, doesn't it?'

'Just a bit. Did you have to do a test? About Rilke, I mean?'

'No, thank God.' He looked around, as if worried that he'd be overheard and marched from the premises. 'I'd have been in trouble if I had.'

And with that, one of the hipster waiters arrived bearing a platter of raw fish. Fortunately, perhaps, for Meneghini, he did not have appear to have heard his confession.

Thin slices of raw seabass, simply dressed in olive oil, lemon and a scattering of pink peppercorns. Followed by *bistecca Fiorentina* charred on the outside and a deep Carpaccio red on the inside.

I think there were some vegetables on the side but, to be honest, they weren't really the main event.

Giuseppe Meneghini may or may not have been a fascist. He was certainly preparing to get into bed with some very unpleasant people. But he also knew how to show people a good time.

'Well,' I said. 'I don't know what kind of special grill your chef got in, but I've got to say that was pretty good.'

Meneghini smiled. 'Pretty good?'

'Okay. Exceptionally good. In a "best steak I've had in Venice" kind of way.' I sipped at my wine and noticed, with some regret, that the half bottle was now empty.

Meneghini must have seen the expression on my face and made an almost imperceptible gesture to the waiter who returned swiftly with another half bottle.

'Oh well, I guess I'll have to be good tomorrow.' He patted his stomach. 'Protein-heavy diet. My doctor tells me it's good for giving me energy.'

'I wish I had a doctor like that. Mine just tuts at me and shakes his head.'

'I'll put you in touch with mine. It took me ages to find him.' He refilled our glasses. 'Well, I'm glad you've enjoyed dinner, Mr Sutherland.'

'Call me Nathan, please.'

'Nathan it is, then. We'll have to invite your wife next time.' He chuckled. 'We do allow women now. It took a while, but we got there in the end.'

'Well, it's been a delightful meal. I don't really understand why you wanted to meet up, but I appreciate it anyway.'

He smiled. 'Look, I'll be honest with you. I'm going to be mayor within a couple of months. Even if it goes to a *ballottaggio* – especially if it goes to a *ballottaggio* – there are votes I can count on. The *Lega* and the *FdI* will be with me and there are enough independents to carry me over the line. Fabris is a good candidate but,' he spread his hands, 'the numbers just aren't there for her.

'And so, as I said, I'm going to be mayor within a few months. You English have this expression about hitting the ground running. Well, that's what I'm doing. I thought it would be good to at least make contact with the various consular services before taking office.'

I took a sip of my wine, and shook my head. 'Can I be honest with you?'

'Of course. The English, of course, have a reputation for their plain speaking. Go ahead. I promise you I won't be offended.'

'Okay.' I took a deep breath. 'I'm sorry, but I don't think that's the reason.'

'No?'

'No. I don't think you quite understand what the consular service does. We're not like Ambassadors, or anything like that. If you come to the Honorary Consul's reception, you're not going to get any Ferrero Rocher.

'Besides, there are about forty Consuls in this city.' I looked around. 'Are you seriously going to take them all out for dinner? Here? I don't think even you have that much money. So come on, *signor* Meneghini, this isn't about hitting the ground running, or about establishing diplomatic relations, is it?'

Meneghini looked me up and down, as if weighing his thoughts. 'Okay. That's very honest of you. So I'll be honest with you. This is about Anna Fabris.'

'Okay. Tell me more.'

'You like her?'

'I do. And her husband. They seem like good company.'

'And politically?'

'Same again.'

He paused. 'More than me?'

'I'm afraid so.'

'Okay. Honest, again. Why so?'

'Because I think she'll be good for the city. I think she'll work for Venetians first and foremost. On the environment. On housing. Maybe there's just a chance she'll be able to stop the population drain.'

'And you don't think I'll do that?'

I shook my head. 'No. I don't. Oh, I think you probably mean well enough, but if you're elected it'll be because of a coalition of fascists and chancers.'

'That's a little harsh.'

'But true.'

'That remains to be seen. I'm not one to be pushed around, Mr Sutherland. Neither by fascists nor chancers. Why don't you give me a chance?'

I shrugged. 'It wouldn't matter. I'm not going to get to vote anyway.'

'You aren't?' Then he snapped his fingers. 'Oh no. Brexit, of course. My sympathies. What about your wife? Is she of the same mind?'

'On many things, no. Particularly with regard to my record collection. But on this, yes, we agree.' He frowned, ever so slightly. 'I'm sorry. This really isn't personal.'

He tried to smile. 'No, of course not.'

'And I don't see why our votes in particular should make any difference. Yes, Federica's worked on some high profile projects but it's not as if she's in the paper every day. And as for me, I shrugged, 'I'm the British Honorary Consul. That doesn't carry any weight with anyone.'

'Well, I think you're being too modest. But I understand.

Just tell me one thing though. What's the first thing that strikes you about Anna Fabris? The one thing, the main thing that people on the street are saying about her?'

I frowned. 'Difficult to say.'

'No it's not. You're being too diplomatic now. I'm reading this in the newspapers every day, remember?'

'Okay then. The thing that strikes me about her is that she seems to be honest.'

Meneghini nodded. He sipped at his wine. 'Honest. Yes, that's what everybody says.' Then he smiled, ever so slowly, as he leaned in towards me. 'The thing is, Nathan . . . is that Anna Fabris is a liar.'

Chapter 29

'I don't understand.'

Meneghini waved a hand. 'All in good time. I'll come to that. Let's just talk for a moment about Anna Fabris. About lovely, honest Anna Fabris and what you think she'll do for the city.'

'Okay.' I ticked them off on my fingers. 'I think she'll try and do something about the maritime environment. That means not just banning cruise ships from sailing down the Giudecca Canal, but getting them out of the lagoon altogether.'

Meneghini nodded. 'Fair enough. I imagine she might at least try and do that. Incidentally, how much difference would it make to your life?'

'Realistically? Very little.'

'Okay. At least you're being honest about it. What else?'

'Limiting the number of holiday apartments. Legislating that a certain number of rentals must be reserved for residents, young people in particular. Encouraging businesses other than tourism to move here.'

He nodded. 'And you think Anna Fabris will do that?'

'I'm prepared to believe so.'

'Me too. Or, as I said, I think she'll try.' He shook his head. 'And the net effect of this all will be precisely nothing.'

'You can't be sure of that.'

'Oh, I can. The population of this city has fallen way beyond critical mass now. Out of interest, when did you move here?'

'Fourteen years ago.'

'2006, then. Still over sixty thousand people in those days. Within a couple of years, we'll have dropped below fifty thousand. A decline pushing twenty per cent just in the years since you arrived.'

'I hope you're not blaming me,' I said.

He laughed. 'Just an illustration. But, seriously, the city crossed a threshold years ago. Now I'm sure Anna is perfectly ready to implement all these schemes you mentioned. And it will make no difference at all. It will be putting lipstick on a corpse.'

'So what's the alternative?'

'Managed decline, Nathan.'

'Blimey. That'll look good on a poster.'

'I'm being serious.' He jabbed his finger towards the window. 'That view out there. That's all very lovely, very pretty. But the future of the city is beyond that. Mestre. Marghera. The mainland. If Venice has a future, that's where it is.'

'In Mestre?'

'Nobody loves it. Nobody even really likes it all that much. But that's where the jobs are, Nathan. That's where the affordable housing is. That's where the new hospitals and schools are going to be.'

'So what are you saying? We just abandon Venice to the holidaymakers and the students?'

'Not overnight. As I said, it's all about managed decline. Demographics will see to it within a generation, and trying to fight against that is like trying to fight against the sea.'

'That's a pretty cynical point of view, if you don't mind me saying so.'

'A cynic is what an idealist calls a realist, Nathan.'

'First time I've been accused of that. But, go on then. Tell me what this has to do with Anna Fabris and her honesty or lack of it?'

'You were in Cavalletto recently, I understand?'

I nodded.

'You found the Englishman, Mr what-was-his-name?'

'Shawcross. Anthony Shawcross.'

'That must have been distressing.'

'It wasn't pleasant.'

'And I understand you met with Andrea Mazzon just the other day?'

'Could I ask just how you happen to know that?'

He waved a hand. 'Andrea and I are in touch quite a lot, as you can understand. He's a historian, as you know. He told me about something – an archive which had belonged to Luchino Visconti – that contains something that would absolutely bury Anna Fabris should it come to light.'

I shrugged. 'I don't know much about it. But unless Anna turns out to be the illegitimate great-granddaughter of Edward, Prince of Wales, I don't see what it could be.'

Meneghini shook his head in irritation. 'I'm trying to be serious here. The archive came up for auction, just before Christmas. Mazzon was going to acquire it.'

'Oh I see. And then you could blackmail Anna Fabris with

the contents, get her to withdraw, and you and Mazzon romp home to an easy victory.'

'Not blackmail. We'd just release the contents.'

I shook my head. 'That's pretty shady stuff, Giuseppe.'

'It's politics, Nathan. Nothing more.'

'So where do I come in?'

'You were at Cavalletto. You're in contact with Shawcross's family, I imagine?' I nodded. 'Good. Well, it's like this. If you can find any information on the whereabouts of the box or even concrete proof of what it contains,' he smiled, 'well, I'd be very grateful.'

'Grateful?'

'I'd remember you. When I become mayor.'

'Politics, again?'

He grinned. 'Exactly.'

'Well, I'm flattered. But short of putting a little extra translation work my way, I'm not sure what you could do for me.'

'Don't be too sure. Where's your office these days? The Consulate, I mean.'

'The Street of the Assassins, San Marco.'

He sniffed. 'I know it. It wasn't always there though, was it?'

I shook my head. 'It moved, a few years before my time. It used to be in the Campo della Carità, near the Accademia.'

'I know it. Lovely building. It has a terrace overlooking the Grand Canal, as I remember.'

'Expensive, though. There was no way it was sustainable going forward, especially considering how little there actually is for the consul to do here.'

Meneghini shrugged. 'I don't think that need matter. I'm sure I could arrange something.'

I smiled. 'Okay. I think I understand.'

'And not just that. Your wife works in art restoration, I understand?'

'Signor Meneghini, it seems you have quite the dossier on me.'

'Nothing that can't be read in the papers. But, seriously, funding for art projects is always so hard to come by. I'm sure I'd be able to help.'

I nodded. 'Again, I think I understand.'

'Good.' He smiled, and poured out the last of the wine. 'Good.'

'But just to be absolutely clear, you want me to help you find this box in order to destroy someone else's reputation and, effectively, cheat your way into power.'

'It's not cheating, Nathan, it's just—'

'Politics. I know. Well, it's crystal clear to me, Giuseppe, and I'm afraid the answer is no.'

'I wouldn't be such a bad mayor. Really. And if I could throw a few favours your way, well, where's the harm?'

'I'm sorry. I can't do this. No matter how lovely that terrace overlooking the Grand Canal is.'

'I understand.' He sighed. 'But I was right about funding restoration projects. They can get cancelled just as easily as they get set up.' I opened my mouth but he put a finger to his lips. 'No, no. It's getting late. We've both had a drink. Just have a think about what I've said, okay? And I'll be in touch.' He pulled his wallet from his jacket, and took out a business card. 'This is my address. Not very far from *Fenice*.'

I took it from him, worrying for a moment that he'd passed me the Runes. I turned it over in my hands. 'Nice,' I said. 'Do you have a canal view?'

'I even have a watergate. I really should get a boat to go with it, but I haven't been back in the city all that long. I thought I needed a Venetian address, you see.'

'Signor Meneghini?' I half-turned round to see a stocky man standing behind me, smartly dressed yet with a woolly hat perched incongruously on his head.

The same man I'd seen in church with Mazzon.

'Francesco? What have I told you about wearing hats indoors? Particularly in the club.'

'I'm sorry sir,' said Francesco, not looking sorry at all. Meneghini stared at him for a few seconds, until he reached for his hat and pulled it off, idly dangling it from one finger. 'Signor Mazzon has been calling.'

'Oh, has he?' Meneghini grinned. 'Anything new?'

'Nothing new, sir. Just the usual.'

'Okay. Well, I see no reason to call him back just yet. Let's just let him wait for a while longer, eh?'

Francesco nodded.

'I think you can call it a day for now, Francesco. Thanks for everything. By all means get a drink at the bar before you leave. Ask them to put it on my tab.'

Francesco turned to go, but not before pulling the woolly hat back on to his bald head.

Meneghini stared after his retreating bulk, and shook his head. 'Someone's going to complain about him breaking the dress code one of these days, and I'll be the one getting in trouble for it.' He drained the very last of his wine. 'Well, I guess we've both got work to do tomorrow, Nathan. Shall we call it a night at that?'

I nodded. My audience, evidently, was over.

He reached across and shook me gently by the shoulder. 'As I said, Nathan, we can help each other out here. Have a think about what I said, eh?'

Chapter 30

Federica stirred her second cup of tea of the morning.

'So, all you have to do is find this Visconti archive, give it to Meneghini and in return I find myself first on the list for the most prestigious restoration projects that come along, and, as a bonus, we get ourselves a lovely apartment overlooking the Grand Canal?'

'That's about it.'

'On the downside, we deliver Venice into the hands of an unscrupulous charlatan who'll do nothing for the city except run it down?'

'Pretty much'.

'So what are you thinking?'

'I'm thinking that, nice as it may be, the Palazzo Querini alla Carità is probably a bugger to keep clean.'

'I imagine it is.' She nodded at Gramsci. 'What do you think, Unfriendly Cat?'

'Hang on, Gramsci gets a vote on this?'

'I think we need to be unanimous, *caro*.'

'Okay, well if I can speak on his behalf, I think he'll be happy anywhere with a comfy well-padded sofa for him to destroy. Oh, and that's another strike against it, it's probably full of antique *signorile* furniture that he really shouldn't be left near.'

'True enough.'

'How about you?'

She wrinkled her nose. 'Well, if I had any doubts before – which I didn't – I think this just cements *signor* Meneghini into place alongside *signor* Mazzon as people who should not be let within a hundred kilometres of the levers of power.'

'Okay. So what are we going to do?'

She got to her feet. 'Well, I'm going to work.' She kissed me on the cheek. 'If you can solve this while I'm out, that'd be lovely.'

'Right. Sure. Yes, I can do that.'

'I'm sure you can, *caro*. See you later.'

She kissed me again, then pulled on her coat and made her way downstairs. I sat there and looked at Gramsci.

'Well now, puss. How are we going to sort this one out, eh? I mean, if you knew where the Visconti Box was, what would you do with it?'

He stared up at me and miaowed.

'You'd sit in it? Well, of course you would. And presumably destroy the contents as well?'

He miaowed again.

'Okay, I understand. But it seems everybody else who's interested in it wants something more than that. Mazzon wants it. Meneghini wants it. And there's something in it that's of interest to the poor deceased Anthony Shawcross, and also, it seems, something that would destroy Anna Fabris's reputation.'

I looked down at him but he'd tired of the conversation by

now, and had thrown a paw over his eyes. I looked down at him, his chest slowly rising and falling.

'Okay then. You sleep on it, eh? I'll work on it in the meantime.'

I turned on my computer.

'Now, I'm just thinking that the man with the tattoo who I saw at Andrea Mazzon's church the other day and at the 1920 club last night might just turn out to be the man who punched me in the face in Calvene. So, let's start with him.'

Mazzon, as I had imagined, was not averse to appearing in the newspapers or on television. An image search then, was going to take some time. And then, when I was on the verge of giving up, I found a video clip of Mazzon appearing on *Dribbling*, the football show that Sergio and Lorenzo had told me about.

I had to say, it was quite entertaining. Mazzon in his rich, dark brown voice drawled on about the merits of the Beautiful Game whilst his co-presenters looked on, evidently trying not to laugh.

And yet, it had obviously done something to rehabilitate his image. The video linked to 'Andrea Mazzon's Best Bits', a compilation of his appearances and then, most bizarrely of all, to his appearance at the Stadio Olimpico for a recent Lazio–Roma derby.

There he was, with a sky-blue replica shirt awkwardly pulled on over his suit, grinning from ear to ear as the stands erupted around him. A banner behind him read 'Mazzon stands with the *Irriducibili*' whilst a bald-headed man stood with his left arm thrown around him. The other one was raised in a fascist salute.

I searched for more images from the match, and there he was again. The arm was still around Mazzon's shoulders but this time the fist was clenched.

There was one more. This time he was holding open the door of Mazzon's car, his arm stretched out towards the waiting press pack in a gesture that very firmly suggested that giving them a bit of room would be a good idea.

I expanded the images as much as I could. The first one was too faint to make out, but in the second there could be no doubt. The same man I'd seen in the company of both Meneghini and Mazzon. And – I rubbed my jaw – the same man who had punched me in Calvene.

This was beyond coincidence now. This was something that needed checking out.

I'd need a journalist. Ideally someone who knew about football.

I smiled to myself. I knew just the person. Even if it was going to push my diplomatic skills to the limit.

Mestre has its charms. From Piazza Erminio Ferretto, with the *duomo* of San Lorenzo and medieval clock tower, to Parco Albanese, a pleasant place to stroll in the early spring or autumn.

Yes, it has its charms. But they're well hidden on Corso del Popolo on a rainy January afternoon.

Roberto Bergamin folded his arms and leaned against the door jamb upon seeing me.

'What do you want?'

Bergamin, from the little I knew of him, had never been confused with a ray of sunshine and his disposition, it seemed, had not shifted in the two months since we last met.

'I thought you might be able to help me, Roberto?'

'Oh yes?' He nodded his head as if wondering whether to slam the door or not. 'Now why would I want to do that, Mr Nathan Sutherland?'

'Because there's a story in it for you. Like last time.'

He nodded. 'Okay. Any reason why me?'

'Well, partly it's because of your happy-go-lucky approach to life. And because there are few things I like more than schlepping out to Mestre on a rainy January afternoon. But mostly it's because you're the only newspaper man I know.'

For a moment, I expected him to slam the door on me but then, to my astonishment, something that might have been a grin flashed across his face.

'Okay. Come on then. Tell me all about it.'

He stood back to let me enter the apartment, which remained much as I remembered it, the signed Venezia FC shirt still in pride of place on the wall.

'So go on then, Mr Honorary Consul. What's it all about this time?'

'You write about football, don't you, Roberto?'

'Not as much as I'd like to. That dickhead Bianchi at the office seems to have that one covered. I only get to cover the matches he doesn't want. So if it's Pordenone or Cosenza, I'm your man. If we get Juve or Milan in the Coppa Italia, well, you can bet your life Bianchi will be the name on the strapline for that one.'

'Sorry about that. Do you only ever cover the football itself? What about the nasty stuff; you know, *Ultra* culture and the like?'

He shrugged. 'Well now, that can be nasty stuff as you

said. And *signor* Bianchi doesn't really like getting involved in that. So, if a bit of chair throwing goes on outside the Stadio Pier Luigi Penzo,' he jabbed a thumb towards his chest, 'matey boy here gets a call to go down to Sant'Elena and check it out.'

'Can't be much fun?'

'Ah, it's not as bad as you might think. It never really kicks off too badly in Venice. Think about it, you're travelling up from Rome or wherever, you've been on a train or a bus for hours and then you've got to queue up to get on a bloody boat to get to this tiny stadium lashed together with scaffolding which feels like it might just fall to the ground if you do anything as excessive as a bit of jumping up and down. I don't think your heart would really be in a fight after all that.'

'Okay. But there's one guy in particular I want to talk to you about.' I took the envelope from my pocket and smoothed out the two clippings I'd printed off.

'Hang on, that's him isn't it? Posh boy? Andrea Mazzon?'

'That's him. But do you know the guy at his side?'

Bergamin nodded. 'I do, yeah. See, you know I told you I always get the shit games? I've got some photos somewhere. Of about a year ago. Two games where things kicked off a bit outside the ground.' He flipped up the cover of his laptop and tapped away.

'Two games, as I said. This one was taken almost a year ago. Home defeat by Perugia.'

A group of *tifosi* were involved in a pitched battle against police outside the Stadio Pier Luigi Penzo. A flare was burning in the background, whilst in the foreground a bare-chested, bullet-headed man was gesturing at the cameras in the universally understood gesture for 'come on then, I'll take you all on.'

He tapped at the screen. 'That's him, isn't it?'

I nodded. 'Pretty sure.'

'Okay then. Second photo. October 2018. Home draw with Hellas Verona.'

This time, two cops were holding the bullet-headed man in a head lock. I shook my head.

Bergamin frowned. 'That's the same guy, right?'

'It is. Sorry, I was just thinking that Saturday afternoons in Sant'Elena don't look much fun.'

'Oh, it's not usually like that. Most of the bad stuff goes on near the station or Piazzale Roma. But this is him, yes?' I nodded, and Bergamin smiled. 'I know who he is, if that's useful.'

'It would be, yes.'

He grinned again and tapped his nose. 'Well now, be careful what you wish for. And the second thing is, what's in it for me?'

'Maybe nothing. Maybe there's nothing to find here at all. But if there is, then it could be something big. Something affecting the mayoral election.'

'Politics? Oh Christ, politics. I don't really do that.'

'Well, now you do. We're expanding your horizons. Tell me about this guy.'

He shrugged. 'Okay, so his name's Bentivoglio. Francesco Bentivoglio. But everyone just calls him Havok. I've got more photos here.'

He clicked away at his computer and I looked at the face staring out at me from the clippings. Bullet-headed and bare-chested, holding an iron bar in one of the photos and, in the other, unmistakably giving the Roman salute.

'I think I'd call him whatever he wanted,' I said.

Bergamin snorted. 'Probably wise. He's on record as saying he'd kill anyone who called him Francesco. Havok is his *Ultra* name. If you're big enough in *Ultra* circles you have to have your own name. It's kind of like being a Brazilian footballer or a superhero.'

'What's that tattoo on his arm? I can't quite make it out.'

'I didn't really want to get close enough to check it out at the time. But I know what it is. It's by a guy called Grinta.'

'You're losing me.'

Bergamin tapped away at his laptop. 'This is what it properly looks like.' He turned the screen towards me. An angry, snarling little cartoon man, swinging a kick and wearing a sky-blue top and a bowler hat that reminded me of Alex in *A Clockwork Orange*. 'It's Mr Enrich.'

'Who?'

'Mr Enrich. It's a logo designed by a guy called Antonio Grinta. Lazio's *Irriducibili* use it as their logo.'

'Lazio's *Ultras*, right? Organised football hooliganism?'

'That's it. And the *Irriducibili* are the biggest, hardest bastards of the Lazio *Ultras*. They like the whole fascist thing, you know.'

I shook my head. 'Hang on, I'm confused now. What's a Lazio *Ultra* doing in Venice?'

'Oh his dad's from Rome. Roman name, isn't it? Bentivoglio. Died over fifteen years ago now. Think he might actually have been murdered. So what do you want to know about Havok?'

'This is where the big story comes in. I want to know why

he's hanging around with Andrea Mazzon and Giuseppe Meneghini.'

Bergamin frowned. 'That doesn't sound very likely. What would they have to talk about? Classical music?'

'Football, fighting and fascism?'

'Okay. One of those, I grant you, might be of interest to *dottor* Mazzon. So what evidence do you have?'

'I saw Havok and Mazzon together in the Church of Angelo Raffaele.'

'Are you sure? He's never struck me as someone likely to be a big churchgoer.'

'It had to be him. I remember that tattoo on the back of his hand.'

Bergamin sucked his teeth. 'Mmm. Okay. That would be kind of unusual, in Venice. Are you sure they were together?'

'Again, I wasn't sure. Until I saw this.' I took out the photograph from the auction of the Visconti Box and placed it next to the newpaper clippings. 'It's him. Isn't it?'

He looked from one photo to another, and then a smile spread across his face. 'You know, Mr Sutherland, I think you might be on to something.'

I smiled back. 'I think I might be. But there's more than this. I know for a fact that this guy is hanging around with Giuseppe Meneghini as well. I saw him last night. He seems to be working for both of them. At least, that was the impression I got.'

Bergamin rubbed his face. 'Okay, too much going on here. Let's concentrate on one at a time. Let's take Mazzon. Now, assuming it's not a new interest in fine art and classical music, what do you think might be in it for Mr Havok?'

'A chance to meet new people and hurt them, I imagine.'

'Well, he's got form for that.'

'And the politics?'

'Lazio have a hard-core Nazi element among the *Ultras*. But there's more than that. Havok has links with *CasaPound*.'

'The fascist group?'

'That's them. You know their story?'

I shook my head. 'Not really. Started in Rome, didn't they?'

'Yep. Started as a social movement to deal with the housing crisis. Squatters, basically. And then they kind of evolved a political ideology.' He shook his head. 'Look, don't ask me too much about that. Like I said, I'm no expert on this sort of thing. But basically they're seen as being a fascist group.'

'Ah, and so Havok's after building alliances between them, Mazzon and Meneghini?'

'I don't think so. *CasaPound* don't operate as a political party any more. Not since about six months back.'

'Which means if you were one of them, you'd be casting around for alternative fascists to piggyback on.'

'Exactly. Well done, Mr Sutherland, you're learning.'

'So what's in it for Mazzon?'

'Votes from the *Ultra* community, but there can't be many of those up here. No, if you ask me, *dottor* Mazzon's just after some hired muscle. Protection, if you like.'

'It might just be that. Well, there's one way to find out I suppose.'

'What, you mean talk to Mazzon?'

'I've met him once. He's smart. He'd just give us some sort

of glib, semi-convincing answer. No, I think we should talk to the monkey, not the organ-grinder.'

Bergamin sat bolt upright. 'You mean talk to Havok?'

'Yes.'

'Are you nuts? This is a guy who did eighteen months in prison for attacking someone with a hammer. Count me out.'

'There'll be two of us. I'm sure it'll be fine.'

'And I'm very much sure it won't be. No way.'

'There could be something big in this for you.'

'There could be a coffin in it for me. No.' He folded his arms. 'No way, Mr Sutherland. There isn't a story big enough that could convince me to do this.'

Chapter 31

'I must be insane to be doing this,' said Roberto. 'Even with Mr Big here.'

Dario looked at him. 'I've got a name, you know. Most people call me Dario. Sometimes people call me *signor* Costa.'

Bergamin sighed. 'Whatever you like, Mr Big.'

Dario shot me a glance. 'Tell me again why I'm doing this, Nat?'

'It's a chance to make new friends, Dario.'

'Yeah. With Mr Happy here. And a guy called Havok. This sounds like an afternoon with the word "Fun" written all over it.'

'Look, there's three of us. It'll be perfectly safe. We just need to talk to the guy, that's all.' I paused. 'Listen, Dario, is Vally okay with you doing this?'

'Well, she wouldn't be if she knew about it.'

'You didn't tell her?'

'Hell, no. Did you tell Federica?'

'Are you crazy? Look, as I said, it'll be fine.'

The vaporetto was pulling in to the island of Sacca Fisola, and we made our way outside, bracing ourselves against the icy wind that blew in off the Giudecca Canal.

'You been here before, Nat?', said Dario.

I shook my head. 'Never had the need to. And tourists don't stay here so there's never any consular business.'

'How about you, Mr Happy?'

'Sometimes, Mr Big. Never for anything really important. Maybe to cover a fight or a break-in. Things like that.'

I stopped walking. 'Can we knock it off with the Mr Happy / Mr Big thing, please? This is making me feel like we're in the worst ever remake of *Reservoir Dogs*. Dario, this is Roberto. Roberto, this is Dario.'

Dario shrugged. 'Okay, I can do that. Hi, Roberto.'

'Hello, Dario.'

'That's better. Now, come on then.' I straightened my back. 'Let's go to work.'

We made our way down the Calle del Vaporetto, lined on each side by modern apartments in shades of pale yellow and green.

'Not like the *centro storico* is it?'

'You can say that again. You ever been here before, Dario?'

'When I was a teenager. One of my pals from the *liceo* lived here. So a group of us would come over from time to time. It was easier to play football here. More open spaces, you know.' He shook his head. 'Don't know what happened to him. Think he moved out to Treviso, years ago. Sad how you lose touch with people, isn't it?

'Anyway, it's kind of a different world here.' He jerked his thumb in the direction of Giudecca. 'Over there we've got the Molino Stucky. Five star hotel, now. When I was a kid it was just a wreck. We used to go and drink beer there. Stupid of us, it was a dangerous place. And now,' he shrugged, 'I probably couldn't even afford a beer there.

'But here, it's all just a bit different. Blue collar, I suppose you'd call it. Houses where people can afford to live, and where people with maxi-yachts wouldn't want to.'

'Someone told me the residents are all a bit lefty here,' said Bergamin.

Dario shrugged. 'I think it was, back in the day. I don't know if that's still true.'

'Seems a bit of a strange place for a fascist to hang out, then.'

'I guess even fascists appreciate a reasonable rent,' I said.

We weren't seeing the island at its best, but I could appreciate that, come the spring, there'd be plenty of green spaces to relax in and the apartment blocks looked well cared for. I'd seen far more crumbling buildings in Venice proper, although I suppose they had the excuse of having been built in the Middle Ages and not the 1960s.

We stopped outside one of the apartment blocks. 'Is this the place?'

Bergamin checked his phone. 'This is it.'

The label on the doorbell keypad read 'Bentivoglio' instead of 'Havok'. I went to press it, but Dario grabbed my hand.

'What?'

'You've thought about what to say to him? When he recognises us, I mean?'

'He only saw you for a moment, and he's not met Roberto at all. He probably won't recognise you.'

'Yeah, that word *probably* is doing a lot of heavy lifting,' said Bergamin. 'So, what are we going to say to him?'

'We'll be honest. Well, partly honest. We just say we're with the press.'

'Oh yes,' said Bergamin. 'Football hooligans are just famous for their love of the press.'

'They might be interested in getting their face in the papers though.' I shrugged. 'So, anyone got a better idea?'. There was silence. 'Okay then. Let's try it. Roberto, I guess you ought to do the talking. You being an actual journalist and all.'

Bergamin rolled his eyes, but pressed the buzzer anyway.

'*Chi è?*' came the voice over the intercom.

'Hi, is that Havok?'

'Who wants to know?'

'My name's Bergamin. I'm from the *Gazzettino*. I wondered if we could have a talk.'

'What about?'

'Just stuff. *Ultra* stuff, if you like.'

There was no answer, although I could still hear the crackle of the line. He hadn't hung up on us, at least. I looked at Bergamin and rubbed thumb and forefinger together.

'There's money in it, okay?'

'You're a journalist?'

'Said I was, didn't I?'

'Hold your journalist's card up to the camera.' Bergamin fumbled in his wallet, and did so. 'What about the other two?'

'I'm a translator,' I said, 'English.'

'A translator?' There was a definite note of interest in his voice now. 'What about the big guy?'

I decided to be honest. 'He's protection, okay. We were a bit scared.'

Havok laughed. 'First floor. But don't be stupid, okay?'

The door buzzed open. As we made our way up, a young woman with a headscarf passed us on the stairs. Havok opened his door, and stared after her. He nodded at us to come in.

The room was relatively spartan, and held what looked like a sofa bed with a pile of laundry at one end. A stereo was pumping out reggae at a volume that might be considered antisocial.

I looked at Havok. Bullet-headed and powerfully built. If he was my neighbour, I thought, I'd let him play music at whatever level he desired.

A small cabinet was fixed to the wall. Six daggers were hanging inside. Even from a distance, I could see each of them had Nazi insignia.

'See anything you like?' said Havok. My eyes shifted to the bookshelf. 'What are you expecting to see? A copy of *Mein Kampf* or something?'

I tried to speak but my throat was dry.

'I don't have it, if that's what you're thinking. I've read it, though. It's bollocks, and it's boring as well.'

Neither Dario nor Bergamin seemed able to speak. It looked like I was going to have to do the talking.

'Look, Mr Havok,' I began.

He burst into laughter. '"Mr Havok",' he replied, mimicking my accent. 'Fuck me, you really are English aren't you?' He stared more closely at me. 'We've met before, haven't we?'

I nodded. 'We have. But I really am a translator and my friend here,' I nodded at Roberto, 'he's from the *Gazzettino*.'

'And your friend?' said Havok, nodding at Dario.

'I sell real estate.'

'You brought an estate agent as your protection? Bloody hell, I've heard it all now.'

'I was in Sarajevo,' said Dario.

'Blimey. Didn't know there was such a good housing market there. Anyway,' he turned to me, 'you. Downton Abbey man. What do you translate, then?'

'Lawnmower manuals, mainly. Academic papers and the like. But I've done stuff for the English papers. The *Telegraph*, *Guardian*, *Express*, *Mail*. All those.'

'Oh yes. So I can find you online, can I?'

'Probably not. They're not good at crediting translators.'

He shrugged. 'Okay then. Out with it. What do you want?'

I was starting to find the level of the music oppressive, and the stink of dope in the air wasn't helping either.

'Could you turn that down a bit, perhaps?'

He gave a little bow, and mimicked my accent again. 'Anything your Lordship desires.' He switched the music off.

'You like reggae?' I said.

'Yes I do.' He caught the expression on my face. 'Oh, don't tell me, you thought I'd be here listening to Norwegian Black Metal or something didn't you?'

'Well. Yes.'

'I just like reggae, okay? Where they come from doesn't bother me. Just as long as they stay there. So what's this all about then? "My life as an *Ultra*"? That sort of thing? Or do you want to talk to me about Diabolik?'

'Diabolik?' I said, and the words were out of my mouth before I could stop them.

Havok's eyes narrowed. 'Diabolik. Fabrizio Piscitelli.

You know?' His eyes narrowed further. 'The top man of the *Irriducibili*. Murdered in Rome last August.' I said nothing. My mouth was dry. 'You've never heard of him, have you? So this isn't about *Ultra* stuff, is it? What's this about?'

I looked over at Bergamin and saw genuine terror in his eyes.

Havok didn't take his eyes off us, but moved to the sofa bed and rested his hand on a cushion, as if about to reach for something beneath it.

Dario held his hands up, slowly. 'Look, this guy's an Englishman, right? He doesn't know shit about *Ultra* culture or anything like that. He's here as a translator, okay?'

Havok's eyes flicked from Dario, to me, to Bergamin and back again, one hand resting on the back of the sofa bed, the other behind the cushion.

'So, your dad was in Kosovo?' said Dario.

'What?'

Dario tapped his forearm. 'That tattoo. Not Mr Enrich, the one on your forearm.' He rolled up his sleeve, displaying a blue heraldic shield with KFOR written vertically on one side and КФОР on the other. 'I've got one as well. I was there in '99. I thought – no offence – that you were too young to have been there. So, I thought maybe your dad was.'

Havok relaxed, just ever so slightly. Then he nodded. 'Yeah, he was.'

'Maybe I met him. Who knows? It seems a long time ago now. But I remember a few of us got drunk one night, just before they sent us home and we all got tattooed just to remind us never to do anything so bloody dangerous in the future.'

'Maybe you'd have met him. I don't know. He didn't like to talk about it very much.'

'Anyway, as I was saying, my buddy here doesn't know much about the *Ultra* thing. So if he asks some dumb-ass questions, that's why. He doesn't know anything about Diabolik or the *Irriducibili*.'

'It's true,' I said. 'Look, I don't even know much about football. Cricket's more my game.'

The three of them turned to laugh at me and Havok stepped away from the sofa; thinking, perhaps, that nobody would send a cricket fan to murder one of the hardest bastards in the *Irriducibili*.

Bergamin spoke up, trying to keep his voice steady. 'We're not here about football at all.'

'No? I think I've gathered that already.'

'We want to talk to you about Andrea Mazzon.'

'Oh. Do you now?' He paused. 'So. Come on then. Who sent you? The Fabris bitch?'

'No. It's just – well, it's a possible story, you know? Why would somebody like Andrea Mazzon hire,' he gulped, 'well, someone like you?'

Havok stared at Bergamin. He was unable to hold his gaze, and looked away, shaking slightly.

'Why didn't you ask me why somebody like me would work for someone like Andrea Mazzon?' said Havok.

'Erm, yes. That as well.'

'You just thought that the smart guy with the good suits and the letters after his name must be the boss, didn't you? Always the same. But the truth is, if you want to be in politics, you've gotta look good. And I,' he looked down at the tattoo of Mr Enrich and flexed his knuckles, 'I don't look too good, do I?'

He moved to the window, and stared outside. 'This place has changed, you know? Since I moved here. After my dad died. There are more of *them*, now.' I followed his gaze and saw the young woman with the headscarf passing by. Havok tapped on the window and she looked up at us. He blew her a kiss, and she quickly turned her head away. 'More of them. Every year. Same as in Rome. Where our kids can't find a place to stay.

'So Andrea Mazzon tells me he just needs someone to look after him for a few months. And that maybe, if I'm good, there'll be a bit of work coming my way after the election. It's as simple as that. And I decide I like the sound of what he has in mind, so I figure, yes, I'll do it.'

Bergamin nodded.

'I can't help noticing that you're not writing anything down,' said Havok.

Bergamin tapped his head. 'It's all up here. Promise.'

I took a deep breath. 'That's it? It's all just a job of work. Protection?'

He looked surprised. 'Yeah.'

'Okay then.' I breathed deeply, once more. 'What about Giuseppe Meneghini?'

Havok, I thought, hesitated for a second. 'Look, Mazzon's not the best payer in the world. Man needs two jobs, sometimes. We're not like them,' he gestured towards the window, 'we don't get any handouts. We don't get given free houses, stuff like that. We want something, we have to work for it. And if that means two jobs, that means two jobs.'

'I understand. Can I ask what you know about the Visconti Box?'

'The what?'

'The archive belonging to Luchino Visconti. I saw you were at the auction with Mazzon and an Englishman called Anthony Shawcross.'

'Oh that? The stuff belonging to the fag film director? Well, that was a wasted journey. All the way down to Rome to find out some fucker had withdrawn it from sale. Still, it was chance to meet up with some of my crew. Have a few beers and the like.'

'Okay. You say Mazzon wants you for protection. Protection from who?'

Havok laughed. 'You don't really expect me to tell you, do you?'

'It's just we think there might be a big story behind this.'

'It could be as big as you can imagine, Downton. I'm still not telling you.'

Dario sighed and reached – slowly – into his jacket, taking out two fifty-euro notes.

Havok gave the thinnest of smiles, and turned to Bergamin. He opened his mouth to protest but Havok's smile grew wider, and so he pulled out two fifties from his wallet.

I thought perhaps I should make a token effort at protesting, but Havok's eyes were boring into mine and he was standing closer to me than felt comfortable. I handed over my share.

Havok filcked through the notes. 'Now, no matter what I tell you, none of this is going to be in the press before the election, is it.' It wasn't a question.

Bergamin cleared his throat, nervously.

Havok turned to him. 'Because if there is, both *signor* Mazzon and *signor* Meneghini are going to be very unhappy. And that would make me very unhappy as well.'

Bergamin nodded.

'Okay then. *Signor* Mazzon asked for my services just before we all went off to Rome for the auction of this Visconti thing. Because he'd said he was being threatened. That there was someone very, very keen on him not getting to see it.'

'Okay. I understand, I think. Who was it?'

Bergamin smiled. 'Gianluca Casagrande.'

Chapter 32

'Well,' said Dario. 'I think we've just wasted three hundred euros.'

'More than that,' said Bergamin. 'We've just spent three hundred euros on a story that I can't use.'

'Come on, Roberto, there's something worth uncovering here.'

'Trust me, this story is never reaching the papers. Did you not see that guy?'

'That's hardly the spirit of Woodward and Bernstein now, is it?'

'No, but they didn't have an *Ultra* called Havok "advising" them not to publish, did they? Anyway, what's in this for Gianluca Casagrande?'

'Meneghini told me there's something in the archive that would ruin Anna Fabris. That's more than enough reason for Casagrande to threaten Mazzon.'

Dario yawned and stretched. 'Okay, I'm heading home. It's been an interesting afternoon. Think it might be a while before I come out to this part of town again, though.'

'Okay. Thanks, Dario. Thanks, Roberto. I'll have a think about what this all means and I'll be in touch.'

'You don't have to bother, Mr Sutherland. Really. I think this is as far as my involvement in the world of politics is likely to go.'

'You won't have another think about it?' He shook his head. 'Ah well. Thanks anyway.'

Dario gave a gentle cough. I turned round to see him holding his hand out. Then I turned back to see Bergamin mirroring the gesture.

'Oh Christ,' I said. 'I don't suppose there's a *bancomat* around here is there?'

'So,' said Fede, 'I've had a nice day at the church of San Polo, and I'm starting to think that, if we can get the funding, there's a project there that could keep me going for the next twelve months.'

'Excellent.'

'And, by contrast, you've been to meet a man called Havok who was once jailed for attacking someone with a hammer?'

'That's about the size of it. Oh, and don't forget having to pay Dario and Bergamin a hundred euros each.'

'Oh I hadn't forgotten that. I really hadn't. Isn't this getting rather expensive?'

'It is a bit.'

'I mean, can you claim any of this back from the Embassy?'

'I don't think you can just submit an expense claim for bribes. It's going to be tricky.'

She sighed. 'Anyway, what did you find out?'

'Look.' I grabbed a piece of paper and a pencil from my desk. 'We have Anthony Shawcross. Andrea Mazzon. Gianluca Casagrande. Anna Fabris. Giuseppe Meneghini.

And Mr Havok, as I'm sure he likes to be known. So what connects them?

'We've got a dead British citizen. Who's been seen in the company of one of the candidates for mayor and his pet thug. Said candidate for mayor is, apparently, being threatened by the husband of one of the other candidates. And in the middle of this,' I drew a box in the middle of the six names with a flourish, 'is the Visconti Box.'

Fede nodded. 'Okay. So is there a next step, which doesn't involve paying social calls on convicted football hooligans?'

I smiled. 'I think the next step can be carried out from the safety of a comfy chair. And I might even treat myself to a spritz as well.'

'Mr Shawcross? It's Nathan Sutherland.'

'Mr Sutherland? Thanks for calling. I was about to call you, actually.'

'Oh, really?' I reached into my desk for the sheaf of papers with the name Anthony Shawcross scribbled across the front. 'Well, this is just to say that I have all the documentation to hand here, it's been scanned and sent to all the relevant parties and so all we can do now, I'm afraid, is wait.'

'Any idea how long?'

'It's difficult to be sure. I would usually expect we'd hear within about two weeks. In the meantime there are funeral services in town I can contact who are used to dealing with situations like this.'

'Thank you. That's good to know.' He paused. 'But there's more. I've been going through my brother's emails.' He laughed, humourlessly. 'Do you know what they call that now? A "digital legacy". I think Anthony would have had a fit if anyone had ever suggested he'd be leaving a "digital legacy".'

'I can imagine. It's not something I've ever thought about myself.'

'I don't feel happy about having done this, I have to say. There were some upsetting things to be found there. If I'd looked at his emails when he first went missing we might have found he was going to Cavalletto in time.'

'But that would have been breaking a confidence. I don't think you should be blaming yourself for that.'

He chuckled, drily. 'Private investigator and counsellor as well, eh? I have to say the life of an Honorary Consul seems to be rather complicated.'

'You could say that.'

'Anyway, I'll send the essentials over to you. Take a look. There are some interesting things to be found there. Things that don't quite add up.'

'How's it going?', said Fede.

I looked up from my laptop. 'Shawcross sent a few emails on to me. Have a look at these, eh?'

I brought up the first. 'This one's from Anthony. *Andrea, I'm sorry to bother you but I'm getting no help at all from Anna Fabris or her husband. Well, to tell you the truth, Ms Fabris is pleasant enough but Casagrande is just downright hostile. I don't think we'll get anything from them.*

'But the most interesting part is Mazzon's reply. *Dear Anthony, it's no bother at all. It's probably to be expected and if Anna and her husband do not wish to meet, then there's little we can do. Nevertheless, I am convinced your grandfather must have known Alvise Fabris. The two of them were certainly at the Villa Godi Malinverni at the same time, and references in the* Archivio di Stato *suggest they did know each other – the problem is, of course, that so much of this material has been lost, presumably forever. Now, if you like the idea, I could probably arrange a ticket for the mayor's event at the Scuola Grande di San Rocco. Perhaps Anna will be more willing to talk at a social event and Gianluca, I imagine, will be less likely to cause a scene. At any rate, it's the sort of place one simply must see when in Venice. (You'll also have the chance to hear Giuseppe Meneghini's singing voice but that, perhaps, is a less essential Venetian experience).'*

Fede smiled. 'I didn't realise people still wrote emails like that.'

'I think the world of text speak and emojis are foreign to Mr Shawcross and *dottor* Mazzon. Anyway, this explains why Shawcross was invited. And then he replies to thank him, and explains that he's hoping to make a brief visit to Cavalletto, and return in time for the event.'

'Except he never did.'

'Exactly. Now then, what else do we have?' I scrolled through the messages that Shawcross had mailed on to me. 'Much of this is just travel arrangements and the like. But here's an interesting one, from Mazzon again. *Dear Anthony, I hope this finds you well. I've managed to find out some more information for you on the contents of what we've come to call the Visconti Box. It does, indeed, contain a number of letters and diaries from British servicemen stationed at the Villa Godi Malinverni during that period of the War. As I understand, diaries means both personal diaries and unit diaries.'*

'I don't understand, what's a unit diary?'

'I had to look that up. A unit diary basically recorded daily movements, map references and similar. Others went further, and recorded operations, intelligence reports and the like. Personal diaries – now that's kind of strange, as soldiers were not allowed to keep them. Although a lot of them did anyway.'

'So what are these doing in a box belonging to a dead film director?'

'Mazzon goes on to explain. *As far as I have been able to ascertain, much material belonging to British Command was left behind when the unit abandoned the villa in late 1918. Much of this lay gathering dust for decades. When Visconti was filming the ballroom scene in* Senso *I understand he spent many evenings in the company of the then custodian of the villa. One can imagine Visconti being taken with the image of the* bon ton *of British society – including the Prince of Wales, no less – wining and dining just a few kilometres from the slaughter of the Asiago Plateau. In the end, of course, he did nothing with the material. Perhaps he simply thought he wasn't the man for a British costume drama. Or, given that he started work on* Le Notti Bianche *shortly after, perhaps he simply didn't have time. At any rate, we have reason to be enormously grateful to him. Without him, some of this invaluable historical information might have vanished forever.*'

Fede nodded. 'Okay. So we have personal and unit diaries from the First World War. Are we assuming some of this is related to Shawcross's grandfather?'

'I think we have to, for the time being. That's the only reason why I can see him being willing to offer twenty thousand euros for it. Or rather, to lend Andrea Mazzon twenty thousand euros.'

'And so, what do we do now?'

I yawned and stretched. 'Right now, *cara mia*, I'm going to fix us two splendid Negronis. Then I'm going to make us a mushroom risotto. And then after watching a suitably distressing film I'm going to try and attempt to have a decent night's sleep that doesn't involve dreaming of dead men lying in the snow at the foot of a gigantic cross.'

'And then?'

'And then tomorrow, well, I suggest we pay a call on Anna Fabris and see if she'll be more amenable to having a chat with us than she was with Anthony Shawcross.'

Chapter 33

St Paul stared down at us from the church that, in *Veneziano* at least, bore his name. Fede shielded her eyes and looked back up at him.

'It's probably not him at all, you know?'

'It isn't?'

'No. He's far more interesting in some ways. As far as we can be sure, the original was sculpted in Greece, from the time when Paul wouldn't even have been a twinkle in his great-great-great-great grandfather's eye. Then they added bits over the centuries to make him a bit more *Pauline*, shall we say. Then they moved him from the *calle* where he originally was, stuck a sword in his right hand, and there you have it – instant St Paul.'

I looked up at him. The lack of a sword was immediately obvious. As, indeed, was the lack of his hand. 'Poor chap,' I said. 'You'd think they'd do something about that?'

'He was restored back in the eighties, I understand. They did the best they could, but the sword was a step too far.'

'So that's why you're here? To give St Paul his mojo back?'

'I suppose so. Or at least to give him his roof back. It might be that it'd benefit from a proper restoration. Perhaps even the exterior as well. We shall see. If it comes off, that would be fantastic. There's so much that could be done. If we had the money, as ever.'

'It'd make it a bit strange living here in the *campo*. I mean the guys working on the exterior would be looking directly into your front room.'

'If only there were some sort of device that existed to close off the outside world. We could call them, oh I don't know, "Venetian Blinds" or similar.' She kissed me on the cheek. 'Okay, *caro*. I'll see you later. I'll just drop into the church to see how things are going.'

'You don't fancy coming up for a chat with Anna?'

She checked her watch. 'I don't think I've got time. Anyway, you'll be fine on your own. Just be your usual charming self. And don't start a fight. You can do that, can't you?'

I smiled. 'I can try.'

She kissed me again, and made her way into the church. A guy in a hi-vis jacket smiled and nodded at her, and passed her a hard hat. Fede, I knew, hated wearing them and I wondered how long she'd put up with it.

I checked the name on the doorbell panel. The three top ones read 'Locazione Turistica' and I shook my head, sadly. The one for the *piano nobile*, however, read 'Casagrande / Fabris'.

'*Chi è?*'

'*Dottoressa* Fabris? My name's Nathan Sutherland. We met a few days ago.'

There was silence at the other end.

'I'm the British Honorary Consul.'

'Oh yes, of course. I'm so sorry. Do come in. Top floor.'

I noticed the presence of two bicycles in the entrance hall, one in bright pink, and one with the Spider-Man logo on the crossbar. Children, then, and presumably still quite young. Cycling, like playing football, was one of those things that only small children were allowed to do in the *centro storico*. A city free of cars, full of spaces in which to play. And then one day *mamma* and *papà* would tell you that you were too old now for bikes and balls, and childish things would be put away. The thought made me a little sad as I made my way upstairs.

'Mr Sutherland?'

'*Dottoressa* Fabris.' I gave a little bow which was, perhaps, overdoing it a bit.

She smiled. 'Anna, please.'

'Anna it is. Call me Nathan.'

'Can I offer you a coffee, Nathan?'

'That'd be lovely.'

'Follow me.' She led me through to the living room. Three large leather sofas were placed around a wide-screen TV. A Playstation or similar was connected up to it with control units and wires trailing across the floor.

Anna smiled. 'Ginevra and Allegra have just been playing tennis.'

'Tennis. Oh, I see.'

'It's a little bit sad, I think.'

I nodded. 'I can imagine. Nowhere to play in the city itself and so they have to play at home in front of a TV screen.'

'Oh it's not that. We belong to a club on the Lido. It's just that they prefer the computer version. They get a little over-enthusiastic at times. You'll notice there are no vases in here.'

I laughed. 'Kids, eh?'

'Do you have children yourself, Nathan?'

'I have a cat. I think that must be quite similar. At least when it comes to having breakables in the flat.'

She smiled at me. 'Come on then, let's get this coffee made.'

'So, are you doing the rounds of all the candidates? I understand you've been out to dinner with Giuseppe.'

'You heard about that?'

'Oh, Giuseppe told me. Part of his "charm offensive" he called it. Just to try and wind me up, I suspect.'

'Well, he asked me out to his club, and I don't turn down invitations like that unless they're somebody I actively dislike.'

She smiled, a little slyly. 'And so, can I ask what you thought of him?'

'He's – well, let's just say I liked him more than I expected. Which is not to say we'll be on each other's Christmas card lists, but we got on well enough.'

'Well enough to vote for him?'

'Ah well, I've lost my vote, remember?'

'Oh yes. I'm sorry. What about your wife?'

'Well, that's up to her. But she has three words for Giuseppe Meneghini, and two of them are "Giuseppe Meneghini". But, out of interest, what do you think about him?'

She put her head to one side. 'That's a pretty good question. I don't think he's a particularly bad man, *per se*. I imagine he could be quite good company. The question is, though, why does he want to be mayor?'

I shrugged. 'I have no idea, beyond "it's a cool thing to be mayor".'

'And I think that's it. Giuseppe's smoothed through life,

from school to university to business and now – now I imagine he thinks public service is the next big challenge. First mayor, then President of the Region, then the Senate.'

'So it's just something he thinks he should do?'

'Something he feels entitled to do. But perhaps I'm being unfair. The trouble is he just thinks you can manage the city in the same way as you manage a business. That plays well with a lot of people. Never underestimate the power of "I'm not a politician, I'm a businessman."'

'Like Berlusconi?'

She flinched, just a little, then smiled again. 'Like Mr B, yes. At its simplest, it's an argument built on "I'm not like them." But, of course, he is.' She sighed. 'On his own, I think he'd be manageable. But it also seems that he'd be quite happy to get into bed with Andrea Mazzon as a minor partner. And that really might be a disaster.'

'Why Mazzon, though? Why not the Greens, or some of the minor socialist parties?'

'The Greens' environmental agenda wouldn't work for him. And the socialists would want him to pay more tax, which he's never going to do. That leaves some of the far-right parties, and Mazzon himself.'

'The cuddly fascist it's okay to like?'

'They're never cuddly. And it's never okay to like them.' She shook her head. 'So, anyway, Nathan. What is it I can do for you?'

'The first time we met, I asked you if you'd ever heard of a man called Anthony Shawcross.'

'Oh yes. Gianluca told me you found the poor man, up in the mountains. That must have been dreadful.'

I nodded. 'Did he ever get in touch with you?'

Anna frowned. 'It's possible. I do get a lot of mail. But – this is going to sound horrible – emails from residents are always going to take priority. But why would he want to talk to me?'

'I think it was something about the war. That's the only reason I'm asking you, really,' I lied. 'It might just be something nice for his family that I could pass on. Perhaps the names of people he'd served with, things like that. Did you have family at the battle of the Asiago Plain?'

'I did. Many of us in this area would have done, of course. My great-grandfather was there.'

'He survived?'

'He survived, but you couldn't say he lived. Grandfather remembers him as a sad man. A man grown old before his time.'

'Your grandfather? He's still alive then?'

'Very much alive.' The voice came from the kitchen door. I turned to see an elderly man, immaculately dressed, sitting in a wheelchair.

Anna smiled, crouched down by his side, and gave him a hug. '*Nonno* Alfredo. Good morning.'

He smiled and patted her hand. 'Good morning, dear Anna. I'm so sorry I'm late joining you, but it takes forever for me to get out of bed and fit to face the world these days.' He looked over at me. 'Does Gianluca know you're entertaining a male friend?'

Anna ruffled his thin grey hair. '*Nonno* Alfredo, don't tease. This is Mr Nathan Sutherland. He's the British Honorary Consul.'

'The British Consul? What have you done now, Anna? Don't tell me, Queen Elizabeth is going to make you a Dame?'

I smiled. 'I wish it was that exciting, sir.'

He waved a hand at me. 'Oh don't bother with that *sir* business.'

'That's very kind of you.'

'And we can use the second person as well, if you like.'

That surprised me. By now, the habit of using the more formal third person in Italian to address someone older than me had become ingrained.

'Thank you.'

'I'm one hundred years old, you know? I might not have time to get to know you well enough to ask you to switch to the informal. Might as well start as we mean to go on. So,' he clapped his hands together, 'if you're not here to invite Anna to Buckingham Palace, what are you here for?'

'It's a bit of a long story.'

'Hmm, I'm not sure I like the sound of that. I can't guarantee I'll be around at the end of it. Could you cut it down a bit?'

I smiled. 'I'll try. Did you read about the British gentleman who died up in the mountains at Cavalletto?'

He nodded. 'I did. Silly thing to do at this time of year. Still sad, though.'

'He was researching his family tree. As I understand it, he thought he might have been in the same unit as Anna's great-grandfather. Your father, of course.'

Anna put a hand on his arm. '*Nonno*, remember you shouldn't be talking about things like this. It only upsets you.'

Alfredo looked surprised. 'Not at all, dear Anna. If this

gentleman's gone to the trouble to come out here to see you, I think it's the least I can do. Why don't we go and sit down in the living room, eh?'

Anna looked at me and frowned, shaking her head ever so slightly.

'And I'm not blind, you know. I can see perfectly well. Up to about ten metres anyway. Come on Mr Sutherland, let me wheel myself back into the living room, you can pull up a comfy chair and we can have a good chat.' He looked up at Anna with a wicked smile. 'That coffee smells good.'

Anna gave a sigh of exasperation. 'You're not allowed coffee, Grandfather, and you know that.'

'Oh well. Can't blame a man for trying.'

'I've got some decaffeinated if you'd like that?'

He shook his head. 'Life really is too short.' He looked up at me. 'You see what I have to put up with? I was going to take up smoking again when I reached one hundred, but they won't let me.'

'Well, and wouldn't that be a fine example to Ginevra and Allegra?' She looked at me. 'I have some work to carry on with, if that's okay? But try not to keep him too long. I'll make you a cup of herbal tea, *nonno*.'

'Oh well. I suppose that will have to do.' He looked up at me. 'Come on then, Mr Sutherland. Let's talk.'

Chapter 34

'So Mr Sutherland, what did you do in military service?'

'Me? Er, nothing. I never had to do it.'

'You don't have National Service in England?'

'Not for over fifty years now.'

'My goodness.' He seemed disappointed. 'We abolished it as well. 2005, I think it was.'

'A friend of mine did it. He ended up with KFOR. In Kosovo, you know?'

Alfredo nodded. 'My father was a soldier, of course. Then I was with the partisans in the Second World War.

'Your family must be very proud of you.'

He smiled. 'Well, it's nice if they are. But we all just did what we thought had to be done. And, of course, I was a young man and thought I was indestructible.

'Every year, you know, every Liberation Day, they wheel us out. Maybe to talk to the public, school kids, whatever. I've even been on the television a few times. And every year, well, there are more and more faces missing.'

'That must be so sad.' I shook my head. 'I'm sorry, that sounds terribly inadequate.'

He smiled. 'Don't worry. I understand.'

'Your father was in the Great War, then?'

'Alvise Fabris. He was a *caporal maggiore*. He survived Caporetto. And then he survived the Asiago Plain.'

'Did he speak much about it?'

Alfredo shook his head. 'If he ever did, it always upset him. So we learned not to talk about it. It was bad towards the end of his life, when he became confused. He'd have terrible nightmares, screaming nightmares. About things he'd seen. About things he'd done.' He shook his head. 'He died before the Second World War. I'm glad of that. I don't think he could have borne it, seeing me go off to fight.'

'He never spoke to you about an Englishman he might have known? A man called Thomas Shawcross?'

Alfredo smiled. 'Mr Sutherland, my father has been cold in his grave for eighty years. If he ever mentioned anyone by name,' he tapped his forehead, 'you'll forgive me if it's slipped my mind in the meanwhile.'

I smiled back at him. 'Of course. Silly of me. What sort of man was he in life?'

The old man looked terribly, terribly sad all of a sudden. 'I wish I knew. I wish I'd known him better. He died when I was a young man. And those memories that all boys should have of their fathers – learning to ride a bike, playing football in the *campo*, having a first beer together as men – I have none of those.'

'I'm sorry.'

'Tell me about your father, Nathan.'

I shook my head. 'I don't have those memories either, Alfredo.'

'You don't?' He sighed. 'Ah, that's too bad.'

'It's okay. We were never close.'

'Is he still alive?'

'I don't know. We haven't been in touch in years.' I changed the subject. 'What did your father do in the army?'

'He was a mechanic. And a driver. Weren't many of them in those days. A properly skilled job. He might only have been a *caporal maggiore* but he would have had some respect. He also spoke some English.' Alfredo chuckled. 'Better than I ever did. That would have been unusual as well. So the British liked him. They even asked for him up at the Villa Godi Malinverni. He never wrote many letters to my mother. He was always better with machinery than with putting pen to paper. But I remember one letter which said he'd seen the Prince of Wales himself. He had an eye for the ladies, he said, which would get him into trouble one day.'

I laughed. 'He wasn't wrong there. Tell me about your mother.'

'She was a wonderful woman. Now, I know what you're thinking, I'm Italian and so I have to say that. But she was, and yet she always seemed so sad. I couldn't understand why – we lived in this lovely *palazzo*, after all. We seemed so lucky. I remember so many children of my age who didn't even have a father. And I had a dad, and we lived in a big house and yet my parents never seemed happy. He died before I went away with the partisans. I'm glad of that in some ways. I think it would have broken his heart. I don't think he ever imagined that one day I would have to go away and fight like he had. He would have been so worried, that war would break me, like it broke him.

'But I've been a fortunate man. I have my lovely

granddaughter and my lovely great-granddaughters.' He chuckled. 'Although I don't understand half of what they're talking about. I suppose the day may come when Gianluca or Anna decide they can't handle the old man living here any longer, and they'll put me out to a *casa di riposo* but more likely I'll just go to sleep one night and then – pffft!'

'Can I ask – and I don't want to be insensitive – but what happened to your son?'

He shook his head. 'Ayayay. Poor Giacomo. Too many years working over in Marghera. Breathing in poison every day. They say nobody knew, of course, but they did. They did.'

'He worked in the chemical plants?'

'A dangerous job. A horrible job.'

'It's just that,' I looked around the *palazzo*, 'with all this . . .' My voice trailed off.

'Ah, you're thinking why would a man who lived in a house like this be needing to work in the furnaces in Marghera?'

'Well, yes.'

'The answer is, Giacomo just felt he needed to work. He felt he was doing something useful. He did a lot of work for the union as well.' He smiled. 'You can see where Anna got her politics from.'

'I understand.'

The old man shook his head again. 'It's a terrible thing, you know, to lose your child.' His eyes focused and he looked into mine. 'Do you have children, Mr Sutherland?'

'No, we don't.'

'No children. Ah, that makes me sad.'

I smiled. 'I don't think I'd be good at it.'

'Heh. You don't think everybody else in the world feels the same way?' The sound of childish laughter came from another room, and he cupped a hand to his ear. 'You hear that? That makes it all worthwhile, you know? Hearing Ginevra and Allegra laughing. They'll probably be through soon, wanting me to read comics with them.' He chuckled. 'And I'll have to ask them who Spider-Man or Captain America is again. But that's okay. Because the day will come when they'll be too old to want to do such things with great-granddad, and it'll all seem a bit too childish for them. Or,' he tapped his chest, 'more likely I simply won't be here. And that's okay too, of course.'

We sat in silence for a moment, as I looked around the room again. I noticed a discoloured patch of wallpaper, less faded by the sunlight than the surrounding area. I looked back at the old man, afraid that perhaps he'd think I was being nosy and finding fault, but his eyes were closed and his chest gently rising and falling. I smiled.

I looked up at the discoloured patch on the wallpaper. Then something caught my eye. I knelt down and ran my finger across the *terrazzo* flooring. It stung, and as I pulled my hand back I could see tiny fragments of glass sparkling in the light. I got to my feet and carefully brushed the specks away.

I stepped back to take another look at the wallpaper, shielding my eyes from the sun that was streaming in. There was no doubting it. That patch of the wall was noticeably darker in colour.

'*Bisnonno*, will you come come and read with us?'

I heard a noise from behind me. A little girl, perhaps ten years old, wearing a Spider-Man T-shirt.

'Hello,' I said. 'Are you Ginevra?'

She scowled. 'I'm Allegra.'

'I'm sorry. My name's Nathan. I'm a friend of your mum's.'

'My mum says we shouldn't talk to strangers.'

'Well, your mum is very wise.'

'Do you like Spider-Man?'

'Of course. He's my favourite superhero.'

She narrowed her eyes. 'Who's your favourite villain?'

'Dr Octopus. He's really cool.'

I was, perhaps, at the limit of my knowledge here, but I seemed to have passed a test and she smiled at me. I nodded at the dark patch on the wall. 'It seems great-grandad's having a sleep. But could you be a brilliant girl and tell me what used to be up there?'

She looked at me suspiciously, but then nodded. 'It was,' she paused, and then started counting on her fingers, 'Great-Great-Grandfather's picture. He must have lived a very long time ago if he was Great-Grandfather's dad.'

'Oh right. What happened to it?'

She frowned, again. 'Mummy says it got broken. I don't know how.' Then she looked over at my hand and saw the tiny flecks of blood on my fingers.

'You want to be careful,' she said. 'You'll get hurt.'

Then she turned and skipped from the room. I looked down at the sleeping form of Alfredo Fabris, and made my way to the door. It opened before I could touch the handle, and Gianluca Casagrande stood there, with an expression of surprise upon his face.

Chapter 35

Grandfather is adamant that he should move into the care home at San Lorenzo. I am equally adamant that he should not. We have space, we tell him, he must move in with us. He'll see more of the grandchildren and that will be good for him.

Father's upstairs apartment, where he spent so many years alone with Grandfather after Mother died, will need to be cleared. We haven't yet agreed on what should be done with it. I tell Gianluca we should try and open it up to the community, perhaps to someone unable to afford the spiralling cost of living in the city. Perhaps it would inspire others to do the same. Gianluca laughs and says, 'What you mean, cara mia, *is that it would shame others into doing the same.' I have to admit he is right.*

Gianluca is more practical than me of course. He favours turning it into a tourist rental. I tell him this is not happening. He shrugs his shoulders and says very well, but I think all I have managed to do is kick the can down the road for now.

I am tired. I have dealt with bereavement just once before, when Mamma died. Father felt unable to do anything, of course, and so it fell to me. Now, it is the same. We gave Grandfather time for one last look around, and then Gianluca took him down to our apartment.

Both of them offered to help, but Grandfather would, I know, find it too upsetting. And Gianluca – well, I am sure that he meant well but neither am I sure that I can completely trust him to take his time and not to throw away something precious in his haste.

Old clothes, I decide, I have to be practical with, and bag them up ready to take to the clothes bank at Santa Marta. Then I make a list of the furniture. Nothing, I suspect, is of any great worth. And how much sentimental value can one really impart to a wardrobe, a chest of drawers? I mark out a small bookcase as something perhaps that we should keep. Father loved reading, so much. It would be a nice memory of him.

The bookcase itself would be completely inadequate for the number of actual books. I pile a fraction of them in the centre of the room, and sit myself down to go through them. History books, encyclopaedias, a set of the Divina Commedia *and the Bible, both illustrated by Gustav Doré, trashy airport novels,* fumetti *and Mondadori* gialli *from the period after the war.*

Some of these, I suppose, might be worth something to collectors, but do I really have the patience to find out? How many of these am I ever going to read?

Perhaps it might be nice to have a family Bible? I set it aside. The children will soon be starting Dante at school, so I put the Commedia *aside for them.*

'Nel mezzo del cammin di nostra vita

mi ritrovai per una selva oscura,

ché la diritta via era smarrita.'

Soon, these words will be engraved on their memory as they are on mine. The one part of the Commedia *that every school-child can remember, imprinted on their minds in perpetuity following months of learning by rote. Wasted on a child of four-teen, perhaps, and yet it is a little part of our history that we will carry with us for always. And Doré's illustrations, I hope, will inspire them when the text becomes too much.*

I flick through the pile of comic books and smile at the covers. Tex was his favourite. We used to read them together when I was little, but then there came a day – I think it might have coincided with my thirteenth birthday – when I decided that cowboys were silly and boring. I switched to Diabolik, which seemed newer, cooler and sexier, but father used to tut when he saw me reading them. And so, for old times' sake, we'd sit down together and read about Tex Willer, Texas Ranger, once more.

I'll box these up and take them down for the girls, I decide. I'm not sure I've seen them reading much beyond X-Men, Spider-Man and the Avengers, and so I wonder how much the adventures of Tex are going to appeal, but I'll do my best. I make a mental note to check that they don't suddenly appear for sale on eBay.

I'm getting tired now and yawn as I flick my way through the rest of the pile. Comics, comics, more comics. And then, right at the bottom, there's a dun-coloured envelope, with faded hand-writing. 'For Anna'.

The handwriting is Father's.

I hesitate for a moment and then slide a nail under the seal and tear it open, as carefully as I can. There's a letter inside, per-haps a couple of pages. Again, I hesitate for a moment. And then I tease it out, and begin to read.

I don't know quite how long I sit there upon the floor, as the shadows lengthen outside and I ignore every last ring from my mobile phone. I just sit there, and think and think and think.

I think of the painting of Great-Grandfather in our home, where he has looked down upon us, in his military uniform, for as long as I can remember . And my body starts to shudder.

I try to raise myself to my feet, but my legs have fallen asleep and I stumble back on to the sofa. Again I think of the picture of Great-Grandfather, and the tears, at last, start to run.

This will kill *nonno* Alfredo.

But only if he finds out.

I tell the family that I have a migraine and need to go to bed early. The children give me a hug and then go back to their computer games. I've forgotten all about the Tex comics. That's a treat that will have to wait for another day. When all this is over.

Gianluca, never having known me to have a migraine, looks at me strangely and I give him a warning glance. Not now.

Later that evening he holds me, and lets me cry, and tells me that he will sort everything out. Father, he tells me, left the letter for me on purpose. So that I could decide what to do with it.

And so we burn the letter, together.

Chapter 36

Gianluca smiled. 'Hello, Nathan. This is an unexpected pleasure.'

I looked back over my shoulder, at the sleeping form of the old man. 'I've just been having a good old chat with *nonno* Alfredo.'

'Oh. Right.'

'About the war.'

'You have?' His expression changed. 'Is Anna around?'

'Hello, *caro*.' Anna entered the room, and kissed him on the cheek. Her eyes narrowed. 'Have you been out with Fabio again? Your jacket smells like there's been a lot of passive smoking going on.'

'Ah, you know what he's like.'

'That shop of his is a health risk, I swear. Anyway, I've been hard at work. *Nonno* was in a mood to talk and so Nathan very kindly took him off my hands.'

Gianluca shook his head. 'He shouldn't talk about such things. It only upsets him.'

I held my hands up. 'I'm sorry. It was my fault. But he seemed perfectly happy.'

Gianluca seemed to relax a little, and smiled again. 'I'm

sorry too, Nathan. He's a great age, as you understand. We worry about him.'

'Well you don't need to.' Alfredo yawned and opened his eyes. 'I just need my sleep a little more these days, that's all. Otherwise I'm fit as a fiddle.'

Allegra and Ginevra ran into the room, all bundled up in padded jackets and woolly hats.

'*Ciao, papà.*'

'*Ciao, papà.*'

He bent down to hug them both, nearly toppling backwards as they raced into his arms.

'Is it time, *papà*?'

'Can we go now?'

He got to his feet, laughing. 'Doesn't daddy even get the chance to sit down for five minutes?'

'No!'

He rubbed his chin. 'Ah, well now. Can you promise me you've been good today?' He looked over at the old man. 'How have they been *nonno* Alfredo?'

Alfredo smiled. 'Oh, they've been good as gold. As they always are.' He winked at them. 'Isn't that right, girls?'

Gianluca pretended to yawn. 'I'm very tired though. A nice little sit down might be nice.'

Allegra stamped her feet. 'No, *papà*, now!'

'We've been good! Promise!'

'Oh well. I suppose we'll have to go out then.'

The two little girls cheered. Allegra smiled at me. 'Are you coming as well?'

'Well, I don't know. Am I allowed?'

Gianluca looked a little surprised, but Allegra leapt in

again. 'He knows about Spider-Man and Dr Octopus and everything.'

He smiled. 'Well in that case I think you'll have to, Nathan.'

'Thank you. I'm honoured. Er, what are we doing?'

'Ice-skating in the *campo*. And then perhaps we'll all bring some pizzas home and eat with *nonno* Alfredo,' said Anna.

'That'd be lovely. Thank you.'

'Or will Federica be expecting you at home?'

'Oh, she's not at home. She's just working over the road.' Anna looked confused. 'At the church,' I explained.

'Wonderful. She can join us as well.' She turned to Alfredo. 'Now, will you be okay on your own, *nonno*?'

'I'll be fine, Anna. My ice-skating days are behind me, I'm afraid. And don't worry, I promise to still be alive when you get back.'

She kneeled down by the side of his chair, and poked him gently in the chest. 'And I've told you before, you're not to say things like that.'

The old man grinned, and pulled her to him, ruffling her hair. 'Have a wonderful time. And don't forget my pizza!'

Federica linked her arm in mine as we steered ourselves through the crowds, Allegra and Ginevra skipping ahead of us, and Gianluca scurrying forward trying to keep them in sight.

Fede smiled at Anna. 'They're so excited, bless them.'

'They are. I don't know why. It seems we have to come here almost every other day, but the novelty doesn't seem to have worn off yet.'

Fede shivered and I pulled her closer to me. 'You cold?'

She inclined her head back towards the church. 'It's freezing in there.'

Anna smiled at her. 'I can imagine. Look, I guess I'm supposed to know about these things but – what exactly needs doing there?'

'Maybe something, maybe nothing. The ship's keel roof is probably worth taking a look at. Also the *stucco*. Just in case there are any problems with residual damp, following what happened in November.'

By the time we arrived at the rink, Gianluca had already kitted out Ginevra and Allegra and the two had set forth onto the ice. He looked up at me and smiled when he saw me reaching my hand into my jacket, and shook his head.

'No you don't, Nathan. My treat.'

'Are you sure?' He nodded. 'Thanks.'

'Just tell the *signora* in the hut what shoe size you are.'

'Are you sure you're okay with this, *caro*?' said Federica.

'Of course. Why wouldn't I be?'

'Well. It's just you've never expressed any interest in this before.'

'Well, neither have you.'

'Only because I thought you . . . Well, you know.'

The *signora* handed me my skates. 'Ah-hah. It's one of those things, is it?'

'What things?'

'One of those "Nathan probably can't do this sort of thing" things.'

She squeezed my arm. 'Not at all. It's just you've never expressed an interest in ice-skating before.' She frowned. 'You have done it before, then?'

'I've been roller-skating. Principle's the same, isn't it?'

'I . . . guess so. When was this?'

'1999, I think. But the laws of physics haven't fundamentally changed in the meantime, have they?'

'Okay. You're sure you actually want to do this?'

'Of course.' I paused. 'You never actually told me when you last did this?'

'I think it was about 2005.'

'Right. I'm sure we'll be perfectly fine as long as we hang on to each other.'

We stepped out, a little uncertainly, onto the ice. Anna and Gianluca actually seemed to know what they were doing as, to a lesser extent, did their little girls. Then I noticed a group of children making their way around uncertainly, using plastic snowmen on runners as stabilisers. I wondered if we'd lose too much face by asking if we could use them too, but then Fede had taken my hand and stepped out. And so we were away.

It would be nice to say we saw Campo San Polo, in all its splendour, revolving around us in absolute silence save for the hiss of our skates on the ice. In truth, it wasn't quite like that. The silence was broken by the excited cries of children, and the occasional thud, scream or curse, but there was still a magic to it.

'Having fun?'

'I most certainly am.'

'You're actually quite good at this.'

'You sound surprised.'

'Well. Just a little.'

'I'm not sure I'm very good at the whole "stopping" thing though.'

'Oh, *caro*, let's worry about that when we come to it.'

And I started to think how much fun this all was, and how nice Anna and Gianluca seemed, and that perhaps we should come back with Dario, Vally and Emily and maybe go for dinner afterwards, all of us . . . and then, in front of the church of San Polo, I saw him.

Havok, just standing there, with his hands thrust into the pockets of his leather jacket and no expression on his face. Staring at us.

'Ow!'

'What?'

'You're gripping my hand too tightly. It's digging my wedding ring into my finger.'

'Sorry.'

'I thought you were enjoying this?'

'I am.'

We finished another circle, and I looked again towards the church. There was no sign of him. I breathed a sigh of relief, and then wondered why. After all, he was allowed to wander through the city just as much as anyone else and, although we hadn't exactly parted as friends, there was no reason to suspect any particular animosity towards me. Then I saw him once more, this time laughing and joking with a couple of young guys on one of the food stalls.

'Nathan.'

He didn't strike me as someone who'd have a particular interest in ice-skating, but then again, why not?

'Nathan, small child approaching. Nathan!'

Fede let go of my hand, and pushed me to one side, just in time to avoid running into the back of a little boy using one of the snowmen as support who, either through exhaustion or lack of interest, had ground to a halt in the middle of the rink.

My balance gone, my arms windmilled uselessly through the air as I prepared myself for the inevitable. To my right, I saw Gianluca, grinning at me. Then his expression changed to one of mock-horror as he braced himself for the crash.

My legs slid out from under me, and I steeled myself for impact; first with Gianluca and then with the ice. Despite a brief moment of pain, I couldn't help laughing as the grey-blue Venetian sky spiralled above my head before I slid into the padded barrier at the side of the rink.

A shame, I thought. I'd been doing quite well up until then. Still, at least I'd found a solution to the problem of stopping.

Fede skated over to me, slowed down as much as she could, and then stopped by grabbing at the barrier and swinging herself into it. Perhaps not a textbook manoeuvre, but undoubtedly more dignified than my method.

'Are you all right, *caro*?'

'I'm fine. Sorry, I lost concentration for a moment.'

'You've dropped your keys. And your wallet.'

I checked my pockets. 'Not mine.' I looked down at the ice. Coins, a mobile phone, and a few business cards were scattered around. I tried to crouch down, but would have slipped had Fede not been there to steady me. With her help, I got to my knees and gathered the debris together.

'These must be Gianluca's.' I swept the cards into a neat pile, and then froze when I caught sight of the one on top. 'What the actual hell?'

'What's the matter?'

'This card here. Look at it. Look at the name.'

'Anthony Shawcross. Oh, that one must be yours then.'

'I never had one.'

'Are you sure? You picked a few things up when you were at that hotel.'

'I never had one of these, I'm certain. Look at the back.' I turned it over for her, where the words *Antico Borgo, Via Roma, Calvene* had been written.

Fede looked down the ice to where Gianluca was struggling, and failing, to get to his feet.

'So if it's not yours, it must be his.'

'It must be. And Anna assured me they'd never met him.'

I looked over towards Gianluca, still laughing as he tried to pull himself to his feet. Then a tall figure strode out of the crowd, and stretched a hand down towards him.

Gianluca put out his hand and then snatched it back, as he saw the face of Andrea Mazzon staring down at him.

I looked back at Fede. 'Come on. I think we need to hear this.'

Gianluca pulled himself unsteadily to his feet, but it was difficult to gauge the expression on his face. Mazzon extended his hand, this time in order to shake, but once again the other man made no attempt to take it.

'We need to talk.'

Gianluca looked back at his family on the skating rink. 'I don't think so.'

'We really do. Please. It's important.'

'Is it now?' Gianluca didn't shift his gaze from his wife and children.

'I'm being serious, Gianluca.'

Mazzon placed a hand on his shoulder, but he shook it off. 'Two things, Mazzon. It's *dottor* Casagrande to you. Second thing, don't fucking touch me.'

It was the first time I'd heard him swear.

Mazzon ran a hand across his brow and I could see that he was perspiring in spite of the low temperature. 'Gianluc— *Dottor* Casagrande, I know why you're upset but there's something you must do.'

'There is? Really? Okay then, Andrea. Tell me what I *have* to do?'

'The box. The Visconti archive. I know you know where it is. And you must tell me. You simply must tell me.'

'Why *must* I, Andrea?'

'Because – because I think someone's going to get hurt if you don't.'

'Another threat, Andrea?'

'It's not a threat, I promise you. Just tell me where the archive is or how to get hold of it, and I swear you'll never hear from me again. I swear to you, Gianluca.'

For a moment, I could have sworn I saw tears in his eyes. And then Gianluca grabbed him by the scruff of the neck, and pulled Mazzon towards him so that the older man was now balanced on the tips of his toes.

'Listen to me, you piece of shit. It's like this. If I ever see you again. If I ever hear you so much as mention my wife's name again, I will end you. I will fucking end you. You understand?'

There was genuine fear in Mazzon's eyes now and he babbled something unintelligible. Gianluca dragged him closer to him, and inclined his head.

'I'm sorry. I didn't hear that.'

'I understand.'

Gianluca grinned. 'Promise now?'

'I promise.'

Gianluca released his grip, and Mazzon stood there gasping for breath. Then he turned and half-walked, half-ran away.

Fede nudged me with an elbow. A crowd had gathered by now, and I could see at least two men with cameras snapping away.

'This isn't going to look good, *caro*.'

I nodded.

'Gianluca, what's going on?'

Anna Fabris, leading her daughters by the hand, looked at her husband in confusion. Immediately some members of the crowd turned to photograph her, save for the ones nearest to Gianluca, who caught the expression on his face and decided it might be best not to.

He smiled at her, and then at the crowd. 'Nothing, *cara mia*, nothing at all.' He turned to the two of us. 'Nathan, Federica, I'm so sorry but I think perhaps we need to skip the pizzas tonight.'

I nodded. 'I understand.' I held out his keys, wallet, phone and business cards. 'You dropped these.'

'I did?' He patted his pockets. 'Yes, it seems I did.' He took them from me. For a moment his eyes rested on Shawcross's card, and then he stuffed them into a pocket. Then he patted me on the arm, and smiled at Fede. 'Thank you. Another time.'

He turned on his heels, and made his way through the crowd, as if oblivious to the presence of his wife and daughters following in his wake.

Chapter 37

Anthony Shawcross does not look as I expected. Gianluca had checked out his profile on the university webpage. Distinguished-looking, greying at the temples, and laughing at some unseen joke off camera. His interests are listed as Military History, craft ales and rugby.

The man in front of me, however, seems to have shrunk in on himself. Some wisps of thin, grey hair still cling to his scalp, and he looks gaunt and painfully thin. He is wheezing from the effort of hauling himself up the single flight of stairs that leads to our apartment.

'Can I bring you anything, Mr Shawcross?'

He opens his mouth to speak, which turns into a coughing fit. He holds up a hand, as if to indicate that he'll be all right. He takes a few deep breaths, and then a smile breaks across his face.

'Thank you, signora. *Perhaps just a glass of water?'*

'Of course. Please, do make yourself comfortable. I'll just be a couple of minutes.'

I go to the kitchen, and let the cold tap run for a few seconds. I think about making myself a coffee, but I don't want to leave Mr Shawcross alone for too long. I don't know why I should feel like this. The company of an evidently ill, frail man should not worry me. I fill two glasses with water, fix a smile to my face and return to the living room.

Shawcross is still sitting where I left him, but staring at the patch of darkened wallpaper above the fireplace. He takes the water from me, and I am shocked by the freezing touch of his fingers against mine.

'Would you like me to turn the heating up, Mr Shawcross?'

He shakes his head, and smiles. 'No need, signora. I'm feeling the cold more and more these days, I'm afraid.' He sips at his water. 'Thank you for agreeing to see me.'

I nod, warily. Gianluca, I know, would be furious if he knew I had let Mr Shawcross into our home. Into our lives. Still, we have some time until he returns home. Shawcross does not strike me as an unkind man. What harm could there be in talking to him?

'You want to talk about the First World War, as I understand? Particularly the campaign on the Asiago Plain?'

'That's correct.' He coughs again, and for a moment I fear it's going to turn into that dreadful, wheezing sound I heard when he arrived, but he holds up a hand. 'I'm all right.'

'Your grandfather was there, I understand?'

'He was.' Then he smiles at me. 'Along with yours, if I'm correct?'

'Not quite. Grandfather was a partisan during the Second World War. It was my great-grandfather that served in the First World War.'

'My mistake. Of course. Signora *Casagrande*, I wonder if—'

I interrupt him. 'Signora *Fabris*.'

'I'm sorry?'

'Casagrande is my husband's surname. Italy isn't like England. Women keep their name upon marriage.'

'I must apologise. Signora *Fabris*,' he spreads his hands wide. *'I'm not a well man, as you can see. My doctor tells me I'm a damn silly fool even for travelling to Italy at this time of year. But there are things I want to do. Or, perhaps, better to say there are things I need to do whilst I still have time.*

'I've always had an interest in military history, signora. *And particularly in what my grandfather might have done during his time in Italy.'*

'Did he never speak about it? I know many soldiers never wished to.' I know the answer to this question already, of course, but if Shawcross is surprised at all by my obvious attempt to lie, he gives no sign of it. He just shakes his head, sadly.

'I never knew him, signora. *He never returned home.'*

'I'm sorry.'

'My father never knew him, either. He was just an infant when Thomas Shawcross left for Italy. To us, he was nothing more than a picture on the mantelpiece.' For a moment, I think his eyes flick towards the patch of discoloured wallpaper. *'Nothing more remains of him. A few letters, that's all. Amazing they survived really. Mail home was very heavily censored at the time and they were never sent.*

'And I started to think – when I heard that I was ill – that sooner or later, the same would happen to me. I would be that photograph on the mantelpiece. And I decided that wasn't good enough. That we needed more of my grandfather than what remained to us.

'So I contacted various organisations. The British Legion. Various regimental associations. Writers. Historians. Throughout England and then throughout Italy. It wasn't easy, my Italian really isn't very good. But then I discovered something about the

Villa Godi Malinverni, and a film called Senso. *You've seen it, I imagine?'*

I nod. *'It's one of those films that I think one has to see. Or at least pretend to have seen.'*

'It wasn't quite what I was expecting. I'm not so sure I'd go as far to say I enjoyed it, but that's my fault not the film's. Cinema's never been my thing. Anyway, I started to hear rumours about something called the Visconti Box from an Italian historian called Andrea Mazzon. You know him, of course?'

I keep my voice even. *'I do.'*

'It's supposed to be an archive of papers that Luchino Visconti had brought back from the Villa Godi Malinverni. Containing all sorts of things. Architectural plans and sketches, historical information from the time of Palladio himself. But more than that, there were letters – actually letters and diaries – from servicemen from the time of the First World War. Including from my grandfather. All of a sudden, we'd found a little bit more of Thomas Shawcross. And I knew I had to have it.'

'And did you?' I try to keep my voice as light as possible.

He shakes his head. *'It was withdrawn from sale at the last moment. Andrea and I are doing our very best to track down who the original owner might be. In the hope we might be able to persuade him to change his mind.'* He smiles. *'I understand Andrea is one of your rivals in the upcoming election.'*

'He's another one of the independent candidates, yes.'

'You must see him quite frequently, then?'

'Less than you might think,' I say. *'Occasional public events where all the candidates happen to be together, but that's about it. We don't see each other socially.'* I smile. *'We're not really the same sort of people.'*

Shawcross takes a deep breath. 'I've spoken to Andrea, a number of times. I think you could say we get on. Oh, we're very different in many ways, but I think one needs to respect his scholarship. And he tells me that – well, that there might be a connection between my grandfather and your great-grandfather.'

There is ice in the pit of my stomach. I take a moment to take a sip of water, praying that he will not see my hands trembling.

'That's possible,' is all I say.

Shawcross leans forward, his eyes are brighter now. 'It's more than possible. I think it's certain. Mazzon tells me that they were both under command of the joint British-Italian force.'

'Oh, that's quite possible. But that doesn't mean they knew each other. I doubt my great-grandfather even spoke any English. Few Italians from his background would have done so at the time.'

He shakes his head. 'I understood he did. But that wouldn't have mattered, anyway. Thomas Shawcross was an interpreter. That's why he was so useful to the army. Why he did relatively little service in the field. It was more important to have him as a translator and interpreter.'

'Of course. But I don't think that necessarily shows they would have known each other. I don't think Great-Grandfather would have been mixing with people like that. His background was quite humble.'

Shawcross takes a deep breath. 'Signora *Fabris*. There's something I have to ask you. What do you know about looting during the Great War?'

I shake my head, but, again, I feel that icy grip in my stomach. 'I thought that was more associated with the Second World War?'

'That's correct. But it happened also during the First. On nothing like the same scale, but it did happen. Now, British Command were holed up in the Villa Godi Malinverni, which held a selection of papers and drawings by Andrea Palladio. The Austrians had advanced over one kilometre in a single day. I think the officers in charge panicked. This archive was one of Italy's cultural treasures. It would be of enormous propaganda value to have it fall into Austrian hands. More than that, there would be the shame of the British being unable to protect their ally's treasures.

'All I have is one final letter from my grandfather. About being called up to the villa for some secret reason.' He screws his eyes shut, and then carries on. 'And then, my grandfather just vanishes from history. Nothing remains of him now. Just a bland letter to my grandmother saying missing in action and presumed dead. Nothing more known about Signor Fabris.' He pauses, and opens his eyes to stare directly into mine. 'And nothing more is known about the Palladio archive.'

I shake my head. 'I don't know what you want me to say, Mr Shawcross.'

'I just,' his voice breaks for a moment, 'I just want you to tell me what your great-grandfather did in the war, signora. That's all. What happened to him? What happened to the Palladio papers? And most of all, I want to know what happened to my grandfather. Mazzon tells me there are references in the State Archive to something called Operation Quattro Libri. I think Thomas Shawcross and Alvise Fabris were involved in that. Please, tell me, do you know what it is?'

I get to my feet and mentally count to ten. I keep my voice as firm as I possibly can. 'Mr Shawcross, I am so sorry but I can't help you with this.'

'Can't? Or won't?' For the first time, his mask of control cracks, just a little; and there's an edge of desperation in his voice for the first time.

'I can't. As I said. I'm sorry, but I think it would be best if you go now.'

'No,' he shakes his head, furiously. 'Please. I just want to know what happened to my grandfather. That's all.' He steps towards me, and I can't help flinching. 'I won't say anything. I swear. Look.' He reaches into his coat and takes out an envelope. 'I hoped I wouldn't have to do this but – well, you're welcome to this. All of it. All I want to know is the truth.'

He holds the envelope out towards me, his hand shaking. I have no idea why, but I take it.

'Anna? What's going on?' I hear the door slamming, and look over to see Gianluca, his face darkening.

'Gianluca, this is Mr Shawcross. He's here – he's here to—'

'I know why he's here, Anna.' Gianluca's voice is low, controlled. 'Mr Shawcross has been in touch. Many times.' He shakes his head. 'I thought I told you to have nothing to do with him?'

'Gianluca, he's not well. I couldn't just leave him out there in the wind and the rain.'

He puts his hands on my shoulders. 'Of course not. Of course not.' He turns to the Englishman. 'Mr Shawcross, I think my wife has said all she has to say to you.'

'But—'

Gianluca holds up a hand. 'Sir, I don't wish to be rude. Or unkind. I am genuinely sorry for whatever might have happened to your grandfather. But we can't help you. We simply can't. And so I think it's best if you go.'

Shawcross's shoulders slump, and the old man looks beaten.

He's about to speak, but Gianluca just shakes his head. He walks to the door, and pulls it open. 'Good afternoon, sir.'

Shawcross half-stumbles to the door. Then Gianluca looks at the envelope in my hands, as if noticing it for the first time.

'What's that?'

I shake my head. 'I don't know, Gianluca.'

He turns to Shawcross. 'Did you give her that?'

He nods. Gianluca takes the envelope from me, and runs a fingernail under the seal. He looks inside. And his face darkens.

He holds up the envelope. 'You thought you could just give us some money, eh? Because everyone knows you can just buy Italians for money. That's what you thought, wasn't it?'

Shawcross shrinks back. 'I didn't mean it like that. It was just,' *he pauses, and then realises he has gone too far to stop now,* 'Mazzon thought it might help.'

'Mazzon. Well of course.' *He's brandishing the envelope in his face now.* 'Did he suggest you give it to us in cash. Even better, yes? Because everyone knows there's nothing the Italians like better than being paid in nero.'

Shawcross, I can see, is shaking. Whether from fear, or simply from the effects of his disease, I cannot say. I also fear he is about to burst into tears, and I think I would find that unbearable.

'Gianluca,' *I say,* 'stop it, please.'

He turns and looks at me, an expression of disbelief in his eyes.

I keep my voice low and calm. 'Mr Shawcross has made a mistake. That's all there is to it.'

Gianluca shakes his head. He turns back to Shawcross. 'A simple mistake. Yes, I'm sure. I'm quite, quite sure that's all it was.' *He thrusts the envelope into Shawcross's trembling hands.*

'Well now. I'm going to the kitchen to make myself a large drink.' He lowers his head, until it's just a few inches from that of the old man. An awful smile is on his face.

My husband, I know, would do anything to protect me, to protect our family. Even to the extent of bullying a sick old man. And that thought makes me want to vomit.

'By the time I return, you'll be gone. Won't you?' Shawcross opens his mouth to speak but the words will not come. 'Won't you?' he repeats, his smile ever wider.

He nods, silently. Gianluca pats him gently on the cheek. Then he turns and, without so much as a word, leaves the room.

I get to my feet and walk unsteadily to the door. I whisper the words 'I'm sorry' to Shawcross but the old man doesn't seem to hear me. Then he gathers himself, shaking his head. He looks across the room in the direction of the kitchen, afraid that Gianluca might reappear at any moment. 'Please,' he says. He fumbles in his jacket for a moment, and takes out a business card and a pen. He scribbles an address on the back of the card, and presses it into my hands. 'That's my hotel. In Calvene. I'll be there for the next couple of days. If you change your mind. Please.' Then he turns and half-runs from the room.

Gianluca returns from the kitchen, whistling nonchalantly. He has a glass of prosecco in each hand. He passes one to me, and we clink glasses, awkwardly.

'Cheers, darling.'

Then he looks up at the discoloured patch on the wall. 'We really must get that seen to,' he says. Then he catches sight of the card, still clutched in my hand. 'Perhaps I ought to take care of that.'

No further mention is made of Anthony Shawcross at all.

Chapter 38

The mobile phone on the bedside table buzzed again and again. I flapped around with my left hand until I felt it, and then brought it to my face, screwing up my bleary eyes in order to make out the number.

'Roberto?'

'Nathan. Good morning. Did I wake you up?'

I screwed my eyes up further, trying to make out the time. 'Yes, you did. Is it important?'

'Absolutely it is. You were right, Nat, there's something going on with Mazzon and Fabris, and those photos of Casagrande picking Mazzon up by the scruff of his neck are going to be in all the papers this morning.'

Nat? We'd moved on to Nat territory now?

'We need to crack on with this straightaway. Grab Mazzon for an interview before those bastards from *La Nuova* get to him.'

'We?'

'Of course, we're a team now. And anyway, you owe me a favour I guess.'

'Oh, do I?'

'You do. Now he's not answering his phone—'

I interrupted him. 'I don't think he ever does. He's very cautious about screening his calls.'

'Okay then. Are you going to call round? He knows you, doesn't he? He'd probably just slam the door in my face.'

'I guess I could. Can you give me an hour? I'll see you in Campo de l'Anzolo Raffael.'

'Nah, I've got other stuff to check out. What I need is you to get him to agree to meet me for an interview. For later this morning, definitely no later than this afternoon. Tell him we'll let him give his whole side of the story. Also tell him he can't trust anyone from *La Nuova*.'

'Christ. How do you feel about going back to football reporting?'

'Not any more, Nat. This is my chance to have a crack at the big league.'

He hung up. Federica padded in from the kitchen carrying a mug of tea. 'Your cat was hungry,' she said. 'Again.'

'So,' I said, 'how do you feel about going to church with me this morning?'

'What do you mean how do I feel? I spend most of my working days in churches. I probably spend more time there than *padre* Michael.'

'Fair point. Okay then, how do you feel about coming with me to see a fascist at morning prayer?'

'Well, this sounds like the sort of thing every girl should see once in her lifetime.'

'Exactly.'

'Only once, mind.'

If the interior of Angelo Raffaele was any warmer than the

exterior, we failed to notice, yet Federica's eyes lit up as soon as she saw the series of paintings by Guardi.

I smiled at her. 'Good?'

She squeezed my hand. 'I don't come here enough, you know? Looking at them, well, it just makes me happy. That's all. They're so gentle, so lovely.'

I looked around but there was no sign of Mazzon. I checked my watch. 'He's late this morning.'

'Is he always here exactly on the hour, then?'

'He strikes me as a man to whom these things are important.'

She put a finger to her lips. 'Well, we ought to be quiet I suppose. Let's just sit here and look at Guardi. I can think of worse ways of passing a cold morning.'

We sat down at the back of the church, Federica's eyes fixed on those five paintings from the Book of Tobit. I kept scanning the church, just in case Havok decided to pay a call. Like Mazzon, however, there was no sign of him. The cold was sinking into my bones now so I snuggled closer to Federica. I checked my watch. Twenty past ten. Twenty-five past. Had he just decided to treat himself to a morning off?

Venice is a city of over one hundred churches. Catholic, Anglican, Lutheran, Waldensian and several flavours of Orthodoxy. The one thing they have in common is their absolute contempt for the bottoms of the faithful. I had yet to find a pew that could be described as anything better than mildly uncomfortable.

I wondered how long it would be until I lost all feeling in the lower half of my body? I checked my watch once more, and then Fede gave me a gentle prod.

'Cold, isn't it?'

'Well, it's – chilly, I suppose.'

'Bloody cold is what it is. It's all right for you. You spend your days in front of a computer screen in a nice warm flat. I'm up scaffolding in icy churches. And now I'm sitting here waiting for Andrea Mazzon to turn up and say his prayers. I thought fascists were supposed to be particular about keeping to time.'

I got to my feet. Yes, definitely still two of them. Still some feeling remaining. That was a good sign.

'Let's go to his flat, then.'

'We could have done that at first, you know?'

'I didn't think he'd be likely to let us in. Given what happened last night.' I stretched. 'Oh, that feels better already. Come on.'

We made our way across the *campo* to Mazzon's block. I rang his bell a couple of times, without success. I looked upwards to his flat. Even with the shutters closed, I could hear loud opera music blaring.

Fede shook her head. 'His neighbours must absolutely love him. What is it?'

'*Tosca*, I think. Just the thing to blow away the cobwebs on a cold morning.'

'And everyone else's as well.'

I was about to ring again, when the door opened and Bruno stood there shaking his head.

'He's really gone too far this time,' he said. 'Everybody in the block can hear it. I don't know how he can sleep through that.'

'Sleep? What makes you think he's asleep?'

'I banged on his door, but he's not answering.'

I took Federica's hand and we headed up the stairs. 'Come on. Let's take a look.'

'Mister, where are you going?'

'Something's wrong, Bruno.'

I sized up the door. Not a *porta blindata*. Just a wooden interior door. There might be a chance of forcing it.

I took a step back and braced myself.

'Mister, are you sure this is a good idea?'

'Not sure at all. If I'm wrong, tell *dottor* Mazzon to send me the bill.'

I took another step back and took a deep breath.

Fede gently stretched her arm out in front of me, shaking her head. She turned the doorknob, and pushed the door open.

'Oh.'

She smiled at me. 'I thought it was worth checking first.' Then she turned to walk inside, and stopped dead in her tracks.

'*Dio.*'

'What's wrong?'

'Nathan. We need to call an ambulance. And the police.'

Vanni set his Newton's Cradle in motion, and sighed. 'Okay, Nathan. Let's go through it again.'

'Pretty much as I said. Fede and I decided to join Andrea Mazzon for prayers.'

Vanni shook his head. 'Can you leave the jokes, Nathan? Please. Because all I really want now is a quiet afternoon and a small cigar. And instead I have to deal with prominent historian and media figure Andrea Mazzon being beaten to a bloody pulp.'

'Sorry. How's it going by the way? Not smoking, I mean.'

'Fine, as long as I'm not stressed. But, as I said, you've brought me an unconscious celebrity fascist who's been on the wrong end of a beating. And so I'm just a little bit tense.'

'Well, as I said, I just wanted to talk to Mazzon again.'

'Okay.' He scribbled away on his pad. 'What about?'

'About his links with Anthony Shawcross, a football hooligan called Havok, and why exactly the contents of the Visconti Box are so important to Giuseppe Meneghini.'

Vanni continued to scribble away for a moment, then sighed and put his pen down.

'Could you just put your head to one side for a moment, Nathan?'

'What? Like this?'

'Just a little bit more if you would.'

'Sure.' I leaned my head to the left. A microsecond later Vanni's pencil went hurtling through the air, smashing against the wall behind me.

'Thank you, Nathan. I feel better for that.'

'Oh good.'

'Really, I do. Now, can you try explaining all that to me once again? Perhaps in thirty seconds or less.'

'Okay. Well, elderly British academic Anthony Shawcross is investigating the death of his grandfather Thomas in the Great War. He contacts Andrea Mazzon, something of an expert in this area, who tells him about the Visconti Box, which might hold further information for him. And there's more. Somehow Mazzon knows that there's a link between the Shawcross family and the great-grandfather of Anna Fabris. Something that might compromise her candidacy as mayor. Shawcross makes various attempts to contact her, but she won't speak to him. Then he journeys to Cavalletto to stand at Thomas's grave, and dies during the extreme weather.

'But it doesn't end there. Mazzon and Meneghini think there's something in the box – proof – that would ruin Anna. But what they don't have is the box. And if we had that – well, things would be a lot clearer.'

Vanni tapped his watch. 'Forty-five seconds. Not bad. Where does Havok,' he made quotation marks with his fingers, 'come into this?'

'I think he's just a heavy that Mazzon hired for security.'

'Hmm. Okay. I'd have thought there might have been easier people to work with.'

'Havok's ex-*Ultra* and ex-*CasaPound*. So he's a tough bastard who shares the same ideology. An ideal job for him in some ways.'

'Could be.' He took out a new pencil.

'You're not going to throw that, are you?'

'This? No.'

'You will tell me, though? If you are.'

Vanni nodded. 'Okay then. Tell me about Gianluca Casagrande.'

'I've only met him a couple of times.'

'And how does he strike you?'

'I think he seems like a nice guy. Except—'

'Oh. There's an "except"?'

'He just seems a little bit over-controlling, you know? If you see the two of them together, he's always kind of fussing with her clothes and hair. "No darling, stand over there." That sort of thing.'

'I imagine he just wants her to be successful. A woman running for mayor is going to get commented on if there's a hair out of place. Sad, but that's the way it is.'

I took a deep breath. 'There's something else, Vanni. When we were ice-skating last night and we ran into each other, all sorts of crap fell out of his pockets. Keys, wallet, phone. I picked them all up and gave them back to him. But there was something else as well. Shawcross's card was there, with an address scribbled on the back for a hotel in Calvene. The same place I stayed with Dario.

'Now Anna said to me she had no memory of ever speaking to Anthony Shawcross. So why would Gianluca have a business card for the same hotel, one hundred kilometres away, that Shawcross was staying in?'

'So what are you saying, Nathan?.'

'That I think Meneghini was telling me the truth. That Anna Fabris is a liar.'

'So Mr Shawcross's death was not an accident, and Gianluca Casagrande is implicated in some way?'

I shook my head. 'I don't want to think that. And I can't imagine him being capable of murder.'

Vanni set the Newton's Cradle on his desk in motion once more, and watched it clack away. 'Gianluca Casagrande. A man who threatened Andrea Mazzon last night on camera. A man who really would have everything to gain from Shawcross and Mazzon being removed from the picture. And, of course, a man who seems ready to use his fists.'

'You're saying Gianluca beat him up?'

'It seems obvious.'

'I don't think he's that kind of guy, Vanni.'

'He's the kind of guy who was ready to punch Andrea Mazzon in the face in full view of his wife, family and a crowd of people.'

'I know. I think that was just stupid and spur of the moment. I can't imagine him doing something like this in cold blood.'

'He goes round to his apartment. He tells him to leave his wife alone. There's an argument, and he turns up the stereo to cover up any noise. And he beats him unconscious.'

'Is that really what you think, Vanni?'

'I don't know. At least, not yet.' Then he looked me straight in the eyes. 'But it's a nice, easy solution and nice, easy solutions are things I'm always in favour of. We're going to need to talk to him, Nathan.'

Part Three

The Candidate

Chapter 39

Fede and I clinked glasses in silence.

Ed looked at the two of us. 'Am I missing something? It's just there seems to be an "atmosphere" here, if you know what I mean.'

Fede smiled, weakly. 'Let's just say we're drowning our sorrows.'

My phone plinged and I reached into my pocket to retrieve it. 'It's Bergamin. He says Gianluca giving Mazzon a beating is going to be the cover story in every paper in the Veneto, and probably beyond, tomorrow morning.'

Fede shook her head. 'As expected. Not that that makes it any better.'

Ed polished a few glasses, and stacked them up. 'Look, I'm trying to be positive here but is this going to make any difference? I mean, it's not Anna's fault if her husband goes a bit mad and gets into a fight, is it?'

'It was more than a fight, Ed. It looks as if Gianluca beat the crap out of Mazzon. So having your husband hospitalise one of the other candidates – well, it's not going to look good.'

My phone buzzed once more and I checked the message.

'Bergamin again?' said Fede.

I shook my head. 'Meneghini.' I glanced around the bar. Fede and I were the only customers. I pointed at the wall-mounted TV. 'Ed, can you put that on, please?'

'I thought you hated that?'

'I do. But I think this is going to be important.'

I leaned over and showed him the message on screen. *You might find there's something interesting on television right now. G.* Followed by a smiley face.

Ed clicked on the remote control. 'Which channel?'

'Televenezia.'

Ed clicked through the seemingly infinite selection of channels until Anna's face filled the screen.

The camera pulled back to reveal a crowd of journalists thrusting microphones towards her and a babble of unintelligible voices could be heard.

She held her hand up. 'Can we do this one at a time? Please?'

'*Dottoressa* Fabris, is it true your husband has been arrested for assault?'

'Is it true *dottor* Mazzon is in hospital?'

'*Dottoressa* Fabris, is your husband at home at the moment?'

Again, she held her hand up, and the camera zoomed in on her face. Her eyes were red, and she looked tired. 'To take those in order. My husband has not been arrested, but the police wish to speak to him. Andrea Mazzon is in hospital, yes, and he has all my prayers and good wishes for a swift recovery. Finally, no, my husband is not at home. But my young daughters are, and so is my elderly grandfather. Could you please, therefore, give them a little bit of respect and a little bit of space?'

A camera flashed in her face, and she put her hand to her eyes to shield herself.

'Anna, will you be stepping down as candidate?'

She shook her head. 'No.'

'Is it possible for you to continue? Given that your husband may have assaulted a rival?'

'Gianluca would not have done this.' Her voice was weary, and on the edge of breaking. 'As you know, *dottor* Mazzon has made no comment on the identity of the man who assaulted him. And so I think there's nothing more to say.'

'You're standing by your man, then?' Cameras snapped again, and the crowd was pressing in on her now.

She rubbed her eyes, and, again, the cameras flashed. 'Okay, I'll finish with this. When my father died last year, I remember the day of his funeral. I remember tourists photographing his coffin being loaded onto the funeral barge. And I remember feeling tired. So, so tired at the realisation that everything we did as Venetians just seemed to exist for the purposes of being photographed by tourists. And I decided that I had had enough. That perhaps I could change things for the better. But now – look at you all. I'd expect tourists to behave like this. But not Venetians.

'So there's nothing more to be said. I will not be standing down. I will not be saying anything else about my husband. And you remember this—' her voice was shaking as she jabbed a finger at the crowd, 'you stay away from my family. You understand? You stay the fuck away from them.'

Then she turned, and slammed the door behind her.

Federica reached across the bar for the remote control, and switched the television off.

'Fede?'

'I've seen enough.'

Ed shook his head. 'Shit. Poor woman.'

My phone buzzed once more and I looked down at the screen.

'Meneghini?'

I nodded.

'What's he got to say?'

I showed them both the screen. *Poor Anna. Honesty really would be the best policy. But I think tomorrow's headlines have already written themselves.*

Federica swore under her breath. 'The trouble is that prick is actually right this time.'

'What do you mean?'

'Of course the headlines have written themselves. They've caught her swearing on camera. And you can bet your life that every front page photo is going to be of her with her hand in front of her eyes. As if she's about to cry. It's just what these bastards like Meneghini wanted. You can't trust a woman to do this, what you need is a big strong man who's capable of keeping his temper and, even better, what you need is a big strong businessman.' She looked at the blank screen again and shook her head. 'Well, they've got what they wanted.' She turned back to the bar. 'Come on, Ed. Two Negronis, eh?'

'Coming up.'

Fede nodded at me. 'And the same for him.'

'Christ. Are you sure?'

'Tomorrow morning, the papers will be patronising the shit out of half the population of the country. And in a couple of weeks time Venice is going to elect another disaster of a mayor. Yes, I'm sure.'

I smiled weakly at Ed. I could only agree.

Chapter 40

Fede was almost correct. Anna, shielding her eyes, was indeed the front page image in the morning papers. She did, however, have to share it with the battered and bloody face of Andrea Mazzon. The words 'foul-mouthed tirade' were also prominent.

Gianluca, Vanni informed me, would be at the *Questura* again that morning. Just to make a final statement and sign a few papers. Nothing more. No, there was no possibility of me being there as well. 'The Honorary British Consul would like a word,' he informed me, was not a request that could be made with any weight of the law behind it. However, we were pals and so he promised to tip me off when they were finished with him, thus saving me hours of hanging around in the cold outside.

I stood in Bar Filovia, eating what might be the best mortadella sandwich in Venice. My phone buzzed and I smiled when I saw the message from Vanni. I texted back a quick 'thx', drained my spritz and put a few coins down on the bar. The *barista* smiled and gave me a wink. 'We're never sure when to expect you, Nathan.'

'Ah, it just depends if there's someone under arrest.'

He wasn't sure if I was joking or not, but smiled anyway.

I made my way outside, just in time to see Gianluca making his way along the Fondamenta Santa Chiara, in the direction of the #1 vaporetto stop.

'Gianluca?'

He paused for a moment, and I saw his shoulders tense, but then he resumed his stride without looking back.

'Gianluca? It's me, Nathan.'

He made his way onto the pontoon, without turning around.

I followed him inside.

'Gianluca. I need to talk to you.'

He turned and looked me up and down, his eyes red and tired. 'I'm sorry, Nathan. It's not a good idea.' Then he turned away again.

I checked my watch. We had a couple of minutes at most before the vaporetto arrived.

Two tourists were poring over a map, and then looking up at the names on the #1 line in some confusion. One of them looked at me, hopefully.

'Excuse me. Do you speak English?'

I nodded. 'Sure. You need any help?'

'We're kind of lost. We've got a hotel booked which we're told is near San Marco.' He pointed at the map of the line. 'It's just we don't know if we want,' he pronounced the words carefully 'San Marco Vallaresso or San Marco Zaccaria'.

'Okay. What's the name of the hotel.'

'I think it's the Novecento, or something like that.'

'Oh yes, I know that. Don't get off at San Marco though, Giglio is better.'

He frowned. 'Where's that?'

'Same *sestiere*. Just get off at the stop before *Salute*.'

He laughed. 'Okay, you're in danger of losing me now.'

'The church of the *Salute*. Big, well, church-ey type thing. You'll have seen it a thousand times on TV, I guarantee it.' I tried sketching it in the air with my hands. I wondered if it was possible to mime a church, but he nodded enthusiastically so I assumed my attempt had been successful.

'But that's near St Mark's, right?'

'Near enough.'

'How long does it take to walk there?'

'Let me see, it's about two hundred metres. Which means somewhere between five minutes and two hours.' He frowned. 'Don't worry, it's all part of the experience.' The vaporetto, piloted by an over-enthusiastic *comandante*, banged into the pontoon setting it rocking. 'And so is that.'

Further passengers had arrived during our conversation, filling up the pontoon and hiding Gianluca from view. For a moment I feared I'd lost him, but then I saw him making his way along the vaporetto, taking a seat halfway down the cabin.

I followed him on board and took the seat behind him. Again, I saw his shoulders tense.

I waited until the boat had pulled away from the jetty before speaking.

'Gianluca, I need to talk to you,' I said, keeping my voice low.

He said nothing. I put my hand on the back of his chair. 'It's important,' I said.

His head twitched, just a little, and then, very carefully, as if afraid I would cry out, reached behind him and clamped his hand down on mine, squeezing it painfully.

He turned to face me. 'It's a bad idea,' he said, his grip tightening.

'Okay Gianluca, it's like this. You either talk to me, or I start talking really loud, right now, about what's just happened. And once I've done that, I'll repeat it all in English as well. How about that?'

He glared at me, his face reddening, but he relaxed his grip and drew back his hand.

'Come on,' I said, nodding behind me. 'Let's sit outside, eh?'

'It'll be freezing!'

'Exactly. Only tourists and mad people sit outside in January. So it'll be nice and discreet.'

He shook his head, and followed me outside, cursing as the blast of cold air hit him. 'What do you want, Nathan?'

'As I said. Just to talk. About you, Anthony Shawcross, and the events of a century ago.'

Chapter 41

I checked my watch. 'Okay, best stop for Campo San Polo is probably San Silvestro. That's about twenty-five minutes. Plenty of time to chat. Unless of course we freeze to death in the meantime.'

Gianluca laughed, bitterly. 'San Polo? Are you mad? I can't go back there at the moment.'

'Oh.' I tried to find the right words. 'Are things a bit difficult?'

'Difficult?' He shook his head in incredulity. 'It's a media circus. The press are camped there waiting to photograph Anna as soon as she steps outside. Do you know what happened this morning? They photographed her taking the kids to school. My kids, for Christ's sake. Whose friends are going to be asking them if it's true what the newspapers say, that their daddy is a violent lunatic and is going to prison.' He slammed his hand into the adjacent seat and then cursed with the pain. 'So no, I'm not going back home. Not for a few days, anyway. I've got a hotel booked, and no, I'm not going to tell you where.'

I shrugged. 'Up to you.'

'And then, when the police announce that I'm not of

interest, perhaps I can go about getting my life back to normal and my wife can get on with hers.'

'Okay. I hope it'll be that easy.'

'Do you have any better ideas?'

'You could tell me all about what happened?'

'I've spoken to the police. I have a good lawyer. That's an end to it.'

'You have an alibi?'

'I was at work.'

'That's just five minutes' walk away. That won't work. One double espresso too many might have been enough to push you into paying him a call. And they know you'd heard from Anthony Shawcross.'

He laughed. 'Because you told them, right?

'What was I supposed to do? Lie? You followed Shawcross to Calvene, didn't you?'

Gianluca closed his eyes, and leaned back in his seat. Then he nodded. 'Yes.'

'Want to tell me about it?'

'He telephoned us a number of times. There were emails as well. Requests to meet. We ignored them. We kept ignoring them. And then he paid Anna a call one day, when I was out. He even offered us money. And I – well I lost it a bit, I admit. But he left us an address in Calvene.

'I swear to you, Nathan, that I didn't go there to hurt him. I met him there at his hotel. And I begged him, I promised him money, whatever he wanted, just to stop digging into this. Because of what it would do to Anna and Alfredo.

'And do you know what he did? He said yes. He said that he understood. And that all he wanted to do now was to pay a visit to Cavalletto and just pass a few minutes there. And that when that was done, he'd return to England and we'd never hear from him again.' Gianluca rubbed his eyes. 'And that, Nathan, is the absolute truth.'

'You told the police this?'

He shook his head. 'I can't. Or the whole truth will have to come out. So I stonewalled the whole thing. *I was at work the whole morning. No, I've never seen that card before.*'

'That's not going to make it go away, Gianluca.'

He stared at me, and then threw himself back in his seat. 'Okay, Nathan. So what can the British Honorary Consul do that the police and my lawyer can't?'

I took out a photo of Havok from my jacket. 'Do you know this guy? Have you ever seen him before?'

He shook his head.

'You're sure?'

He nodded. 'It's not the sort of face you forget. Who is he?'

His name's Francesco Bentivoglio. But if you call him Francesco he'll kill you. He prefers to be known as Havok. A Lazio *Ultra* and ex-member of *CasaPound*. Oh, and it seems he's good pals with both Andrea Mazzon and Giuseppe Meneghini.'

Gianluca looked at me with interest. 'Why?'

'I don't wish to stereotype but I don't think it's for the conversation.'

'Protection?'

'That's what he says. You see, I think Mazzon discovered the truth about the Visconti archive and realised he could use that as leverage with Meneghini. The only trouble is, he was expecting to acquire the box at auction and then the owner withdrew it. Now he's made a promise to Meneghini that he can't keep, and Meneghini starts losing patience. He starts offering Havok more money in order to work for him, instead. Maybe, he thinks, Mazzon really does have the box and he's stringing him along in the hope of getting a better deal.

'And then, Gianluca, and then – well, you give Meneghini a perfect excuse. You're photographed on camera assaulting Mazzon. And the next morning, Meneghini sends Havok around to Mazzon's apartment to ask him – politely, and one last time – just where the box is. Havok doesn't really know the meaning of subtlety, and so it ends with Mazzon in hospital and you at the *Questura*.'

Gianluca shook his head. 'Is there any way of proving of this?'

'I don't know. But there's one thing you've got to do for me, Gianluca. You must tell me where the Visconti Box is.'

'Nathan, I don't know where it is.'

'Don't lie to me, Gianluca.'

'I'm not lying.'

'You are. You were at the auction along with Shawcross and Mazzon.'

'I wanted to bid for it myself and then burn the bastard thing.'

'That would have been too risky. You had no idea quite how much money the pair of them had access to. No, you contacted the owner beforehand and either persuaded or bribed them to withdraw it. And so you've got to tell me who it is. Because whoever has the box is sitting on a time bomb.

Sooner or later, Meneghini is going to ask Havok to pay a house call on them as well, and next time it might not just finish in a beating.'

Gianluca shook his head. 'Why are you doing this?' he said.

'Because it can be one final act of closure for the Shawcross family. Because there are two little girls at home missing their dad. And because I really don't want Giuseppe Meneghini and Andrea Mazzon in charge of this city.'

He took a deep breath. 'Whatever I've done, Nathan, I did to protect my wife. You must understand that. And that is why I cannot tell you anything about the contents of the box.'

'I do understand that, Gianluca. Really. So come on then. Who has it?'

The vaporetto was pulling in to San Silvestro now. Gianluca got to his feet and, for a moment, I feared he was going to walk away from me without another word. Then he patted my shoulder, and looked down at me.

'It's Simonetti,' he said. 'From *Settima Arte*.'

Chapter 42

Fabio Simonetti's apartment was a deep shade of yellowy-brown. It had probably been some other colour at first, but it was difficult to be absolutely sure through the thick fug of cigarette smoke.

He took another from the packet of cheap MS and offered me one.

I shook my head. 'Given up.'

He raised his eyebrows, and looked disappointed.

I made my way over to the window, in the hope that there might be a draught of fresh air from the outside. I peered through the murky glass, my eyes stinging.

'That's a lovely view,' I said.

And it was. The southern lagoon stretched out uninterrupted before me, with the exception of a few small islands, as far as the eye could see.

'It is. I'm a lucky man, you know. Bought this place back in the seventies. Not so many people wanted to live here then. Tourists sure as hell never came here. And now it's all mine.'

'Giudecca's changed a bit, I imagine.'

'More that you can imagine. You know the old Junghans factory? That's flash new housing now. The *birreria*? Housing, again, and art spaces. Change is good, I know, but it's something we're not very good at in Venice. All those new apartments, and no Venetians to rent them to.'

I nodded and turned back to the window, looking out at the islands. 'My geography's rubbish. What am I looking at here?'

He pointed to the left. 'That? That's the San Clemente Palace. Posh hotel.'

'Uh-huh.'

'And then, you look over to the right from that, straight ahead. 'That's the Marriott. And that's the island of Sacca Sessola. Of course, the owners don't like to call it that. That would link it too much with its original purpose.'

'Fuel storage depot, wasn't it?'

He smiled, and might even have looked a little impressed. 'That's right. For a while, at least. Then it had cholera patients. Oh, and then TB patients. Now, if I was the owner of a posh hotel, I'm not sure that's the sort of information I'd be printing in the glossy brochures. So now they call it the Island of Roses.' He laughed, which turned into a great, rumbly cough. 'Island of Roses,' he repeated. 'Imagine that. Anyway, you're not here to talk about the geography of the lagoon, are you?'

'No.' I took a deep breath and wished I hadn't. 'If you don't mind, I'd like to talk to you about Luchino Visconti. And the archive.'

Simonetti sighed, and fumbled for another cigarette. 'Okay, perhaps you'd better sit down. You need a cup of coffee?'

'Maybe just a glass of tap water.' Anything, I thought, to try and clear the stale smoke out of my throat. And yet part of me was quite enjoying the whole passive experience.

He nodded, and returned from the kitchen with a glass of water which I gratefully half-drained.

'Well now, I met Visconti back in 1970. Before that I was just a young punk reporter. But I'd written a piece on *Anonimo Veneziano* which got picked up by one of the papers. Don't ask me which one, I can't remember now. Anyway, out of the blue I get a call from Guido Aristarco. You know him?'

I shook my head.

'The guy was a legend. Seriously. First professor of cinema in Italy. And he founded a magazine called *Cinema Nuovo*.' He looked at me expectantly, but his face fell when he saw my expression.

'No?'

'I'm sorry. You must think I'm terribly ignorant.'

'Ah well. You're a young guy. Now Aristarco was a Marxist, see. And he tells me he likes my Marxist critique of *Anonimo Veneziano*. I didn't even realise that's what I'd done, but I figured that even if I'd done it by accident, all well and good.

'Aristarco tells me, he'd like me to do a piece on Visconti, because he's out on the Lido filming *Death in Venice*. And I have to ask him to repeat what he's just said, because I don't believe what I've just heard.

'He tells me that he trusts me to do a good piece on Luchino fucking Visconti. That he thinks I'm a talent. Well, maybe I am, or maybe he just knows he can get this done on the cheap and he won't have to pay any hotel costs or train fares. But I don't care. A few days later I'm on the boat out to the Lido and there they all are. First person I see is Dirk Bogarde. Then it's Silvana Mangano, and now I'm having to be really careful not to babble a load of nonsense because I'm a young guy and I've seen *Riso Amaro* and I'm more than a bit in love with her. There's the young blond guy ,' he scratched his head, 'you know I can't remember his name?'

'Tadzio?'

'That's the character. You remember the actor?'

I shook my head.

'Me neither. Poor guy. Anyway, there's crew running up and down, and I recognise the cinematographer. Because he's a legend, and he's worked with Fellini and Losey and Bresson and – all I really want to do is run away and go back to *mamma* and *papà* on Giudecca. Because I'm just a punk reporter who got lucky with a single piece, and now I'm going to meet Luchino Visconti and arse it up and that's my career ruined before I've even started.

'And I'm really thinking maybe I can sneak away, just go home and tell Aristarco that I'm sick and he'll have to send someone else. But then it's too late, and some guy in a suit comes over and looks me up and down – he's thinking this kid's too young, I can tell – and he says Mr Visconti will see you now. And that's it. I'm in a room at the Excelsior Hotel, and I'm talking to the second most famous Italian director in the world.'

'Wow. So what was he like?'

'He was – okay, you know. I think he realised quite early on that I wasn't an idiot. That helped. Oh, and I'd actually read *Death in Venice* which helped even more. He talked a lot about the past. His health wasn't good, you know, even at that time. Did you know he smoked over one hundred cigarettes a day? Assuming he slept for eight hours, that means lighting up about every ten minutes.'

'Blimey.'

I took a look around the nicotine-stained apartment. He caught the expression on my face and smiled. 'I'm doing my best to keep his average up. Not so easy now I'm not allowed to smoke in the shop any more. Anyway, he wasn't in good health but he was happy to talk. So I asked him about his past. About the war. He was an anti-fascist, and he really walked the walk, you know? He hid escaped POWs and partisans. He was nearly executed.' He dragged on his cigarette, and nodded. 'He was one of my heroes. As a filmmaker. As a man. He still is.'

'You got on, then?'

'Pretty well.' He grinned. 'We even went clubbing a couple of times. That was back in the days when Piccolo Mondo was fashionable.'

'You went clubbing with Luchino Visconti?'

Simonetti looked a little hurt. 'Sure. I was a good-looking guy in those days. Not as pretty as Tadzio, of course, but then again who was? We kept in touch for a few years. We were supposed to meet up again when he was filming *Ludwig*, but Aristarco wouldn't pay for me to go to Germany and I didn't have the money myself. And then, well, he had a stroke and he was never quite the same again.' He lit another cigarette, shaking his head.

'When you met him, did you ever talk about *Senso*?'

Simonetti smiled. 'That's what you really want to talk about, isn't it? Sure, we did. He said it was still a film he was proud of.'

'And?' I left the question hanging.

'And – you want to know about the box, right?'

'That's why I'm here, Fabio.'

He shook his head. 'People come along wanting to talk about Luchino Visconti while all they really want to talk about is the goddam box.' Then he grinned. 'It's not so much of a secret, really.

'The Brits moved out in 1919. They cleared up most of their stuff but it seems they weren't quite so scrupulous as they might have been. You see, there were all sorts of documents and photos relating to the Prince of Wales. And plenty of these ended up in the hands of collectors, you know? Locals thinking they'd be a nice souvenir to have. And so maybe a little money changes hands and that's why lots of houses in Calvene have a picture of Edward VIII on the wall.

'Now Visconti's heard about all this. He's just made *Senso*. It's ten years in the future, but he's already starting to think about *Il Gattopardo*. What's that all about if not the decline of the old order and the birth of the new? Anyway, the villa was undergoing reconstruction at the time and one of the custodians just happened to have a box of memorabilia from the war years that he was prepared to let Luchino have for a very reasonable amount.'

'He never did anything with it, though?'

He shook his head. 'No. I think he decided he just couldn't properly get into the heads of the English.'

'Well, we are very impenetrable.'

Simonetti laughed. 'Besides, can you imagine Burt Lancaster as the Prince of Wales?'

I grinned. 'It's a stretch. But he was a pretty good Duke of Salerno. And so, the big question is – what happened to the box?'

'Oh, it passed to me. Years later.'

'How so?'

'I did an interview with Franco Zeffirelli. Not long before he died. We talked about Visconti, of course. He'd lost interest in the Villa Godi project – if he ever really had much to begin with – shortly after *Senso* and so he turned it over to Zeffirelli.'

'And what did he do with it?'

'Kept it in his library gathering dust. He'd pretty much forgotten about it by the time we spoke. We took a look through the contents together. Photos and letters from the Prince of Wales, that sort of thing. His eyesight wasn't what it was so I read them out for him. It made him a little sad. He told me that, once upon a time, there might have been the germ of a film in them. Remember, this is the guy that made *Tea with Mussolini*. But he was far too old by then.'

'And what else was there?'

'Well, this is the interesting part. My English isn't that great, you understand, so it took me a while to get round to working my way through them. There were letters from a young English captain to his wife. The usual things, life at the villa and the like.'

'Which she never received. Those letters would have been censored.'

'There was more. Official documents. Operations reports. God knows how they ended up there. Just misfiled, or lost I imagine, when the Brits were packing up to leave. They were about something called Operation *Quattro Libri*.' He smiled. 'Now, where do you think that title comes from?'

I shook my head.

'No? Antonio Palladio. *The Four Books of Architecture*.'

'Oh, I see. Palladio, who was credited with the Villa Godi Malinverni.'

'One of his first projects.' He grinned. 'You know, here's me being Venetian and I didn't know any of this stuff. No, I've had to find this all out for myself. The villa was commissioned by the Godi brothers who acquired quite an archive of Palladio's material. Including his handwritten notes and original drawings for *The Four Books of Architecture*.'

I whistled.

'Indeed. Imagine how much that would be worth to a collector, eh? And this archive remains there, at the villa, down through the centuries, right up until the moment that the Brits come marching in.

'Then, one day, the Austrians advance almost a kilometre. And the Brits start to worry, just a little. Everybody's telling them that this is just the dying gasp of the Austrian army, but they don't want to risk it. They're sitting on top of a chunk of Italy's artistic heritage and they don't want to risk it being looted. That'd all be just a bit embarrassing.

'So they plan to have the Palladio archive – and this is something you could probably fit in a modestly-sized suitcase or trunk – evacuated to Venice. And there's one man for the job. Step up, Captain Thomas Shawcross. He speaks Italian, he's been on whatever the early twentieth-century equivalent of The Grand Tour is, and he even knows a little bit about art. They give him a driver as well, just for that extra bit of security, but the route to Venice is relatively safe and they don't see any great danger in a single vehicle travelling on its own. Then, in Venice, Shawcross will deliver the archive to the Accademia and enjoy a couple of days' rest and relaxation before returning to his unit.

'Except he never makes it. His Lancia's found outside Castelfranco, a burned-out shell. Inside is the charred body of Shawcross. He's been shot, multiple times. The driver is the lucky one. He's been shot in the leg, and sees out the last few months of the war in hospital.'

'And the Palladio papers?'

He shook his head. 'Gone forever. Sold to a dealer in Austria just after the war. The story has it they're somewhere in Belarus now.'

I shrugged. 'Okay. It's a good story, I'll give you that. But why so much interest in it now?'

Simonetti grinned. 'Well, this is where it becomes really interesting. It's all down to the identity of the driver. His name was Alvise Fabris. And he was the great-grandfather of Anna Fabris.'

Chapter 43

Simonetti passed a yellowing letter to me.

Hello Ma. Well, I'll be home before this letter will, that's for sure. I suspect I'll get into a spot of trouble even for writing it, but it'll probably be all right. They do rather need me, after all.

Turns out the Austrians are making more of a game of it than anyone expected. Now, you mustn't worry about me in that regard. I'm not even in the field. Far more useful, it seems, to have me up at the villa.

Anyway, it seems tomorrow the young Captain Shawcross is being sent on holiday. No, not back to England, sadly, but that'll be soon enough. It seems I'm off to Venice for a couple of days. Now this is all rather exciting. I've never been there, but I'm told it's the sort of city one should visit.

As to why I'm going there? The brass have decided, it seems, that there are some artefacts at the villa that need to be relocated. Just in case the Austrians make one push further than anyone expected. Now, most everyone seems to think this is a load of nonsense, but the diplomats seem to have been getting into a bit of a state. Be terribly embarrassing, it's thought, if we let some of Italy's treasures be stolen right from under our noses.

It should be straightforward. Chap called Alvise is going to be my driver. *It's just a few hours to Venice, and then I make contact with Prof somebody-or-other at the Accademia. Everything gets securely put into storage. Nobody's seriously worried about anything too bad happening to Venice at this particular stage.*

Alvise seems to be a decent enough chap. Speaks English, and apparently he's a bit of a marvel with his hands. Slightly more educated than I expected. He'd actually heard of Andrea Palladio, and seemed to have a proper idea of the worth of the papers we're transporting.

I'll try and bring something home for you all. Perhaps a little wooden gondola for the Boy (it'll have to be a model, I'm afraid. Not sure I can stretch to the real thing just yet). Alvise tells me I should get something in glass for Margaret. Apparently he knows the best places to go. He also says Venetian girls are the most beautiful in Italy. He also says he knows the best places to go for that as well but, never fear, your boy will be tucked up in bed at the Embassy whilst Alvise is out playing Casanova.

As I said, I'll be home before you read this. I'll write from Venice, of course, telling you all what a wonderful time I'm having. If it's as lovely as they say, perhaps we should all go back some day.

My love to Margaret and the Boy,

Your loving son,

Thomas

Chapter 44

'So Anna Fabris's great-grandfather murdered a British serviceman and sold part of his country's artistic heritage to a
dealer in Austria. Is there any proof of that?'

Simonetti shrugged. 'Actual proof? That's difficult to say.
But there are documents in the archive showing that's what
the British suspected.'

'So why didn't they do anything?'

'It was the end of the war. They had better things to do
than pursuing some little Venetian guy over a box of papers.
Besides, it was embarrassing for them. They'd sent Shawcross
off on a pointless mission. One that killed him. If they'd stayed
put at the Villa Godi Malinverni everything would have been
all right. Except that Alvise Fabris would not, somehow, have
acquired the money to buy a *palazzo* that would normally
have been beyond the range of a humble mechanic.'

'How many people know about this?'

'Difficult to say. Mazzon suspects it, of course – I think he's
seen some references in the State Archive – but he's never seen
any actual proof. That leaves you. Me. Anna. And Gianluca.'

'They know?'

'Sure they know. I've known Gianluca for years. Anna's

father found out the truth and left a letter for her to find after his death. He never spoke a word of it to *nonno* Alfredo. So when I put the box up for sale, Gianluca asked me – no, he begged me – to withdraw it. Just for a couple of months, he said. At least until after the election, or at least until Anna's grandfather had died. *Nonno* Alfredo didn't need to know the truth about his father.'

'But this is a hundred years ago. None of this is Anna's fault.'

'No. But she's based a campaign on being honest.'

'Is this really enough to finish her?'

'Maybe not. But it doesn't have to. Remember, she has to win outright in the first ballot. Otherwise Meneghini will clear up the far right votes in the *ballottaggio*. All he needs is an edge of a couple of percentage points.'

He made his way over to the bookcase, and ran his hands over the spines. He adjusted his spectacles, as if to be absolutely sure that he was in the right place, and took down a stack of paperbacks. Then, reaching into the gap behind them, he took out a box, smiling as he blew dust from the lid.

A shoebox. That's all it was. A shoebox that had passed from the custodian of the Villa Godi Malinverni, to Luchino Visconti, to Franco Zeffirelli, to Fabio Simonetti.

The Visconti Box.

He placed it on the table and tapped the lid. 'There's more than enough in here to finish Fabris's career.'

'What are you going to do with it, Fabio?'

He shrugged. 'Gianluca's a friend, as I said. I can't pretend the money wouldn't be useful. But I told him I'd sit on it for

now. Perhaps I always will, I haven't really thought it out yet.'
He smiled. 'I think Mazzon always suspected. At least, he
kept offering me ever-increasing amounts of money. Which
I kept turning down for some weird reason called "friend-
ship". And then one day you came into my shop talking about
Visconti this and Visconti that, and I thought no English guy
can be that interested in him. So the first thing I did when
you were out of the door was to call Gianluca to tell him
somebody else was sniffing around.'

I looked down at the box. 'So what now, Fabio? There
are people, bad people, who want to get their hands on this.
What are we going to do?'

He opened his mouth to speak, but was interrupted by a
sound from downstairs.

'What's that?', I said.

'Shh.'

I listened. From below came a rhythmic hammering
against the front door, followed by the sound of splintering
wood.

'Shit.'

'What is it?' said Fabio.

'If we're lucky, it's just someone breaking in.'

'And if we're not?'

'Then a man called Havok is coming to kill you and take
the Visconti Box.'

'You're serious?' Simonetti took out his phone. 'So let's call
the cops.'

'No time. What about your neighbours?' I heard the tread
of feet upon the stairs, and ran over to the apartment door
and locked it.

'Every other flat is a tourist let. There's nobody here at this time of year.'

I dragged a chair across the room and wedged it under the handle. It rattled, and then the entire door shook as the intruder applied his weight to it. 'That's not going to hold him for long.'

'What are we going to do?'

'We could fight him, but that'd end badly.' I ran my hands through my hair. 'Okay. We just need to buy ourselves some time. Get me a box. Any sort of box.'

Fabio ran to the bookshelves, grabbed a box file and tipped out the contents. 'Will this do?'

'Perfect. Now give me a large book. Preferably something you don't mind losing.'

'Telephone directory?'

'Excellent.' I grabbed it from him, and dropped it into the box file. 'Lighter fluid, matches, anything like that. Quickly.'

He yanked open a drawer in his desk, and tossed a Zippo to me, followed by a small can of butane.

'You know, Fabio, smoking might actually be about to save your life,' I said, as I emptied the contents of the can into the box file.

'Mister, does your plan involved burning down my house?'

'I hope it won't come to that.' I made my way over to the window, and pulled it up, looking out at the scaffolding. 'Can you get down there?'

Fabio shrugged. 'I can try.'

'Good. Then you take the Visconti Box, climb down and run like a bastard.'

'Mister, I'm seventy-three years old and I smoke eighty cigarettes a day. Run where?'

The door shuddered. 'Anywhere. We haven't got much time, Fabio.'

'I've got my boat. Would that help?'

'A boat? Just the thing. Now get going, I'll hold him as long as I can.'

'Are you sure about this?'

'Get going, Fabio.'

I helped him through the window and on to the working platform, and watched as he made his way, painfully slowly, down the ladder. Behind me, I heard the sound of wood splintering. That just left the chair, and that wouldn't hold him for more than a few seconds.

I swung my legs over the sill, and on to the platform. Then I balanced the box file on the windowsill, and waited, lighter in hand.

The door gave way as Havok forced his way into the room. I stared straight into his eyes, and flicked the lighter.

'One step, Havok. One step more, and it all goes up.'

He took a half-step forward, but I shook my head.

'Do you think you can get to it in time? Maybe you can? Maybe you'll be able to save the contents? But maybe you won't.'

The flame wavered for a moment and Havok took another half-step before stopping. 'It's a Zippo, Havok. These things stay lit even in a gale.' I hoped that was true.

'I'm going to hurt you for this, you English ponce.'

'Me? I'm the ponce? Listen, I'm not the one at the beck and call of a couple of posh boys. You don't even get to wear your stupid woolly hat indoors unless your boss says you can.' I moved the lighter closer to the box. 'Come on. Have a go, if you've got the balls. Come on, Havok. Or should I say, *Francesco.*'

I heard the roar building in his throat as he threw himself across the room. And then I dropped the lighter into the box, and turned and ran. From behind me I heard a *whumph* as the contents went up in flames, and the sound of Havok crashing through the window.

I took the steps of the ladder two at a time. From above I could hear Havok screaming and cursing as he tried to extinguish the flames. Then he swore once more upon discovering that the box held nothing more than a charred copy of the Venice telephone directory, and I heard the clang of boots against metal as he set off in pursuit. His mood, I suspected, would not have improved, and I tried to put out of my mind the numerous terrible things the *Irriducibili* had done to their rivals.

I jumped to the ground, slipped and fell. I scrabbled back to my feet, and ran along the jetty to where Fabio was waiting. He'd cast off and the motor was already running. I let myself down into the boat, and he gunned the engine.

I heard footsteps thundering along the pontoon, and took a look back. Havok reached the end of the jetty and, for a moment, I feared he was about to jump after us. Then he stopped short and stood there, silhouetted against the lights of the surrounding apartments, breathing deeply and cursing in his thick Roman accent.

We motored on in silence until we were out into the midst of the lagoon. Fabio idled the engine.

'You okay?'

He nodded. 'How about you?

'Not too bad.'

'So what do we do now?'

'What you said. Call the police.' I took my phone out but he grabbed my hand.

'We can't do that. They'll ask too many questions. I promised Gianluca I wouldn't say a word about this.'

'You can't go back home. Not when it's dark.'

'I could ring Gianluca and Anna. They've got a spare room.'

'Gianluca's in a hotel somewhere. You can stay at ours. If you can sleep on a sofa, that is.'

Fabio shrugged. 'I can sleep anywhere.'

'Good. You'll have to smoke outside though.'

Chapter 45

Fabio Simonetti sat at the tiller of his boat and smoked furiously, as if making up for his enforced abstinence over the past twelve hours. He guided us down the Rio di San Luca, past the baroque facade of the church of San Moise which conspired to make even the Versace store opposite the Hotel Bauer look understated, and out into the mouth of the *bacino*.

It was chillier here, and a stiff breeze made me pull my coat tightly around me. Fabio didn't appear to notice the cold, and carried on quietly and systematically smoking his way through the pack, as he steered us around the Punta della Dogana and into the Giudecca Canal.

San Giorgio della Maggiore. Zitelle. Redentore. The churches slid past us as I reflected that, nice as it might be to actually have a boat, it was undoubtedly both colder and rougher than travelling by vaporetto.

Fabio turned us under the bridge, just before the Palanca vaporetto stop, down the canal that led to the open lagoon, and pulled into his mooring.

He hadn't said a word the entire journey. Then he tied the boat up, hauled himself on to the *fondamenta* and extended a hand down to me.

'Are you all right, Fabio?'

He muttered something that might have been 'we'll see'. He pushed open the door to the apartment block, and we made our way upstairs. He laid his hand upon the door and took a deep breath.

'Come on then,' he said. The door swung open at his touch.

I hadn't expected it to be good. I hadn't expected it to be that bad, either.

Every poster had been torn from the wall. Those in frames had had their glass smashed.

Havok had evidently gone back to see if he could find any trace of the box. When he couldn't, he'd decided to destroy as much as he could. Just *because* he could.

Fabio swayed on his feet for a moment. I tried to take his arm but he shook it off.

'Just let me sit down for a minute, okay?' He looked around. 'It seems he never got around to smashing the furniture at least.' He sat down, his hands shaking as he lit another cigarette.

'Fabio, I'm so sorry.'

He shook his head. 'Not your fault.' He sighed, and his voice cracked as he spoke again. 'But this was everything, you know? A lifetime of collecting. And now—' He shrugged. 'Just because the spiteful bastard couldn't find what he wanted.'

I dropped to my knees, and smoothed out the poster next to me. Fellini. *Juliet of the Spirits.*

'That's signed, you know? By Fellini and Giulietta Masina. His wife.'

It was torn, but perhaps repairable. I folded it as best I could. 'Come on then, Fabio. Let's get to work.'

'I don't understand?'

'Clearing up. We rescue whatever we can. And I'll get a locksmith round to fix the door.'

'Nathan, you're trying to be kind and I thank you for that. But what's the point?'

'The point is we're going to rescue as much of this stuff as possible. And you're going to need a lock on your door.'

'And what if he comes back?'

I shook my head. 'He won't be coming back. I guarantee that.'

Fabio shook his head as if he wasn't convinced. In all honesty, I wasn't either.

We sat in the middle of the room and surveyed what we'd managed to rescue. He was trying to put a brave face on it but there was no denying the 'destroyed' pile was bigger than the 'could be saved' pile.

He sighed. 'Thank you, Nathan. I think that's all we can do.'

'I'm sorry, Fabio.'

'Some of this stuff was going to be my pension, you know. Oh well. Guess I can keep the shop going for a few more years.'

'You still have the Visconti Box. At some point you'll be able to sell that.'

He shook his head. 'No. That's for you.'

'I don't understand?'

'Take the damn thing, Nathan. I don't want it in the house any more. I'm not saying I'm superstitious, or I believe in fate or any of that bollocks. But it doesn't seem to make anyone happy, does it? I don't want it. So you take it. And you decide what to do with it.'

Chapter 46

Gramsci curled up inside the Visconti Box, as I leafed through its contents. Sketches and watercolours from officers stationed at the villa. A few scribblings by the Prince of Wales, mainly complaining about the food. Some not terribly good poetry. And a few letters from servicemen, aware that the end of the war was now in sight, but scarcely daring to hope that they might be the ones fortunate enough to return home.

There were also papers from the last days of the British occupation of the villa, mainly inventories and logistical papers. And there I found it, a report into the death of Captain Thomas Shawcross who had been killed whilst transporting papers belonging to Andrea Palladio to Venice.

His car had been ambushed, and Shawcross had been shot through the head, following which the vehicle had been set on fire. His driver, Alvise Fabris, escaped with a flesh wound and managed to call for help at a nearby village. Of the papers, there was no sign.

It was convenient. Too convenient. The area of country between Calvene and Venice had been safe for months. And rumours persisted about a dealer in Austria who had acquired original papers by the great Italian architect Andrea Palladio, just a few months after the armistice.

There was, it had been agreed, little to be done. The British had neither the time nor energy to pursue this further. All everybody wanted was to return home. Captain Thomas Shawcross, therefore, would now be considered to have been killed in action at the battle of the Asiago Plain.

I sighed. What to do with the damn thing? Havok, I feared, might be interested in paying a call on me in the not too distant future. I supposed I could just burn it, in the same way that I had burned a copy of the Venice telephone directory, but that didn't sit right with me. I didn't care what the future Edward VIII thought about the catering arrangements at the Villa Godi Malinverni, but there were letters there by ordinary servicemen that needed to be preserved. Few as they were, banal as they might have been, they were all that remained of men long since cold in their graves. They deserved to be cherished for that.

Gramsci yowled as I tipped him out of the box, and replaced the papers.

Keys rattled in the door, and Fede came in, looking tired and red-eyed.

'*Ciao, cara.*'

'*Ciao, caro.*' She kissed me on the cheek, and then flopped down on the sofa.

'What's the matter?'

She looked up at me. 'You haven't heard?'

I'll make this as quick as possible, and I won't be taking any questions afterwards. I'm tired, and I'm really not in the mood.

I'm sorry. Maybe sometime later, but not now.

It is as simple as this. I have not been honest with you, and I have not been honest with myself.

Following the death of my father, I came across documents from my great-grandfather. Documents in which he expressed regret for his actions during the war.

I have to accept that my great-grandfather was not the honest soldier, wounded in the service of his country, that our family believed him to be. Instead, he was a man who murdered a British serviceman and sold part of our country's national heritage to a dealer in a country that we still considered to be the enemy. What my family have – our money, where we live – is a result of this.

I knew this. And I kept it quiet. More than that, I destroyed the evidence of what had happened. I told myself that it was for the best, that the actions of a century past had no relevance for today. I told myself that it was to protect my grandfather.

I wonder if I was being completely honest with myself.

And a British gentleman, a good man in poor health, went to his grave without ever knowing the full story about the death of his ancestor. I could have given him that closure and I chose not to. I lied.

I've based this campaign around honesty. And you all deserve somebody who will be honest. I've fallen short, and so I'm here to announce that I will not be contesting the mayoral election.

Fede clicked off the TV.

I stared down at the papers in the box. 'So this was all for nothing. Meneghini and Mazzon, hunting for it for months, and it turned out they didn't even need it. Half of Simonetti's archive destroyed.' I picked up the papers and riffled through them. 'For nothing. I may as well have burned them.'

Fede slipped her arms around my neck. 'There's nothing we can do now, *caro*. Except perhaps get the bunting out for Meneghini.'

I shook my head. 'Maybe not.' I patted her hand, then made my way to the door and grabbed my coat.

'Where are you going?'

'I'm going to have a little chat with our prospective mayor.'

'And what are you going to do?'

'I don't know. But I'm pretty sure it's going to make me feel a whole lot better.'

'Nothing stupid, though?'

'Nothing stupid.' I wasn't one hundred per cent sure of that.

Chapter 47

I pressed at Meneghini's doorbell again and again, until he picked it up with a weary '*Chi è?*'

'It's Nathan Sutherland, Meneghini. I need to talk to you.'

'Nathan?' He paused for a moment as if trying to remember my name. 'Look, does it have to be now? I'm a little busy. Could you ring my secretary, make an appointment perhaps?'

'I could. Or I could just stand here all afternoon with my finger on your buzzer. Which I'm prepared to do.'

He swore under his breath, but the door buzzed and clicked open. 'First floor.'

I walked through into the main hall, where the bright winter sun shone through the watergate, casting dancing blue shadows on the ceiling.

A watergate. How very appropriate for a politician.

I made my way upstairs. Meneghini was waiting for me, casually dressed and holding a glass of prosecco.

He pressed it into my hand. 'Come on in then, Nathan. Seeing as you're here.'

He waved me through into the living room. A flat-screen TV, mounted on the wall, was showing footage of Anna's press conference.

. . . and so I'm here to announce that I will not be contesting the mayoral election.

Meneghini chuckled, picked up the remote control, and turned the volume off. He raised his glass. 'Not going to congratulate me?'

I did my best to smile, and raised my glass. It was probably good prosecco, but it had a sour taste.

'You haven't won yet, Giuseppe.'

'Nathan, it's all over bar the counting. Most of Anna's supporters will be transferring to the *Partito Democratico* I imagine, but there'll be plenty left over for me. They won't be counting the votes so much as weighing them. Come on, let's be friends. I meant what I said about the *palazzo* by the Accademia. And you never know, I might not be so bad.'

'You've pushed and bullied and manipulated a good woman into stepping down. And who knows what you've done to her family. To her kids. To her grandfather.'

'At least she's been honest for once, Nathan. When we first met I told you that Anna Fabris was a liar.'

'About events from a hundred years ago.'

'I know. But she lied about it. She covered it up. People won't forgive that.'

'She's a politician. People expect it.'

'Not of lovely Anna Fabris, they don't. If you make a big point of being the only honest candidate, then you'd better make damn sure you've never told even the whitest of little white lies in your life.' Meneghini held the tips of his thumb and forefinger a millimetre apart, as if to indicate just how tiny this particular white lie would have to be. 'But perhaps you're right. People might get over the fact that her great-grandad wasn't a war hero after all, but actually a grubby little murderer. Face it, we've all got embarrassing relatives in the closet, haven't we?' He smiled at me. 'Even your wife, as I understand?'

I smiled back at him, and shrugged.

If I do this, I thought, *I'll have lost the moral high ground. Ah, to hell with it.*

I punched him in the face as hard as I could.

Meneghini fell backwards, sprawling across his leather sofa. He tried to get to his feet, failed, and sat down heavily. He screwed his eyes shut, shaking his head and then, unsteadily, raised himself up.

'Bastard,' he said, balling his fists.

'You want a fight, Giuseppe? You want to appear on TV with a black eye or a split lip.' I looked around. 'You really want to trash your lovely apartment? Well, come on then. I'm game.'

'You stupid English prick. I'll make you pay for this.'

'Oh no. Should I withdraw my application for the 1920 Club?'

'When I'm mayor, I'm going to enjoy every last minute of making life very, very difficult for you, Sutherland.'

He clenched his fist again, as if wondering whether to chance his luck or not. The thought struck me that I had no idea if Giuseppe Meneghini was actually any good at fighting and that, just possibly, I might have pushed my luck a bit too far.

We were interrupted by the buzz of the door phone. Meneghini waved a weary hand at me. 'I'd better take this, okay? *Chi è?*' I heard the crackle of a voice on the other end, but could not distinguish the words. 'Andrea? Andrea, now's really not a good time, okay? Can we meet tomorrow? Give me a call, yeah?'

He hung up. Immediately the door phone buzzed, and buzzed again.

'Oh Christ.' He pressed the entry button, and leaned back against the wall, breathing deeply.

There was a knocking, and then a hammering, from outside.

'Christ,' Meneghini repeated, shaking his head. He opened the door.

Despite the cold, I could see beads of sweat on Mazzon's forehead. He was formally dressed, as ever, but his tie was not as immaculately knotted as was usual. His face was badly cut and bruised. Someone had, indeed, done a very good job on him.

'Giuseppe, we need to talk.' Then he noticed me for the first time, and did a double-take.

'As Giuseppe says, Andrea, now isn't a brilliant time. We were kind of having a fight.'

'I don't understand.' Then he waved a hand, and turned away from me. 'No matter. Giuseppe, you've not been answering my calls.'

'Haven't I? I'm sorry Andrea, things have been a bit crazy over the past few days. As you can imagine.' He nodded towards the TV and grinned as Anna Fabris silently repeated her resignation speech again. 'Look, perhaps it might be better to give my secretary a call. I'm not quite sure how clear my diary is at present, but I'm sure he'll be able to sort something out.'

Mazzon ran a hand across his face. 'Look at this, Giuseppe. Havok did this to me. You paid him, didn't you?'

Meneghini smiled. 'I'm afraid I don't know what you're talking about, Andrea.' His smile grew ever wider. 'Although, you were rather taking your time about making good on your promise to find the box. Which is almost funny. As it turns out, we didn't need it after all.'

Mazzon spread his hands wide. 'Look Giuseppe, here's what's going to happen. Given all I've done for you. Given what I know. I thought perhaps we might arrange a press conference together. Formally announce things, perhaps even start discussing what position I might take in the administration.'

Meneghini rubbed his forehead. 'Yes. Yes, of course. As I said, speak to my secretary. He'll find a date for us.'

Silence hung in the air.

'Well, this is awkward,' I said. Both Meneghini and Mazzon turned to stare at me. 'Look, I'm sure you've got lots to talk about, so I'll be off.'

Meneghini moved to the door, and pulled it open. 'I think you should both go.'

Mazzon shook his head. 'I'm sorry, Giuseppe, but I'm not going anywhere. Not until this is sorted out.'

'It's not the best time, Andrea. Really.'

'After everything I've done for you, Giuseppe. You owe me this.'

'Oh Andrea,' I said. 'Don't you get it? He's just not that into you.'

Mazzon merely smiled. 'You think I didn't know that?' he said.

'You were expecting this?'

'I did wonder. Especially in the past couple of days. Fabris's poll ratings start to slip and Giuseppe's closing in on that magic fifty per cent barrier. Because I keep my mouth shut. Because we need the voters to think that Gianluca Casagrande beat me up, and not just some cheap football lout for hire. And then Fabris pulls out, and all of a sudden, Giuseppe isn't returning my calls. Because, perhaps, he's starting to think that he can manage without me.' He smiled again. 'And so, I'm here to tell him that, no, he can't.'

Meneghini sighed. 'Andrea, I'm tired, I'm pissed off and my head is ringing like a bell since that son-of-a-bitch punched me. So if you don't mind, I'm going to have a drink and go to bed early. Call me in the morning, eh?'

I looked over at Mazzon. 'See? It's "I'm washing my hair tonight" all over again.'

Mazzon ran a hand through his hair. 'No. I'm not going to call you in the morning. We're going to talk about this right now. I want a commitment from you that you're going to honour every promise you made to me.' He jabbed a finger in my direction. 'Mr Sutherland, I'd like you to stay here to witness this please.'

I shrugged. 'Okay. If you think it'll be useful.'

Meneghini shook his head, and walked over to the drinks cabinet. He poured himself a generous measure of whisky, and downed it in one. Then he looked at the empty glass, shrugged, and poured himself another.

'I don't suppose there's any chance—' I began.

He jabbed a finger at me. 'You. Shut up.' Then he pointed at Mazzon. 'Okay, Andrea. Why don't you sit down?'

Mazzon took a seat on the black leather sofa, his right leg twitching.

'It's like this, Andrea. We had an agreement, okay? That's politics. People do this sort of thing all the time. And sometimes they even honour those agreements.' He shook his head. 'But not this time, Andrea. You see, with Fabris now out of the race, I don't really need you. In fact, it might be even better if I formally rule out any sort of coalition with you at all. The idea could scare off some of the lovely voters I might inherit from her. I don't think you have much of an intersection on a Venn diagram.'

'Nevertheless, you're going to keep this promise, Giuseppe.'

'I am? Tell me why?'

'Because I know where all the bodies are buried.'

'But that's just the thing, Andrea. There aren't any bodies buried. We have the accidental death of a very sick Englishman in a cemetery in Cavalletto. That's all.' He leaned forward. 'The brilliance of this is that we haven't actually done anything wrong.'

I coughed. 'I think attempted blackmail is kind of doing something wrong, Giuseppe.'

'Shut up. Look, Andrea. It's nothing personal. It's politics.'

'We had a deal, Meneghini.'

'He's right, you know,' I said. 'You really couldn't have done it without him. He was the one who was contacted by Anthony Shawcross. Poor, sad, dying Anthony Shawcross who just wanted to find out what had happened to his grandfather. Just to have a few memories of him to leave to the rest of his family.

'Mazzon's researching the battle of the Asiago Plain. He

finds a trail that leads to Anna Fabris's great-grandfather and the sale of papers that once belonged to Andrea Palladio to a private collector just after the war.'

Mazzon shook his head. 'As Meneghini says, there's nothing wrong in what we did. We just made sure the truth came to light. The public had a right to know.'

'You manipulated a sick man into doing your dirty work for you. So you could pretend you were keeping your hands clean. Inviting him to that event at San Rocco, giving him the contact details for Fabris and Casagrande. In the hope that eventually he'd break the story. Except that didn't happen. The poor guy did the decent thing. He decided that nobody else needed to have their heart broken over the whole affair. And he got his final wish to visit his grandfather's grave but it was too much for him. You manipulated him. You tried to manipulate Anna and Gianluca. It's disgusting, whichever way you look at it.'

Meneghini shrugged. 'You call it disgusting. I call it politics.'

'And Mazzon's price for this information was, simply, a ride on your ticket. Deputy mayor, perhaps, with the power to put some of his nastier little ideas into practice. Except now,' I looked over at Mazzon, 'that's not going to happen is it? In fact,' I turned back to Meneghini, 'was it ever going to happen? There are other, more mainstream parties you could have worked with. Ah, but I remember what you said to me at the 1920 Club. About being able to control people. You thought Andrea Mazzon would be easier to manipulate than an actual seasoned politician. Who might be as big a bastard as you. I'm right, aren't I, Giuseppe?'

Meneghini said nothing.

Mazzon laughed. 'Well, we'll see. We'll see how easy I am to manipulate. Because all I have to do is go to the press and tell them everything.'

'You won't do that, Andrea. You'll ruin what little reputation you have left.'

'We'll see. We'll see.' Mazzon turned to the door. 'Get out of the way, Giuseppe.'

'You're not going to go the police, Andrea.'

'Oh? Aren't I?' Mazzon reached into his jacket and took out a revolver.

Meneghini raised an eyebrow. 'You've got a gun?'

'He's a fascist obsessed with the war, Giuseppe. He's probably got a collection,' I said.

Mazzon raised the gun and levelled it at Meneghini.

'You won't shoot, Andrea.'

'Won't I?' Mazzon's hands were shaking.

'Put the gun down, Andrea.'

Meneghini reached out towards Mazzon.

And then Mazzon, his hands shaking almost uncontrollably, shot him.

Meneghini clutched his arm, and then dropped to the floor. We stood there, in the silence, as the roaring in our ears diminished.

Mazzon continued to shake. 'Oh Christ,' he said. 'Oh Christ.'

I dropped to my knees beside Meneghini. 'Giuseppe?'

He took his hand away from his arm, and looked at the blood that was dripping onto his immaculate white marble floor.

'You stupid bastard, Andrea.' He clenched his teeth against the pain. 'I'll bury you for this.'

Mazzon raised the gun once more. 'No you won't. I'll bury you, Giuseppe.' He turned to me. 'Both of you.'

I threw myself at him, reaching for the gun, and toppled him over. Mazzon was first on his feet, and kicked out at my face; and I lost my grip as I cried out in pain. He raised the gun, and I threw my hands, uselessly, in front of my face.

Then Meneghini was grabbing at him, trying to wrestle the gun away. Mazzon was slight in comparison, but the bigger man was bleeding profusely now. The two of them staggered backwards and forwards, as Mazzon did all he could to turn the gun on his adversary. Then, in an instant, Meneghini pulled him close, and another shot rang out.

Mazzon said nothing, but merely clutched a hand to his chest and staggered through the door. As Meneghini and I watched, he toppled down the staircase, across the hall, and into the water.

Meneghini slumped to the floor as I stood there and watched Mazzon's body spiral in the water, his blood turning it a deep crimson.

Meneghini's breathing was ragged, but he managed to smile.

'If there was any doubt, I've just won the election, Sutherland,' was all he said, as the reflected light on the ceiling turned from blue to a rusty red.

Chapter 48

'How's the head, Nathan?'

I touched the bruise above my eye. 'Not too bad, Vanni. It's a bit sore, though. Fede says I probably shouldn't hold any surgeries for a few days. Might look bad if people think the Honorary Consul has been in a fight.'

'Well, you have been in a fight.' He reached into his desk drawer for a cigar, and then remembered that was something he didn't do any more and sighed.

'Quite a collection, the late *dottor* Mazzon had. The one he used on Meneghini is,' he consulted the papers in front of him, 'a Beretta M1915. Probably hadn't been used in over a century. He must have taken very good care of it.' He smiled. 'Fine piece of Italian engineering.'

'How's Meneghini?'

'Doing well. They say he'll be leaving hospital in a couple of days. I imagine his approval ratings will be going through the roof. Mayoral candidate attacked in his own home. Bravely fights off intruder despite being shot. It's going to take a lot to stop him now.'

'Shit. Maybe I should just have left the two of them to shoot lumps out of each other.'

'Nothing to be done now, Nathan. And who knows, maybe he won't be such a bad mayor after all.' He smiled but was, I thought, trying a bit too hard.

'Nathan! Hey, Nathan!' Ed called out to me from the Magical Brazilians.

'Hi, Ed.'

'Thought your head seemed to be in the clouds there. You didn't even look up.'

'Sorry. Mind's on other things at the moment.'

'Come in for a minute, eh? I'll fix you a Negroni.' He looked at my face and winced. 'On the house, even. Looks like you might need it.'

'Ah, thanks, Ed. I think I do.'

'Bitter?'

'Very.'

'Angostura bitters, I mean?'

I shook my head. 'God, my head's all over the place at the moment. Thanks, Ed, that'd be good.'

'Anyway, I'm glad you've come in. Always good to see my famous buddy.' He drew a *Gazzettino* from the rack, passed it to me, and turned back to mixing my cocktail.

I saw the headline, and swore when I saw the name beneath. 'Bastard.'

'What's wrong, man?'

'You've seen the headline, I take it?'

'Sure. Sorry, I thought you had as well.'

'I've been at the *Questura* all morning. No, I hadn't. Oh Christ, look at this.'

Meneghini injured in frenzied attack. Mayoral candidate

saves life of British Consul.

Meneghini was pictured in his hospital bed, grimacing through the pain as he gave a thumbs-up for the camera.

'I just did what anyone else would have done.'

'Roberto Bergamin.' I shook my head. 'You absolute prick.'

It is understood Meneghini and British Consul Nathan Sutherland have become firm friends in recent weeks.

Ed's Negroni's are good. His free ones are even better. But never had I wanted to finish a drink so quickly . . .

'Pronto?'

'Bergamin. You bastard!'

'Nathan! How are you?'

'You son-of-a-bitch. You stupid, stupid son-of-a-bitch. Do you know what you've just done?'

'Erm, I've got my name under a big front page headline for the first time in months?'

'If there was any doubt about it before, you've just gone and won the election for Meneghini, you know that?'

'Nathan, Nathan. It's not like that, okay? All I do is write the story. Headline's not down to me. That's the sub-editor's job.'

'And Meneghini lying in bed bravely smiling through the pain? Oh, and not forgetting, saving his life of his best buddy the British Honorary Consul. You had nothing to do with that?'

Bergamin sighed. 'Look, it's not down to me what sort of spin a sub puts on a story. But everyone here has kind of decided that Meneghini is going to win the election and so they all want to be on his side. You know, invites to parties, front seats at the Regata Storica and the fireworks at Redentore. You know how it is.'

'You seem mighty sure he's going to win.'

'Look, Fabris has withdrawn. Andrea Mazzon is dead. There's hardly anyone left to vote for. I guess the *Partito Democratico* will pick up most of Anna's votes, and the *Lega* will get Mazzon's, but nowhere near enough. Anyway, there's two ways I look at it. Either he's just another shit mayor – who cares, we've had plenty of those and we survived – or he turns out to be okay. Either way, everyone wins in the end.' He paused. 'Anyway, Nathan, why worry? You don't get a vote, do you?'

'I don't get a vote but it bloody well affects me all the same.'

'Calm down, man, calm down. You'll do yourself a mischief getting in a state like this. Look – and I'm being serious here – thanks for the heads-up on this. Really. It's done my career the power of good. And, you know, if I can help you out in the future, give me a call eh?'

'Oh, be sure of it, Roberto.'

He showed no sign of picking up on the sarcasm in my voice. 'Thanks again, Nathan. I owe you one. And you were right, politics is more interesting than I thought.'

I was lying on the sofa, half-asleep when I heard Federica come in.

'Ciao, caro.'

'Ciao, cara.'

She sat on the arm of the sofa, and leaned over to kiss me, her hair damp with rain and cold against my cheek.

'You're freezing.'

'Yes, it's a bit cold out.' She held my face in her hands, and I shivered and laughed at the same time. 'That's better. That's warmed me up a little. Come on, shift up.'

I lifted my legs up, making space for her to sit down, and then draped them across her lap.

'You've seen the newspapers, I take it.'

She nodded.

'Are you cross?'

'What about?'

'I seem to have won the election for someone you despise.'

'Oh, that? No, I'm not cross. You tried to do the right thing.'

'Let me see now. In the past week I've dealt with politicians, fascists, journalists, oh, and a football hooligan. I wonder if there's anyone I've missed. You know, serial killers and the like. At least they're horrible within established parameters.'

She sighed. 'Come on then. What's going to cheer you up?'

'Unplugging Meneghini's life support?'

'Okay. Perhaps something that isn't first-degree murder? What about some of your horrible music?'

I shook my head. 'Believe it or not, I'm not really in the mood.'

'Okay. Things are worse than I thought. What if I go out to get pizza tonight and we watch one of your horrible films?'

'Even *Suspiria*?'

'Even *Suspiria*.'

'Aww. You really are the best wife in the world.'

'I know.' She checked her watch. 'Still a bit early to eat though. Maybe there's something else we can do as well.'

I grinned. 'You mean?'

'Yes. Get your coat.'

'Oh.'

Chapter 49

The vaporetto journey from Sant'Angelo to San Silvestro takes about four minutes.

Federica felt every one of them, checking the online edition of *La Nuova* on her phone, and cursing as she saw the headline. She swore more loudly than I was expecting, and I winced as some of the passengers in nearby seats turned reproving glances on us. Two little girls laughed out loud, mentally adding some new words to their vocabulary. The grey-haired woman at their side shook her head and wagged a finger at them both. They did their best to look contrite but, as soon as her back was turned, they whispered excitedly to each other.

I couldn't help but smile, which was the wrong decision as grandma saw the expression on my face and scowled.

'I don't want their *mamma* to think they learned those words from me.'

'Sorry.'

I caught sight of the newspaper headline and photograph. Meneghini, smiling as best he could through the pain, waving from his hospital bed. His ratings, according to the headline, had indeed gone through the roof whilst Mazzon's had, for obvious reasons, disappeared altogether.

The woman jabbed a finger at the photograph. 'There's a good man. *Un vero Veneziano*. He'll be so good for this city.'

Fede, I could see, was about to say something regrettable. I hooked my arm under hers and, as gently as I could, pulled her to her feet.

'What are you doing?'

I smiled at her and then at the *signora*. 'We're getting off soon.'

'It's raining outside.'

'Well, the fresh air will do us good.' I smiled at the *signora* who gave me a nod best described as courteous, and then turned back to the little girls. They'd been giggling and whispering to each other, but – in fear of another furious finger-wagging – turned off their smiles as soon as grandma turned her gaze upon them.

We made our way outside the cabin. Immediately, the wind whipped at us, and irate cries of '*La porta!*' came from within. I smiled, and nodded, apologising to the entire cabin, and pulled the door shut.

'What was that all about?'

'I'm sorry. I didn't want you to start a fight. Or have a corrupting effect upon the younger generation.'

Fede huffed.

'Anyway, a bit of fresh air will do us good. Blow the cobwebs away, eh?' I took a deep breath of the cold air. 'Bracing, isn't it?'

Fede was about to answer, but the wind changed direction, blowing her hair this way and that across her face.

'Am I being too English again?' I said.

She nodded.

The *marinaio* kept staring at us as the boat crawled its way along the Grand Canal, wondering why we were not availing ourselves of the warm, dry cabin. Presumably he thought we were tourists anxious not to miss a moment, no matter how inclement the weather.

The canal itself was quiet. The delivery barges had finished work for the day. And yet, even on a rainy January afternoon, a couple of gondoliers still plied their trade, their passengers wrapped up in plastic ponchos and shielding themselves as best they could with umbrellas.

We disembarked, finally, at San Silvestro. Fede took shelter in the pontoon cabin for a couple of seconds, in an attempt to sort her hair out, and then realised it was a hopeless task.

She shook her head, grabbed my arm, and marched me through the chilly streets to Campo San Polo and the *palazzo* that Alvise Fabris had bought with the proceeds of murder, a century past.

'Nathan. Federica. Come in.' Gianluca looked at the wound above my eyebrow. 'That looks nasty.'

'It's worse than it looks,' I said.

'He's being very brave,' said Fede.

'I am. But I'm self-medicating with Negronis so, you know, it's all good.'

Ginevra and Allegra ran into the room, attracted by the unfamiliar voices.

'Girls,' said Anna, 'why don't you go and have a chat with great-grandpa for a while?'

'He's asleep, *mamma*,' said Ginevra. Or was it Allegra?

'Okay, then. Just go and play quietly in your room for a bit. *Mamma* and *papà* have some things to talk about with Federica and Nathan.' She smiled. 'We won't be long. Promise.' The two of them turned on their heels and scampered from the room.

'How is your grandfather?' I said.

'He's better than you might expect. It's all been a shock – a dreadful shock to him – as you can imagine. But he's not too bad. I wonder if perhaps he knew more than we thought.'

'It's not something he should have to live with, though, is it?' said Gianluca. 'Not in his last days.'

I shook my head. 'No. Of course it isn't.' I turned to Anna. 'Why did you do it? Confessing everything on air and resigning like that?'

'Because of Luchino Visconti and that wretched box. Fabio called Gianluca, and told him what had happened. Sooner or later somebody was going to be killed because of it. And I couldn't have that on my conscience. So the only way was to confess everything. And by doing so, the box ceased to have any value.'

Fede put a hand on her arm. 'But that's not really why we're here.'

'No?'

She took a deep breath. 'I need to ask you something. And I'm afraid it's a big ask.'

'It is? I don't think I can manage that without caffeine. Gianluca, could you go and make us all coffee?' She smiled at me. 'You do drink coffee at this hour? I know the English are all supposed to have a cup of tea at five in the afternoon.'

'Coffee's good,' I said.

'Tea, if you have it,' said Federica, and Anna smiled again. 'Sit down. Please.'

We sat on the battered leather sofa, facing the discoloured patch on the wallpaper where the portrait of Alvise had once hung.

Anna saw the direction of my gaze. 'I imagine we'll be needing to redecorate' she said. Then she sighed. 'I suppose we'll have plenty of time.'

'That's why we're here,' said Fede. 'Or rather, it's especially why I'm here.'

'Oh yes?' Anna's voice was guarded, as if she knew what was coming next.

'I want you to contest the election. That's why I'm here.'

Anna smiled, sadly. 'I've been asked that quite a lot over the last day. And my answer, I'm afraid, is going to have to be the same. No. I think I'm done with politics.'

'Anna, you can't do this.'

'I have to.' She nodded in the direction of the girls' bedroom. 'For them. The last few days have been horrible. Press everywhere. At the door, on the phone. They don't understand it. It's frightening for them.' She shook her head. 'There were even photographs of them in the newspaper yesterday, on their way to school. I can't do this to them.'

'I know it's difficult. But you have to. You have to do this, because if you don't it's going to be spun as the little woman staying at home to look after her family and putting her children first. No matter how unfair that is, it's what the press will do. And the next mayor will be some ossified party apparatchik or, worse, some chancer of a businessman seeing this as a stepping-stone on the path to greater things.'

'I know all that. But it's asking a lot of my family. Maybe too much.'

'Anna,' I said, 'your little girls are going to find out what's happened within weeks. Days, even. There are probably kids at school giving them the eye already, whispering behind their backs. One day they're going to come home from school and ask you just why that portrait of great-great-grandfather is no longer hanging there.'

'And I'll tell them the truth. This time, at least.'

'They'll understand. Of course they will.' Fede nodded towards the window. 'And so will they. Everyone out there. You think you're the only one with relatives who did something despicable during the war?'

Anna shook her head. 'That's a dirty little secret for many families. But it's a secret that we like to pretend is hidden in someone else's attic. Not our own.'

'I wonder. People might appreciate the honesty.'

'I think the time for that has long since passed. Now, I'll forever be Anna Fabris, who covered up her family's shameful past in order to try and preserve her political career.'

'Or you could be the Anna Fabris who's that rarity amongst politicians – the one who admits they've done something wrong.' Fede sighed. 'But I'll be honest. It's not really about that. Not for me. I want you to run because I'm tired, just so tired of a succession of identical, uninspiring, second-rate men having a monopoly on this job. So tired that I don't even know if I can be bothered dragging my arse along to vote. Unless you're there. Come on, for once, we could have an intelligent woman – an intelligent Venetian woman – running things instead of another mediocrity who's only there because he's served enough time in the *Partito Democratico*, or the *Lega,* or the *Fratelli*.'

'Federica, I don't think I can win.'

'Maybe you can't. It's probably going to be that idiot Meneghini whose one tactical masterstroke in the whole campaign was managing to get himself shot. But maybe it won't be. And even if it is, for the next month at least a whole load of us in the city will at least be feeling a little bit of enthusiasm. That maybe things can actually change. That even now things can be turned around.'

Anna smiled, and turned to me. 'She's very good at this, you know?'

'I know. I should do what she says. That always works for me.'

'Or maybe, just maybe, you should be doing this yourself, Federica?'

'What?'

'Seriously. Why not?'

'Because— Well because I've never been involved in politics before. And all I know how to do is criticise stuff I don't like. I'm not sure I'd be any good at building things up from scratch. Also I don't have the right sort of hair and I'm a terrible diplomat.'

Anna turned back to me, and I threw my hands up in the air. 'Don't look at me. I'm not getting involved.'

She closed her eyes, and nodded to herself. 'Okay then. Maybe not this time. But think about what I said. And if you at least do that, then,' she took a deep breath, 'then I'll run.'

Fede smiled. Then she went over to Anna to hug her. 'Thank you.'

Gianluca chose that moment to enter the room. 'I seem to have missed something?'

Anna checked her watch. 'I think you have. Never mind the coffee. I was thinking perhaps we should share a bottle of prosecco together.'

'Prosecco? I don't understand.'

'*Dottoressa* Ravagnan has done a very good job of persuading me that I should re-enter the campaign.'

'Has she?' Gianluca raised an eyebrow. 'Oh Christ, does that mean we have to go through all this again?'

'Yes. Hopefully without murdering any of the remaining candidates. So, from tomorrow, we'll be back hard at work again. But this evening, I think, we can celebrate just a little. Oh, there are a couple of journalists I'll need to ring, of course. So that we can make the papers tomorrow morning. Poor *signor* Meneghini will just have to get used to not completely being the centre of attention.'

Gianluca sighed. 'Anna, I don't like saying this, but there is no way you can possibly win now. There are too many people lining up behind Meneghini. Do you really want to put yourself through this?'

'You know what, Gianluca? I think I do. Now, I think there's at least one bottle in the fridge. Be a darling and bring it out, would you? Oh, and four glasses of course.'

Gianluca shrugged. 'Ah well. Maybe I'll end up being Venice's first first gentleman after all. A shame. I was rather hoping to avoid the spotlight for a while.' He turned, and made his way back to the kitchen.

Anna shook her head. 'I don't think he needs to worry. Meneghini is going to win.'

We could only agree. But in the meantime, at least, there was prosecco.

Chapter 50

The adrenaline had worn off by the time we returned to the Street of the Assassins, and Fede slumped onto the sofa with a tired expression on her face.

'Would a Spritz Nathan help?'

'It would.'

I returned from the kitchen with our drinks to find her tapping away at her phone.

'Doomscrolling?'

'You could call it that. Some of the papers have the story already. The words "unlikely comeback" are being used. And some less kind words as well. "Fabris Flip-Flops". That sort of thing.' She yawned. 'You know, I'm really tired. Could you move that vase off the mantelpiece?'

'Er, yes.'

'Good. Now, can you throw a cushion across the room as hard as you can? I'm not sure I've really got the strength for it.'

'Okay.' I took one from the sofa and hurled it at the wall with all my strength. Gramsci yowled in delight as it dropped to the floor, and jumped on top of it, his claws scrabbling away.

'Better?'

'Much.' Then she sighed. 'Ah, but this is tough.'

'I know.'

'She'd have been so good. So, so good.'

'She would. But who knows what might happen?'

'I think we know. Realistically. Either Meneghini or some grey-faced time-serving party apparatchik will happen.' She sipped at her drink, her hand shaking and the ice cubes clattering. 'A man, of course. A middle-aged man. It's always a bloody middle-aged man. Just this once, just this bloody once, there was a chance to change the record. But no. It'll be another middle-aged man.' She looked at her glass. 'Oh look. My drink's vanished.'

'Do I need to be the Spritz Fairy again?'

'I think you do.'

'Do you think that's wise?'

'No. But we're going to, aren't we?'

I nodded and made my way back to the kitchen. The level in the Campari bottle, I noticed, was ominously low. There was, however, a full bottle of Aperol. It had taken up residence in the fridge several years ago now, waiting for visitors who preferred an Aperol spritz to Campari. It had remained unopened all these years. It seemed we just didn't have those sorts of friends.

One of us, therefore, was going to have to make the big sacrifice. I made two Spritz Nathans, one bitter, and one with the sickly orange stuff. My phone plinged, and I swore when I saw the contents of the message. I was on the verge of texting something abusive in reply and then paused. No. Perhaps not. And then I smiled.

I took our drinks through, red in my left hand, orange in my right. I stretched out the Aperol towards Fede. Disappointment flashed across her face and, without missing a beat, I passed her the Campari as if that was what I had intended all along.

'Thank you, *caro*.'

'So what now?'

'I think we get a little drunk.'

'And then?'

'Then you either cook us a fabulous dinner or we go out for pizza. I think the second is the better idea.'

'And then?'

'Well, we could watch a film I suppose. Maybe not one of your horrible ones. And certainly not anything by Visconti.'

'And then?

'And then we wake up tomorrow with a filthy hangover and just in the right mood to see whatever disastrous stories are in the newspapers. So, yes, that's one idea.'

'Or?'

'Or we could just go to bed now?'

I grinned, and drained my spritz. 'Yes. Maybe that's exactly what we should do?'

Fede got to her feet and grabbed my hand. 'Come on then. You might need to go out for pizza later.'

'Why not now?'

She rolled her eyes. 'No. later.'

'Oh. Right. But don't keep me up too late. I've got a busy day tomorrow. The next Mayor of Venice has invited me for a drink.'

'You what?'

I grinned. 'He absolutely has.'

'You said no, of course?'

'I absolutely didn't.'

'You're going to go for a drink with that bastard? Just so he can gloat.'

'Oh yes. I imagine a lot of gloating is going to happen.'

'Okay, I've got to be honest, I'm not sure I'm in the mood now.'

I smiled again. 'Okay. I'll go out to get pizza. And then I'll tell you all about it. But first of all, I need to phone Roberto Bergamin. I think the two of us need to go and have another chat with Mr Havok.'

Chapter 51

Harry's Bar.

I suppose you could call it the Venue of Legends. Ernest Hemingway, they say, had his own table here. If the many stories about him are even halfway true, he probably had one to sleep under as well. Truman Capote, Alfred Hitchcock and Arturo Toscanini had all sampled a Bellini or two. Orson Welles had dropped by in search of a restorative sherry. Even Charlie Chaplin had been in, but whether in civvies or in costume I couldn't be sure.

Giuseppe Meneghini sat across the table from me and smiled. 'Bellini?'

'I find them a bit too sweet. Spritz?'

'I don't think you come to Harry's Bar for a spritz, Nathan. They might despise us for that.'

'Perhaps not, then. Well, why don't you decide? What would Charlie Chaplin have had? No, better still, what would Hemingway have had?'

'Hemingway? More than I can aspire to pay for, I'm afraid. I'm not mayor yet, after all.'

It was my turn to smile. 'Why don't we have a brace of martinis, eh?'

Meneghini nodded at the waiter.

'So,' I said, 'how are things? How's the arm, for one thing.'

'Not too bad. Not too bad at all. The doctors tell me there was no long-term damage done.' He rubbed his jaw. 'I owe you for this one, of course.'

'I don't suppose we could just hug and make up over martinis?' He shook his head. 'Come on Giuseppe, what would Hemingway have done?'

'Probably shot you the next time he went hunting.'

'Well, I've never really been interested in that sort of thing.'

'Perhaps that's just as well, Nathan.'

Our martinis arrived. 'Cheers, Giuseppe.'

'Your continued good health, Nathan.'

We clinked glasses, setting the martini levels slopping perilously near the brim. I shuddered to think how much money could have spilled on to the table.

'Thank you for coming to meet me,' he said. 'I wasn't sure if you would.'

I shrugged. 'Well, I've never been here before. It would have seemed a waste of an opportunity not to.'

'And what do you think?'

I looked around at the immaculately polished tables, the white-jacketed waiters and the range of optics behind the bar, all glowing in the soft amber light. It was smart, yes. But at the end of the day, it was just a bar. More than that, it was a bar with no view.

'It's nice enough,' I said. 'I don't quite understand why exactly you wanted to meet here, though.'

'Well, I didn't want you to come round to my apartment. Not after last time.' He rubbed his jaw again. 'Besides, I wanted to be somewhere where we could be sure of not running into any Venetians.'

We both laughed.

'So, what now?'

'Well, it looks as if I'm going to be very busy over the next few weeks. This seemed the best chance we might have for a little chat.'

I nodded. 'You mean you've seen the polls and you've already been measuring the curtains for the mayor's office?'

He chuckled. 'That's a lovely English expression. But, yes, I suppose I have. Look, there's something I want to show you.' He clicked open his briefcase and took out that morning's edition of *La Nuova*. 'Perhaps you've already seen it?' I shook my head. 'No?' He smoothed it out on the table. 'The latest opinion polls. Look at that, eh? Over sixty per cent, now. No need even for a *ballottaggio*. I'll win comfortably in the first round.'

I nodded. 'I see. So, you just asked me out so I could offer my congratulations in advance.'

He grinned. 'That's about it. But don't feel so bad, Nathan. I'll pay for the drinks.'

I sighed. 'Well. I suppose that's something at least.'

He reached over and gently shook me by the shoulder. 'That's it. A bit of that famous English sangfroid.' Meneghini, I was coming to understand, evidently had quite a long list of things he considered to be quintessentially English. 'The stiff upper lip. Being a good sport even in defeat.'

'You're trying a bit too hard now, Giuseppe.'

'Don't feel too bad, Nathan. You might be surprised just how good a mayor I'll make.'

'I suppose the odds of us moving into the Palazzo Querini have receded?'

He nodded. 'Oh, and that restoration project at San Polo? Well, budgets might need to be cut over the next few years. Let's leave it at that, eh?'

'I understand.'

'You've been in Venice sometime now, as I understand? Maybe long enough? Maybe it's time you thought about moving on elsewhere?'

I nodded. 'You mean we go away, and don't create any more trouble and maybe, just maybe, you'll forgive me for being a pain in the arse. Is that right?'

'That's right.'

'Given that I know what actually happened.'

'That's what's so brilliant, Nathan. There's no proof that anything happened at all.'

I sighed. 'That's the problem, I suppose. No proof. Anyway, there's something we should talk about.'

He raised an eyebrow. 'Oh yes?'

I took the laptop case from over my shoulder, unzipped it, took out an A4 envelope, and passed it to him.

He smiled. 'The Visconti papers? As you know, I don't need them any more.'

'It's not that.' I chewed on the olive from my martini. 'Go on. Take a look.'

He carefully teased the top sheet from the envelope. As he read, the smile slowly vanished from his face. I did all I could to keep a neutral expression.

He read it again. And again. I could see his lips moving as if he couldn't quite believe what was there.

He pushed back his chair. 'The fuck is this?'

'It's your resignation statement, Giuseppe. From the election. You're going to withdraw your candidacy. I thought maybe you might like to state unspecified personal reasons. That sort of thing always goes down well enough. Now my Italian is good, but if you find any mistakes just let me know and I'll email you an updated copy.'

'Why the fuck do you think I'd do this?'

I winced. 'Look, do you think maybe you ought to mind your language? Just a bit. You know, there might be tourists here who speak Italian. They want to go away with a nice impression of Venice and the Venetians. I mean, you're the prospective mayor. You have an image to uphold.' I paused, and then grinned. 'Oh, I'm sorry. I meant to say, you *were* the prospective mayor.'

Meneghini screwed his eyes shut and gripped the edges of the table. Slowly, he opened them again, and looked once more at the sheet in front of him. Deliberately, slowly, he tore it into pieces.

'I'm sorry. As I said, my Italian's imperfect. I'll get my wife to proofread it and send you another one.'

'The fuck you will.'

He'd raised his voice a little too much this time and there was no avoiding the look of annoyance by a group on a nearby table. The white-jacketed waiter raised a hand, ever so gently, and mouthed the word *Signori!* in admonishment.

Meneghini leaned towards me and, for a moment, his hands reached towards me as if to grab the lapels of my coat. The waiter started, this time in genuine alarm, looking back over his shoulder to the rest of his team behind the bar. One of them, burly and bearded, gave him a nod.

Then Meneghini relaxed and sat back in his chair, breathing heavily. Again, he closed his eyes, and I could see his lips moving, as if counting to ten.

'Why should I do this?' he said.

'Take a look at the rest of the contents, Giuseppe.'

His hands scrabbled away at the envelope until he lost patience, tearing it apart and grabbing at the pages inside.

'That's a mock-up of the front page of tomorrow's *Gazzettino*, Giuseppe. But it's not going to end there. This story is going to go national. How you conspired with Andrea Mazzon to use a one-hundred-year-old scandal to blackmail Anna Fabris into withdrawing from the race. And then, when you got bored of waiting for Mazzon to come up with the goods, you bribed his own bodyguard to beat him up in the hope of throwing the blame on to Gianluca Casagrande.'

He laughed. 'You think this will be enough? There's no proof of any of this.'

'We have a witness, Giuseppe. A man called Francesco Bentivoglio. Well, we didn't call him that, or else he'd have killed us. But Havok has given us a complete statement detailing exactly what you paid him to do and why.'

Meneghini shook his head and looked down at the sheet. 'I don't believe you. This is some sort of trick.'

'Well, you could always wait for the papers to hit the stands tomorrow. The thing is Giuseppe, I know this guy at the *Gazzettino*. Truth be told, he's a bit of a bastard. But right now, Giuseppe, he's *my* bastard and he's sitting on the biggest story he's ever had.'

'There's no way Havok would have spoken to you, Sutherland.'

'Oh, he did. He was surprisingly vocal. You see, he might be committed to the glorious revolution and the supremacy of the white race; but right now, right at this moment, he's also a bloke who'll do anything for a bit of money. You found that yourself, right, by bribing him to double-cross Mazzon? So when we told him just how much money he could expect from a story like this, well, he was surprisingly happy to co-operate.'

'He's a known thug, a fascist and, what's more, you have no proof.'

'There's enough proof, Giuseppe. And once one story is out, well, stories always seem to follow one upon the other, don't they? I wonder what else is still to be revealed?'

'This isn't a smart thing to do, Sutherland.'

'Ah yes. We've reached the "unspoken threat" part of the afternoon.'

'Oh, it's not a threat. It's a promise.'

'So it's the "unspoken threat" mixed with a certain amount of bullish machismo.' I chuckled. 'I'm sorry Giuseppe. It's all rather predictable, don't you think?'

Meneghini sat back in his seat, and closed his eyes as he counted to ten once more.

'I won't forget this, Sutherland.'

'I don't imagine you will.'

'But do you think I'm going to slink away having learned my lesson?' He leaned towards me, ever so slightly. 'No, I don't think so. ' He smiled. 'You're not getting rid of me quite that easily.'

I reached over, and patted his shoulder. 'Well, there we go. I'm not going anywhere either.'

'So I imagine we'll be seeing each other around?'

'Oh. Depend on it, Giuseppe. Depend on it.'

He waved at the waiter, making a signing motion with his hand. The white-suited waiter nodded, and bowed, and returned with a hand-written receipt on a silver plate. Meneghini picked it up, and looked at it. He nodded.

'I'll treat you.'

'Thank you.'

He peeled off some notes from his wallet and then sighed. 'You know what's going to happen now, of course. It'll be some party idiot from the centre-left or the centre-right who wins.'

'I imagine so.'

'That pisses me off.' He frowned, as if displeased with himself for having sworn. 'I'd have been okay if Fabris had won. Seriously. But another dull party man?' He shook his head. 'Christ. No wonder the city's going nowhere.'

'You really think you'd have made a difference?'

'Oh, I'm sure of it. But now we'll never know.' Then he smiled. 'Well, perhaps not. Never say never. There'll be another election in five years. Memories are short. And unlike your country, there are always second acts in Italian politics.' He got to his feet, and turned to leave. '*Arrivederci,* Mr Sutherland. I'll see you around. And thank you for coming out. As I said, I wasn't completely sure you would.'

'I wasn't completely sure either.'

Meneghini looked back over his shoulder at me. 'Did you think I was going to have you killed?'

'Worse. I thought you were going to make me pay.'

We both laughed. Meneghini waved a hand in farewell, and left.

I swirled the remains of my martini, holding the glass up to the light, and then took a final look around my surroundings. At the end of the day, it was just a bar. An expensive bar. Once the haunt of celebrities, but now, perhaps, more frequented by tourists who'd just come in off the boat. It was nice enough, but it wasn't the Brazilians.

The white-suited waiter came over to me, casting a glance behind him at a group of tourists waiting for a table. 'Can I bring you anything else, sir?' he said, in a tone of voice that suggested he hoped not.

I shook my head. 'I don't think so.' I took a few coins from my pocket and laid them on the table as a tip. The disappointment in his gaze was palpable. '*Grazie. Buona serata.*'

I made my way out into the evening. The low winter sun was setting, turning the sky a blazing red and illuminating the church of the *Salute* in a pale, pink light. I breathed in the cold air, stretched my arms wide and smiled, still feeling the warmth of the alcohol spreading through me.

Back then to the Street of the Assassins. Back to the Magical Brazilians, where Ed and Fede would be waiting for me, and where Negronis could be bought for affordable prices.

Somewhere in Venice, a man called Giuseppe Meneghini was not feeling kindly towards me.

But that was okay. I wasn't feeling kindly towards him either.

Chapter 52

'You wanted to see me, Anna?'

'Yes, Nathan.' She patted the bench. 'Sit down for a while, why don't you?'

I winced slightly as the cold of the bench cut through my clothes. Next winter, I promised myself, I really would treat myself to a better coat.

We sat there, looking at the handful of skaters on the ice rink in the middle of Campo San Polo. Ginevra seemed nervous, tippy-tapping her way across the ice, whilst her older sister swirled round and around in effortless circles.

I smiled at Anna. 'Allegra seems quite good.'

'She is, isn't she? She just seems to naturally take to things like this.'

'Perhaps she thinks "What would Spider-Man do?".'

Anna laughed. 'Perhaps she does. Ginevra's not quite the same.'

The little girl seemed to be having an unhappy time of things. She lost her balance for a moment, and her arms flailed, but then her big sister was there to catch her arm and steady her. She crouched down next to her, and gave her a hug. Then she took her hand and, slowly, guided Ginevra around the rink, the little girl laughing with delight as she finally found her rhythm. Allegra looked down at her as if to say 'is this okay?' and then released her hand, the two of them now moving independently of each other in ever-widening circles, the hiss of skates against ice mixing with their laughter.

Anna smiled and applauded. Ginevra looked over for a moment, and almost lost her footing, but, once again, Allegra was there to take her hand.

'I envy kids in Venice,' I said.

Anna looked surprised. 'You do? Why? It won't be too long now until Allegra will be too big to go out on her bike. And a few years after that they'll be too old to play football in the *campo*.' She shook her head. 'That's not a conversation I'm looking forward to.'

'I know. But I remember growing up in Britain, and hoping Christmas and the holidays would go on forever. But then one day you'd wake up and you'd have to go back to school. The anti-Christmas, if you like. But that wasn't the worst thing. The worst thing was coming home after school and finding that Mum and Dad had taken all the decorations down. As if they'd been waiting for you to be out of the house to cancel Christmas.'

Anna laughed. 'I'm sure they didn't mean it like that, Nathan.'

'But here in Venice, you kind of have that emergency back-up Christmas. It lets you down gently, before you have to go back into the real world. Almost as if you're decompressing.'

'You don't think you're over-analysing this a little?'

'Maybe I am. But here we are, in the second week of

January, and kids are ice-skating in Campo San Polo. And the decorations are still up.'

'Only because the city doesn't want to spend money on taking them down.'

'Oh, I see. And that'll be your first act as mayor will it?'

She laughed. 'I don't think so. I don't want to go down in history as the mayor who cancelled Christmas. More importantly, the girls would never forgive me.'

'And quite right too. But as I was saying, the decorations are still up and they'll stay up until the end of Carnival. Kids here get almost two months of the festive season. I think that's amazing.'

She wrinkled her nose. 'Oh God. *Carnevale.* I suppose I'll have to be making costumes again for them.'

'So your second act in office, after cancelling Christmas, is going to be doing away with Carnival?'

We sat there, and laughed, and watched the girls circling round and around.

'It's not going to happen, of course,' said Anna. 'There are stories going around that Rome might even have the election cancelled and put someone in while we sort ourselves out.'

'Like they did a few years ago. When the mayor-before-last resigned in order to spend more time with his lawyers.'

'Exactly. One could hardly blame them. One candidate dead, one resigning in the midst of a scandal, and one who doesn't seem sure from one day to the next if she's going to stand or not.' She shook her head. 'So I'm probably not going to be mayor. And I can live with that.'

'You could try again in five years?'

'Perhaps. But there are other things I can do. Less showy,

perhaps, but equally important.' She shivered. 'Right, I need to get these two home. Hot chocolate on the way, of course.'

'Well, I must be getting back as well. To see my lovely wife and my unlovely cat.' I paused. 'Why did you want to see me, Anna? Not just to chat about the election?'

She shook her head. 'No. There's something I have to do. I know it won't put things right, but I need to do it. And I need you to help me with it, because I don't think I can do it alone.'

Epilogue

My name is Anna Fabris, and I am probably not going to be the next Mayor of Venice. It will more likely be a party apparatchik from the Left or Right. As like as not, he – for it will almost certainly be a he – will be elected by the mainland. Venice, again, will be forgotten, seen only as a cash cow to be milked by terraferma. And so nothing – in Venice at least – will really change. We will continue to pollute the lagoon. We will continue to disappear amongst the ever-increasing throngs of tourists. We will continue to deny our children a possible future in their city.

Perhaps I would have made no difference. Perhaps things have gone too far now for the city to be successfully, or even adequately, governed.

The four of us stand alone in the graveyard, shivering with cold before the Cross of Sacrifice and the grave of Thomas Shawcross. Time to reflect, in the silence, on the injustice that my family did to the Shawcross family.

Nathan pulls Federica closer to him, the two of them doing their best to shelter from the freezing air and swirling snow. The big man, Dario, looks at his watch, and then up at the sky.

'Nat, man, we need to go soon. The weather's closing in.'

Nathan nods. *'You're right.'* He looks over at me. *'Are you ready, Anna?'*

I nod. Then I cross myself, and mutter a few words of a prayer under my breath. I am afraid that the flowers will be whipped from my hand, and so I kneel down and place them as close as I can to Shawcross's headstone. A bouquet of red roses. Then I get to my feet, dust the snow from my clothes, and cross myself once more.

'Ready?'

I nod, and we turn to make our way back to the Land Rover. But not before I take one final moment to look back over my shoulder at the grave of Thomas Shawcross and the flowers I have left.

A flash of red against the white of the snow.

Glossary

acqua alta	the phenomenon of seasonal high tides in the Adriatic sea and Venetian lagoon leading to periodic flooding of areas of the city
acqua granda	The name given to the exceptionally high floods that struck Venice in 1966 and 2019.
agriturismo	typically a small farm converted for use as a restaurant or holiday accommodation
Babbo Natale	Father Christmas
bacino	basin, as in an area of water. In Venice this refers to the San Marco basin, that area in front of Piazza San Marco where the Grand Canal and Giudecca Canal merge
ballottaggio	the final run-off between the leading two candidates in an election, should neither have passed the 50 per cent threshold in the first round.
La Befana	in Italian folklore, an old woman who

	takes gifts to children on the eve of Epiphany
birrificio	a small brewery (what we might now call a craft brewery)
bisnonno/bisnonna	great-grandfather/mother
boh	'I don't know.' Perhaps best accompanied with a shrug.
caffe corretto	a coffee 'corrected' with a shot of alcohol, usually grappa
calle (pl. *calli*)	a narrow street, alley
campanile	the bell tower of a church
capo	boss, chief (can used in the sense of 'pal', 'buddy')
casa di riposo	rest home / nursing home
CasaPound	a neo-fascist social movement and occasional political party, formed in Rome in the early part of the century.
cazzo	expletive (relatively strong!)
centro storico	historic centre. In Venice this is typically used to refer to the main area of the city and not the outlying islands
chi è?	literally 'who is it?', a common way of responding when answering the entryphone
Cinepanettoni	cheap and cheerful farcical comedies, traditionally released around the Christmas period
Comandante	commander, here the pilot of a *vaporetto* or water bus
Di Montezemolo, Luca	Italian businessman, former head of Ferrari

fondamenta	typically the street alongside a canal
frutti di bosco	'fruits of the forest', a common filling in a brioche.
furbismo	craftiness
Irriducibili	Notorious gang of Lazio *Ultras*, active between the late 80s and 2020
Il Gazzettino	a daily newspaper of Venice and the Veneto
macchiatone	a coffee, somewhere between a *macchiato* and a *cappuccino*. Don't try asking for one outside the Veneto, it'll only confuse people.
marinaio	sailor, here, the 'conductor' of a *vaporetto* or water bus.
Negroni sbagliato	a 'mistaken' Negroni, with the gin element replaced with prosecco or sparkling wine. A mistake indeed!
nonno/nonna	grandpa/grandma
Oddio	oh God!
piacere	a pleasure
piano nobile	the principal floor of a *palazzo*, typically the second storey in Venice.
Pagine Bianche	the telephone directory
Pagine gialle	the Yellow Pages
Per colpo di qualcuno, non facciamo credito a nessuno	literally 'because of someone's fault, we don't give credit to anyone.' Perhaps an equivalent to 'Please do not ask for credit, as a smack in the face often offends.'
Pesce crudo	raw fish

porta blindata	reinforced door
pronto	literally, 'ready', but in this case used as a telephone greeting
Querini Stampalia	a Venetian cultural institution, housing an archive, a library and a museum
questura	main police station
RAI	the Italian state broadcaster
Scarpa, Carlo	20th-century Venetian architect
sestiere	Venice is divided into six *sestieri* or neighbourhoods
settima arte	the 'Seventh Art'. A suitably reverential term for 'cinema'
signorile	noble, refined, gentlemanly
tesoro/caro/cara/vecio	terms of endearment
terraferma	the mainland
terrazzo	typical Venetian flooring, made of marble or granite chips set in ground limestone or concrete and polished until smooth
tramezzino/i	the traditional Italian-style sandwich; triangles of white bread with the filling typically heaped up in the middle
Ultras	fanatical bands of football supporters, often (but not always) associated with violence and extreme political views.
vaporetto	the style of boat used in the public transport system in Venice
Veritas	the organisation responsible for refuse collection in the city

Notes and Acknowledgements

The Villa Godi Malinverni, later used as the setting for the ballroom scene in Luchino Visconti's *Senso*, was indeed used as a base by British Command during the Battle of the Asiago Plain, and once hosted the Prince of Wales, later King Edward VIII. As far as I have been able to determine, however, no unit diaries from this part of the campaign survive.

CasaPound, a neo-fascist social movement, began with the occupation of state-owned buildings in Rome by squatters in 2003, and operated as a political party between 2008 and 2019. They had and continue to have links with other fascist groups such as the *Irriducibili*, the most notorious of Lazio football club's *Ultras*. Effectively founded by the graphic designer *Grinta*, the group came to be run by Fabrizio Piscitelli, also known as *Diabolik*. His murder in 2019 led to the *Irriducibili* disbanding in February 2020. I am indebted to Tobias Jones's book *Ultrà*, a peerless source of information on the Ultra subculture.

I continue to be amazed by the number of messages I receive, via Twitter, Facebook or email. My apologies, I've never quite got on with Instagram, and TikTok, I suspect, will always remain alien to me. But however you've got in touch, thank you. It means a great deal.

I finish, as ever, with my thanks to my agent John Beaton; to Colin Murray; to Krystyna, Rebecca, Jess and everyone at Constable; and, of course, to Caroline. None of this, *cara mia*, would be happening without you.

Philip Gwynne Jones, Venezia 2022

www.philipgwynnejones.com